EMERALD LAKE PREP

BOOK THREE:
SHATTERED PIECES

BY: ALISHA WILLIAMS

For more information, please address:
alishawilliamsauthor@gmail.com

Book cover design: Alisha Williams

AUTHOR'S NOTE

Please be advised. This is a reverse harem/why choose romance, meaning the heroine of this story does not have to pick between her love interests.

This book contains explicitly described sexual content and the excessive use of swear words. Some parts may have darker themes.

Even though this is a prep school based book, this story is focused heavily on the characters' relationships with each other, as well as other exciting events.

This is a fast burn romance, but you already know that if you've gotten this far... So, hold onto your panties or you might end up feeling the breeze a little more intimately than expected - cuz these pages are on fire!

DEDICATION

I'd like to dedicate this book to anyone who has ever had a dream but grew up thinking they will never make anything of themselves because of the environment they were raised in. If you have a dream, go for it. You never know what you can do unless you try...

PROLOGUE
Tyson

MY FEET POUND against each step as I run the fastest I ever have in my entire life. I have one thought in mind: *save my brother.*

I won't let him die. Not like this, not ever. Not if I can help it. I need him. Emmy needs him, and so does his daughter.

Fuck! Our daughter. She's probably here by now. It was my job to protect them, and here Emmy is giving birth in the fucking school library. Well,

I failed to keep that fucker from kidnapping her, and then his batshit crazy daughter almost killed her, so what's one more let down?

Really, Tyson. Two for two. Time to step up there, buddy.

The emergency door alarm is blaring as I reach the top of the steps. Bursting through the door on the floor that holds the girls' dorms, my face pales and my stomach drops as I take in the sight of my brother lying in a pool of his own blood, his skin paler than normal.

"Oliver!" I shout, checking his pulse. It's weak, but it's there. *Thank fuck.*

The wound is still bleeding, but the flow of blood has lessened. Whether it's from losing too much blood or not, I have no clue.

I don't touch him, not wanting to make things worse. We need the EMTs.

Knowing they are right outside the school, all I need to do is get their attention. But calling to guide them to our location will take too much time, and I don't want to leave Oliver.

Looking around, I see Emmy and Charlie's bedroom door cracked open. Getting up, I rush into their room, straight to the window. Throwing it open, I look around and see the front lawn of the school littered with SWAT team members, and behind them are two ambulances.

"Hey!" I cup my hands and shout to the people below. Every gun quickly aims at me. Raising my arms, I shout. "The threat has been eliminated—room thirteen.

My name is Tyson Kingston; I'm the gym teacher here. I need an EMT now. My brother's been shot, and he's lost a lot of blood."

The SWAT team moves quickly into the school. "Also, there's a student who is in labor in the library. I'm not sure if she's given birth yet, but she needs to get to a hospital too."

As the EMTs all spring into action, I rush back over to my brother.

"You got this, man. Stay with me. You have two amazing ladies down there that need you. Don't put Emmy through any more pain than she's already been through." I plead. My heart is racing, and I feel tears forming in my eyes. I don't cry. The last time I cried was when I saw Emmy look so small and fragile in that hospital bed last summer. But *fuck!* I can't lose my brother. My best friend.

I know we had some issues because of my feelings for Emmy, but we're finally back in a good place. Our little family is just starting, and I can't wait to see how everything comes together, but it won't be whole without him.

Chatter and a rush of footsteps reach me from the stairwell. A moment later, two SWAT and three EMTs file into the hall.

I move out of the way, so they can do their job. They start working to save his life immediately, getting him on the stretcher, lifting him up, and leaving to take him downstairs.

"I'm here, brother. I'm with you. Hold on." I demand as I follow down after them.

I wanna scream, cry, and beat the shit out of someone. Brittany's death was all too quick. If I had the choice, I would have kept her alive, so I could hand her over to Harlow and then ask my best friend if I could take part in one of her little playdates. I'm not really into her form of torture, but I would have made an exception for that fucking bitch.

I want to rush to Emmy's side, but I don't. She has everyone else helping to take care of her. Oliver needs me. I know his stubborn ass would have told me to go to Emmy, but too bad; he doesn't have a say at this moment.

When we get out to the front lawn, I see everyone gathered around one of the ambulances.

Talon, Ben, and Charlie stand around watching as they begin to load Emmy into the back. Charlie has something in her arms and as we get closer, I hear a baby cry.

My heart bursts and sinks all at the same time. *Dammit!* I missed the birth of my daughter. I wanted to be there so bad. To hold Emmy's hand as she pushed. To see my baby girl's beautiful face the moment she made her way into this world.

But I'm not the only partner Emmy has. I know she was in good hands.

Talon locks eyes with me, then sees his best friend lying on the stretcher. He lets out a curse as a look of horror takes over his face.

Emmy looks from the baby in Charlie's arms to Talon, before following his line of sight to Oliver.

"Oliver!" Emmy shouts, her face contorted in pain, panic, and terror. "Olly!" She sobs.

She scrambles to get up from the stretcher, but Ben and Talon try to hold her down as she fights against them.

"Let me go!" She screams, her voice cracking, sobs racking her chest as she tries to get to her lover.

"I got him, Princess. Everything's gonna be okay!" I shout to her as they load him up into the ambulance. I want to run over to her, gather her into my arms, and tell her everything is gonna be okay, but I need to stay at my brother's side. I'll see her once he's stable.

"Don't leave him!" Emmy demands. "Don't you fucking leave his side, Ty. I can't lose him!" Her voice breaks, and my heart does the same right along-side it.

"I won't! I'll be with him right up until I'm not allowed." I tell her.

"We need to go." The EMT says to me, holding the door open. With one last look at my girl, I climb in the back with my brother and close the door shut behind me.

The door locks and the vehicle starts to move. I watch out the window as they load Emmy into the back of her own ambulance. I don't move until she's just a small dot, and out of sight.

Moving over to sit next to Oliver, I take his cold, clammy hand in mine and give it a squeeze.

"I got you, brother. Just hold on a little while longer."

Chapter 1
Oliver

WITH A JOLT, my eyes snap open. It takes a few moments to get my bearings. Blinking a few times to get the blurry haze out of my eyes, I find myself standing alone in the middle of a meadow.

Where the fuck am I?

The tall grass sways in the warm breeze, tickling the tips of my fingers. Spinning in circles, I see that I'm alone, with miles and miles of rolling hills in every direction.

How did I get here? Why can't I remember?

Giggling in the distance catches my attention. Turning around, I see a little girl running through the grass, her bright red hair bouncing with every step she takes.

I look around to see where her parents are, but there's no one else in sight. The need to help her, to go to her, is strong.

I start to run towards her, never taking my eyes off of her. She continues to giggle, and it sounds like a musical melody.

Melody... Melody... Why do I feel like I should be remembering something important?

I feel like I've been running forever, but I'm not getting any closer to the little girl. What the fuck is going on?

And just like that, she's gone in the blink of an eye.

"What the...?" I whisper to myself, rubbing my eyes and checking the spot where she was just standing. "Hey!" I shout, hoping to bring whoever that was back.

"Olly..." A voice whispers in my ear, making me shutter. I spin around to see who it is, but no one is there.

"Olly..." The voice repeats from behind me, this time louder. Turning around again, I find Emmy standing off in the distance.

My eyes go wide, and I breathe a sigh of relief. "Oh, thank God, Emmy. I thought I was going crazy for a moment." I say, taking a step closer, then furrowing my brow in confusion.

"What a minute, what are you doing here? What am I doing here? And where are we?" I ask.

She smiles wide at me, but it's not one of her sweet, loving ones; no, this one is much more sinister. A wave of unease blankets my body, and the strong feeling that something is not right pounds a steady rhythm through my mind.

"Where did the little girl go?" I ask.

"What little girl?" She asks, tilting her head to the side.

"The little, red-haired girl who was just there a moment ago." I tell her. At least, I think she was here. Fuck, maybe I am going crazy because none of what's happening right now makes any sense.

"There's no little girl, silly." she giggles. "And there never will be."

Wait a minute.

Everything comes rushing back all at once, and I feel like my head's about to explode.

The school. Brittany. The shooting. I was shot... I'm dying... but then how am I standing here?

"Am I dead?" I whisper. But if I'm dead, then how am I seeing her? Oh god, please no. Don't tell me she's dead too?

"The baby?" I say, looking down at her belly.

"Gone." she growls, her eyes turning black. "Dead and gone because you couldn't protect us. Just like all of the other times before this." Shock and dread freezes my insides.

The belly of her white dress starts to bloom bright red with blood. "You failed us, Olly. Now you must pay the price."

No, no. Please, God, no. This can't be happening!

A sharp pain in my side makes me crumple in on myself. The pain is unbearable, like I've been shot. Wait, I was shot.

Looking down, I see blood soaking my own shirt. Lifting it up to get a look at what's causing me to bleed, I find the little bullet hole. How can something so small cause so much blood?

It starts to gush out of me. Putting my hands on it and adding pressure does nothing.

My knees give out, and I collapse to the ground. Emmy is gone, my daughter is gone, I'm dying, and it's all my fault. I couldn't keep them safe. I never could.

My vision starts to blur, and all I can hear before everything goes black again is the echoing giggles of the little girl who was running away from me.

Emmy

Rapid beeping jolts me out of my sleep. I suck in a hiss of pain as I sit up too quickly, but I'm careful not to pull on any of the wires attached to Oliver.

Oliver. My love. My best friend.

Tears sting my eyes as I look down at his pale face.

He starts to stir, and my eyes go wide with excitement. The machine starts to go crazy. He's waking up!

"Olly, Baby, wake up. My Love, please. We need you." I coax, gently caressing his cheek in a calming manner.

When he doesn't wake, but keeps moving, I start to panic. Not wanting him to hurt himself, I press the call button frantically, needing a nurse in here right away. A few seconds later, three rush into the room.

"What's wrong?" One asks, looking from me to Oliver.

"I think he's waking up. The machine started to go crazy, and he was tossing and turning in his sleep."

Just as I finish my sentence, looking back at Oliver, his eyes open, pupils filled with fear.

"Emmy!" His scream comes out broken and filled with terror. He frantically looks around with wild eyes, searching for me.

"Shh. It's okay, Olly. I'm right here. You need to relax, or you're gonna rip your stitches." I tell him with a smile in my voice and tears in my eyes. I'm fucking happy beyond belief that he's awake.

His eyes find mine. "Firefly," he breathes, reaching out his hand that has the IV inserted. "Please tell me this is real." He whispers pleadingly.

Taking his outreached hand, I bring it to my lips, giving it a kiss before cradling my cheek into his palm. Taking a deep breath and closing my eyes, I do the best I can to get a hold of myself.

"It's real, Olly Bear. I'm here. I'm okay. You're okay. We're both fine." I chant, opening my eyes and finding his. He instantly looks relieved.

"I dreamed you were dead. That both of you were." He whispers, and his eyes go wide again. "The baby!" He shouts and tries to sit up, grunting in pain.

"Mr. Price, please lay back. You're only going to hurt yourself more." A nurse says, trying to get Oliver to lay back. He jerks away from her touch.

"She's fine." I tell him, knowing that right now I am the only one who can calm him down. "She's so beautiful, Olly. You're gonna love her." My voice breaks a little, and my smile takes over my whole face as I think about my baby girl.

"She's okay?" He sounds like he's ready to cry.

"Yes." I laugh, overwhelmed by the moment we're sharing, and wipe the tears that started to fall from my eyes. "She's with Amy, Charlie, and Tyson right now."

"Why isn't she here?" He asks, looking around.

"Because, Olly, you've been out for a few days now. Melody was released yesterday. Amy thought it would be best to take her home."

"Oh," he says, settling back into the bed. "How come you didn't go with them?"

"Because," I smile. "As much as being away from her right now sucks, I know she's in good hands. I couldn't leave you here alone. I didn't want you to wake up by yourself. I had to see for myself that you were going to be okay." I tell him, my voice cracking as I try to hold back the tears that are threatening to spill again.

Leaning over, I place a soft kiss on his lips, not giving a fuck about the nurse in the room. Oliver lets out a groan as my lips move against his, but this isn't enough for him. His hand comes behind my head, pushing my lips harder against his. When he moves his hand to get a better grip on my hair, the wire catches on a few strands.

"What the fuck?" He asks, trying to pull his hand away. I laugh as I detangle my hair from the wires.

"Fucking cock blocker." Oliver grumbles at his hand. I can't help but bite my lip letting a giggle slip past.

He looks at me with heated eyes, but the humor in them is clear.

"Well, normally hospitals are not a place to get physical with our partners, Mr. Price." A doctor says upon entering the room. He gives us each a smile before looking down at the chart in his hand.

"No, but I think almost dying earns me a little action." Oliver mutters.

The doctor continues to read his chart, but I can see the little tilt of his lip at Oliver's remark.

Leaning close, I whisper in his ear. "Don't worry. When you get out of here, I'll give you all the action you want.

I can't really do anything for six weeks, but I may as well keep my men pleased in other ways." My voice ends up coming out a little huskier than normal, and Oliver sucks in a rugged breath. Moving away, my eyes find his which are filled with lust as if he's ready to yank me into him and take me here and now.

7

Giving him a little grin, I move off the bed. His eyes go from lustful to panicked.

"Where are you going?" He asks, his voice coming out in a rush.

"Hey, it's okay," I say, taking his hand. "I'm not going anywhere. Just getting off the bed so that the doctor and nurses can look you over to make sure everything is okay." I tell him, my heart hurting at how much that dream must have affected him. That if I leave his sight for one moment, then that dream might become a reality.

I pull the chair closer to the side of his bed and take his hand in mine while the doctor starts to talk to him.

"Well, it's good to see you awake, young man. You had this little lady worried. You were both put in terrible situations, but she didn't let that stop her from being by your side, not even after just having a baby." the doctor chuckles. Oliver looks at me with questioning eyes.

"What does he mean?"

"Well," I say, shifting in my seat. "I was kind of overwhelmed with everything and I didn't want you to be out of my sight, so I asked him to put me in your room with you. Melly and I were right next to you for the first few days." I shrug.

"Asked? No, that feisty lady of yours demanded. She even threatened to punch your brother between his legs if he kept telling her to calm down." The doctor reiterates with a chuckle. "We didn't want her to overwhelm herself or the baby, so we didn't see an issue with putting her in here."

Oliver smirks at me. "I bet Tyson just loved that, didn't he?" Oliver chuckles.

I grin widely at him. "He was pissed, but hey, I had just given birth in the middle of a school shooting; who would be stupid enough to argue with me?" I joke, but it falls flat as Oliver's eyes turn dark with anger and regret. I shake my head at him, not wanting to get into everything with others around.

"Later, okay?" I beg him. He looks like he's about to argue, but the doctor keeps going.

"You had to undergo a serious surgery, and it was touch and go for a while.

You lost a lot of blood, but thankfully you got here in time. We removed the bullet, but it did leave you with some damage. Your recovery is going to be a minimum of a few weeks, but after that, you should be good as new. Although, as much as we tried to stitch you up nicely, being shot at close range like you were, it's going to leave a pretty big scar."

I can't help but think about my own scars on my legs and side. Oliver has just as much ink as I do on his body, and I know some of his amazing artwork is going to be affected like mine was.

"That's okay. Just means I have another thing in common with my girl. Her scars make her look sexy as fuck, so this just means I get to be a little bit sexier than the others." He says, giving me a cocky wink and giving my hand a squeeze. It's like he can read my damn mind.

I roll my eyes at him, but can't help the smile that stretches across my lips.

The doctor talks with us a bit, while the nurses check his vitals and other things, before leaving. I crawl back into bed with Oliver, and he holds me tight against his body, stroking my hair as I get him up to speed on what he missed.

I tell him all about what I can remember of the delivery. How gorgeous our little redheaded girl is. He grins against my head at that and says something about how we are in for it. With my sassy side and her fiery red hair, she is going to be a force to be reckoned with.

He doesn't point out the fact that there's a good chance that Ben is her biological dad. I can tell he doesn't care. And neither do I.

Watching how Tyson, Ben, and Talon take care of our daughter melts my heart every time. They are so amazing with her.

Ben's mother came to get Ben and Talon after everything calmed down. They didn't want to leave, but with everything that happened at the school, they had to go back home until the school board decided what was gonna happen in regards to the rest of the school year.

As of right now, the school is closed. All remaining students on probation are suffering house arrest.

Talon had a few things to say about the fact that Charlie and Tyson would be able to be with me at all times and by default, the baby.

I promised that we would video chat every day, but I can tell that with everything that's happened and how Melly was brought into the world, Talon and Ben have become over-protective daddies. And fuck if it doesn't make my heart swoon with how much they love her already.

Oliver asks if Amy can bring Melody over so he can meet her, but because of how late it already is, we decide that tomorrow would be better, and he isn't the only one sad about that. I've missed my baby girl, and my boobs really need to be pumped again.

"Fuck." I groan as I sit up to go pee and look down at where I was cuddling with Oliver.

"What?" He asks, looking down at the wet spot on his gown, then to my chest. His smile grows wide, and he lets out a chuckle.

"Um, Babe, I think you're leaking." He jokes.

I glare at him. "No, really? I would never have guessed." I say sarcastically, gesturing down at the two massive wet spots on my chest.

I press the call button, and a nurse comes in. "Hi, I need to pump again, could someone please come back in about ten minutes to get the bottles and put them in the fridge?"

"Of course." She smiles and leaves.

"So, how is that going?" He asks, and I know he's referring to breastfeeding.

I sigh and climb out of the bed, heading over to the bag that's sitting on the window sill, containing the pump and bottles I need.

"Not bad. I mean, I'd much rather be breastfeeding her myself. I want to have that bonding time with her as much as I can before we head back to school." I pout. "She's taken to the bottle fine, but I'm afraid she's gonna get too used to it, and I won't get that few weeks of skin to skin contact with her before we return."

I take a seat in the chair next to the bed and begin hooking my boobs up to the pump. When the machine starts doing its job, I look up and find Oliver's eyes glued to my tits; not in a sexual way, but more out of curiosity.

"Does it hurt?" He asks.

"Not really. Feels a little weird, but my milk supply has been heavy, so it doesn't take me long to fill the bottles. We already have a good month's supply in the freezer at home," I laugh.

"I'm sorry." He says, his voice soft.

"About what?" I ask, leaning my head back against the chair.

"For everything. But right now, it's because you don't get to do all the things a new mother gets to do with her baby. That you're in here with me when you should be with her. She's more important."

"Hey," I say, narrowing my eyes. "Enough of that. You're both important. And as I said before, she's in good hands. I wanted to be here when you woke up. You didn't ask to get shot, you know."

I look at him with determination, trying to convey to him that even though I miss Melly and my body aches for her, I'm right where I want to be. Right here by his side.

"None of this would have happened if it wasn't for me." he growls.

"How the hell are you the one responsible for that crazy bitch coming back and shooting up the place?" I snap back at him. I'm not mad, but I am getting agitated that he's blaming himself.

"I should have protected you! I should have kept you safe. But, yet again, I failed you." he insists. His machines start to speed up, beeping faster and faster as his breathing grows heavy. Without saying a word, I unhook the pump and bottles, cap them off, and set everything on the table next to me, then climb back into bed with him, not caring that I'm still in a wet bra and shirt.

I cuddle close to Oliver and kiss him deeply, conveying all the love I have for him, and hoping he understands how much I care for him, how much I need him.

"Please don't. Don't talk like that." I whisper against his lips. He lets out a sigh. "What happened that night, there was nothing you could have done. And, Oliver, I didn't get hurt this time." I smile as I pull away enough for him to see my face. "Sure, giving birth on the couch of a school library wasn't exactly on the top of my list, but I'm fine, and we're okay. YOU did protect us. Both you and Tyson did. You distracted her so that she didn't come looking for me. So please, stop thinking you can't protect us. Stop thinking of the past. Think of the fact that we have a beautiful daughter to love and raise. Think about the fact that we only have three months left until we are free of all this and we can officially start our lives together like we're meant to."

I put my head on his shoulder, trying not to think about the fact that my father is still out there, and that he is still a problem that we will have to worry about at some point.

I haven't gotten any more texts from him. It's been radio silence since the shooting. No more texts, no calls, no presents.

I'm not sure if I should be happy about that or suspicious, but I can't think about any of that right now. Plus, Tyson has appointed himself Melody's bodyguard.

It's quite adorable seeing her tiny body in his massive arms. And fuck, my heart melts every time I see him look at her like she's his whole world.

No, I won't worry about my father right now. Right now, I'm going to enjoy the fact that everyone I love is healthy and okay.

"I love you, Olly." I whisper, starting to drift off to sleep.

His arms tighten around me. "I love you too, Firefly, so fucking much." I can hear the emotion of how true his words are as he kisses the top of my head.

Tomorrow is going to be a good day. Tomorrow, Melly gets to meet the last of her daddies, and everything will be right in the world... for now.

CHAPTER 2
Tyson

HUSHED COOING WAKES me from my sleep. Slowly blinking my eyes open, I look around and find Charlie sitting on the edge of my bed with Melody bundled in her arms. Charlie stares at her with love in her eyes and a wide smile as she softly rocks her from side to side while she talks to her.

I can't help but smile to myself at the sight. Only, I wish it were Emmy holding her and not Charlie. Don't get me wrong, I love Charlie like a sister, but being away from Emmy has been hard.

A few of the guys from the MC are standing guard at the hospital, and even though I want to stay there with Emmy and my brother, I've felt torn between being the one to watch them or keep an eye on our daughter. Emmy wasn't the one hurt this time, but that doesn't lessen the need for me to be there and protect her at all times. We still have a threat on our hands, after all.

One that none of us have heard from since the shooting. Emmy asked me if maybe, that meant he's changed his mind about wanting to take possession of her and the baby, but then quickly realized how highly unlikely that would be. There's just something about that man that is so unhinged that it didn't even surprise me that he's doing this. He doesn't need valid reasons to do things, he just does them, no matter how deranged.

A part of me has always wondered if that's where Harlow got her crazy from. But she's nothing like him. Sure, she's fucking terrifying if you get on her bad side, but she would never harm anyone who doesn't deserve it. And never her own family, unless it was the last resort.

Things have not only been quiet with Dagger and his creepy messages to Emmy, but we haven't had any issues with the Savage Hellhounds either. From what we've heard, no one has really seen any of them outside their compound in the past week. It screams fishy, and makes me want to keep my guard up even more.

I had a talk with my dad last night when he came to visit the baby.

We think the main reason why Dagger wants anything to do with Emmy after all these years is because his original plan to get Oliver away from his daughter has failed, and in the end, it did the complete opposite. It drove her into his enemies' arms.

He doesn't want Emmy and the baby because they are his family, and he loves them. No, he wants them so we *can't* have them. As a prize, as property, as something to hold over our heads in a childish way. Simply put, he wants to be able to say, 'She's mine, and you can't have her!'

But that's never gonna happen. He will *never* get my girls, and I will die trying to keep them safe.

"Oh look! Daddy Ty is awake, and perfect timing too." Charlie says to Melody in an overly dramatic baby voice.

Sitting up, I smile and shake my head. She hands me the baby, and I carefully take my precious, little princess in my arms. I smile down at her, as she looks up at me with her big blue eyes blinking at me. Based on her hair color, those baby blues are most likely going to turn green. Maybe.

Emmy didn't care what color her eyes were, but I hoped they were brown, just like hers. She always grumbles about them being poop colored, but she's wrong. Emmy's big, beautiful, brown eyes are one of the many things I love about her.

Something foul hits my nose, making me scrunch it up in disgust. "Oh, and she just took a shit, so good luck with that." Charlie cackles as she darts out of the room to avoid the impending poop bomb she just left me to deal with.

"My God, Little Princess, how can something so small and pretty smell so bad?" I ask her, laughing as I head over to her changing table.

I had a bed set up in her nursery, wanting to be near her, just in case. The living room is too far away for my liking, and Emmy and Charlie share a bed, so that was not an option.

I grab everything that I need to change her, before laying her down on the table. She lays there, silently watching me, like she's waiting for something. I lift a brow at her before opening up her diaper. Cringing at the nasty sight of what this little human made, I rear my head back, trying to get away from the odor without taking my hands off her.

One thing I'll never enjoy about parenting is changing dirty diapers. Taking one last deep breath, I hold it as I get to work.

And I swear the little stinker smirks at me, like she enjoys watching her daddy suffer.

Just as I start slipping the clean diaper under her, Melody lets out a little grunt and then a stream of crap shoots out of her and right onto my shirt.

I just stand there. Blinking at the baby crap dripping down my black tee.

"I thought this would be a cute outfit for Melly Belly to meet Daddy Olly in." Charlie says, walking into the room. I look over at her with a horrified look on my face.

"What's wro-" She starts, then looks down at my shirt, then over at the baby, and back at my shit covered shirt. She bursts out laughing, like deep belly laughs.

"Oh, that's fucking gold." Charlie laughs. Still amused, she makes her way over to Melody. "Right on, Little Miss." Charlie praises the baby with a little fist-bump to her tiny hand.

"I'll finish up here. You go shower and get ready to take this little miss to her mama. Emmy just called and said she's going crazy and needs some baby cuddles." Charlie laughs.

Still in shock, I leave her with the baby and head to the bathroom to clean up.

This parenting thing is gonna be one long, interesting ride. As much as that little situation was traumatizing, I can't wait for every part of this journey we are on. And I'm glad I get to do it with my brother and the love of my life.

Charlie is not happy that she has to stay behind. She has Melody in her arms, refusing to hand her over while she bitches in baby talk about how the school system is fucked up and how the big bad judge needs to go fuck himself. Little Princess just stares up at her Mama C and blinks, not understanding a word.

I have to agree with Charlie on that one. That judge has dealt with too many of my father's men. But unlike the old judge he replaced, who would have probably seen how much shit my girl and brother have been through and let them off the hook, this one wanted to make us suffer any way he could. And that meant Emmy by default. *Fucking prick.*

When I finally manage to get Melody from Charlie, I just stand there looking at her, then the car seat.

This is the first time I'm going to be caring for Mel alone. I'm taking her to the hospital to meet Oliver and bring Emmy back home. I'm so nervous to drive with her in the backseat. What if we get in an accident? I'd fucking kill anyone who tried to put my baby girl in danger. Unintentionally or not.

"Just give her to me." Charlie huffs out a laugh, taking the baby from my arms again, then strapping her carefully into her car seat. She gives her a kiss on the cheek before standing up and looking at me proudly. "See? Easy-peasy."

"Yeah, maybe for you, but I'd probably hurt her with these big meat cleavers." I say, holding up my hands, then looking down at the tiny human who is looking up at us with big eyes. She's such a good baby.

"You'll get used to it after a while. I have experience with my cousins, since they're so little." Charlie shrugs. "I've always loved kids." She says, looking down at Melody with a soft smile and eyes radiating love.

"Alright. I'll get her seat hooked up in the car, but then you gotta take it from there, big guy." Charlie says, bending over, grabbing the handle of the car seat, then slapping my back on the way out.

"Goodbye, my sweet girl. Be good for Daddy Ty." Charlie says, kissing the baby again. "Who am I kidding? You're perfect!" Charlie coos, booping her on the nose lightly.

"She's all yours. Here's the diaper bag." Charlie slips the bag off her arm and places it on the passenger side of the car. "There's enough diapers in there, but we didn't make any bottles because, well, Emmy can just breastfeed her there."

"Thanks." I say, as she closes the car door. "We won't be too long. I'll find out how long Oliver needs to be in the hospital, then I'll bring Emmy home." God, I am so fucking excited to have her back. It's only been a few days short of a week since she gave birth, but she hasn't been home yet. We've had no alone time since before the shooting, and I just wanna hold her in my arms and know that she's safe.

Amy has given me the okay in regards to staying here at the house, not just being posted outside to guard. With Dagger being a major threat, even if he has been silent, I'm no fool, so I want to be as close to my girls as possible.

I don't like not being able to help out my brother, but he will be okay being back at the compound with all the Reapers to look after him.

Charlie waves goodbye one more time to the baby before heading back into the house. I round the car and slip into the front seat.

Sticking the key into the ignition but not starting it up just yet, I relax back into my seat, letting out a sigh.

"Alright, Little Princess, we're off to see Mama and Daddy O. We got this." I say, looking over my shoulder and seeing her in the reflection of the baby mirror that's attached to the seat. I can't help but smile at my beautiful, little girl when I see that she's fallen asleep. Hopefully, she's out for the rest of the ride.

Two hours later, we finally pull up to the hospital. Oliver and Emmy were admitted to the hospital closest to the school, and Oliver was in no shape to be moved to the one closer to home. As for Emmy, that woman was not gonna leave him. And after she threatened to punch me in the balls when I tried to tell her what to do, I let her be.

Charlie gave Melody a bottle before we left, but based on the high-pitched screeches coming from the back seat, I'd say it's time for another feeding. She was sleeping the whole car ride, but she's wide awake and pissed now.

Hating to hear her cry like that, I put the car in park, grab the bag, and rush to the trunk to pull out the stroller.

I try to get the stroller to open, but I can't figure out how to unlock it. I'm getting stressed and frustrated, and I can't think because all I can focus on is Melody's crying.

"Need some help, Handsome?" Emmy's soft, comforting voice comes from behind me as I feel two small hands rest on my tensed shoulders. She gives them a squeeze before kissing the middle of my back.

I let out a sigh, relaxing a bit at her touch. Dropping the stroller to the ground, I turn around and pull her into my arms.

"I missed you, Princess." I murmur into the top of her head. "So fucking much."

"I missed you, too." She snuggles into my embrace.

Breaking apart, I cup her face in my hands, needing to feel her lips on mine. She moans into my kiss as my tongue swipes along her bottom lip, needing to taste her.

A full-on banshee cry snaps us back to reality.

I look at her with a wince. "Someone's a little hungry. I was trying to get her up to you as quickly as I could, but I can't get this damn stroller to unlock." I grumble, kicking the stupid thing on the ground. She just shakes her head with a smile and laughs.

"I'll show you how later. Just put it back in the trunk, and grab her bag. I'll just carry her up."

She opens the back door to a now red-faced Melody. Fuck, I feel like shit that I let it get to this point.

"Hi there, my little Melly Belly. Mama missed you so much." Emmy says softly. Unbuckling her, Emmy takes Melody out, cradles her in her arms, and right there in the middle of the parking lot, pulls out her breast so Melody can latch on.

My eyes go wide, not at the fact that she's breastfeeding, but that there could be someone watching.

Emmy sees me looking around and slaps my arm with her free hand. "I don't care if anyone sees me. It's just a boob, and I'm using it for what they were made for. If anyone has a problem, they can fuck off."

"Or I can kick their ass." I mutter, stroking the feeding baby's cheek as she greedily eats and suckles down her lunch.

"That would work too." Emmy says, her voice a little husky. My eyes snap up to hers and I see them wide with lust.

Fuck, that kiss from before has me hard, but with the way she's looking at me right now, it's testing all my restraint. I can't wait until her six weeks of healing time is up. Although, I might have one of the other guys worship her body before I do because I know I'm bigger than them, and I don't want to hurt her by being the first one to be intimate with her after having the baby.

But when I do get to make love to her for the first time, it's gonna be everything I've been fucking dreaming of and more. When I take her, I don't want to hold back. I don't think I could, even if I wanted to.

That time in my cabin, when she made me cum just by dry humping me, I gave myself a big pat on the back for not flipping her over and rutting into her like a mad man.

"You're gonna need to stop looking at me like that, Princess." I growl. She shivers at the sound.

"Or what?" She sasses back, her eyes lighting up with excitement and a challenge.

"You're a brat, you know that?" I say, narrowing my eyes at my sexy, little minx.

"Yes, but you love me." She winks, before turning around and heading towards the hospital entrance.

Locking the car, I jog up to her, giving her ass a little swat and making her squeal. She turns to look at me with wide eyes full of shock. I chuckle low in my throat, stepping into her, making sure not to crush the baby.

17

"You're right, I do love you, Princess. So fucking much. So much I would start a war just to see you smile. But that doesn't mean I won't punish your sweet, sassy ass." I bite her lower lip, then back away with the cockiest grin ever while she gapes at me. The desire is clear as day and that excites me so fucking much. I'm gonna have fun with my girl, soon. So. Much. Fun.

"Olly, are you good?" Emmy asks, peeking her head around Oliver's door. Emmy finished feeding the baby on the way up the elevator. When we got to the nurses' station, they said he was just getting a sponge bath.

Yeah, the look on Emmy's face was fucking terrifying. Reminded me all too much of one that Harlow makes. One that says, "Touch my man and die." The idea of one of these nurses touching Oliver is not something she likes.

"You can come in." A female voice says. Emmy tenses. When we walk in, Oliver has a big smile on his face as he takes in me and the baby. I look over at Emmy, but she is not sharing the same look he is. No, she's glaring at the nurse who is unnecessarily still fussing over him.

"Hello." Emmy bites out, forcing a smile.

The nurse looks at Emmy with her own forced smile. "Oh hi. You must be Oliver's... sister?"

Oh boy. Run, lady, run as fast as your skinny legs can carry you.

Emmy's smile gets bigger, and *fuck*, yup. I can totally tell Harlow and Emmy are related.

"I'm his girlfriend, actually. Also, the mother of his child." she deadpans.

"Oh. Well, it's nice to meet you." The nurse lies out of her ass. She turns back to Oliver. "You're all good here... for now. If you need anything, anything at all, just buzz, and I'll be happy to help." She runs her hand down Oliver's arm, giving him a lingering look of attraction before turning away.

"Hey, wait." Oliver calls out to her. She stops and looks back with hopeful eyes.

"If I do end up ringing the buzzer, make sure it's one of the other nurses who comes. I don't want to see you in my room again. And if it wasn't for the fact that I'm about to meet my daughter for the first time, I would be encouraging my girlfriend to kick your ass." Oliver looks at her like she's nothing.

18

Sure, you might think that what he just did was rude, but she deserved it after the way she blatantly disrespected Emmy like that.

I kind of wish I could see Emmy kick her ass. Oliver told me about the time in the bathroom at the clubhouse when she bashed in Mariah's face using the sink.

Kind of like the story Harlow told me about when she bashed some chick's face into the bar at a club for flirting with Dean. *God. I'm really in for it.* These two seriously are gonna turn me gray before I'm thirty.

The nurse looks at Oliver with wide eyes, and a blush of embarrassment brushes her cheeks. She turns to give Emmy a glare before huffing and storming out of the room.

"So, now that that's out of the way, I believe you have something for me?" He says, looking at the now sleeping baby in my arms. Emmy rushes over to Oliver, carefully crawling into his bed with a bright ecstatic smile on her face.

"Oh, you mean this little ball of cuteness?" I chuckle as I take his other side, sitting on the side of the bed. Oliver gets more comfortable while eyeing Melly with a sudden case of the nerves.

"Here." I say, handing him the baby. He takes her like I'm handing him the most precious thing in the world. Fitting, because I am.

"She's so beautiful, so tiny." Oliver breathes as he looks at our daughter like she hung the moon, slipping his thumb into her little hand.

"She's perfect." Emmy says, beaming down at Melody.

"I promise to always love and protect you, little one. You will never want or need for anything in your life." Oliver says in hushed tones to the baby.

"Um, Babe?" Oliver says, looking up at Emmy. She cocks a brow at him. "Two things."

"Okay?" Emmy smiles.

"One: I love you, you're my best friend, my love, my heart. But I'm afraid you're gonna have to share your spot as my number one girl."

Emmy bursts into giggles.

"That's okay. I can't think of anyone I'd rather share it with."

"And two: What is that awful smell?" Oliver says in disgust, scrunching up his nose.

I burst out laughing because as soon as he says that, the smell of Melody's dirty diaper hits my nose.

"Not it!" I say, raising my arms in the air in surrender. "I need a break after this morning."

Emmy smiles and rolls her eyes, heading over to the diaper bag. She looks over her shoulder with a pinched brow.

"What happened this morning?"

So, I tell them the story, and by the end Oliver is winching in pain from laughing so hard.

Emmy is giggling so much that she has to try a few times before she eventually gets Melody's diaper on properly.

Once the baby is cleaned up, Emmy gives her back to Oliver. We sit and talk until the doctor comes in and tells Oliver that he is healing well. That he's okay to go home in a few days but is on bed rest for the next few weeks. He is okay to go back to school, if that becomes an option, but has to limit himself until he's fully healed.

Once it starts getting late, I mention to Emmy that we should probably get going. She looks sad, but agrees.

With tears in her eyes, she says her goodbyes to Oliver.

I hold her hand the whole car ride home as she looks out the window with a forlorn look.

When we get to her house, Charlie sticks to Emmy like they are super-glued together. Giving them some space, I take care of the baby for the night.

Once I have Mel in her crib, I check in on Emmy. She and Charlie are asleep in their bed, TV still on, with the blanket fallen to the floor.

Shutting off the TV, I pull the covers back over them and kiss Emmy on the cheek.

"Sleep well, Princess. You're safe now."

CHAPTER 3
Emmy

OFFICIALLY BEING AT home with Melody has been interesting, to say the least. I'm not complaining. I'm loving every moment with her. She's the light of my life, my new reason to keep fighting whatever battles life plans to throw at me, but is waking up every hour on the hour screaming like a banshee really necessary?

I've already fed and changed her and I've spent the last hour rocking her to sleep; nothing's working.

It's four in the morning, I'm half asleep, exhausted both mentally and physically, and I'm very close to crying right along with her. "Sleep, Melly Belly." I beg. "Mama will give you anything you want."

"Why didn't you come get me? I would have helped." Charlie says, her voice cracking a bit from sleep. "And Babe, she's two weeks old, the only thing she wants are the two milkshakes attached to your chest." She jokes, giving me a half sleepy smile.

"Sorry." I sigh with Melody still fussing as I rock back and forth. "No point in both of us being awake. And she already had something to eat, so I don't think it's that."

"How come I didn't hear her crying?" She asks. "I woke up and the bed was empty."

"I turned off the baby monitor." I say, as Charlie takes the baby from me. She rocks her and sweetly hushes her.

"Again?" Charlie narrows her eyes at me with a sigh. "Babe, you have to stop doing that. How are we going to help if we don't know you need it? I don't mind getting up with her too."

"I know." I say, laying down on the bed that's set up for Tyson. "It's just that you guys have already done so much while I was in the hospital with Oliver. I want to do as much as I can before we have to go back to school."

"She's all of our daughter, meaning she is all of our responsibility. We don't mind at all." Charlie says, then looks down at the red-faced Melody. "Helps that she's pretty damn cute too." She coos, but it does nothing to settle the baby.

"What's going on in here?" Tyson asks from the bedroom doorway. I sit up on my elbows to look at him.

"Our pain-in-the-sexy-ass girlfriend doesn't seem to understand that we enjoy caring for our daughter just as much as she does, and that the bonus of having so many lovers is that everyone can help out, so that no one gets overwhelmed." Charlie looks at me, and I think she's trying to be intimidating, but she just looks sexy as fuck. "So let us." She growls.

A shiver takes over my body, apparently it's not too tired to get turned on. I give her a lazy smirk. Maybe it's because I've been without sex since the epic fuck fest that the guys and I had before the baby or maybe it's the lack of sleep fucking with my brain, but I feel bold. "Oh, I have something you can help me with." My voice is low and seductive.

Charlie's eyes widen slightly at my words, and her pupils grow lustful. "Not fair." She grumbles. My smile gets wider. "You can't say shit like that, Babe. You have another four weeks before I can worship your body again. You teasing me isn't helping." She whines. I can't help but laugh.

"Alright you two. Enough S-E-X talk around my Little Princess." Tyson grumbles and gathers Melody into his arms, taking her from Charlie.

"Hello there, My Little Lady." Tyson says, his face lighting up with pure joy, making my heart melt with the look he's giving her. Like she's the most important thing in the world. "Daddy Ty missed you very much. But Daddy O was being a grumpy butt and complaining the whole time I was there." Watching this sexy-as-sin man baby talk is, oddly, a turn on.

And just like that, at Tyson's voice, Melody stops crying. She gives him a few hitched breaths, calming down from her erratic crying, and after a few moments she starts to drift off to sleep.

"How did he do that?" Charlie whispers, astonishment taking over her tone as she looks at me with wide eyes.

"Some kind of Voodoo bullshit, if you ask me." I mutter, slightly annoyed that I spent an hour trying to calm her down, then this big, tattooed biker dude got her to not only calm down but fall back to sleep in under a minute.

Tyson lets out a soft chuckle. "I just have the magic touch." He grins over at me. "Hi, Princess." He finally greets me.

"Hi," I pout, walking over to him and kissing our daughter on the forehead. "Well, maybe you can use your magic touch on me sometime soon." I say, giving him a sexy smirk of my own.

He lets out a low growl that makes me bite my lip and clench my thighs.

"Alright, little horn dog." Charlie laughs, pulling me into her arms so that my back is to her front.

"Sorry." I laugh. "I don't think I've been this long without sex in over a year, so my brain is making everything dirty."

Tyson carefully places Melody in her crib. He puts his finger to his lips, indicating for us to be quiet, and nodding his head to the door.

We leave and head down to the living room so that we don't wake up anyone in the house.

Charlie sits down on the couch and pulls me onto her lap. "What's the verdict?" Charlie asks Tyson.

The Phantom Reapers called church, and Tyson was called in. He left us with another member who watched over the house, and was not happy about having to leave us for any amount of time. But I was glad he could check on Oliver.

"Well, I'll start with Emmy's father." Tyson says, taking a seat on the chair next to us. My body tenses at his words.

"He's no father of mine." I spit. Just the idea of that man makes my stomach turn. I still can't believe that the crazy fucker who has been sending me those gifts and text messages was my dead-beat dad all along. Who just decides out of nowhere that they want someone's baby?!

I knew that the president of the Savage Hellhounds was not a sane man. He's an unpredictable, cold-blooded killer; and knowing that my sperm donor has some delusional idea that he's gonna take my child from me, makes me wanna channel my inner Queenie. I'm not one for violence, but I don't hold back if you mess with the ones I love. I'm not a pushover.

And now that I'm a mother? Oh, watch out buddy, you're poking at the wrong mama bear because I will bite the fuck back!

"Sorry, you're right. Dagger and the Savage Hellhounds have been quiet. No one has seen any of them in a while. Dad doesn't like it. He thinks they are planning something big.

We don't know if it has to do with the Phantom Reapers or if it has to do with the fucked up shit Dagger has been doing to you." Tyson growls.

Once everything at the hospital calmed down and Olly was stable, I told Charlie and the others about the phone call I received just as I went into labor.

Tyson was on the phone right away with his dad. Steel was already on his way down because of the shooting, but he brought along a few extra men to keep an eye on everything. Ever since, Tyson hasn't allowed me or the baby to go unwatched by him or one of his men.

He hated not being there with me at the hospital, but Dagger said that he wanted Melody for himself, she is number one to be watched.

"We are stuck at this point. We don't know if we should bring the fight to them and get it over with, or wait until they strike and just be ready for when it comes."

"Well, you always have Harlow for backup if you need it. I know she's been itching to come up here and handle everything herself." I smile.

Let's just say that Harlow did not like what happened at the school and even cursed Tyson out for not keeping Brittany alive so that she could add her to her next show.

I've heard about her shows and her playdates. Brittany got off easy with a bullet to the brain. Although, a part of me would have liked to see that cunt suffer.

I don't care what the reasoning was for that crazy bitch being the way she was, and after everything she did, after all the hurt she caused my family, I can't find it in me to care. I'm just glad she's gone. It means there's one less threat to me and my family.

Yeah, get rid of one, gain another. Isn't life just grand-fucking-dandy.

"After what I saw her do to Talon's dad..." Tyson shivers violently at the thought. "Anyways, involving *her* in all this is probably not the safest solution for any of us, however well-meaning she may be."

"She's been texting me non-stop about seeing the baby. It took a lot of convincing for her to wait until summer to come visit." I tell him. He smiles softly in response. It's clear that he adores her, even if she freaked him out a bit on her last visit.

"And then there's school." Tyson says, getting back on track while giving the baby monitor a glance, turning it back on, and making sure Melody is still sleeping soundly. "I got a call from Mr. Tucker."

That gets both Charlie and me to sit up a little straighter. "And?" she urges.

"And, as of next week, you're all due back to school." Tyson says, irritation taking over his face.

"You're fucking kidding me, right? Please tell me you're joking? After everything, we are not even gonna be let off three months early, or at least finish out in another school?" Charlie asks, growing angrier by the minute.

"There's more." Tyson sighs.

"Fucking great. Of course there is." I grumble.

"Every student, who isn't on probation and is just there because their parents don't want to deal with them, are being sent to schools closer to their residences."

"So the school is gonna go from what, sixty students, to like thirty now? What's the point of keeping all the staff on for such a small amount?" Charlie asks.

"I don't know. Mr. Tucker says that it's not fair to put all the teachers out of work this early, and that the easiest solution for the remainder of the students who are on probation, is for them to finish out at the school rather than try and deal with all the legal stuff." He exhales with a sigh.

"Wow, just wow." Charlie says, shaking her head.

"Yep, and that means Felicity won't be there when you get back." Tyson says, looking at me with regret filling his eyes as he breaks the news that Charlie's and my best friend won't be there to graduate with us.

"No." I breathe out in horror, ready to cry.

Charlie wraps her arms around me, snuggling me back into her chest. Closing my eyes, I blink back the tears.

"Anything else you wanna tell us, big guy? Wanna shit on our parade some more?" Charlie snarks.

"Hey, don't get all pissy with me. I know it sucks, but I have no control over this. I'm just the messenger. We will go back to school, you guys will work your butts off, study hard, and then we can all move the fuck on from Emerald Lake Prep. I'm starting to think that damn school is more of a curse than a blessing." Tyson says.

"It wasn't always this bad." Charlie says.

"Not until I got there." I mumble into her chest, then peek up at her. "Everything started going to shit the moment I got there."

"Hey." Tyson says, getting my attention. "You were *not* the reason any of that shit happened. That bitch had been unstable long before you arrived at that school. Hell, if you didn't show up and help Brittany show her true colors, she probably would have snuck into Oliver's room at some point and either killed him or kidnapped him. I would not be surprised if she had some kind of shrine for him somewhere."

I scrunch up my nose in disgust at that idea.

"Come here." He commands. I shiver with delight at his words. Charlie feels what Tyson is doing to me and chuckles lightly in my ear.

"I'm gonna head back to bed. If the baby wakes up again, you will *not* get up, okay? I'll bring her to you, and you can feed her in bed while we do everything else. I know you want to do as much as you can with her before you're only able to see her on the weekends, but you need to let us help, so you're not burning yourself out trying to do everything by yourself. A healthy and happy mama equals a happy and healthy baby."

"Alright, alright." I say in defeat, too tired to argue. Charlie kisses my cheek before we both stand up, and she walks away, heading up to our room.

Looking back at Tyson, I see the heat in his eyes as he eyes me up and down. I don't know what he sees because I'm only in my sleep shorts and one of the guy's shirts, which I think even has some baby puke on it. I don't exactly know which of the guys' shirts I ended up borrowing, but at this point, they are all mine.

My hair is in a messy bun. Not one of the cute ones that girls try so hard to get just right, no, the one where half of my hair is hanging out, and the scrunchie is barely hanging on for its life.

But here this man is, looking at me like I'm some kind of snack.

"What?" I ask, raising a brow at him.

"I told you to do something, didn't I?" He asks, voice low and scratchy. Fuck, the sound of it has me instantly wet. God, I need to get laid, and soon, before I become a walking sex freak.

"And?" I ask, giving him the last bit of sass that I have left in me for the night.

"And... don't make me repeat myself." His tone leaves no room for argument.

Doing as he told me to in the first place, I shuffle my way over to him and straddle his lap. I wrap my arms around his neck, as he brings his around my waist, crushing me to his body. I love the feeling of being surrounded by his warm, strong, protective arms.

"I love you, Princess." He says into the top of my head before giving it a kiss.

"I love you, too." I whisper into his neck.

"Everything is going to be okay. I won't let anyone hurt you or our baby girl, okay? And I'll die trying."

"No. No talk of dying." I say, hugging him tighter to me, scared at the idea of losing him, or any of them.

"Nothing will take me away from you. I finally have you after all these years, and I never plan on letting you go. You're stuck with me forever." He states.

"And you're stuck with me even after forever." I counter.

26

"I'm not stuck with you, Princess. I'm blessed to have you. There's a difference. The universe, for some unknown reason that I don't plan on questioning, gave me you and because of that, I plan on spending every day for the rest of my life showing you that I'm worthy of being someone you love."

Fuck, his words have me crying again, but this time, they are happy tears.

"Thank you." I say, kissing his neck.

"For what?" He asks, stroking my hair.

"For everything. But most of all, for just being you. For choosing me. You could have had any woman you wanted."

"I did get the woman I wanted. Why choose one of them, when I could have the goddess herself." He says with a confident glint in his eyes.

Oh, he's smooth.

"Let's go to bed. The lack of sleep is making you corny." I joke.

Tyson just chuckles. Holding me up by my ass cheeks, he carries me to bed and tucks me in. I'm almost passed out by the time he's done, but I still feel the warmth of his kiss on my forehead and his whispers of goodnight before sleep takes me fully.

CHAPTER 4
Oliver

"THANK FUCK, I'M getting out of here. I've been going crazy sitting in this damn bed all the time." I complain.

We're all heading back to Emerald Lake Prep today. Woo-*fucking*-hoo. I don't get why they opened that damn school back up again. The place should be shut down for good. Clearly no one there is good at their job. But that doesn't matter when money is involved, and that's all that the school board sees when they look at this place. It's just a dumping ground for rich people to drop their kids off, so they can run off when they don't want to deal with the responsibility of being a parent to a troubled teen.

Sure, the idea of helping troubled youth is an honorable one, but the direction that this school has been heading in over the past few years, makes it seem like that is no longer their goal.

When I first started at this school, it was honestly a lot of help. We had a different counselor, an older woman who actually cared about all the kids, kind of like the new one we have now. The other teachers also cared about their jobs and all of the kids got the help they needed, but over time everything changed. The only thing that seems to matter now is money.

The school only takes a certain amount of kids on probation a year. The limit was probably put in place because of the school not getting enough money from the government. Mr. Tucker might be an okay guy, but I have a feeling he's in on it too. But really, that doesn't matter anymore, when we have less than three months left before we are done and out for good. I can't wait to be able to just move on with our lives and have some real control over my own future.

"Dude, you got shot like, what, less than three weeks ago. The outer wounds might be mostly healed, but you still got shit that needs to heal on the inside, you know." Tyson says, snatching the bag from my hand and forcing me to sit back down on the bed.

"I can pack my own damn bag." I argue.

"You can sit your stubborn ass down and shut up!" Tyson smirks, shaking his head in amusement at the pissed off look on my face.

"Emmy is at home, waiting for us, and as much as it's killing her to leave Melody behind, she's really excited to see you. This house arrest bullshit has been hard on her."

It's been hard on me too. I've been going crazy not being able to hold my Firefly. To feel her safe in my arms. Ever since the accident, when I woke up from that nightmare, I've been waking up in cold sweats, screaming Emmy's name, and looking around for Melody. I always have to look at the screensaver on my phone with all three of us to remember that they are safe.

No thanks to you.

Shaking my head to get out of my own mind, I look up at Tyson who's just shoving everything in the bag.

"You know, I wanna kick your ass." I casually throw out.

Tyson looks back at me with a raised brow. "And why the fuck do you wanna do that?" He chuckles.

"Because, you lucky bastard! You've been living with her. You've been around her all day, helping with the baby. I should be there too. You're new, so go to the back of the line and wait your turn," I say, glaring at him.

He barks out a laugh. "It's not a competition, you asshole. And of course I'm there every day. Why would I put someone else on guard, when I can do it myself? It's bad enough that I'm not going to be there to watch over Melody myself after today. I wanted to do as much as I could before we all had to head back."

"So, who is going to be taking your place?" I ask, needing to know who's in charge of keeping that crazy fucker away from our daughter.

"We will have three people watching the house at all times. And yes, when Amy takes her out of the house, they will be on them like flies on shit. I don't care how it looks. This town knows who we are; they won't fuck with them if they know what's good for their health. I want eyes on that house every single moment of the day. I won't risk our daughter's safety. Until we are able to do it ourselves, they will be there in our place." Tyson says, the protectiveness in his voice over our daughter makes me proud to call him my brother.

"You know, I thought having my brother join our little rag-tag, oddball, brother-boyfriend group thing we have going on would be weird, but it's not too bad," I say, grunting as I get up and head over to him snatching my boxers from his hand as he raids my underwear drawer. "I can do that." I mutter under my breath while taking over packing the bag, but he takes it back from me and places it on the bed.

"The whole thing is... different, that's for sure. And I thought I'd need more of a chance to get used to everything, but with all the time we've spent together, even all of us as a group, getting ready before the baby was born, it got me used to things. It's nice, you know, to be a part of a little family that loves and cares for each other so much like you all do."

I can't help but grin. "Aww, is the MC Enforcer getting all mushy?" I say in a joking baby voice.

"Fuck off." Tyson huffs out a laugh and puts me in a headlock.

"Ouch! Gunshot victim here, remember?" I shout.

He lets me go, and I straighten my hair. "Whatever." he says and rolls his eyes. "Is that everything?"

Looking around the room, I mark off all the items on my mental checklist. "Yup."

"Alright, let's go get our girl, then."

Tyson

Seeing Emmy break down when we said goodbye to Melody broke something in me. Fuck, I hate seeing my Princess cry, and all I want to do when that happens is whatever it takes to make her happy again. But as much as I tried, and trust me I did, I can't change this.

We get to go back every weekend, and Amy can come to the school sometimes too, but it's still gonna hurt to be away from a piece of our heart. Hell, she is the biggest piece of it.

From the moment I got a good look at her big blue eyes in that hospital room, she owned me. I don't give a single fuck that she doesn't have any of my DNA. That little girl is just as much mine as she is anyone else's in our little family.

Each of my girls owns half of my heart, and I would not change it for the world.

Never in a million years, no matter how much I craved Emmy since meeting her in the tattoo shop, did I ever think she would actually be mine. I'm one lucky bastard. She changed me for the better, and I'm gonna fight like hell to make sure I'm the man she deserves. I will do everything in my power to be the best damn dad I can be.

Soft sobs from the back seat have me looking in the rear-view mirror. Emmy is back there with Oliver, clutching his good side like he's her lifeline as she cries into the crook of his neck.

Oliver's arms are tightly wrapped around her as he strokes her hand with one of his while rubbing her side with the other, and whispering words of love and support in her ear. I've never been so damn proud of my brother than I have been since Emmy came back into his life.

He might think every shitty thing that has happened to Emmy is his fault, but it's not. He's been one of the reasons why she hasn't broken down and given up.

Looking over at Charlie, I can see tears in her own eyes as she tries to be strong for Emmy.

She decided to let Oliver have her to himself for the car ride, but I can see how badly she wants to be the one back there consoling her girlfriend with how tense her body is and the sad look on her face.

The love that Charlie and the guys have for Emmy, and the love Emmy has for them in return, can't be put into words. It's life changing. And I'm honored I get to be a part of that.

Charlie sniffs and wipes her eyes. Taking my hand off the steering wheel, I give Charlie's shoulder a squeeze in an attempt to comfort her. She looks over at me with watery eyes and gives me a pained smile.

I know how they feel. My heart is breaking right alongside theirs. Having to hand Melly over to Amy, after saying my goodbyes, was like I was handing a piece of myself over.

I know she is in good hands with Amy and Rick, but I can't help and worry about all the little things that other people might think are silly.

Like, is she eating enough? Does Amy know what song gets her to sleep? Does she have the right blanket or the right soother? Does Amy know which cry means what?

Taking care of my Little Princess almost full time the past few weeks has been some of the best times of my life. Hearing her sounds of contentment. Rocking her to sleep. Just spending hours holding this tiny little girl in my arms has become a huge part of my life. It's gonna feel strange, *wrong*, to just go back to the way things were before. Well, as much as it can.

The rest of the ride is depressing as fuck. Eventually, both Emmy and Charlie fall asleep.

When we pull up to the parking lot of the school, Talon and Ben are waiting there, hand in hand with excited and anxious faces.

Before I even shut off the car, Talon is opening the car door on Emmy's side.

"Shh." Oliver says in a hushed tone. "She's having a hard time leaving Melody behind and is not taking it very well. She cried almost the whole two hours, so she's probably exhausted and drained."

Talon nods and carefully gathers Emmy into his arms. She doesn't wake but stirs a bit in his arms, before snuggling into his chest.

Talon lets out a breath as his body relaxes at her touch. He looks down at her like she consumes his whole world. Giving her a lingering kiss on the forehead, he turns and starts to take her into the school.

"Hey, man." I greet Ben with a nod as I make my way to the trunk.

"Hey." He says back before opening the car door for Charlie. I hear a few hushed words, probably Ben waking Charlie up, and then she gets out and hugs Ben tightly. To see the kind of friendship they have formed and know that it's not just everyone learning to get along for Emmy's sake is nice. We truly are a little family.

"I'll help you with these." Ben says as Charlie helps a grunting Oliver into the school. He swats at her, telling her to go away, but she just narrows her eyes, lightly slaps him upside the head and tells him to get the fuck over it.

Charlie really is one of my favorite people. And God help us all when she becomes friends with Harlow and Evie, because we all know that's bound to happen.

I really don't stand a chance with all these women in my life, do I? *Fuck.*

"So how's everything? Are you guys doing okay?" I ask. That's a stupid question though, because how could they be? They met their daughter once and won't get to see her until the weekend.

Amy is coming up here for their first visit so that Talon and Ben can spend more time with Melody.

Emmy has video chatted with the guys for hours on end since leaving the hospital. Most of the time they just went about their day while still on call, just so that they could feel as close to each other as possible. When Emmy would sing Melody to sleep, the guys would be there to sing right along with her through the phone. We even gave them access to her baby monitor, which I quickly regretted, when I got a call at 2 am from Talon bitching that Melody was awake and that I hadn't gotten to her fast enough for his liking.

I was sleeping in the same room, but heard no crying. I checked on her, and she was just lying there looking up at the ceiling. Talon would not shut up unless I picked her up and held her until she fell back asleep.

He said he didn't like her just laying there wide awake while we were all sleeping. He said that if she's up, one of us should be too.

I never wanted to punch that man more than I did in that moment.

"The best we can be. It helped that Talon and I had each other, but it hurts not to be there, you know? To be able to do what you guys are doing for her. To not be able to hold our girls and take care of them."

I didn't know, because I got to do exactly that, but I understand what he means.

"And Oliver must have been a pain in the ass." he laughs. "Being so close but not being able to be there either."

"Oh, don't even get me started." I groan. Ben just laughs and shakes his head. He looks towards the school at his lovers, with a look of longing as they head up the front steps.

"Go." I say, nodding my head in Emmy and Talon's direction. "I'll take these."

He hesitates for only a moment before jogging over to them. Talon stops when he hears Ben. Ben leans over smiling down at a sleeping Emmy and kissing her forehead as Talon did before, then smiles up at Talon and places a loving soft kiss on his lips before they disappear into the school together.

I follow everyone up to the girls' dorm, trailing behind them. I'm the last one to get to the top floor, and when I open the door that leads into the hallway of rooms, I bump into Oliver, but he doesn't budge. He just stands there stiff as a board, staring at a spot on the floor.

Following his line of sight, I stop when my eyes reach a very light stain on the flooring, which I can only assume is Oliver's blood. The building is old with wooden floors, so when Oliver was shot, the boards soaked up some of his blood, and I'm guessing they were unable to get it all out.

"You okay, man?" I ask Oliver, stepping in front of him, snapping him out of his trance.

"What?" He asks, blinking up at me. "Yeah. I'm fine." He says, shaking his head. "I'd be better with my girl in my arms, though. Come on."

He steps around me, and follows the others into the girls' room.

Charlie crawls into the bed next to a still sleeping Emmy as the guys and I work together to clean up the best we can.

Turns out, the bitch trashed the room when she went on her little hunting and killing spree. Emmy and Charlie are sleeping in the spare bed that was oddly untouched unlike the rest of the room. The other beds had the blankets and pillows ripped off. Clothes were left hanging out of the dresser drawers and scattered across the floor. Photo frames were smashed, and many other items ruined.

We try to salvage anything we can. Thankfully the photos were still in good shape, and the blankets and clothes only need washing.

"She's sleeping in our room tonight." Talon says, crossing his arms as he looks at our girl. "You had her this whole time, since the shooting. It's my and Ben's turn."

"Umm. Not everyone has had time with her. I've been recovering from a fucking gun shot wound and on house arrest too, asshole." Oliver grumbles, taking a seat at the end of the empty bed.

"Well fine, but these two did." Looking from me to Charlie, Talon replies, "And you share a room with us anyways."

"We could always push the beds together like before." Ben suggests.

"Before?" I ask.

"Yeah, when we all worship her body at the same time." Talon gives me a mischievous smile. "Too bad you're not down for that. It's one of the hottest, most erotic things. And *she* makes it even better."

Narrowing my eyes at him, I scoff. "I don't need to be involved in your sex-capades, thank you very much. I plan on loving her, and praising her body all on my own. I want her all to myself when we are together."

"Hey, don't knock it until you try it. I know she would love a brother sandwich. You should have seen how her face lit up like a Christmas tree when I mentioned it." Talon says, coming up behind Ben and wrapping his arms around his boyfriend, giving his neck a kiss. Ben shivers, and a blush creeps up his face when his eyes meet mine. I just smirk as he quickly looks away.

"It's a lot like the looks she gives us when we're about to share her." Talon's smile turns dreamy as if he's remembering. "Anyways..." Talon says, moving away from Ben and adjusting his crotch. I huff out a laugh and shake my head. "I like the bed idea. We'll let them get some sleep and set up our own room, get everything ready."

"What about Charlie?" Ben asks.

"I think she will be okay on her own for the night. As long as Emmy is with one of you, I don't see why it would be a big deal." I say.

"I just feel bad that Felicity is gone. Charlie would always hang out with her while Emmy was with us.

She hates it when Charlie is alone while we are together doing other things." Ben says, with worry etching his face as he looks at the girls.

"Well, Charlie is a big girl, and this is our life. Charlie can't be with someone at all times, and I think she knows that. It's Emmy who feels bad. Once we are out on our own, Charlie can hang out with Melody." I chuckle.

"I mean, that's what I plan on doing whenever she spends time with just you two." Oliver says, looking from Ben to Talon. "Have you seen that face? We are in so much trouble, guys. She's gonna have us wrapped around her little finger."

"Too late." I grin. "That little girl owns me. But I wouldn't have it any other way."

After leaving the guys to do their thing, I head down to the main office to talk with Mr. Tucker. He tells me that classes will start tomorrow, and they are supposed to go on as if nothing happened. To pick up right where we left off. I can't help but scoff at how easy he can just sweep this under the rug.

I used to think Mr. Tucker was a good guy. My dad knew him growing up and said he was a decent man, but I'm starting to think that Mr. Tucker is not the stand-up-guy he tries to portray. I mean he's nowhere near as shitty of a person as the last two nasty fuckers who got fired, but he's not someone I'd trust to have my back either; and that makes him someone to keep an eye on.

Sighing as I make my way into my cabin, I toss my keys on the counter and place my bag on the couch. Looking around, I feel like this place isn't mine anymore. I mean, I never really felt at home here because I knew this was just a temporary place, but now it really feels like I don't belong. I started to feel content spending so much time at Amy's, like that's where I was meant to be. Not Amy's house exactly, but anywhere that my girls are.

Now this small little cabin just feels cold and empty.

My phone rings, jolting me out of my own thoughts. Looking at my phone, I see the name "Crazy Bitch" pop up.

Knowing I can't avoid her forever, I pick up.

"Hello." I greet her, waiting to get chewed out.

"*It's ALIVE!*" She cheers on the other side of the phone, dramatically. I can hear a *'for now'* come from Neo in the background, followed by a chuckle and then a giggle. "*Well, well, well, look who decided to grace me with the decency of answering my call. It's not like my sister just gave birth during a school shooting or anything.*"

"Low, she's fine. Well, as fine as a new mother can be while having to leave her baby behind to come back to this hellhole of a school." I mutter, starting to undress as I make my way to the bathroom.

"*I could always get rid of the judge and put someone who is under my thumb in his place.*" she chirps. "*That way she can be done with her time, and be at home with that cutie pie.*"

"Personally, I'm not completely opposed to that idea, but you know Emmy. She's not used to your world, and I don't think she would enjoy you killing someone in her honor unless he really, *really* deserved it."

"*You're no fun!*" She says, sounding disappointed.

"What can I do for you, oh great one?" I say playfully, hoping to keep her in a good mood.

"*Well, first off, you can convince my sister to let me come up sooner.*" She says.

"Low..." I sigh.

"*Fine! She's lucky there's so much shit going on, or I wouldn't be afraid to get my own way.*" She snarks back.

"Really?" I deadpan.

"*Oh, come on. At least this time it wasn't her getting hurt. I call that a win. So, how's your brother?*" She asks.

"Annoying as fuck. But he's healing well."

"*I still wish you saved me that bitch so that I could enjoy her pain for myself.*" She purrs.

"Not really the thing I was thinking about at that moment. All I wanted to do was put down the threat to my girl, my daughter, and my brother. I'm just fucking pissed I didn't do it before the cunt caused the damage she did." I growl.

"*Oh Ty Ty, be careful! You're gonna piss my pet off with all that foreplay you're trying with me.*" She says in a voice of amusement. "*I love hearing my bestie being all blood thirsty.*"

A growl comes from the other end, followed by a possessive *'Mine'*. To which she replies. *'Actually, you're mine'* in a demanding no-nonsense voice. God, if they keep talking like this to each other, I'm going to have to listen to them have sex on the phone.

A lusty moan filters through the other end, followed by some male grunting. *Fuck, never mind, too late.*

"*Well, keep me updated.*" She says in a breathy tone, and I cringe as I hear skin slapping together. "*I'm gonna let you go. People to do, orgasms to have. Bye!*" And just before she hangs up, my ears are met with a high-pitched scream.

Why do I have friends like this? Who would have thought my best friend would be a fucking serial killer and sex maniac? But I'd rather be on her good side, than any other.

I shower and crawl into bed, my mind on fire with the memories of that day. Seeing my brother get shot. Watching him start to slip away in my arms. I never felt so helpless in my life.

It felt amazing to be able to be the one to take that bitch down.

When everything settled down at the hospital, I had to talk to the police, and because I was the one who actually killed her, they were questioning me for hours.

I told them that she was going after my loved ones, and I followed her. That I was gonna do whatever it took to keep her from harming any more of my family.

In the end, they saw it as self-defense. I don't know what the report originally said, but Harlow made sure I came out scot-free, and I didn't question it.

With that out of the way, I was free to be with Emmy, by her side and keeping her safe.

Grabbing my phone, I switch on the camera feed for the baby's room. Amy sits in the rocking chair, singing softly to Melody as she gives her a bottle.

"Good night, my Little Princess." I say, placing my hand on the screen. "Daddy Ty loves you so fucking much."

CHAPTER 5
Emmy

JOLTING AWAKE, I sit up, confused about where I am. It's dark, but as my eyes adjust I see that I'm not in my room at home. Reality hits me hard as I remember I'm back at school while my baby girl is two hours away from me.

Tears start to burn the back of my eyes. Squeezing them shut, I try to get a hold of myself. I've cried for hours already, and it's not going to change the situation.

A light snore grabs my attention. Looking beside me, I see Talon cuddled into Ben, mouth hanging open as he drools onto Ben's chest.

Grinning, I look to my other side, seeing Oliver. He's sleeping on his back, with one arm under his pillow and the other over his gunshot wound.

As I'm watching, Oliver grumbles something in his sleep. His face looks tight with worry as whatever he's dreaming about gets him worked up.

Cuddling into him, I place my head on his chest, listening to his heart beat. Bringing my hand up, I caress his worried brow until he starts to relax at my touch.

Ben shifts closer, curling into me so that my back is to his front, and I can feel his cock against my ass.

How is he hard in his sleep, and it's not even morning yet?
"Emmy..." Ben moans in his sleep. I smile against Oliver's chest. I guess that answers my question. *Whatever he's dreaming about sounds like something I might want to try while awake. I wonder if he'll remember so we can do a replay in real life.*

As much as my heart hurts to be away from my daughter, I can't help but feel beyond happy to have my guys within arms reach again. I missed them so fucking much that it hurt my heart and soul to be away from them.

My goal is to work hard and get good grades while spending time with my loves to keep myself as busy as I can, so that my mind isn't thinking about being away.

I'll do my video chats with Amy and Melly, or watch her on the camera feed, as much as I can for peace of mind, and hope that the weeks fly by.

Feeling a little more at peace, I close my eyes and allow the warmth and love of my guys to make me feel safe and protected. All that's missing is Tyson. It's going to take some getting used to, building a relationship with him that mirrors the same dynamic as Charlie and mine.

"Emmy!" A blood-curdling scream pierces my ears. Oliver shoots up into a seated position, knocking me off his chest and onto my back, as he looks around frantically.

"Oliver. It's okay, I'm right here." I say, placing my hand on his back in a calming gesture. He flinches at my touch as he becomes aware of his surroundings.

His eyes meet mine and my heart breaks with all the fear I see in them.

"Emmy." He croaks, pulling me into his arms and hugging me tightly, like he needs the contact to tell himself that I'm real, that I'm there and not just a figment of his imagination.

"I'm here, Olly Bear. I'm okay. You're okay, shhh." I soothe as I rub his back in a circular motion.

It feels like hours before either of us move. He needs this, and I'll stay here as long as it takes for him to trust that I am actually safe and in his arms.

Clearly, his reaction was not one of a normal bad dream or nightmare. Something tells me this is a recurring thing, and my soul aches for him. *Fuck*, my heart splinters more at the realization that I wasn't there for him all the previous times he has woken up with that pain and fear in his eyes.

He had a few small panic attacks in the hospital besides the first one when he woke up, but despite that, I thought it was a one-time thing. Nothing I should really worry about, until now. I won't ask him about it, at least not yet. I want to see if he comes to me on his own.

"What time is it?" He asks, pulling away from me.

"6 a.m." Ben says in a sleepy voice from beside me. Looking over, I see that Oliver's outburst woke them up too.

"Perfect. My alarm was about to go off anyway." Oliver says, climbing out of the bed.

"Where are you going?" I ask with a pinched brow.

"To the bathroom, wanna come?" He asks, looking back at me with a cocked brow and a smirk. "Gotta drain the lizard. I think I can do it myself, but I mean if you wanna help, by all means."

I scrunch my nose up at him. "Nah, I'm good, that's all you." I say, waving my hand towards the bathroom.

He chuckles deeply, mirth painting his face, and all evidence of what just happened is gone. He leans over and places a soft, but passionate kiss on my lips making me moan and causing my body to wake up, in more than one way.

"Careful, Firefly, or this morning wood won't be going away on its own." He says against my lips.

He pulls back with a heated look, before turning around and heading towards the bathroom. "I'm gonna take a shower while I'm in there." He says looking over his shoulder and throwing me a wink in a joking manner.

"Want any help?" I ask, fucking with him just a little bit more.

"Fuck!" He groans before shutting the bathroom door.

I fling myself back onto the bed with a sexually frustrated sigh. These next 4 weeks need to fly by, or I'm gonna explode from the sexual tension.

"Would me sucking Ben off in any way help with the situation you're finding yourself in?" Talon asks in a husky tone, seeing how wanting and turned on I am. I turn my head and narrow my eyes at him, flipping him off.

"Fuck you." I grumble.

"Soon, Baby Girl. Very soon." He promises and fuck, I just grow wetter.

The first day back felt weird. Being away from school for so long then coming back felt like reliving the first day of the school year all over again.

So much has changed. The classes are smaller. The school went from having sixty students to only thirty.

We are allowed to have our cell phones back, but I'm thinking it's a little too late for that. Maybe if we were allowed our phones before, someone could have called 911 as soon as they saw Brittany with a gun, instead of waiting until she shot a few guards, killed a girl, shot Olly, and almost got to me and my loved ones.

I never liked Krissy, but she didn't deserve to die. And poor Joe. I'm so glad he is okay and healing well.

At lunch the guys joke around and talk about nothing in particular, while Charlie is chatting with some girl who she got assigned a project with in English, but all I can do is stare at the chair across the table that Felicity used to sit in. I miss my bestie. With everything going on this past year, I feel like we started to drift apart and I hate it. And now with her being gone, it stings like a bitch and leaves me with so much regret.

"I was a shitty friend." I say, speaking for the first time since we sat down. The guys stop talking and look at me.

"What?" Ben asks.

"To Lissy. With spending so much time between you guys, I never had any for her, not really anyway. Charlie was the only one being a good friend to her since this school year started."

Talon grabs my hand and brings it to his lips, placing a kiss to the back of it. "You had a lot going on, babe. She knew that, and she understood. Yes, she had Charlie, but she had you too."

"Still, I wish I spent more time with her. And now she's gone, and God knows when I'll be able to see her again."

We've been texting a lot since the shooting, and I've been trying my hardest to be a better friend, but it's not the same.

"Once we get out of here, you are going to be able to see her whenever you want. Even when she goes off to university. You want to go spend the weekend with her? We got Mel. You want her to come out to visit us? We will make sure we have a big enough house for a guestroom." Ben says. The earnest look in his eyes makes my heart warm, thawing my self-hatred. He loves me so much and really does want to do whatever he can to make me happy.

"You know what? You're right. Once we are out of here, everything will be so much better. We will have our freedom back." I smile.

"When we are done with this school, Shorty, we plan on taking you to places you can only imagine in your wildest dreams." Talon says, adding to our fantasy about what our future will look like in just a few short months.

It sounds like heaven.

41

"Miss Knox." The teacher calls out, getting my attention. I'm sitting here in math class which is my worst subject, and I have absolutely no interest in this shit whatsoever. I mean, sure, we are going to need basic math in our lives, but half of this shit we won't even use.

"What?" I ask, pulling my gaze away from the window where I was watching a butterfly sitting on the ledge.

"I asked you if you knew the answer to this question." He repeats, pointing to the board.

"Umm... no?" I reply.

"See me after class." He says, with a look of disappointment on his face, but what the hell did he expect? With all the bullshit going on in my life, math was the last thing on my mind. Who needs the square root of bull-shit when you have crazy bitches trying to kill you, and a fucked up delusional father who wants your damn baby?

Groaning, I lower myself in my desk, avoiding the worried look from Charlie, and the pissed off look from Oliver, who also looks seconds away from punching the teacher in the face. His protectiveness, even over something so small, such as this, was kind of hot. Sometimes it's annoying, but it's also nice to know he cares about me with this kind of intensity.

"Maybe if you spent more time paying attention, then off in your own little dream world, you would be able to answer questions when I ask."

Okay this new teacher is a fucking dick. I have no idea why the old one left with only a few months left in the year, but I would not be surprised if it was because of all the fucked up shit that happens here. *I'm over it too buddy, I feel ya.*

Oliver growls low, growing more irritated, and Talon coughs out "prick" under his breath from the other side of the room where he sits with Ben at his side.

Ben shakes his head, and the room of maybe ten other students start to snicker.

"Mr. Knight, is it?" The teacher asks, stopping in front of Talon's desk.

"The one and only." Talon grins.

"Detention after school. Meet me in the dining hall for supper." The teacher says.

"Aw, are we gonna have a nice meal together and get to know one another? I don't know, teach, I gotta say you're not really my type. I like them tall, tattooed with red hair. Or, drop dead gorgeous with curves for days and you, sir, have none of those."

I smother a grin. God, Talon really did choose the worst times to open his mouth.

The teacher just glares at him, then goes about his lesson. Talon looks back over his shoulder and gives me a wink. My belly flutters and I bite my lower lip. His pupils go wide, promising me all the deliciously dirty things he's gonna do to me once my doctor gives me the go ahead to fuck my men like a succubus who just came into her powers.

"Alright. Since half of you are missing, and there are less than twenty of you, for the remainder of the year, we will be spending the time in this class a little differently. You have the choice of going to the weight room, pool, and, when the weather permits it, we will be canoeing or hiking. Today, since it's pouring outside, I'll give you the option of going to work out, or swim in the pool."

Tyson was explaining things and although I could hear everything he was saying, I was distracted by the way his muscles flexed when he crossed his arms, or how his brow twitches as he looks at all the other kids with annoyance.

When his eyes land on me, they soften and I can tell he wants to smile, but with all eyes on him, he keeps his professionalism in place.

"Come on, Butterfly. Let's go get our bathing suits." Ben says, offering his hand. I smile at him and his newest nickname for me. I guess 'cocoon' doesn't work since I'm not carrying something inside me anymore.

"You're not going to work out?" I ask Ben and Talon. They love working out. It's one of the few ways they get their frustration out. And being home, they didn't have access to the type of equipment that they have here.

"And miss the opportunity to see you in a bikini? Nah, Shorty, I wouldn't miss that for the world." Talon smirks. I roll my eyes at him, but give him a smile in return.

Hand in hand, we all head up to the changing rooms. Damn, I was so fucking happy to be back around my guys.

Tyson

God, I hate being back here. I mean, I'm glad I'm here because I get to be close to Emmy and the others; but I hate being a teacher. Hell, I'm only the gym teacher, that barely qualifies. *Right?* I mean, no hate against them as a whole, and all the power to whoever enjoys their jobs, but this shit sucks. And teenagers are annoying.

Most of the guys, including Oliver, went to the gym, but Ben and Talon walk through the boys' changing room doors and I'm surprised to see them here. I thought they would take a chance to work out without giving up free time with Emmy, or waking up at a crazy fucking hour like Oliver does.

But I quickly understand why they chose swimming when the girls' changing room door opens and Emmy walks out looking so fucking delicious that it takes everything in me not to march over there, push her against the wall and ram my tongue down her throat.

"You alright there, Mr. Kingston?" Charlie asks, popping up next to me, coming out of nowhere. "You might wanna avert your gaze there, or little Johnny is gonna be standing tall and proud any moment now." Tearing my eyes off my goddess of a girlfriend, I turn to Charlie with a look of annoyance. She just grins at me, her eyes wide and knowing.

"Go swim, Miss Ross. Mind your own business." I grumble and walk away to go sit down on the bench.

Ben and Talon are messing around in the pool, but Emmy isn't in the water yet. She's standing by the pool watching the others.

Her arms crossed as if she's trying to hide her body, biting her lip as she contemplates if she wants to go in, or go back in the locker rooms to get dressed. I don't know if it's her scars or the stretch marks from having Melody that has her so unsure, but she has nothing to worry about. She's fucking perfect, a vision. And even though she bounced back to her original weight, if she hadn't I would still think she's gorgeous. It doesn't matter her size because she will always be stunning to me.

She looks up, locking eyes with me. I stare at her down, trying to hide the heat in my gaze.

I give her a pointed stare that causes her worried look to change into a sassy glare before she takes the bait. Trying to prove she's stronger than this, she unfolds herself, standing a little taller.

A whistle sounds from the pool. "Hot damn!" Talon calls. "Fuck me, Baby Girl! You are the definition of MILF." He bites his lip and groans. The others in the pool turn to look at Emmy. Thankfully, they don't look long and no-one seems interested in continuing to gawk at her, so Emmy relaxes and gets into the pool.

When she gets closer to the guys, she splashes them. Talon grabs her by the hips, making her laugh out a squeal, before he picks her up and tosses her into the water.

She pops up, wiping droplets from her face. "No fair." She glares.

"She's right." Ben says, before tackling Talon into the water.

"My Hero." Emmy says, in a fake Southern Belle accent as Ben wraps his arms around Emmy, pulling her in his chest. They start to kiss softly, but it quickly turns heated.

"Hey!" I call out. "Enough of that. This is school hours, do that shit in your own time." I warn, partly because I wish it was my lips on hers right now, and because if I didn't do my job, I'd have to deal with Mr. Tucker, and every time I see him I want to punch him in his face. So to keep my job, I'll have to actually do it.

They break apart, but I don't miss the bulge in Ben's swim trunks.

"Oh don't worry, Mr. Kingston, we plan on it." Talon says, giving Emmy a heated look.

Rolling my eyes, I distract myself with some pointless paperwork for the rest of the hour. When class is almost up, I tell everyone to go get changed.

Ben and Talon each give Emmy a kiss before heading into the men's locker room and instead of going straight to the women's locker room, Emmy takes the long way around so that she will have to pass me.

"You know Mr. Kingston," Emmy says as she looks at me with a playful glint in her eyes. "If you're jealous, all you gotta do is ask. I don't mind making you feel included." Her eyes turn hooded. "Sir." She says, her voice low and seductive.

Well, now my cock is wide the fuck awake.

She looks down at my crotch, grinning as she looks back up to meet my eyes. "If you need any help with that situation you have going on, I'd be more than willing to help."

She bites her lip as she slowly backs away. When she gets to the locker room she gives me one last look before darting through the door with a vigorous laugh.

Looking around, I check to see if anyone is paying attention, but I am in the room alone. She must have known we were the only ones here.

This is going to be so fucking hard. Trying to keep the professionalism as a teacher and still be her boyfriend? She sure as hell isn't going to make it easy.

But that little stunt she just pulled, acting like a little brat and calling me sir? Yeah, I liked that. I liked that way too much.

I'm going to have to spank her ass for that, later, and I'll be looking forward to it.

Chapter 6
Ben

"THIS IS FUCKING bullshit!" Talon grumbles, and I grin at him in his pissy mood.

"Babe. You have only yourself to blame." I say, smiling over my shoulder as we head to the dining hall.

After swimming in gym class, we all hung out in Emmy's and Charlie's room watching a movie to wind down from the school day.

Even though we just got back from a two-week break, it didn't stop the teachers from diving right back into our studies, as if they are trying to cram in those weeks we missed so that we can be back on track to where we should have been if we didn't leave the school.

It's fucked up if you asked me, but there's nothing much we can do. We're all passing our classes, and as long as we keep trying our best, we should be able to graduate with a mix of Bs and Cs.

Talon was due for whatever detention the new asshole-of-a-math teacher had planned for him.

"Well, he was being a dick to Emmy." He growls.

"I know, and it made me want to knee him in the balls. But if I did that, I knew it was just going to get us in trouble, like it did you. We only have a few months left, then we're free. Let's try to keep it as low drama as possible until then. Please?"

Emmy releases my hand and stands next to Talon, taking his and leaning her head against his arm. His gaze softens at her touch, and he leans over to kiss the top of her head.

"As much as I loved the fact that you wanted to take the heat off me in class, Ben's right. I want as little drama as we can get for the rest of this year. We have enough going on. And now you gotta spend your dinner in detention without us. Be good for me, please?" She grins up at him, fluttering her lashes.

He groans. "Fine. I'll try, but it's not gonna be that easy. He just gets under my skin."

"Thanks, babe." She kisses him on the cheek before skipping off to catch up with Charlie.

"You know, after you're done we can always head back up to the room and I can help you relieve some of that stress you've been holding in." I say, stopping Talon and wrapping my arms around his waist to pull him against me, so that his cock is pushed up against my hard one.

He winds his arms around my shoulders, tucks his head into my neck, and groans as I feel his dick hardening against mine.

"Fuck, Ben. You know I want that. So fucking bad." He bites my neck lightly and my body shudders at the bit of pain mixed with pleasure. "But you know I feel bad about doing anything more than making out. I don't think it's fair we get to fuck when she needs to wait another month."

Sighing, I pull back to look him in the eyes. "You know she wouldn't care. She's not selfish like that. She knows that we have our own thing. She supports that, supports us. And I know she would never ask us to wait like this."

It's not that I don't feel bad that Emmy can't have sex, because I do. And even though I see how easily she's gets turned on these days, which is most likely due to the lack of sex and massive amount of hormones coursing though her body, I also know *her*. She would feel bad if she was the reason why Talon and I weren't being as intimate as we want to be.

A throat clearing causes us to break apart, and we look at the dining room entrance. Our math teacher stands there with his arms crossed, giving us a death glare.

"You're late." He snaps before turning around and heading back into the room.

"Fuck." Talon mutters. "Let's go before he gives me another detention for being late to this one. Fucking prick."

When we get into the room, Talon gives my hand a squeeze before following the teacher into the kitchen.

Emmy and the others are already sitting at the table. "Where's your food?" I ask when I reach them, looking at the empty table.

"They haven't opened the kitchen yet. Something about waiting for a student to help." Oliver chuckles, knowing that student is Talon.

"Attention, students. I'd like to apologize for the late start to supper. A student was meant to help out these hard-working ladies in the kitchen, but he so rudely kept everyone waiting. Now that he has finally graced us with his presence, we can start serving food. Please, line up." Mr. Prick, which is what I will now be calling him, says from the kitchen door.

"I don't like him." Charlie states, glaring at Mr. Prick.

"I don't think anyone likes him after the stunt he pulled with Emmy today." Oliver says, standing up and holding out his hand for our girl to take.

We all line up and wait by the serving window.

The window opens, and the line starts to move. When it's our turn and we reach the window, Charlie bursts out laughing. "Oh fuck, this is pure gold. Hold on, I need a photo."

"Don't you dare," Talon growls. My eyes go wide and a grin threatens to break out on my face when I take in his appearance.

He's dressed in a white chef's coat and apron, but that's not what has Charlie laughing, it's the hair net that Talon also has on.

"No really, this is something we'll *all* want to remember." Charlie says, snapping a photo.

He looks at me and sighs. "Just don't."

I raise my hands up in a surrendering gesture. "I wasn't gonna say anything."

"Good, because don't think I wouldn't spit in your food." Talon says, directing his comment at Charlie. She just grins wider, snapping another photo before picking up a tray. Talon places a few plates on it, then moves on to plating food for our trays.

"You know, I have other places you can spit on." Emmy says, biting her lip as she fucks with him.

Talon's eyes flash with heat. "You're a dirty girl, Shorty. You know that?"

"Don't act like you don't know how dirty I can be." She says seductively.

"Move along, Miss Knox. You're holding up the line. Other students would like to eat too. It's bad enough one of your little boyfriends has already made them wait." Mr. Prick says.

Talon glares at him and places a bowl of fruit, a plate of pizza, and a can of pop on her tray before doing the same thing for me, and we head back to our table to eat.

"Why do I feel like he doesn't like me more than most? I mean, I've noticed he's an ass to everyone, but he's a little extra asshole-y to me." Emmy says, taking a bite of her pizza.

"He better watch himself. We might not be able to do much without stirring shit up, but Tyson, is a whole other story. Something tells me he's not gonna let things go as easily as we do." Oliver says, looking over at his brother.

Tyson is sitting at the teacher's table with a murderous look on his face as he stares daggers into the back of Mr. Prick's head.

We sit and eat our meal in relative silence. Talon joins us afterwards muttering something about how he did end up spitting in Mr. Prick's food, which sent Emmy into a fit of giggles.

"Fuck." Emmy says, getting our attention.

"What's wrong?" Oliver asks with concern.

"I need to go pump. My breasts are engorged, and it's starting to hurt." She says, while adjusting her nursing bra.

Talon snickers. "Engorged. That's a funny word."

"What are you, ten?" Charlie asks, diving back into her second serving of food.

"What? It is!" He chuckles. "But it can also be used in other ways. Like how *engorged* you make my cock." He says, looking at both me and Emmy.

"Stop." Emmy laughs.

"Come on. I'll go with you. I'm done eating anyway. They can stay and finish." I say.

Emmy says goodbye to the others, giving them all a kiss before taking my hand and we head up to her together.

Hopping up onto her bed, I get comfy as she gets everything set up. She brings everything over to the bed, then strips off her top. My eyes go right to her breasts and my cock starts to stir as I take in how large they have gotten.

"Eyes up here, babe." Emmy huffs out in a laugh.

A grin splits my face as I look up at her. "Can't blame me. I just want to lean over and take your nipple into my mouth." Yup, there goes my cock. I really fucking missed her being wrapped around it. Mouth and pussy.

"Well, you can't really do that right now. Unless you want a mouthful of breast milk." She says, cocking a brow with a daring smile.

"You know. The idea doesn't turn me off. But I think I'll leave all the liquid gold for our baby girl."

"Oh, come on. Aren't you just a little curious?" She taunts, before taking her breast and giving it a little squeeze. Milk shoots out and almost hits me in the eye.

Emmy bursts out laughing. "Oh my god. I'm so sorry." She tries to catch her breath as I wipe the milk from my face. "I guess they really are ready to burst. I didn't think that would happen."

She smashes her lips together, trying to hold back more laughter. I shake my head. "It's fine. Almost took an eye out, though." I joke back.

She settles between my legs and hooks up the breast pump.

"One time, Melody was feeding and moved her head. The flow was too much for her, and was so powerful it went shooting across the room."

"You know, I feel like you could have fun with that. Like your own built-in water guns." I tease her.

She slaps my leg while laughing, but then goes quiet and the mood quickly grows somber. "I miss her." Emmy whispers. My arms go around her, pulling her up my chest and tucking my face into her neck, kissing her softly.

"I know, Butterfly. So do I, but this week will fly by. We will keep each other company and distracted. The weekend will be here before you know it, and our baby girl will be back in your arms where she belongs."

"Yeah, you're right. Now, let's talk about something else. Tell me all about the dirty things you and Talon have been up to while we were on house arrest."

Sighing, I pull away from her, leaning more into the pillows behind me. She shifts so that she can look at me.

"What's wrong?" She asks, concern showing on her beautiful face.

"Well, Talon and I haven't exactly gotten into... well, anything really. Nothing more than some hot and heavy make out sessions." I run a hand through my hair.

"Why the heck not?" She demands.

Pausing for a moment, I try to think of a way to say this without pissing her off.

"He doesn't think it's fair that we get to cum daily when you can't even orgasm without risking your pussy breaking. His words, not mine." I say with a grin.

She cracks a smile. "Okay, that's not what happens. But anyways, that shouldn't be stopping you. I don't want you guys to ever hold yourselves back from each other because of me. You guys have your own thing, and you damn well know I'm okay with that." She growls and fuck if it doesn't cause my cock to perk back up at the sound. She's so damn sexy.

"I know. That's almost exactly what I've been telling him. But you know Talon." I shrug.

"He's getting more stubborn. I don't like it." She laughs. "It's hard enough to deal with Oliver's pain-in-the-ass self without Talon being the same way."

"Don't worry. We can gang up on him." I joke.

Heat flashes in her eyes. "You know, that doesn't sound like a bad idea. You take him from behind while he fucks me."

It sounds like fucking heaven. "That's if I ever get the chance to take him." I mutter under my breath, averting my gaze.

Emmy unhooks the pump and caps off two bottles. She slips off the bed and places the pump on the dresser, and the bottles in the mini-fridge. We got her a little mini-fridge with a freezer so that she can pump and save the milk for Melody while we're away.

Emmy grabs a new bra and top, and I feel a little sad when she hides her perfect breasts. Climbing back onto the bed, she straddles my lap, and takes my face into her hands.

"You guys haven't done that? You haven't made love to him yet?" She asks softly.

"No." I whisper.

"Why? Does he not want you to?"

"No, it's not that. It's just, he loves being in control. He loves being the one to fuck me. And, don't get me wrong. I love it. It's just..." I trail off unsure how to best explain it.

"You want to be able to bring him the same pleasure that he brings you." She says, stating the words I couldn't find.

"Yes."

"I think you should just do it. March right up to him, shove his front against the wall, rip down his pants, and ram your cock in his sexy ass." She grins, and her eyes look dreamy and full of lust as she imagines everything she just described.

My cock grows at the thought and Emmy's smile widens as she feels the evidence of how her words are affecting me.

"You totally want to." She teases.

"I mean. Yeah, I'd be down for that. But not for our first time." I chuckle.

"Good, but when you do, make sure I'm around." She bites her lip.

My phone chimes next to me and I open up the text message.

"It's Talon. He says he's going straight to the weight room to work out some anger from the day." Another text chimes. "And apparently he has the whole place to himself and is going to blast music, so don't expect him back anytime soon." I convey.

Emmy's face lights up. She crawls off me and leans over to the bedside table. She searches through it for a moment before pulling out a bottle of lube and handing it to me.

"Here." She says with an excited look.

"What's this for?" I ask, raising my brow at her.

"You're gonna go down there and watch your man work out. He'll be all sexy and sweaty. Muscles rippling all over. He's gonna make you so fucking hard. Then you're gonna take what's yours." She groans at the thought. "Damn it! Now *I* want the D!" She whines, dramatically throwing herself down on the bed beside me. "Do you know how hot that's gonna be? Fuck. Maybe I'll come watch you guys."

Chuckling at her antics, I lean over her, and capture her lips with mine. She moans into my mouth, making my cock twitch. I pull back before I get her worked up any more than she already is. She lets out a small sound of protest.

"You mean fuck him right there in the weight room?" I ask in disbelief. "What if someone walks in?"

"Lock the door behind you, *duh!*" She sasses, rolling her eyes, but her lips twitch with a smile.

Her idea, though bold and totally out of my norm, does sound fucking amazing.

If this shooting taught me anything, it's that we aren't guaranteed tomorrow. I've spent a lot of time in my own head thinking about all the things I wanted to do and the things I regret not taking a chance on. Being with Talon this way is one of them. The fact that I'm so horny and have so much pent-up sexual energy that I'm surprised my balls haven't popped yet, also helps me in my decision making process.

"I'm gonna do it." I say, standing up.

"Fuck yeah!" She says, sitting up and fist pumping. "You go get some ass." She stands up and hugs me tight. "I'm proud of you, Ben. For going out of your comfort zone and taking not only what you want, but what you deserve."

This woman. How fucking perfect is she? She's building me up to go fuck our man. She's the best cheerleader to have on your side, that's for sure.

"Wait!" She yelps, rushing over to the bedside table and grabbing her phone. She makes a call and waits for whoever it is to answer. "Hi." She greets. "Yes, everything is fine. I need to ask you for a favor. Where are you right now?" She waits for an answer. "Perfect." She chirps. "I need you to shut off the camera feed to the weight room, in about five minutes." At this point, I'm going to assume she's talking to Tyson. "Yes." She giggles. "Thank you, Ty. I love you."

She hangs up the phone and smiles. "All set. Go get'em, tiger." She says and playfully punches me on the arm.

"You're amazing. You know that, right? I'm so damn grateful to call you mine." I say, placing kisses up the arm she just punched me with. "Have I told you that lately?"

"No, but feel free to reassure me as much as you want."

"I will. Every. Fucking. Day." I promise. I leave the room and take a deep breath.

Gathering up the nerve, I head down to the weight room. When I get there, I can hear the faint sound of music coming from the space. Placing my hand on the handle, I take a deep breath. I can do this. It's nothing we haven't done before, only the roles are reversed. *Right?*

Opening the door, I realize that the music is louder than I first thought, but I can still hear the sounds of Talon grunting as he lifts the barbell. He doesn't have a shirt on, and I can see the beads of sweat dripping down his back as his muscles flex and ripple. Fuck, I want to lick them off. He looks so sexy right now. And the sounds he's making cause my cock to become harder than ever before.

Closing the door behind me, I flick the lock, closing me and this sinfully magnificent man in together.

Wish me luck. I have a feeling things are about to get a lot more hot and sweaty in here... just from a different kind of workout.

CHAPTER 7
Ben

THERE IS A lull in the music as the next song on the playlist loads before starting, so the room is quiet for only a moment, but it's enough for Talon to hear the lock click shut.

His eyes snap up to mine in the mirrored wall in front of him, and we both pause for a moment, the barbell placed against his thighs.

He looks at me in question, not sure why I locked the door, but the need to find out is written all over his face.

Taking my eyes away from his, I silently move over to one of the chairs against the wall to watch him work out.

My cock is already stiff in my sweatpants, so foreplay isn't needed. Not that it ever is when it comes to my guy and girl. They always manage to get me ready to go in a matter of seconds. All it takes is one look. Watching him work out is its own brand of foreplay.

Talon keeps looking at me for a few more moments before going back to his workout.

The sounds of his grunts have me squirming in my seat. My eyes roam over his body, unable to look away. I feel as if I'm trapped in a spider's web and his body is the one ready to consume its prey. And, fuck, do I ever want to be consumed. But first, I need to be the one to take what my body needs, before I let my dominant man use me in the most delicious ways.

His muscles flex, his skin glistening with sweat. His perfect unmarked skin is on display for me like an all-you-can-eat buffet, and I plan on having my fill plus more.

When his ass tightens as he brings the barbell up, fuck, it almost makes me cum right here from just watching him.

Unable to take the torture that I'm putting myself through any longer, I take a deep breath, swallow the nerves warming my belly, convince myself not to pussy out, and slowly stalk over to him.

Breathing heavily from his workout, Talon places the barbell back onto the rack and watches me in the mirror.

When I get to him, I don't even think about the sweat pouring down his back, as I wrap my arms around him, pulling him to me, and placing my chin on his shoulder.

"Hi." I say.

"Hi." He grins, and we stare at each other in the mirror for another moment.

Fuck! My brain is going blank, and I'm just looking at him with these blinking, awe-struck eyes. Think of something to say!

"You're sweaty." I blurt. *Fucking perfect, dumbass.*

"Well, that kind of happens when you work out hard for a long time." He chuckles deeply, the sound making my cock jerk.

"How about we work out together?" I say, running my fingertips along his toned abs.

"I was actually pretty much done when you came in, and was going to go shower, but if you want to work out, I can stay and wait for you?"

God, am I really that bad at sexy talk, or has it just been *that* long since we had sex that we are both losing our touch?

Needing him to pick up what I'm putting down, I stop beating around the bush and do what Emmy said and just take what I want.

"That's not the kind of workout I was talking about." I say, cupping his cock, and giving it a squeeze, finding it's almost as hard as mine.

Grinding my ready and wanting cock against his ass, he drags in a lungful of air as his pupils dilate, finally understanding what I mean.

"We can't." He whispers.

"Oh, but we can. I was just with Emmy, she knows."

He sighs. "And let me guess. She said that she doesn't want us to hold back because of her? That she's more than okay with us having sex, even when she can't."

"You know our girl so well." I say as I kiss the side of his neck. He tilts it to the side, granting me access.

I get to work, sucking and nipping at his skin, causing him to push his ass against me as he moans.

"I still don't-"

"Stop." I say, cutting him off. "Stop overthinking things, and just let go. Be *here* with *me*, Talon. Be here with me, in this moment. Just you and me."

He closes his eyes, leaning back into me. I know he wants me. I can feel it with the way he places his hand over mine, giving it a squeeze.

"I want you." I breathe against his neck as I graze my teeth and drag the pad of my tongue along his sensitive flesh.

"I want you, too." He moans.

"No, *I* want *you*." I repeat. "I want you here." I thrust my cock harder between his ass cheeks again. His eyes fly open and meet mine in the mirror.

"You do?" He asks, genuinely curious with a hint of surprise.

"Of course I do. I've wanted you in this way for so long."

"Then how come you've never said anything before now? I just assumed you didn't want to, so I've never brought it up. I figured you would if that was something you wanted to try."

"I've never really bothered to push the idea because of how much I love and crave the way you make me feel. I love when you take control. I love everything you do to me. But the shooting made me realize how short life is, and I want to start doing things that I've been wanting to do. And I want you, Talon. All of you."

He holds my gaze as I see his mind going over my words, trying to decide what to do with them.

When he doesn't say anything I start to panic, thinking that he hates the idea. That he doesn't want me in that way. I'm about to pull away when he says, "Then fuck me, Ben. Fuck my ass and make it yours. Only yours."

Excitement fills me, and my balls start to tingle in anticipation.

"Only mine." I whisper before reaching into my pocket and pulling out the small bottle of lube.

Talon barks out a laugh. "Prepared, are we?" He grins.

"Thanks to our girl, I am." I grin back.

He arches a brow. "That woman never ceases to amaze me. We are so fucking lucky to call her ours."

Humming my agreement against his neck as I give his cock a rub, makes him moan "Ben..."

Needing to be inside him, I guide him to the bench next to us, pushing lightly on his back to get him to brace himself on it.

"Wait." He says, looking back at me over his shoulder. "What about the cameras? I'm all for our girl watching us, hell, I even encourage it, but I don't need some dude watching us alone in some room."

I chuckle. "Another gift from our girl. She took care of it already. They're off."

"Tyson?" He grins and I nod. "Okay then." He takes a deep breath.

I yearn to kiss him right now. I want to savor the taste of his lips on mine. But we don't know how long we have before someone comes beating down the door, and I don't want to wait any longer.

Leaning over, I kiss down his spine and a whole body shiver takes over him. Leaving little kisses all over his back, I push down my sweats, just enough to take out my swollen cock, pre-cum already beading at the tip.

Squeezing a handful of lube onto my palm, I start to slide my hand back and forth, working my cock, and moaning against his back at my own touch.

When I'm slick and ready, I take my clean hand and pull down Talon's gym shorts, getting a nice view of his beautiful ass. It's an ass women dream of having.

Moving back a little, I place a kiss on each cheek before slightly sinking my teeth down into one, like he always does with me.

"Fuck!" He partly hisses, partly moans.

Taking the bottle, I squeeze out a good amount in his crack, gliding my finger up, down, and around his puckered hole, making sure he's fully coated.

Slipping a finger in, I work it gently to loosen his tightened muscles. "Ugh." He grunts.

"Are you okay?" I ask, freezing.

"Yeah... I'm fine." He pants. "It's just... different... but... a good... different."

Taking that as a green light to keep going, I add another finger, stretching him just a bit more.

He moans as I continue to work him, making sure he's good and prepped. I stand up and remove my fingers, teasing his ring, I replace them with the tip of my cock.

Nervous flutters take over me again. I don't want to hurt him. *What if I cause him pain, or he hates it?*

"Ready?" I ask.

He takes a deep breath, moving one hand from the bench to take his cock into his own hand. I can see him rubbing his shaft in the mirror, and the sight has me aching to be inside him.

"Yes. Fuck me, Ben."

Nodding, I start to push into his very tight hole slowly, letting him adjust. "Just relax." I soothe as I feel him tense slightly.

"Fuck." He hisses. "God, that feels so fucking weird."

"A good weird?" I let out a strangled laugh as I try my hardest to hold myself back. He feels amazing around my cock. So fucking tight. So amazingly perfect. So *mine*.

"Yes. God. Have you always been this big?" He asks.

"Umm yes?" I say, inching further into his tight ass.

"How the fuck does Emmy take all of us like this? God, she really is Superwoman." He moans as I bottom out. "Fuck. I don't think I've ever felt so full in my life."

I give him a moment to adjust, but I need to take him. I need to fuck him. To cum deep into his ass as I bring both of us to new heights.

"I need to move now. Are you okay with that?" He says nothing, but nods his head frantically, gripping his cock harder.

I pull back all the way, before gently thrusting back in. Groaning, I go slow for the first few pumps, but start to pick up the pace as Talon starts to murmur words of encouragement until I'm pounding into him with savage need.

"Sweet god, Ben. This feels amazing." He moans as he pumps his cock in sync with my thrusts. "Harder." He demands, his breathing ragged.

Giving him what we both want I grip his hips hard, digging my fingertips into his skin. It's probably going to leave bruises, but the sound of his approval tells me he won't mind.

I find myself in another universe, the feeling of him gripping my cock taking me to a whole new world. I toss my head back and savor the most delicious, delirious sensation.

"Ben." He moans. "Yes! Yes!"

I can feel my balls start to draw up as I rock in and out of him. I know I won't last much longer. It's been way too long since I've had anything more than my hand, and my man feels way too good to be able to deny the epic orgasm I know I'm guaranteed.

"I'm gonna cum." I tell him through gritted teeth, my chest heaving as I feel his body grip mine.

"Cum, Ben." He demands breathlessly. "Mark me; cum deep in my ass."

Fuck, his dirty talk always does things to me. "Talon!" I cry out, thrusting faster and harder until I come to a complete and total stand still, grasping him as close to me as I can before cumming so damn intensely in his ass I think I'm going to pass out from dehydration because of everything I'm emptying into him.

Breathing heavily, I lean over him, still deep inside, kissing his back then resting my cheek against him. "I think my balls are prunes now... no, make that raisins, because they just got sucked so dry, I'll be surprised if there's anything left of them."

Talon chuckles, causing his back door to clench around my shaft, making me groan.

I slowly pull out and Talon hisses lightly. When I'm free, I quickly pull up his shorts so that none of my cum spills out onto the floor, before pulling up my own.

Talon stands up straight and pulls me into his arms, kissing me so hard that I'm sure he's going to bruise my lips. But I don't care, I love the pain when it's from him and especially if it ends in pleasure.

"You're so fucking amazing." He says against my lips.

"No, you are. Thank you for letting me take you like that."

"I loved it." He grins. "But I also love being the one to bend you over and fuck *your* ass. Especially as you're fucking our girl too."

I groan at that thought, craving Emmy just as much as I crave Talon.

"I can't wait until we can worship her body again. Have you seen her stretch marks on her belly and boobs? Talon, it's so fucking sexy. Like a powerful tigress. God, she's a vision."

"You got to see her without a top?" He gapes at me.

"Yup." I wiggle my eyebrows.

He narrows his eyes at me. "On your knees." He demands.

I look at him with surprise. "What?"

"I said... On. Your. Knees. Don't make me tell you again. You got to cum, and now it's my turn."

Oh, shit. He didn't finish, probably thinking the same thing I did about making a mess.

A flush of excitement takes over. I've missed 'demanding Talon'. As much as I loved taking him in the way I just did, and I do plan on doing that more in the future, but this is what we both need now.

Obeying my Greek god of a boyfriend, I drop to my knees. He yanks down his pants just enough for his cock to spring free. It slaps his belly, and as I go to reach for it, craving the feeling of his slick hot length in my hand; but he doesn't let me, grasping it before I can.

"Hands to yourself." He says, letting go. "And open wide." He gives me this heart-stopping, sinful grin and my cock wakes up from its pitifully short nap.

He grasps his cock, giving it a few strokes before bringing the tip to my lips. He smears his pre-cum against them, then taps my lips, signaling for me to open up.

I open wide as instructed, and he wastes no time threading his fingers into my hair, to get a good grip, and sliding himself into my mouth, not stopping until it hits the back of my throat.

"*Fuuuck.*" He groans. "So hot and wet. God, I missed these sexy lips wrapped around my dick."

The look of awe and love in his eyes, mixed with the raw lust, has my heart beating faster and my skin tingling. I love this man with everything I am. Without him, I'm only half of the man I aim to be. With him and Emmy by my side, I can become more than I ever thought I could be.

He fucks my mouth hard, just how he knows I like it. I gag a little when he holds me still, buried deep down my throat before pulling back and repeating the movement.

He finds a steady rhythm as he clutches my hair tightly, keeping me at the angle he likes.

"Fuck, fuck, fuck. I love you, Ben. So fucking much. God, I'm sorry, I was stupid. I should have accepted that our girl just wants us to be happy. Fuck." He's close, I can tell by how choppy and desperate his movements are.

"I want to fuck our girl while you fuck me in the ass. I want you to fuck me so damn hard that I'm forced to fuck her into the mattress while she screams our names before we send her over the edge. Fuck! I'm gonna cum."

His words have me wanting to reach into my pants and grab my own cock, but I'll take care of that later. Right now, my king needs his release.

Reaching up, I grab his ass cheeks to hold him in place on his next thrust down my throat, squeezing them hard and swallowing as he tosses his head back, making one of my favorite sounds. Like a fucking symphony to my ears. His long fingers tighten in my hair as if he's afraid that I'll move. Jets of cum hit the back of my throat and I struggle to devour as much as I can. But hell, it's a lot. I can feel some dripping down the side of my mouth.

When he has nothing left to give me, he slowly opens his eyes and pulls back, tucking himself into his shorts. I just stay there, on my knees, looking up into his bright blue eyes. The love he has for me right now makes me want to preen at what a good job I just did.

"My sweet, sweet Ben..." He says, cupping my face and wiping his cum from the corner of my lip with his thumb. "So perfect. So mine."

He brings his thumb up and into his mouth, sucking his own cum clean. "Such a good boy for me. Come. Let's take a shower, and I'll reward you."

Eagerness to have him fill me has me scrambling to my feet. I'm about to get a head start on that shower, when Talon grabs my hand and pulls me to his body.

He grabs the back of my head and crushes his lips to mine. His tongue does dangerous things to my mine, while I taste his own release some more. I moan into his mouth, leaning into him, drunk off him.

When he pulls back he gives me a sinful, dirty look. "Let's get cleaned up."

That look in his eyes tells me we're about to get even more dirty before any actual cleaning gets done.

He takes my hand and drags me towards the locker room, the music follows us to the showers by the connected speaker system. *Animals* by Maroon 5 plays and I can't help but smirk at how perfect that song would have been a few moments ago.

Talon quickly strips me bare, making sure to glide his hands all over my body as he does, paying extra attention to my pecs and cock.

"You know, I think it's time I get my first tattoo." He says, running his hands up my body again before locking them behind my neck. "You look so fucking edible with all that ink. I see why our girl enjoys all of your art. Plus, everyone has some and I don't. I feel a little left out." He pouts, and I bite his lower lip, making him growl.

"Don't get anything because we have some, do it because you want to. Once you get a tattoo, it's on you for life."

"I could always get it lasered off." He points out, but I just roll my eyes.

"I think you're perfect, a blank canvas, or covered in beautiful artwork, as long as it's what you want. Now, you have far too many clothes on for that shower you were talking about." I point out, looking him up and down.

He gives me a cocky smirk before stepping back and shoving his shorts down and his cock bobs free, smacking his abs like before.

"Well, I guess that makes the both of us ready for round two." I say, licking my lips as I remember the treat I just had.

"Always, for you and our girl. But this time it won't be in your mouth."

He says, a predatory look on his face as he starts to stalk towards me like I'm the prey he's getting ready to catch and conquer. You're not gonna see me fight it. I'm all his in any way he wants me.

My back hits the shower wall, and I suck in a breath as the cool tiles touch my hot skin.

Talon turns on the shower, his breathing picking up as the hot water rains down on us, wetting his already sweaty hair and making it stick to his face. God, he looks so good standing there soaking wet, with water rolling down his toned abs.

He doesn't do anything, just hands me the bottle of body wash. We squeeze some on our hands and get to work cleaning each other... thoroughly.

Next, he quickly does his hair before doing mine. The feeling of his fingertips running over my scalp as well as the little tugs on my hair makes my cock jerk, needing to be relieved again.

He guides me under the water, rinsing my hair. The way he's taking care of me right now fills me with so many indescribable feelings. No matter all the bullshit we've been through, it was all worth it because it gave me the two loves of my life, some of the best friends a man can ask for, and the most precious, amazing little girl.

"Turn around." He demands. My eyes flutter open as I see that the soft, gentle man from seconds ago is gone, and the hungry predator is back.

I turn around only for him to shove me up against the tile.

"Now it's my turn." He growls into my ear, making me suck in a breath. Just using the water of the shower, he wastes no time before thrusting his cock deep into my ass.

I cry out at the sudden intrusion, but it quickly turns into a needy moan as I soak in the bite of pain.

Talon isn't slow and loving right now. No, he's everything I need and want him to be. Fast, hard, and dirty.

He pounds into me, letting out a string of curses. "Fuck babe, you're so damn tight for me. You like my cock buried deep inside that tight ass of yours, don't you?"

"Yes," I moan. "So fucking much."

"Good, now take it like the good boy you are." He says before fucking me ruthlessly. It doesn't take long before he roars his release, triggering mine as I cum hard, streams of it painting the shower wall as my trapped cock finds its release.

Putting his forehead against my back, we stand there breathing hard, coming down from that amazing high.

He pulls out slowly. "Yeah, I think you're gonna need another shower." He says, looking down at my ass. His jizz drips from me onto the shower floor, washing away with the water down the drain. "But I do enjoy the sight of my cum running down your thigh." The look in his eye tells me if we don't get the fuck out of here now, were gonna be in here for hours.

I chuckle at him, pushing him under the water so he can wash himself again, before telling him to get out and get dressed. I clean myself up again also before following him out.

Once we're dressed in clean clothes from Talon's bag and are ready to go, we head out through the weight room and unlock the door.

When we exit the room, we find that we are not by ourselves.

"What makes you think you have the right to lock that door? This room is for everyone." Mr. Prick chastises, giving us a death glare.

63

"Oh, was it locked? Our bad. We had no idea." Talon says, shrugging his shoulder, grabbing my hand and dragging me in the direction of our room, leaving the asshole standing there looking ready to murder someone. Dude's weird as hell.

When we get to our room, Oliver is there playing on his phone, but he's not alone, Emmy is there too, sleeping in Talon's and my bed.

I smile and join her in the bed. She snuggles into me, placing her head onto my chest.

"How did it go?" She whispers in a sleepy voice.

Kissing the top of her head, I smile into her hair as I remember the events of tonight. "Amazing."

"Good. Next time I want a front-row seat." She says, drifting back to sleep. I chuckle as Talon joins us, cuddling into her back.

Perfect ending to a perfect night. In the arms of two of the most important people in my life. Now, all that's missing is the little girl who completes my heart.

CHAPTER 8
Talon

"WHERE IS SHE?" Emmy says, biting her thumbnail as she stares past the courtyard to the parking lot as she waits anxiously for Amy to arrive.

The rest of the week went by quickly. We made sure to keep ourselves busy and tried to keep Emmy from going too stir-crazy.

We did homework, watched movies, and played video games. Ben and Emmy started reading to each other again, and sometimes I just sat and watched them. Seeing how Ben smiles at her like she's his everything, and how Emmy laughs, sounding genuinely happy. It filled my heart with happiness to see them like that. And when they are that way with me included, everything is right in the world.

The epic weight room fuck will forever be one of the best sexual moments of my life. And since then, we have taken every chance we could to do a few repeat performances. Emmy, unknown to us at the time, even watched a few of those exchanges. Can't blame her, we kind of did it in the same bed as her.

It made me feel bad that she looked so turned on and we couldn't do anything about it. But when she saw the change in my mood, she shut me down hard and told me how fucking hot it was to watch, and that she was more than happy to be woken up that way.

"My love, she texted you two hours ago saying she was on her way. And it takes two hours to travel here. She will be here soon." Ben says, taking the hand she was nibbling on and bringing it to his lips, kissing it softly. She relaxes at his touch, sighing in defeat.

"I know." She groans. "But I'm just so excited. I even skipped my lunchtime pumping so that I would be good to go when she got here. Amy said she fed her before they left and she will be hungry again."

Oliver comes up behind her, taking her into his arms, and places his chin on her shoulder. "You need to relax, Firefly. Babies can feel when you're stressed. We need a happy, relaxed mama for a happy baby, okay?"

"Fine." She grumbles and gives us an adorable pout. I take her chin into my hand and place a soft kiss on her lips, trying to distract her.

"Hi." I grin, when I pull back and see her eyes flutter open.

"Hi." She breathes, smiling back.

"I love you." I say, kissing her nose.

"I love you, too."

"She's here! She's here!" Charlie squeals. Charlie jumps up off the school steps, grabs Emmy's hand, and they start racing towards Amy's car.

Ben, Oliver, and I just stand there waiting, not wanting to crowd them. Oliver saw Melody two weeks ago, but Ben and I haven't seen her since the day after she was born. We watch the video feed whenever we can and look at photos all the time, but it's not the same. I just want to hold our daughter in my arms.

I never liked babies, or kids for that matter, until I laid eyes on her. From that moment on, she consumed my heart and soul, right alongside her mother and father.

Amy reaches us first, the girls are further back. I can see Melody nursing. Emmy didn't waste any time, but the way her face is split into a wide grin right now is giving me all the feels.

"Hey, boys." Amy greets with a smile, giving each of us a hug. "Looking good, Oliver. How are you healing?"

"All he's done is bitch that he can't do anything. Poor gym rat can't even work out. Probably afraid he's gonna lose all those muscles that have his girl drooling over him." Tyson says, messing with his brother as he greets Amy and gives her a hug.

"Ignore my brother." Oliver says. "I'm doing fine. Practically healed."

"You need to stop acting like you didn't get shot in the side and almost die." Amy says with an eye roll. "Take the time you need to heal. You need to be strong and healthy for your girls, don't you?"

I can't help but grin as Amy mothers Oliver. Oliver simply mutters a "*fine*" in response.

"Say hello to your daddies, Melly Belly." Emmy says in a soothing, soft voice as they reach us. We crowd around Emmy and a still nursing Melody. My heart fills with so much happiness as I take her in. She's gotten bigger since we saw her. It's crazy that she's already three weeks old.

Her red hair has gotten brighter and longer, while also starting to curl on the sides of her head, and it's so damn adorable.

"Hi, my Little Caterpillar." Ben says, in awe of our little girl, as he strokes her cheek. "She's so perfect." Ben says with a big grin, looking up at Emmy.

"She is. And she's gotten so big since I last saw her." Emmy says, looking back down at the baby.

"Come on, guys, let's take this inside." Tyson says, looking around at a few students who are passing by the courtyard.

As we all head into the school, I hang back and help Amy with some bags and Tyson does the same. Just as I'm about to enter the school, I feel like I'm being watched. Looking around, I find someone standing off to the side of the building, looking at me with a blank stare. Mr. Park. Or Mr. Prick, as Ben likes to call him. What the fuck is he doing out here? Was he watching us? This dude gives me the creeps. Not only is he a dick, he's a weirdo too.

Glaring back, I follow after our group.

Amy left to go check into the hotel that she will be staying at this weekend. Tyson had a chat with Mr. Tucker, and he agreed that Melody could stay on campus with us. In an official statement, he made sure to say that none of us guys were allowed to stay the night with her, but we all know that was just for show because he couldn't care less at this point. We're all over eighteen and in a relationship with each other. I mean, we've already had a baby, what more could happen? Emmy can't have sex anyways.

"Sooo, it's your first sleepover, how ya feeling, guys?" Charlie asks, jumping on the spare bed next to Emmy, who is staring at Ben, Oliver, and me with this gorgeous grin on her face as she watches us crowded around Mel, who is in Oliver's arms right now.

"Excited." I say. "I've seen what you guys do on the camera feed, I got this."

"Listen to this." Charlie says with a laugh, hitting Emmy lightly on the arm and pointing at me. "He says he's got this. How cute." I look at the two of them with confusion. Emmy bites her lips like she's holding back a giggle.

"Oh, stop." Emmy says, knocking shoulders with Charlie. "They are gonna be just fine. They are gonna rock at being daddies."

I grin proudly at my girl, puff my chest out, and then look over at Oliver.

"Okay, you had her long enough. Gimme." I say, motioning my hands like a greedy child. "It's my turn."

Oliver growls... like a legit growl. "Bite me." He says, then looks back down at our little girl, face soft again. Ben just looks at us in amusement.

Fuck him, fuck them both. They both have gotten a good, solid twenty minutes with her. So, if this dickhead wants me to bite him, I damn well will.

Leaning over, I bite his upper arm, hard. He lets out a pained grunt, then looks at me with wide eyes, surprised that I actually did it. I smirk at him with a cocked brow. "Baby. Now." I repeat again, holding out my arms.

Emmy and Charlie start laughing. Ben shakes his head, gets up, comes to my side of the bed, and kisses me on the cheek before sitting down next to me.

Oliver gives me a death glare, but gently hands over the baby. I gather her in my arms carefully because I'm so afraid of dropping or hurting her. I've only held her once in the hospital. Before that, I'd never even held a baby before.

Oliver grumbles something under his breath before grunting as he gets up and heads to the bathroom, reassuring Emmy that he's okay when she asks.

Melody makes a few cooing noises, but doesn't fuss as I hold her close to my chest. "She's so damn cute." I say, using my free hand to run it over her soft hair. "She totally has your hair." I grin up at my man who looks at our daughter with so much love my heart skips a beat.

We all accept that Ben is the father. I mean, we plan on getting a DNA test done at some point just to be sure because Emmy wants a baby from each of us, but only a blind person could miss how Ben and Melody were practically twins.

Charlie said she didn't care if any of our children shared her DNA because they would all be hers anyways. I have a lot of respect for that woman. I'm glad to call her one of my best friends and have her on our side.

"Maybe, but everything else is Emmy. I mean look at how adorable she is." Ben says, kissing the baby's forehead.

"He's right, no way she gets that from Ben." Oliver responds with a chuckle, coming out of the bathroom and going to sit on the bed where the girls are. He crawls into bed behind them and Emmy snuggles up with him. Charlie puts on a movie, and we all just relax for the night.

I was wrong, oh so very wrong. I did not have this, and we were not fine, not fine at all.

"Maybe she's hungry again?" Ben suggests, rocking the screaming baby.

"She just ate." Oliver growls, running a hand through his hair in frustration.

"Well, maybe she needs to be changed?" I say. "Check." I tell Oliver.

"You check." He snaps back.

Ben lifts the baby up so that her butt is facing us. "Someone, smell."

"You want me to fucking sniff her ass like a dog?" Oliver looks at him in mock horror.

"Well, Emmy does it!" Ben defends.

Emmy ended up falling asleep early so when she woke up, she was wide awake. It's one am now, and she stayed up with Melody while we all got a few hours of sleep, but when Melody woke up for her feeding, everyone else did too. And after Emmy was done, we told her we had this taken care of. So, she took the time to go take a bath. Right after Emmy shut that door behind herself, Melody started crying; and the longer we failed to calm her down, the more she started sounding like a mandrake from Harry Potter.

"Oh, I'll do it." I grumble and check to see if she has a dirty diaper. "Just smells like baby powder to me." I say with a shrug.

"Maybe we should try singing." Oliver says, removing Melody from Ben's arms and taking his turn at trying to calm her down.

"Do any of you know an appropriate song to sing to a baby?" I ask, knowing that my musical preference is not really appropriate for a lullaby.

"Not really." Ben says, biting his lip as he looks at Oliver. "You're the other singer in this family, you sing something."

"Oh yeah, I'll just make up a song on the spot." He says sarcastically. "I can't just pull one out of my ass you know."

Trying to think of a song to sing, I go with whatever comes to the top of my head.

"It's time to sleep and you wanna know why. Because if you don't, you're gonna make me cry. It's 1 a.m., and you're up again," I start to sing, and the damn song is coming out like a bad remake of *Baby Got Back* by Sir Mix-A-Lot.

The guys look at me weird, but then they see that Melody is starting to calm down.

"Hey!" Ben says, smiling. "It's working. Keep going." Oliver keeps rocking her as I continue.

69

"Baby, please tell me what I can do to get some sleep in the other room. Is it because you have to go poo?" The guys say eww in a playful way. *"Or do you want more food? You don't want to bug your mama."* The guys say 'No' in unison.

"Because, Baby Girl, that just makes more drama. I'm begging you, please, I'll get on my knees. So just close your eyes to this lullaby. We'll be right back, after this short track. See I think you're fine and just enjoying this rhyme. But, Baby Melly, it's bedtime."

"It's bedtime." The guys echo. Taking a deep breath to continue, it becomes glaringly obvious that it is quiet.

When I see that she is now fast asleep in Oliver's arms, I grin a smug grin and do an air mic drop.

Oliver sighs, handing Ben the baby and kissing her on top of the head before going to lay back down. Ben waits a moment then places her in the bassinet that we have set up for her.

A snort from behind us has Ben and me looking towards the bathroom where Charlie and Emmy stand in the doorway with looks of amusement on their faces.

Unable to hold her giggles in any longer, one slips free. "I don't know what that was, but next time I'm totally recording it." She whispers. She walks over to us, hair wet, and only in a towel.

"But it did the job." I point out, then look down at our sleeping daughter.

"Yes it did. Thank you." She says, getting up on her tippy-toes to place a kiss on my lips.

"How was your bath?" I ask, wrapping her in my arms as she puts hers behind my head.

She just shrugs. "Hearing her crying made it hard to relax. Also, sometimes my breasts leak when she cries, so there was that." She huffs out a laugh.

"It was starting to look more like a milk bath." Charlie laughed, crawling into her and Emmy's bed.

Emmy smiles and rolls her eyes at her girlfriend as she sticks her tongue out, then looks back at me. "I wanted to come out and help, but Charlie said it was good for you guys to try and do it on your own. She was right though, you guys did awesome." She kisses my lips again.

"I wouldn't go that far, Butterfly." Ben says, trapping her towel-covered body between us and kissing her neck. "She cried like crazy for the longest time."

"Yes, but you guys found a way to calm her, no matter how cute and silly." She says, mirth dancing in her beautiful brown eyes. "We should get some sleep too. Melly will be up in another hour." She groans.

"When she does, feed her and then we will take over." Ben says.

I nod in agreement. "I think we are starting to get the hang of it."

Emmy climbs into bed with Charlie, and Ben and I get in the spare bed with Oliver.

"I swear if one of you grabs my cock again mistaking it for each other, I will be chopping off yours. Got it?" Oliver says, rolling over on his side facing the wall. Emmy giggles from her bed and I can't help but poke the bear.

"You know you like it, just like you loved it when Emmy stuck her finger in your ass." Oliver's body goes stiff and Emmy curses.

"You weren't supposed to tell him I told you!" She hisses.

"Firefly, you're lucky you're my whole damn world, or I'd be spanking that ass until it's tanned red." Oliver growls.

"Oh no, please. *Anything* but that." Emmy says sarcastically.

Oliver chuckles deeply. "Good night, baby girl. I love you."

"I love you too, Caveman. I love you too, Tal and Benny Bear." She says.

"You own my heart, Butterfly." Ben says.

"You own my soul, Shorty." I say.

"You guys make me sick." Charlie scoffs, but I can hear her whisper to Emmy. "I love you, my Queen."

"Emmy!" A roar comes from right next to me. Oliver shoots up in bed.

"I'm here, I'm here." I hear Emmy soothing him. The bed dips and I blink the sleep from my eyes as I feel Emmy crawling over to Oliver before straddling him. Oliver grabs hold of her body and crushes her to his chest. "It's okay. I'm okay. I'm in your arms, safe and alive."

The grip he has on her can't be too comfortable, but she doesn't protest, holding him just as ferociously.

His face is tucked into her breasts and he clings to her like she will disappear if he lets go.

I knew he had nightmares, but since we got back, he only woke up screaming once. I thought it was getting better, but I guess not.

Emmy whispers something into his ear and he nods his head against her chest. They both lay back. She pets his chest, letting him know she's real and there with him.

Looking over at Ben, I see concern and pain on his face for our brother who is struggling with his inner demons.

"What time is it?" I ask him. He looks at me, then reaches for his phone. "A little after six." He says, laying back down and closing his eyes.

Even though I know it's the weekend and we don't need to be up, I get up anyway. Crawling out of bed, I grab my sweats.

"I'm going to get a workout in while Melody is still sleeping." I say, looking over at our sleeping beauty, surprised she's still passed out after what just happened. Ben mumbles something before cuddling into Emmy's other side. Oliver and Emmy have already passed out again.

When I get to the weight room, I see it's not empty. Tyson is there, running on the treadmill and he's not alone. On the other side of the room is Mr. Park lifting weights. He gives me a death glare as I enter the room. What the fuck is this guy's problem?

Ignoring him, I head over to Tyson. He stops the machine when he sees me. "Hey. How was the first night with our Little Princess?" He asks quietly, wiping the sweat from his face with a little towel, then he takes a big mouthful of water from his bottle.

"I don't know how you did it when it was just you and Charlie for that week. It's hard with all of us." I say, taking the treadmill next to him.

He chuckles. "I don't know. She likes me." He winks. "Never really gave me a hard time."

"Maybe we just need to spend more time with her, have her get used to us." I say as I start up the machine.

"That's probably all you need. Did she sleep well?"

"Actually, other than the 1 a.m. scream fest she slept through the night."

"Then why are you here so early when you could be getting a few more hours of sleep?"

"Oliver had another nightmare." I say.

"Fuck." He sighs. "I thought they were getting better."

"So did I. But I think he needs to see someone. Someone outside this school. He was shot, and after everything he's seen with Emmy in the past, I think it's all catching up to him. He watched her almost drown, get stabbed to the point she almost bled out, and then he got shot while she was in labor. It's a lot to deal with." I remind him.

"You're right. We should say something to Emmy. If anyone can get him to do it, it's her. He would just bury it deeper if it were us."

Agreeing with him, we finish our work-outs. When we leave, I see Mr. Park is still here, but working out with another set of equipment. As if he knows I'm watching him, he looks up giving me another glare.

"What do you know about Mr. Park?" I ask Tyson as we head into the showers.

"A lot actually. I made Mr. Tucker let me look at all the background checks on the new and existing teachers. He's clean. Husband to a wife for 10 years, 3 kids. Nothing out of the ordinary. But that doesn't mean I like the guy. Just because his past is clean doesn't take away from the fact he's a dick. I don't like how he talks to you guys. And don't think I don't know exactly what happened in math; I heard some of the other kids talking about it. If he keeps it up, I'll be having a talk with him and he really doesn't want that."

"Well, if you make a plan to kick his ass, let me know when and where. I'll be sure to bring a chair and tub of popcorn." I grin. He shakes his head with a smile.

For the rest of the weekend we get as many baby cuddles in as we can, making sure that everyone has equal time with her. Almost every time it's my turn she's either puking all over me, or crapping like she ate a bar of ex-lax. But I just suck it up, shove some tissue up my nose and do my daddy duties by well... cleaning the doody.

When Amy comes back for Melody, we all have a tearful goodbye, but my strong woman holds it together the best she can. Even when I see the tears threatening to spill as she watches the car disappear down the path.

"Less than a week and you see her again." I say, hugging her close.

"I know. But I miss her already." She sniffs.

"Me too. How about we go do something to take your mind off it."

"How about we all go swimming? Break out the beach ball and nets for the pool?" Ben suggests.

"Yes!" Charlie cheers, wiping her own tears from her eyes, putting on a brave face for our girl. "Emmy, Tyson and me against Oliver, Ben, and Talon."

Tyson high-fives Charlie. "Hell yeah!" He says.

"Hey, you're giving us the injured guy. How is that fair?" I whine as we all start to head into the school.

"Because I said so." Charlie says with a shrug as if it was just that simple, before taking off with Emmy to go get changed.

This weekend was amazing and I enjoyed every moment of it, but my heart hurts seeing our baby girl leave. I can see Ben feels the same way. I plan to do everything in my power to keep us busy until we see her again and I can tell the others are willing to do the same. Sadly, this coming weekend Emmy and Tyson are going back down for the weekend. But if that means my love gets to be the one to see her, I'm more than okay with that. I'll just need Ben to keep me extra distracted. You know, with his dick?

CHAPTER 9
Emmy

"OKAY, CLASS. YOU'VE had a few weeks to get back into a routine, and now it's time to get on with our projects for the rest of the year." Mr. Gregory announces to the class as he walks in. Everyone groans, but the guys look at each other and me with hopeful smiles. We always end up with each other, so class projects were never as dreadful for us.

"And I think we need to change things up a bit. When I call your and your partner's names, please move to a desk next to each other. Also, starting tomorrow, I will have a new seating arrangement for everyone."

Mr. Gregory starts calling out students' names. I tune him out, jotting down a few things I wanted to get the next time I go back home. It's been two weeks since the guys had their first sleepover with Melody. I came back from my second weekend at home last night. Tyson and I took a little detour and stopped at a little park on the side of the road and made out on the driver's side like a couple of horny teens. By the end of it, his cock was hard as stone. I tried to offer to take care of it, but he used a lot of self-restraint and refused all my attempts. He said he wanted to wait until he could take very good care of me in return.

I felt bad, leaving him in that state, especially seeing how uncomfortable he was for the first half hour afterwards, but my out-of-order vagina was flattered.

Now I only have one week left until Amy takes me for my six-week check up. It's crazy that Melody is already five weeks old. She went from being this little six pound baby to ten pounds. I guess all my milk is doing its job. She's beautiful, happy, and healthy and that's all I ever wanted. I'm so blessed to have two amazing parents to help me raise my baby girl.

"Amelia Knox, your partner will be Ethan Cooper." That causes me to jerk my head out of my little daydream. I just blink at the teacher, not sure if I heard him right.

"Miss Knox, did you hear me? I said, your partner is Ethan Cooper." Mr. Gregory repeats, pointing to a guy sitting in the far back corner. Ethan gives me a friendly smile and a little wave. I smile back, still a little confused as to how I didn't get any one of my lovers with such a small class, I gather my things and make my way over.

Risking a look at the guys, I see them all giving Ethan a death glare. Biting my lip to hold back a smile, I take the open seat next to Ethan.

As much as I would have loved to have been partnered with Charlie or one of the guys, I honestly don't care too much about having to work with someone new. All I ask for is that he's not crazy, or an asshole.

"Hi." Ethan says, still giving me a friendly smile.

"Hey." I say back.

"Should I be worried?" He asks, raising a brow and looking beyond me.

"Excuse me?" I ask. He nods his head, and I look over to see that my men are still staring down the poor guy. As if they are trying to use the force and do some Jedi mind trick that will make his head explode or something.

"Nah." I laugh, shaking my head and looking back at Ethan. "They're harmless, for the most part."

"What about the purple haired one?" He says,

"Ah, that one you might actually have to worry about. She looks all bubbly and cheery, but piss her off and she just might stab you." I say with a shrug.

He looks at me with horror. "Really?"

"I'm just fucking with you." I chuckle, and he relaxes. "But the guys might." This time I was not joking. I would not put it past Oliver, especially after everything that's happened to me. At this point, he would stab first, then ask questions later.

"Noted." He says. The teacher gives out the countries for the assignment, which for us happens to be France. Our assignment is to learn about its history and culture, and by the end of the month we will have to do a presentation in front of the class as well as cook a dish from that country. Sounds like fun to me.

We read for a little bit in our textbook before Ethan asks me a question. "So... is it true?"

"Is what true?" I ask, looking up from the book.

"That you're dating all of them? And the purple haired girl, too?"

I just stare at him, unsure how he doesn't know this already. It's become common knowledge. I take in his shoulder-length brown hair, his hazel eyes and then realize I don't think I've really seen him around before. His face isn't one I remember. Not that I really know anyone here anyways; we mostly keep to ourselves.

"Yup. The guy with the black hair." I say, looking over at Oliver who's sitting with some guy I also don't know, "That's Oliver Price, my childhood best friend turned bad boy." I grin and Ethan laughs.

"The two over there who are looking at each other like they are about to rip each other's clothes off and fuck on the desk, that's Ben and Talon. They are my boyfriends as well as each other's."

"Lucky." He mumbles to himself as he looks at my guys with a hungry glint in his eyes.

"Down, boy. They're mine, and I *will* stab you if you try anything." I say, only half joking. I mean, have you met my sister? I'm sure it runs in the family to some degree.

"Don't worry, I won't touch. But I'm not blind... I just mean it's hard not to look or watch them you know?" He sighs, averting his gaze.

"Oh trust me, watching is one of my favorite things to do." I say, grinning at the double entendre.

"You lucky bitch, can I be you?" He begs jokingly.

"You wish." I laugh.

"Do I ever!" He exclaims.

"I hope this doesn't sound rude, but how long have you been here? I was sure everyone knew about my...unique situation by now."

"I've been here since January. On probation until the end of the school year. Was hoping to be let off after the shooting since my sentence is short, but here we are." He slouches down in his chair, tucking his hair behind his ear.

"Don't get me started on that. This school has been nothing but hell for me. I'm so over everything and just want to be done so I can be home with my baby girl."

His eyes light up at that. "You have a daughter?"

"Yup. Her name is Melody. She will be six weeks old this Friday." I can't help but smile as I talk about her. "She's back home with my foster parents."

"Must be hard being away from her." He responds with sympathetic eyes. My mood sullies at his words. Seeming to see that too, he asks, "Got any photos?"

I grin again. "Tons."

We spend the rest of the class looking at photos of Melody from behind the textbook we set up to hide my phone.

"You ready?" Oliver's deep voice stops our conversation.

"Hi, Olly." I grin at him, finding his pissed off face kind of funny.

Talon, Ben, and Charlie come to stand behind him.

"Guys, are you for real right now?" I laugh, rolling my eyes. Standing up, I gather my things. "I'll see you tomorrow, Ethan. We can make plans for the library then."

He looks at everyone behind me with his own smirk of amusement. "Sounds like a plan." He looks back at me with a genuine smile.

"I don't like that guy." Talon says as we head to the guys' room to get our homework out of the way.

"You don't even know him." I say.

"Well, I don't need to. Did you see how he was smiling at you? He wants you."

"Oh, enough of that. He does not. He's nice. And even if he did, it doesn't matter because I already have every piece of my heart put together. I'm whole. I have everyone I could ever possibly want and need already. Each of you are more than I could have ever hoped and asked for." I say, stopping Talon and wrapping my arms around him. "Do you want me to show you later just how much I appreciate *you?*" I whisper against his lips.

"I mean, you're not gonna hear me say no." He grips my ass, grinding his growing cock into me, causing me to let out a moan as he captures my lips with his in a heated kiss.

"Enough of that you two, before you guys go at it right here for everyone to see." Tyson says, standing in the middle of the hall.

"That would not happen." Talon scoffs. "You know she can't have sex yet."

Tyson just glares at him. And I decide to poke the bear; breaking away from Talon, I walk over to Tyson. He follows my every move with interest.

"Say I got down on my knees right now and sucked his cock in the hallway, what would you do to punish me, *Sir?*" His nostrils flare, and my belly flutters at his reaction. He likes it when I call him Sir, and so do I.

"You wouldn't want to find out." He says, his voice low, but I can hear the strain in it.

"Oh, but I would." I grin before stepping around him, brushing my hand against his.

Talon starts laughing as he and Ben turn to continue down the hall.

"Oh, brother. Good luck with that one." Oliver says over his shoulder at Tyson, before following.

"Bye, Sir." Charlie sings songs, with a little bit of a mock to her tone, as she drags me along behind the guys.

When Tyson and I finally get together in every way we ache to be, I know it's going to be something completely different than what I have with the others.

Talon and Charlie are sexy and playful.

Ben is tentative and loving with a dirty side, which I am all for.

And Oliver is a little sweet, a little dominant.

But Tyson? He's not like the others. Making love to him is going to be wild, sinful, and so much *more*, and I can't fucking wait.

Charlie

I'm nervous, why am I nervous? I shouldn't be. It's not like this is a first date or anything. Hell, we have a child together. But even still, every time I see her, butterflies flutter in my belly and I feel all warm and giddy inside. And when she smiles, *fuck me*, I'm done for.

Wringing my hands, I pace back and forth throughout the main lobby waiting for Emmy. I told her after we were done with our homework I was going to go back to our room and get ready. When she asked what for, I just told her to be ready by 6 p.m.

"Hello, you." Emmy says, coming up from behind me, to wrap her arms around me and bring me to her chest. She kisses my cheek and just like that the nerves are gone. She has this way about her that makes you feel safe, loved, and wanted all at once.

"Hey." I say, turning around in her arms to face her. Once we are face to face she wastes no time bringing me in for a kiss.

She licks my lips, and I open for her, granting her tongue access. I groan at the taste of her tongue on mine.

The kiss grows heated as she brings one of her hands behind my head as she holds me in place to deepen the kiss.

As much as I fucking hate to do this, I break the kiss. "What's wrong?" She asks, brows pinched with concern.

"Nothing." I smile, breathing a little heavier from the kiss. "It's just, I have something planned and don't want to get side-tracked. But we can do more of this later." I say, zeroing in on her lips. She bites the lower one, earning another groan from me.

"You look delectable, my love." Emmy says, looking me up and down. "If I knew we were supposed to dress up, I would have put something else on." She frowns, looking down at her outfit. She's dressed in leggings and a baggy hoodie, one of mine, which is a change.

I was dressed in a flowy, flower print, summer dress. I don't care what she wears, she's perfect in anything, but I wanted to look a little extra special for her. It's been far too long since we had this much downtime with no one trying to harm us, or causing unnecessary drama. Just normal school for once. Well, as normal as you can get at Emerald Lake Prep.

"You look amazing. There's no dress code, I just wanted to wear a dress. It's April and spring is here." I shrug. She doesn't say anything else and accepts my answer. "Come." I say smiling wide as I take her hand, guiding her down the hall to the side door that leads to the beach.

She lets out this musical giggle that makes my heart skip a beat, and when we are almost at the beach, I lead us in a different direction.

"Where are we going?" She laughs again, enjoying just being on this random adventure with me.

When we get there, Emmy lets out a surprised gasp as she takes in the sight before her.

We stand in a cluster of birch trees with fairy lights strung from the low branches. Below them on the ground is a blanket laid out with a picnic basket.

"What's this?" she asks, tears in her eyes.

"Well, after everything we've been through lately, with the stress of being new parents, and as amazing as it is, I thought we could take advantage of the downtime. I wanted to do something special for you. You deserve it." I say, taking her hand when she holds hers out, silently asking for it.

"It's perfect." She breathes, bringing me in for a soft kiss. "You're perfect. I love you so much, Charlie."

"I love you more than your beautiful brain could ever comprehend. You're my life, Emmy. You and Melody. Hell, even those meat-heads of yours have come to mean something to me."

"Well, what do you have planned for us?" She asks, huffing out a laugh and taking off her glasses to wipe away the tears before putting them back on.

"An Emmy-approved picnic, of course." I say, holding my arm out as I present her with the blanket.

"Oh, really?" She teases. "I think Emmy should be the judge of that."

We sit down next to the basket and she pulls out the first thing.

"Pop." She says, nodding her head in approval at the cans of Coke. She goes for the next thing and pulls out a box. "You did not!" She exclaims, her eyes wide with excitement.

"How the hell did you get a box of Honey Garlic chicken wings from Pizza 73?" She asks, opening up the box and moaning.

"I had some help from Tyson. There's one in town and he went to get these right before you came down." I grin at her excitement.

"Only we would eat chicken wings on a picnic date." She says, taking a bite of a wing and sighing in contentment. My body flushes at the sounds of pleasure she is making as she devours the wings one after another. How the hell is eating messy wings so damn hot? I'm so ready to lean over and lick all that sauce off the corner of her mouth.

"Stop looking at me like that." She says, her voice filled with desire. My eyes snap up to hers. She has a smile on her face, but her eyes are saying she's reading my mind and is very on board with the plan I have going on in my head. "Want some?" She asks.

"You're actually willing to share your wings with me?" I ask in mock surprise, putting my hand over my heart.

"Oh, I'm not that bad." She defends.

"*That bad*? Remember the time Talon tried to take one and you growled at him; like full on ready to strike growl, and then you threatened to chop off his hand."

"Well, they really are heavenly." She points out, taking another bite. "And you know I can eat all twenty, no problem."

"I know, that's why I got a ten-pack for myself."

We sit and eat, talking and laughing about anything and everything. When we are done, we clean up with some wet wipes.

"That was so damn good." She sighs, laying back on the blanket and looking up into the trees. "I don't think I could eat another bite."

"Oh, that's too bad." I say, digging into the basket. "Guess I'll just have to eat this cheesecake all by myself." I smirk, taking a big piece and bringing it up to my mouth as Emmy shoots up into a sitting position.

"What kind?" She asks, eyes wide with renewed excitement.

"Strawberry." I say.

"Gimme!" She practically screeches, leaning forward and opening her mouth. I laugh as I feed her the bite I was about to take.

When we finish, we take a walk barefoot in the sand, hand in hand as we watch the sun set, before making our way back to the picnic area.

"This is perfect." She says, as we both lie back down on the blanket and face each other. "I love being out here. I wish we could just sleep under the stars, but you know... bugs and shit."

I smile, and lean over to kiss her. We make out for a while, keeping things soft and slow. I'm enjoying every stroke of her tongue, and the touch of her fingers as they glide over my body.

"I want to taste you." Emmy breathes against my lips.

"Babe-" I start.

"Shhhhh..." She says, pushing me onto my back. She straddles me and starts kissing me again. My arms come up to her thighs as I rub them, enjoying the feeling of her weight on me. She removes her lips from mine, moving down to my neck as she starts to nip and suck. I moan for her, needy for my queen. It's been way too long.

She pulls down my bra cups, and uses both hands to massage my breasts with her small soft hands. She rolls my peaked nipples with her fingers, giving them a little pinch and tug, causing my core to dampen. Fuck, what is she doing to me?

"I know you wanted to wait. Talon was just as stubborn, but I go to the doctor in a few days, and even if we have to be gentle for the first few times, I'll be able to have sex again. So, I don't have to wait much longer. But you, my love, have been waiting weeks, and knowing these guys, once I'm told I'm good to go, you know they are gonna be on me like a horny and hungry pack of wolves."

I laugh, because that is the understatement of the year. The permission from her doctor is going to set them off. I know she can't wait, but I don't think I'll be seeing much of her the first week.

But hey, she's gonna need a va-jay-jay vacay at some point and that's when I swoop in like a knight in shining armor. Or a lesbian with a tongue that makes Emmy sob out her name. Same thing.

She moves down my body, leaving a trail of kisses over my dress covered body, stopping when she gets to my knees. Placing her hands on them as she slowly slides up my thighs, taking my dress along with her, and causing my breath to hitch as she gets closer to my wet and waiting center. Her fingers glide over the sensitive skin and my body shivers at her touch.

When my dress is all the way up to my hips, she glides her fingers back down my inner thighs while pushing and parting my legs. I feel so open and exposed but in the best possible way. Her eyes light up as she takes in the drenched fabric between my legs. The way she's looking at me has my pussy clenching at what she might do next.

"You know, this is one of my favorite meals. Not being able to feast upon you for these past few weeks has been pure hell. You're my drug, Charlie. You all are. Like my own personal brand. Without you all, I felt like something was missing. I need you, and I need you. Right. Now." She growls before tugging my panties down my legs.

"Next time, don't feel bad for not being able to do this to me and denying yourself pleasure. I'm okay with missing out on orgasms if it means I get to taste you while you scream my name."

Okay, so sex deprived Emmy is kind of scary, and I'm not gonna lie, she is reminding me a bit of her sister, but it's a major fucking turn on and I'm all for it.

She wastes no time diving between my legs and when her tongue makes contact with my pussy I jolt at the feeling. It's been so long but my body quickly remembers its master and surrenders to Emmy's sinful lips and tongue.

"Fuck." Emmy groans, taking the word right out of my mouth. I'm not able to process how to form a real word with how mind-fucked my brain is right now, and she's just getting started. "I could eat you for hours, for days without being full."

She goes back to fucking me with her mouth, and I'm just forced to lay here and take it. Fuck, it feels so good.

My legs lock around her head as I grip her hair, holding her closer to my pussy because I need more, more of anything and everything she's willing to give.

"Emmy..." I moan. "Fuck, I missed this." I'm panting hard now, my breaths coming in short, quick bursts. I can already feel the orgasm building in my belly, a storm raging before its culmination.

Since Emmy has been out of commission, I took any chance I could get to take care of things myself. But it's not the same, and my body is reminding me just how much we miss our girl's mouth, fingers, and touch.

Emmy sucks my clit into her mouth making me toss my head back. One hand tangled in her hair, the other with a death grip on the blanket.

"Oh, god. Yes... yes. Please, don't stop." I beg, grinding my pussy into her face.

She forces me back down to the blanket and pulls back just enough to insert her fingers. I let out a loud, embarrassing moan into the silent night around us.

She pumps her fingers, hooking them just perfectly in all the right spots. "I'm gonna cum." I say, almost as a cry. "I need to cum. God, Emmy, don't stop, please."

She mumbles something against my pussy, but my brain is going haywire and all I can focus on is my orgasm that's right there, like a ticking time bomb ready to explode all over her face any minute now.

The vibrations from her talking only add to the pleasure. Her tongue and fingers work together in perfect harmony.

One more flick of her tongue and my back arches off the ground as I scream out my release. Only it quickly gets muffled as Emmy's hand shoots up and clamps over my mouth, smothering my cries so no one but us can hear. My eyes roll back and my body twitches, no doubt soaking my girl's tongue with my release.

As I come down from my high, my whole body is humming from the event. I feel happy and content. I feel at home.

I lay there with my breasts out, as a light breeze blows against my dripping pussy and all I can do is blink up at the sky.

"I'm dead, right?" I breathe, causing Emmy to giggle somewhere between my thighs. "I have got to be dead, because that was unbelievably heavenly." I say, lifting up my head to see my girl hovering over my center and it has me almost ready to go again to see my juices coating her lips and chin.

"I'm more than willing to have a second helping, but we have to move this sexy party to our room. It won't be long before someone comes looking for us, and I'd rather not have them catch us with my head between these luscious thighs." She says, smirking as if she knows what this sight is doing to me.

"Oh, don't think I won't take you up on that offer."

"I'm counting on it." She says, leaning over and placing a kiss on my lips. I groan as I taste myself on her.

"You can't tell me you don't taste like the sweetest candy." She breathes. "That would be an argument you won't ever win."

I'm gonna marry this woman someday. Fuck the guys, there are four of them and only one of me. So, I win. Fuck them.

Emmy takes my panties the rest of the way off and tucks them into the front pocket of her hoodie before pulling the dress back into place. I raise my brow with a questioning smirk.

"What?" she shrugs. "They're ruined. Did you want to put wet panties back on? Plus, it's dark and no one else is around; you're fine."

Shaking my head with a grin, we pack everything up leaving the fairy lights for the guys to come and collect them tomorrow.

With the basket in my hand and the blanket in hers, we lock our free hands together as we run all the way back to the school, laughing and smiling. I haven't felt this carefree in a really long time.

She makes everything right in my world. One look at her beautiful face, just one glimpse of her stunning smile, makes my heart skip a beat and that is all I need for the rest of my life. Her. My Emmy.

CHAPTER 10
Emmy

"HEY EMMY." ETHAN calls to me in greeting. I look up from my book and smile.

"Hey you!" I say, closing the book I was reading. "Ready to learn some more about France?"

"Actually, I know a little about it already. My grandmother is from Paris and I've been there a few times growing up, to visit her." He says, plopping down next to me on the couch, flicking his head to the side, getting his long hair out of his face.

"No way!" I say, eyes wide with excitement. "That's so cool. Have you been to the Eiffel Tower?"

"How do you go to Paris and *not* go to the Eiffel Tower?" He says with mock offense.

"You don't. It would be criminal to do so." He grins at my response but it quickly falls with his next question. "So, are they going to be attached to you like creepy stalkers or something?"

I look at him with confusion, then look behind me. My face deadpans as I sigh at the sight of Oliver and Talon standing a few shelves over, pretending to look at books. "They are just looking out for me. A lot of bullshit has happened since I came to this school and they want to make sure nothing else does."

He nods his head in understanding. "Don't you think there might be a little bit of jealousy mixed in there?" He grins.

Looking back over I find them peeking over the books, but then quickly cover their faces back up when we're looking. "Okay, yeah, maybe a little bit."

"Well, they have nothing to worry about. I'm more interested in the blonde one than I would be you. I mean you're gorgeous and all, but I'm not into tits. Cock is more my flavor."

I choke on a laugh, eyes going wide. He just grins and shrugs. "Good to know." I say.

"You gonna tell them I'm gay? Maybe then they will back off a little?" He asks.

"Nah. They should trust me. Besides, I can handle myself. They love me, but they can be smothering sometimes." I sigh.

We spend the next hour reading as many textbooks we can find that mention France. When time was up, we each split up the remaining books and took them to the checkout counter.

"See you tomorrow?" Ethan asks.

"Yup, we can come back here during history and talk about what each of us has read and compare notes."

"Sounds like a good idea." He says, tucking his books in his bag and putting his long hair in a man bun. "See you then." He heads towards the exit, nodding at my not-so-subtle lovers. "See ya later, Oliver and Talon!" Ethan waves before disappearing out the door.

I giggle as I walk over to the guys. "You can come out now." I say with amusement.

"Did you know we were here the whole time?" Talon groans.

"Uh, yes, babe. You both suck at hiding. It was kind of obvious."

"Well, it was the only place we could see you." Oliver grumbles.

"What are you doing here anyway? You should have used this time to research your own assignment." I say, raising a brow. "And where's Ben?"

"He's in the room. He said this was stupid, and we should trust that you're fine. And we do, we trust *you*. It's *him* we don't trust." I can't help but giggle, knowing they really have nothing to worry about. At least not when it comes to Ethan getting in my pants. I don't know his story or why he's here, but I do plan on finding out, especially if we will be spending so much time together. I get a good vibe from him. He seems like a really good guy and from what I've seen so far, I think I'll be okay.

"You guys are too hard on him. He's a nice guy."

"Yeah, because he wants to get in your pants. Why else would he be laughing and smiling at you like that?"

I look at Oliver with annoyance.

"Not all guys want to fuck every girl they meet. Guys and girls can be friends without anything sexual between them. It hurts you know, that you just assume he only wants to hang out with me because he has an ulterior motive. As if I'm not good enough to be friends with without him wanting my body too."

I push past them, needing some space. I love them more than life itself, and I understand where they are coming from, but I lost my only friend outside of them and sometimes it's nice to just talk to a person who I'm *not* intimate with.

I end up at Tyson's office and knock on the door with a little more force than I should. A moment later he opens the door. "Are you okay?" He asks, looking behind me.

"Just dandy." I snap, pushing past him and storming into his office. "Your brother's a fucking dickhead sometimes, you know that?" I'm a little more worked up than I should be. And maybe it's not as big of a deal as I'm making it. Blame all the pent-up sexual hormones.

"What did he do?" Tyson asks as he takes hold of my shoulders, which stops me from pacing.

"He seems to think that I can't have a guy friend because guys only want one thing. Is it so hard to believe that someone might want me for my personality and not just my body? Not everything has to be about sex." I huff.

"No, you're right. One of my best friends is a woman, and we have a completely platonic friendship."

"You fucked her once." I deadpan.

He chuckles. "Once, that's it. We have been best friends ever since." He challenges, raising a brow at me.

"Okay, point taken, but still. Ethan is a nice guy. He's been nothing but respectful to me and the guys. Not once has he tried anything and I don't think he ever will."

"I'll talk to them, okay? Tell them to back off and trust you." Tyson says, rubbing my shoulders before bringing me into a hug.

I melt into his warm, strong body, wrapping my arms around him as he holds me. "I love you." I mumble into his chest.

"I love you too, Princess." He rubs my back. "Try to calm down. I don't like seeing you so worked up. Is there anything else I can do to help?"

I know he's serious, but the only thing I want at this moment is his lips on mine. "Kiss me?" I ask, pulling back so that I can see his face. His eyes grow darker, pupils dilating.

"Always." He growls before gripping the back of my neck and crashing his lips into mine. There's nothing soft and sweet about this kiss. Only pure raw lust, passion, and love.

Lips and tongue battle their own war as things start to get more heated than intended.

Tyson grips my ass while grinding his massive, hard cock against my belly. *Fuck!* I have yet to taste him. I want him. Right now. Fuck waiting anymore. I go to the doctor tomorrow, and I know I've healed up just fine. There was no tearing or anything when I gave birth. Melody was small, but thankfully not too small.

Not giving him a chance to say no, I pull back from the kiss, leaving us both panting. "Sit." I breathe, pushing him towards his office desk.

He looks at me with surprise. "Why?"

"Just sit." I demand, feeling bold and sassy.

"Watch it, Princess. Talk to me like that and I might have to spank your bratty ass." He growls, but moves to his chair and sits down, doing as I ask. A rush of excitement floods through my veins when he obeys my request.

He sits down, leaning back in his chair to get comfortable. "Now what?" He smirks.

I stalk forward with a hungry gaze. Never breaking eye contact, I slowly lower myself to my knees in front of him and run my hands up his thighs. "What are you doing?" He asks, looking at the door then down to me. "This is risky, Emmy." He warns, his voice growing more serious, but he does nothing to stop me as my hands reach for his belt. I say nothing as I unbuckle it, followed by the zipper.

When I have enough room, I reach into his boxers to take him out, and my hand is met with a fucking sausage the size of my fucking forearm. My eyes go wide, snapping up to Tyson's.

"He said you were ten inches, he failed to tell me it was as thick as a fucking coke can." I say in disbelief.

Tyson looks at me with humor. "What's wrong, Princess? Don't think you can handle me? You take these guys like a champ, I'm sure you will be just fineeee." I squeeze his cock as hard as I can at his last word, causing him to moan, and his eyes to roll into the back of his head. "Fuck." He hisses as I start to pump him.

"No more waiting, Ty. I want to taste you." I say, looking down at his cock. "Even if I might have to unhinge my jaw just to fit this in my mouth."

Yes, he's massive, but it has my core dripping. I can't wait to feel him stretch me, but I think I'll have one of the others ease me back into sex before attempting to take his massive cock.

At this point he is too far gone to protest, so I take both my hands and wrap them around his cock before locking eyes with him, licking the pre-cum off his tip.

"God, Princess, you look so fucking perfect. On your knees for me like a good girl." He praises, and I find myself loving his approval. His words make me want to please him, so I start taking him in my mouth.

It's a bit of a stretch for my jaw, but he still fits. I bob my head up and down, only managing to get half his cock in my mouth.

He takes my glasses off for me, placing them on his desk; then gathers my hair up in his fist and starts to guide me on his cock.

"Just like that. Good girl. Take my cock." He groans when my tongue swirls around his tip before I take him deep again. "Fuck! You feel amazing. Do you know how many nights I stayed up thinking of this very moment? Of having my incredible woman show me just how much she wants me, craves me. Like I do her."

I pick up my pace, loving all the sounds I'm coaxing from him. I really want to slip my hands down and play with myself right now but I want this to be all about him, so I just squeeze my legs shut and focus on my man.

"Knock, knock!" A cheery woman's voice says from the doorway. I can't see anything from the angle I'm at, but I know I'm mostly under Tyson's desk. Tyson's eyes fly open in panic before looking at the door, then me. I just grin around his cock and shift back a little so I'm completely covered. He pushes his chair forward and I'm back to having the perfect angle.

"Sorry to bother you Mr. Kingston, but the door was unlocked. I'm sorry if I woke you, it looked like you were having yourself a little cat nap." It sounds like Mrs. Kippland, our part-time school librarian.

"Umm, yes." Tyson clears this throat, strain appearing in his tone. "I mean, no. I was just resting my eyes."

"Oh, perfect. I was wondering if you had a few moments to discuss something?"

"Ah!" He shouts as I scrap my teeth up his cock. "Um, this is not exactly the best time."

"I'm sorry. Do you have somewhere to be? This won't take too long."

"I guess. Yes, sure." Poor dude must look really fucking awkward right now. I'm going to be paying for this later. But that idea alone excites me.

Mrs. Kippland starts to babble on about something, but I don't really pay attention because I'm concentrating on keeping the noise down so she doesn't find me under here.

I keep my sucks slow and relaxed. Lightly humming every few seconds, amused at the way his voice sounds when I do and I try hard not to laugh. But I can tell he's getting close by the way his body is starting to tense up.

One of his hands snakes under the desk to grip my head, and he starts forcing me to go harder and deeper.

"Yes. Yes. God, yes!" Tyson chants.

"Really?" Mrs. Kippland asks, excitement laced in her voice.

"That's wonderful. I'll get you all the details when I have them. Oh, this is so exciting! Thank you so much Mr. Kingston. I'll see you later!" She squeals.

The moment the door closes behind her, Tyson lets out a long groan as he thrusts his hips up, making me gag as he forces me to take him. "Fuckkkkk." Hot cum shoots down my throat, and I try my best to swallow, but it's hard because he's so big and I can barely breathe.

When he's done, and I've made sure to get every last drop, he pulls out of me and falls back into his chair.

Tucking his cock away in his boxers, he looks under his desk and I burst out laughing at the look on his face. "You think this is funny?" He growls. I laugh harder in response. "Get out here. Right now." He demands.

I move out from under his desk, then hop up on it, swinging my legs back and forth as if I have no idea what he's talking about.

"Do you know what you just made me agree to?" He asks, narrowing his eyes.

"Nope!" I pop the P, a big smile taking over my face. "Too busy sucking my sexy man's cock."

His face softens slightly. "I just agreed to put together a book sale fundraiser for a local charity." He says. His face looking less than impressed.

I'm biting my lips hard, trying to keep in the laughter.

"Damn, that... blows." I say, snorting as some giggles slip free.

"You little brat." He says, his voice containing a promise for the punishment to come. "Your ass is gonna be so red by the time I'm done with you."

I jump off his desk and start heading for the door. "Well good luck with your new project. I'm sure you will make that little old lady oh, so happy."

"Get back here." He demands.

"Sorry, gotta go, gonna be late." I say, raising my hands then turn to open the door.

"For what?" He asks.

"Anything but this." I start to laugh. "Bye, Mr. Kingston. Thanks for the afternoon snack." I tease, giving him a heated stare. He gets up and charges for me, but his pants are around his ankles and he is shuffling more than anything. God, this whole sight is too funny, and I almost feel bad for how I'm leaving him. Almost.

"See you later, Sir." I say in a sultry voice before closing the door behind me. I quickly leave to go find the others. I know Tyson won't risk tracking me down just yet. I have a little time before I can't sit for a week.

"What did you do to Tyson?" Oliver asks. It's Friday, meaning Amy and Melody are on their way down for the weekend. My doctor's appointment is in an hour, so hopefully they should be arriving any minute now. The guys and Charlie will be watching the baby as Amy and Tyson take me to my appointment.

"Oh you know, just sucked his dick under his desk while he talked to Mrs. Kippland and it resulted in him having to run a whole charity book sale." I say with a mischievous grin.

"You didn't!" Talon roars with laughter. "Fuck, you're perfect."

I just shrug. "You know it's gonna be hell for you, right?" Oliver says, grinning and shaking his head. "You're playing with fire, baby girl, and you're gonna get burned."

"That's the point. And I can't wait." I wiggle my eyebrows making him laugh.

"Soooo. Like, how is this gonna work?" Charlie asks, coming into the room from our bathroom.

"What do you mean?" Ben asks.

"Well, I don't see any reason why the doctor would say no to Emmy being able to start having sex. So who's gonna go first?"

They all look at each other, then to me. "We are not drawing straws." I narrow my eyes at them. "We will let everything happen naturally. As much as I want to jump you all the moment I get home, we still have the rest of the weekend with Melody, so no sex until she's gone."

Talon mumbles something about sneaking a quickie while Melody naps, but Ben slaps him on the arm saying that their first time with me in weeks isn't going to be something that we rush into, to just get it done and over with and that a few more days won't hurt.

"Also, I'm still mad at you." I say to Oliver, narrowing my eyes at him.

"Still?" He sighs.

"Well, are you going to apologize or not?"

"What do I have to apologize for? I'm right and so are you. I know anyone would be lucky to be friends with you because you are an amazing human. You're loving, kind, strong, and badass. You love so hard. But you're also sex on legs, and even a blind man would want you. And anyone who doesn't, is most likely gay."

Little does he know, Ethan *is* gay. Oliver is wrong because he's clearly judging Ethan without even knowing him. That is why I won't let this go so easily.

I'm not going to tell him either. It should not matter what gender Ethan is attracted to, and he deserves the benefit of the doubt. He shouldn't be seen as a dog only wanting sex just because he's a guy.

As for Oliver, I'll let this go when he apologizes.

"What about birth control?" Talon asks, drawing my attention away from the brooding, raven haired boy in front of me.

"I wanted to talk to you guys about that." I say, biting my lip and looking between everyone.

"Talk to us about what?" Tyson asks, standing in the doorway to my room.

My eyes snap up to his, and I see the threat to tan my ass lingering behind them, but I also see his adoring love for me shining brighter.

"Birth control."

"Okay... What about it?"

"I was thinking of trying something new. Like the shot, or the implant. The Pill I was on was causing my periods to be much worse than before. I don't want to go back to having pain like that again."

"Of course." Tyson says. "You do whatever you feel is best for your body. But is it safe to use those forms of birth control while breastfeeding?"

"That's what I'm going to talk to my doctor about today. I looked it up and it says there are some that are safer than others, but I'll know more after speaking with him. But that means if we plan for another baby in the future, it won't be as easy as just not taking my pill for a few days. This means we would have to plan ahead. Also, sometimes certain birth control can make getting pregnant harder."

"We will agree with whatever you want to do, Butterfly." Ben says, pulling me into him for a hug, and kissing the top of my hair. "Your body, your choice. Always. On everything and anything."

I relax into him, soaking up the love and warmth of his strong, tattooed body.

"Amy's here." Tyson says, looking up from his phone.

"Eeeekkkk! Little Miss!" Charlie squeals, zipping past us.

"It's like we no longer exist." Talon laughs.

"Not unless you're Emmy, when Melody is involved." Tyson says.

I smile at how much my girl loves our daughter. It makes my heart swell every time I see them together, anytime I see any of my lovers with her. That little girl is so loved and protected.

We all head down to meet Amy and Melody, finding them in the lobby. Charlie is baby talking to Melody as she just stares up at her mommy with her big blue eyes, not understanding a word she's saying but loving every moment.

"Hello, Sweetheart." Amy says, giving me a hug. "How is everything?"

"Good." I say, happy that I actually mean it for once. "Not being able to be with her every day is hard, but life here is pretty good."

"Any word on Dagger?" Amy asks Tyson, using his MC name, not even bothering to refer to him as my father.

"Nope. And we're getting pretty antsy. It's quiet. No one has been seen coming or going from their compound. We did, however, stop the truck that goes there every week. When our guys intercepted it, all they found was food and supplies. It's like they are stocking up for a war."

"Oh, no!" Amy says, eyes wide. "What does that mean for the Reapers, for you guys?" She asks, looking at all of us. "We all know he's not done with Emmy.

He may not be calling, texting, or sending gifts anymore, but he would not have done all that just to give up and move on."

She's right. And that's something I think about late at night when everyone else is asleep.

"We are doing the same to a certain extent. Men are watching you and Melody twenty-four seven. I'll be here with these guys, as well as a few other guards that my dad picked out himself. But everyone else will be staying in the compound until we know more. War is coming. That, we know for sure."

I look at Tyson, who won't meet my eyes. He has been keeping me updated, but he tries to keep Dagger's name out of it as much as he can. I think it's because he doesn't want to worry me, but this is my life, and it's my daughter he wants. I don't want to be kept in the dark, no matter how stressful it might be.

"We will be talking about this later." I tell Tyson. He finally looks at me, giving me a nod.

I get some snuggles in before handing Melody over to her daddies and mommy.

This is their first time without me around and I can tell they are nervous, but Charlie will be there to help. Oliver is still healing, although he's practically back to his old self, but I still told Charlie to make sure he takes it easy and to let the others help out.

We say goodbye and head out for my appointment.

Time to see if I can take the 'Out-of-Order' sign off my vagina.

CHAPTER 11
Tyson

EMMY IS MOSTLY quiet during the car ride to the doctor. Amy chats about everything and anything as Emmy mindlessly says a few mmhmms and uhhuhs. I can tell that the earlier mention of Dagger is bugging her. I have been pretty good with keeping her updated on everything, but this was some new information I haven't had the time to tell her yet. She did not look pleased. And she has every right not to be.

Things with the Savage Hellhounds are far from over. We know something big is coming; Dagger wouldn't have wasted his time doing what he did with Emmy if it wasn't worth his time. He's coming for her. It's just a matter of when and where. That's why anytime we are outside this school, I will be with her. I don't care what the others think. Her and Melody's safety is my first concern and main priority.

When we get to the doctor's office, I take Emmy's hand in mine as we make our way into the building. Outside of school, I don't give a fuck about who knows that we are together. It's never been an issue of people knowing, it's just making sure it's not anyone from the school.

"You mad at me?" I ask her as I lean over to kiss her on the top of the head. She hugs my arm, leaning her head against it.

"No, but how long did you know this new information?"

"Just found out last night. I was going to tell you today, I promise, but with Melody coming to visit I didn't want to put a damper on the mood. I want us to be as happy and as stress-free as possible when we are with her. Our time is special and short."

"I believe you. And you're right. Let's just put this to the side for now, nothing's going to change in the next two days right?" She asks, looking up at me.

"Nah, I don't think so, Princess."

"Good. Let's get this appointment over with, then we can go spend time with our daughter. I want to take her for a walk in the carrier on the beach. It's nice out today and the sounds of the waves will soothe me."

"Anything you want, Princess." I say, kissing the top of her head again.

We don't have to wait too long before the nurse is calling Emmy into one of the patient rooms. Amy stays in the waiting room, but Emmy asks me to come in with her.

"Hello, Emmy." The doctor greets her with a big smile. "How is motherhood treating you?"

"Hi." Emmy smiles back. "Amazing. Melody is perfect. And having all the extra hands is a blessing. I love every moment I'm with her." Emmy smiles so bright when talking about Melody that it triggers my own smile to spread across my face at seeing how happy she is. I love my girls so much and seeing Emmy happy is like floating on a cloud of contentment.

"That's wonderful. I've talked to her doctor located back in your hometown. She says Melody is healthy and happy. I'm glad everything is going smoothly, given how she was brought into the world."

"So am I, and I'm grateful it wasn't worse than it was."

"Very true. So let's take a look. I'm sure you're eager to get back to life as it was before giving birth, physically." Emmy blushes and I smirk.

"Um, yeah." She says. "That would be nice."

I snort a laugh, knowing full well that Emmy has been a little horn dog and itching to have a dick in her again. And I can't wait until one of those dicks is mine.

She narrows her eyes at me, cheeks turning a darker shade of red.

Emmy is already in her dressing gown, so all she has to do is lay back and let the doctor do his job. Me, I just sit there with a scowl on my face. I don't like this. Specifically, him being down there looking at her private areas. Emmy sees the frown on my face and holds out her hand for me. I wrap my hand around her soft, delicate fingers, bringing them up to my lips and placing a soft kiss on them, earning myself a stunning smile.

"Well, it looks like you have healed up perfectly. Now, I don't suggest participating in any crazy sexual activities but you should be okay to have regular intercourse." He says, placing the covering back over Emmy's bottom half and discarding his gloves. Emmy brings her hands up to cover her face and groans in embarrassment.

"So you're giving your official word that she's healed enough to have sex again?" I ask. Emmy peaks out at me through her fingers. I grin, giving her a wink.

"Yup, you're good to go. Just remember not to push your limits and listen to your body when it tells you it's had enough. Now, what about birth control?"

Emmy and the doctor talk for several minutes about what is safe to take while breastfeeding. In the end, she chooses a birth control implant and is able to get one right then and there. He says it should be good to go within a few days. We thank him and head out to meet Amy so we can go back to the school.

"You know, I plan on getting my revenge for the little stunt you pulled the other day." I say, sitting next to her on the couch. We all thought it would be more comfortable to hang out at my place today, since Amy is going to stick around for supper. It's not weird when it's your brother and his girlfriend and her mom, so no one should be asking questions.

"Oh, no! I'm so afraid." She says sarcastically as she grins up at me.

"Keep it up, Princess. Each time you sass me it will be another smack I add to that sweet ass." I grin back. Her face falls to something more sexually excited, and fuck me, I'm ready to say fuck it all and just take her in the back to make her mine.

"You can't look at me like that." I say, cupping her face.

"Like what?" She asks, her eyes growing hooded.

"Like you're ready to bend over and offer yourself to me, right here and now." I growl.

"Maybe I am." She counters.

"I think someone is hungry." Charlie says, bringing a fussy Melody over. I offer my arms out to take her and Charlie looks at me with a raised brow. "Do you have milky titties we don't know about?" She snorts.

"No." I roll my eyes. "I want to hold her for a moment while Emmy gets comfortable.

"Sureeeee." Charlie teases. "But lift up that shirt and show me your man boobs to be sure."

"Fuck off." I snort, taking the baby from her.

"You love me, just admit it." She says, before heading back over to Amy.

"You do." Emmy says, lifting up her shirt, and unhooking her nursing bra.

"I do what?" I ask, giving Melody a kiss and placing her in Emmy's arms as I help her latch on. Once she starts feeding I give her little head a rub before kissing her mama's cheek.

"Love her." Emmy gives me a sleepy smile, resting her head about against the couch.

"She's okay, I guess." I shrug, making her grin wider.

"You're outnumbered now."

"Don't remind me." I groan, leaning my head back next to hers so that we are nose to nose. "But if I'm stuck with all you ladies, at least I have some of the best ones in the world." I kiss her softly, and with so much love.

"Thank you." She whispers, closing her eyes and putting her forehead against mine. "For picking me to be the one to tame the manwhore that was once Tyson Kingston."

A snort slips free. "Those days are long over. And ones I never want to remember. They were all placeholders. None ever came close to making me feel what you make me feel. You changed me, Amelia Knox. For that, I owe you my life."

"You can repay me with lots of love and kisses."

"I'd be more than happy to."

"And lots of orgasms." She adds with a wink.

"I mean, it sounds like a pretty damn good deal to me." Talon says, sitting down next to Emmy.

"You can fuck off, too." I growl as Emmy hits my leg.

"Nah, Bro, when Melody is here, they are fair game." He says, looking down at our nursing daughter.

The others gather around, and we settle into a comfortable conversation. When Melody is done eating, I don't give Emmy an option before I take her so that I can burp her myself.

"You know, and keep it in mind that I'm totally not into cock, but there's something hot about a tattooed man caring for a tiny little human." Charlie not so quietly whispers, making Amy giggle.

"Oh, trust me, I feel the same way." Emmy says, biting her lip and locking eyes with me. She is so damn beautiful.

"Dude, go be sexy somewhere else." Oliver says, making shooing motions with his hands.

"All I'm doing is burping the baby." I scoff.

"Right, then just hand her over and go."

"You're all getting on my last damn nerve." I mumble, taking Melody with me to my room, ignoring the sounds of protest from Talon and Oliver.

I place a now sleeping Melody on my bed, and carefully lay down next to her. I tuck my arm under the pillow and lay on my side. I'm so entranced with this tiny, perfect girl. My little Princess. She may not have my blood, but she has my heart.

I would die for her and her mother. I will spend every day making sure she is loved and protected. And God help anyone who tries to harm my family. It will be the last thing they ever do.

Emmy

"Well, who do we have here?" Ethan asks with a smile, sitting down next to me on the couch in the library.

"This little cutie pie is Melody." I say, smiling down at my little girl. I have her propped up in my lap so that she's sitting up, with my legs as support. She's just staring at me, sucking on her hand, and I'd be content to just sit here and watch her do that for hours.

"Hello, Melody." Ethan says in a baby voice. "So they let you have her here overnight?" He asks, looking from the baby to me.

"Yup. I mean, the girls' dorm is pretty empty now that there's not many of us left. Our room is on one end, and the rest of the girls are on the other side of the hall, so we're not too much of a bother. But she was pretty fussy, so I came here so that Charlie and Ben could sleep a little longer."

It's 8 a.m. on a Saturday. Talon and Oliver are at the gym, so I needed a place that should be empty at this time of day.

"What are *you* doing up so early?" I ask.

His face turns grim. "Got an upsetting phone call." He sighs, running his hand through his long hair.

"Want to talk about it?" I ask. "I know we haven't known each other very long, but I'd like to have you as a friend. I'm pretty good at listening. Maybe I could even help."

He's quiet for a while, like he's thinking things over in his head.

"I'd like to be friends." He says. "I don't have many of those, and something tells me you would make a good one." He gives me a half grin.

"I try my best." I smile back.

"Ugh. Where to start." He sighs. "Alright. Well, there's this girl named Leah. My best friend in the whole world. We grew up together. Our mothers met in church when they were pregnant with us, and they became best friends. We did as well, by default you could say." He grins at me.

"Growing up, our parents always said we would get married someday, build a life of our own, and have lots of babies.

We never thought anything of it, we were just kids at the time but as we got older, they really seemed to believe that we really would. So once we became teenagers, we started feeling pressured. She was my best friend, but my parents wanted her to be my girlfriend. And the same went with her parents wanting me to be her boyfriend. So we started dating. But it never felt... right. After a while, we decided that we weren't meant to be more than friends, but decided to keep our parents believing we were a couple.

"As time went on, I started to notice I wasn't attracted to girls, it was always a guy who caught my eye. With Leah being someone I told everything to, I told her I was confused." His face changes expression and fills with humor. "She, being her crazy silly self, offered to help me test it out to see if I really wasn't into girls by having sex with her."

"She didn't!" I ask, eyes going wide.

"Yup. And I, at the time, said what do I have to lose? Also, she said she wanted to lose her virginity to someone she trusted. So, in a way, I was helping her out too. It was also my first time and I felt the same way."

"So did you guys have sex?" I ask, invested in the story now.

"We did. And it was nice. I mean, everything was working. But afterwards, it made me realize I really was into guys instead of girls. She understood and was supportive of that. We laughed it off and moved on. But little did we know that night changed our whole life."

The look of pain on his face told me there was no happy ending.

"What happened?"

"Well, a few months before I was sent here, Leah started feeling sick. She told me she missed her period."

"Oh no." I gasp, seeing where his story is leading.

"Yup. So I took what little money I had, went to the store and bought her a test. It came back positive. We decided that we wanted to keep the baby, and I would help her raise him or her. I love kids and this was my child, I wanted to do the right thing. We were afraid to tell our parents because they're pretty strict and religious, so we kept it to ourselves. I tried my best to take care of her. One day she ran out of prenatal vitamins and I knew how important it was for her to take them. But I didn't have the money at the time, so I stole them. I got caught and then arrested. When my parents bailed me out, I was forced to tell them everything. They told me that I should have told them. They told Leah's parents and we all sat down and talked. They were happy but they told us we had to get married before the baby was born.

That's when Leah said no. She said that she loved me like a best friend but that was all we were ever gonna be.

"Her parents told her that we were still young and she would learn to love me. Seeing that they were not going to back down, I told them that I couldn't marry her because I was gay."

"I take it they didn't react the way you would have liked?"

"Nope." He huffs out a humorless laugh. "They disowned me. Told me that I was going to hell. That I was a disgrace to our family. And to top it off, they managed to convince the store owner to press charges, perks of being from a small Christian town. So they charged me with theft, and the judge sent me here."

"I'm so sorry." I say, taking his hand in mine, giving it a squeeze. "What are you guys going to do about the baby?"

"She's still keeping it. But her parents don't want me to have anything to do with my son. They said they don't want their grandson raised by a faggot boy."

I'm fuming now. I'm ready to find these parents and slap some sense into them on his behalf.

"Leah and I don't care what they think. Once I get out of here, we plan on getting our own place and raising him together. And when we both find someone to add to our lives, we will deal with that then."

I smile at how amazing this Leah is. And how amazing of a man Ethan is for being so dedicated to his best friend and son.

"That all leads up to the phone call I just got. It makes me want to beat the shit out of the next person who looks at me wrong." He sighs in frustration, leaning his head back against the couch with his eyes closed. "She just called to tell me she went into labor."

"Fuck." I say. Looking down, I see Melody fell back to sleep, and I move her to cradle her into my arms. "Where is she right now?"

"She's at the hospital in the next town over." The same hospital I was at. Biting my lip, I take a moment to think.

"I have an idea. It's crazy. But it just might work."

"Okay..." He says, eyeing me warily.

"You're going to need to break something. Like your nose, or your hand. Something that would require you to have to go to the hospital to get a cast."

"Okay, I see where you're going with this. And I'm not saying I won't do that, but when I get there, how will I go see her? Her parents are up her ass and won't leave even if she is pissed and doesn't want them there."

"I can help with that." I say smiling. "Hold her, please." I say, handing over Melody. He takes her happily.

I move over to the window and call Tyson. I tell him my plan. At first he says no, but then I promise him all the dirty sexy things he could think of and that got him to change his tune very fast.

"Done." I say, sitting back down on the couch.

"So, what *is* the plan?"

I tell him that Tyson will be the one to bring him to the hospital, and he will bring one of the guards his father hired. When they get there and Ethan is all bandaged up, Tyson will work his magic and find a way for Ethan to be there with Leah while she gives birth or, at the very least, get to meet his son and not have to wait the next month and a half until he's out of here.

"Thank you, Emmy." Ethan says. "You really are a good person."

"Why, thank you." I say, handing the baby over to Tyson, who just showed up a few minutes ago.

"Make it quick. They will realize the cameras are down soon." Tyson says.

"Ready?" I say, cringing at what I'm about to do.

Ethan takes a deep breath. "Yup."

Tyson takes off down the hall, not wanting the baby to be near this.

"Alright." Ethan places his hand on the frame of the metal library door. "Do it." He says.

And just like that, with all my strength I slam the door on his hand, making him roar in pain.

What a weird bonding experience to have with a new best friend. At least it will make an interesting story to tell our kids someday.

CHAPTER 12
Tyson

"THANKS MAN." ETHAN says as he gets into the passenger side of the car. "I wish I could have been there with her for the whole thing, but I'm glad I at least got to see him being born and spend some time with him before we had to go back."

"You're welcome, but this was all Emmy." I say, starting up the car and backing out of the hospital parking lot.

"I know, but you lost time with your daughter to take me to see my son. I really appreciate it."

My head snaps over to look at him, not caring to keep my eyes on the road. "She told you?" I ask, narrowing my gaze at him.

"That you are part of her little harem? Nah. But I'm not blind. I see how you look at Melody. It's not how an uncle looks at a niece, it's how I look at my son. And don't even get me started on the way your eyes consume Emmy when you don't think anyone is watching." He laughs.

I chew on the inside of my lip, directing my eyes back to the road. "You can't tell anyone at the school." I growl. "I don't give a shit who knows outside that building but I can't have anything fuck up me staying with them until school is over."

"Hey, I'm not going to say anything. Emmy is my friend, and I would never do anything to jeopardize that. She's a special one."

"She is." I smile, eyes still on the road. "She cares about her friends and loved ones hard. That's why I wasn't all that surprised when she called me with her crazy plan." I chuckle, looking down at his plaster encased hand.

"I mean, sure it was pretty on the spot. And I'm a little concerned how she came up with it so easily. But it worked."

"If you knew who her sister was, that would be child's play compared to her." He looks at me with questioning eyes. "Don't ask. You haven't earned that information."

He just nods his head. "She did a good job on it. My hand looked like someone ran over it." He shivers.

"Three broken fingers. I hope it doesn't affect my use of it. I mean I don't do anything special that would require my hand to be perfect, but I'd like to hold my son properly."

"You will be fine. Might take a while to heal, but you're good." There is a short pause before I open my mouth to say something.

"So, I might sound like a jealous boyfriend, but Emmy *is* only a friend to you right?" I ask, side eyeing him. I need to know the answer to the question all the others have been wondering about.

"Yes. One I'd now consider a best friend. Next to Leah, of course." He smiles.

"Your girlfriend, right?" I ask.

"Nope. Just one of my best friends. Maybe even a soul mate."

"But you just had a baby with her?" I ask, confused.

"Long story." He laughs. "But let's just say it was a friends-with-benefits thing, and out of your group of friends, Emmy and Charlie would be the last ones to catch my attention if you know what I mean."

My mind mulls over his words. "Wait. So you're gay?" I ask.

"You have a problem with that if I was?" He asks in a defensive tone.

"No. I mean, I'm not into guys, but Talon and Ben have their own thing, and Emmy is with Charlie. I have no issues with loving the same sex."

"Then, yes. Yes, I am gay."

I bark out a laugh. "Wait until Oliver and Talon find out. They have been so fucking annoying about the whole thing. They're gonna feel so stupid."

He grins. "Don't tell them. Emmy wants them to come around to me on their own before finding out. She doesn't want them to just accept me because I'm gay and no threat to them."

"What an Emmy thing to do." I shake my head.

"Something tells me being friends with her is never going to be boring." He says with amusement.

"Nothing involving Emmy is ever boring. But maybe a little 'boring' might be a nice change. Even if it's only like this for a little while."

When we get back to the school, Ethan says goodbye before heading up to the guys' dorm. I track down Mr. Tucker and give him a run down of everything and let him know how Ethan is doing. I left out the parts where I bribed some staff members, threatened others, and caused some drama-queen 'Karen' who was known as Leah's mother, to demand to see the hospital's manager when they told her she was not allowed in the delivery room because her daughter denied her access. It's a hospital, not a fucking Walmart.

In the end, I was able to get him in the room just as she was about to start pushing. I didn't stay long, but I did see the fear vanish from her eyes as soon as she saw Ethan.

I have respect for that man. I don't know his whole story but I can tell he is a dedicated father, and that's hard to see in guys his age. He was willing to hurt himself just to be there. So, even if he wasn't gay, I would have accepted Emmy's friendship with him.

"Hey, man." I greet Oliver as he lifts weights. He places the dumbbells back on their rack.

"I heard what happened." He says, wiping the sweat off his face. "How did everything go?"

I look around. "Not here, too many prying ears." I say.

"I was just finishing up here. Let me go shower, and then we can head back to your place and talk."

"Brotherly bonding, I like it." I grin, clapping him on the back as he heads towards the changing room.

He quickly gets ready and we head to my place, joking around as we walk.

"So, Emmy didn't tell me too much, just that she helped a friend out. She is hanging out with Charlie right now, so I didn't get the chance to talk to her, just got a text. Mind filling me in?" Oliver asks, taking a seat on the couch.

I head to my fridge and pull out a couple of beers and offer him one as I take a seat next to him.

"Out of respect for Ethan, because it's not my story to tell, I'll give you a vague recap. I got a call from Emmy. She asked me if I could help get Ethan to the hospital. He had a friend there that he really needed to see. And it being Emmy, how could I say no?" I grin, taking a sip of beer.

"Simple. You don't." He laughs.

"Exactly. So, she told me all about her crazy plan to smash the guy's hand in the door so it was damaged enough to be sent to the hospital in need of a cast. Crazy as it was, it worked, and he got to see his friend."

"So Emmy did all that for a guy she just met?" He asks, pondering the question.

"Oliver, this is Emmy. She doesn't do anything half-assed. If you're good enough to be her friend, then you must be a good person. She is smart, and she doesn't fight for just anyone. That should tell you the type of guy Ethan is.

But it seems that all you are able to see is that he has a dick and isn't ugly, so he must want in her pants. And dude, guys can be friends with girls. And the other way around, without catching feelings. My best friend is a girl." I explain.

"Yeah, a batshit crazy one. Fuck, she scares me." He says, blowing out a breath and taking a drink.

"Me too, brother, me too. And want to know the scary thing?" I ask.

"What?"

"I feel like the more shit Emmy goes through, and the stronger she becomes, the more of Harlow I see in her."

"Oh god, don't say that! I don't need my dick chopped off or anything!" He exclaims, quickly placing his hand over his crotch.

"I don't think she would go that far. But she's not that innocent girl you grew up with. She might only be nineteen, but she has grown up a lot in the past two years. Ben doesn't seem to be too bothered by her having a guy friend. Why are you and Talon? Hell, even I'm not losing my mind over it. He's a pretty good kid."

"I don't know. He was just all smiles and charm from the moment Emmy sat down next to him. Then always asking to hang out."

I grin at him. "Are you jealous that she's spending time with someone other than one of you? Not that he would try anything."

"Maybe." He mumbles, taking a drink.

"Okay, I'm gonna give it to you straight. I love you, but you are a fucking idiot. One, she's hung out with him mostly to do a school assignment. Two, she lost the only other friend outside the people she's in a relationship with. We all need time to ourselves, or time away from our lover. It's healthy. So if that means hanging out with Ethan, then so be it. She can be friends with whoever she wants. She's a good judge of character. Don't insult her by thinking she doesn't know what she's doing."

Oliver blinks at me for a few moments and I see his brain processing my words. "FUCK!" He shouts, tossing his head back against the couch. "I was a fucking dick, wasn't I?'

"Yup."

"I need to grovel at her feet, don't I?"

"I mean, it wouldn't hurt."

"I should probably apologize to Ethan too, huh? I mean, if he *is* gonna be Emmy's new bestie, I'll have to get along with him."

"Probably a good idea."

"Well, better late than never. I'm gonna do it right now, before I change my mind." He sighs, placing the now empty beer bottle on the coffee table.

"Good luck." I call out to him.

"Yeah, yeah." He says, not looking back, waving me off.

I had a talk with Emmy about his nightmares, and spoke to her about convincing him to see someone outside the school, someone better equipped at handling what's going on. She said she would. Hopefully it gets brought up during their little heart-to-heart, but something tells me Oliver is just going to end up flipping Emmy's 'Sorry, we're closed!' sign over to 'Come in, we're now open!' Lucky bastard. On the other hand, I know my time is coming soon, and it's gonna be worth every agonizing moment that I've waited. Oh, all the dirty things I'm going to do to my bratty, little princess and that sassy mouth of hers.

That sinful, blissful, mind-blowing mouth. I still have to punish her for that little stunt she pulled in my office, but as awkward and risky as it was, *fuck*, was it hot. She took my cock like the good girl she is. And fuck, if it didn't do shit to my heart with the amount of love she had in her eyes as she did it. I'm so damn lucky she's mine. I may have to share her with the others, but she doesn't show me any less attention or affection than I think she would have if it were only the two of us. That's another thing I love about her. She always tries to make everyone feel equal.

I just want to make her happy, and I might even be open to sharing her every now and then in the future, but I'm a selfish man and my time alone with her is precious. Can't blame me for wanting her all to myself.

I finish off my beer before heading into the shower. I take extra good care of my cock as I replay what happened in the office, moaning her name as I cum.

Soon I'll be doing that with my cock buried deep inside her perfect pussy.

Oliver

I know I was an asshole about this Ethan guy, I know I should have trusted her judgment and not just assume the worst about someone I don't know, but I'm all kinds of fucked up these days.

Everything bad that's happened to her since she's come back into my life, on top of almost dying myself, has my mind in a never-ending loop of fear. Reminding me of all the *what ifs*. What if she did die, what if I did, and what if something is lurking in the shadows ready to strike next.

Add these new nightmares on top of it, and I'm a hot mess. I'm trying to hold it together for my girls, but every night that I wake up screaming is another weight added to the never-ending pressure of my problems.

The first nightmare I had when I woke up after the shooting is the only one I remember; it's the only one that's stuck with me. Every other one I've had is a distant memory the moment I open my eyes, but there are always two things that linger. The need to know Emmy is okay and the little girl's laughter echoing in the back of my mind.

I leave Tyson's place and head straight for the guys' dorm, passing my room and heading for Ethan's. It's around 10 p.m. so I hope he's not already asleep.

After I give the door a few knocks, he answers. He's shirtless in only a pair of sleep pants, his long hair pulled up in one of those man buns as his broken hand hangs at his side with a bright white cast.

"Can I help you?" He smirks.

I run a hand through my hair and look inside his room, then back to him awkwardly. I didn't really think much past this point. "Can we talk?"

He opens the door wider to let me in. "Sure."

Slipping past him, I look around and see three messy beds. He walks past me and heads over to the only tidy part of the room.

"My roommates are next door gaming with some other people. It's just us." He says when he sees the question on my face.

"Cool." I nod.

"You can sit." He says, motioning to his bed. I hesitate for a moment but then take a seat on the edge. "So, what's up?"

"Sorry about your hand." I say.

"Well I kind of did it to myself, so..." He shrugs.

"I know, but I'm sorry that you had to go through that just to be able to see your friend in the hospital. I hope they're okay."

"Thanks. Emmy is a pretty quick thinker. I was on a time limit and she wasted no time thinking up some crazy scheme to get me there."

"Yeah, she's pretty awesome." I laugh.

"She is. And I'm glad she's my friend. If it wasn't for her, I would not have been able to see my son being born. The broken hand was worth it."

My eyes go wide. "Your son?" I ask.

"Yup. So while you've been thinking I'm out to steal your girl this whole time, I really just needed a friend." He says and gives me a sad smile.

"Fuck." I sigh. "About that. I wanted to apologize. I was a dick. And I gave her a hard time over it. I should have trusted you, and her judgment."

"Plus the fact that the only reason we even started talking was because of a school assignment." He points out.

"Yeah. True. But if Emmy thinks you're good enough to be her friend, then it should be good enough for me. I don't know how much Emmy has told you about what has happened these past two years, but it has been a lot. And, I guess, I'm just overprotective of her after everything she's been through."

"I get that. And I understand. I won't hold it against you. But I hope you're okay with me being friends with Emmy. Because I don't have many of those, and she seems to be just who I need in my life."

"I'm good with it... now." I grin. "And I don't think the others will have any issues. As long as you have no plans to steal our girl." I say, narrowing my eyes.

"Nope." He laughs. "Other than to make her my new BFF." He winks.

"Good." I nod. "Well, it's late. I should be going. Thanks for hearing me out."

"Thanks for being man enough to admit you made a mistake and judged me too soon."

"That, I did." I agree.

After saying goodbye to Ethan, I went to my room to crawl into bed for the night. Ben and Talon passed out about an hour ago watching a movie, and I've been laying here in bed thinking about Emmy. I don't like her being mad at me, and it's killing me. I just want to hold my girl in my arms.

Taking my phone from my bedside table, I text her.

Oliver: Hey baby, are you up?

Firefly: I am.

Oliver: Can you sneak over? I need to see you.

I chew on the inside of my cheek as I wait for her to answer, seeing the little dots that mean that she's typing something, but then they disappear. I wait and wait. But nothing.

She must still be pissed at me. And she has every right to be.

Sighing, I put my phone back as I feel a pang of sadness stabbing me in the chest. Closing my eyes, I try to will my mind to shut down, and my heart to fuck off.

Just as I'm about to drift to sleep, I hear the sound of a key turning, and the door clicks open. My head turns towards the door, and I see Emmy closing it behind her before making her way over to my bed. The moonlight streams through the open curtains, casting a glow over her perfect body. Her hair is up in a messy bun and she is wearing one of my baggy t-shirts along with a pair of sleep shorts.

My face splits into a massive smile. The pain in my heart slips away, replaced by joy that my girl isn't ignoring me.

She crawls into bed, then drapes herself over me. Tucking her face between my neck and my shoulder, she snuggles into me. My arms automatically wrap around her, holding her to me, never wanting to let her go, enjoying the warmth and pressure of her body on mine.

"Ethan told me you talked to him tonight." She whispers against my neck.

"I did. I was wrong, Firefly. I am so fucking sorry for being a dick. It's just with everything that's happened, I'm driven by fear." I admit.

"What are you afraid of?"

"Losing you. In any way." I say, rubbing my hand up and down her back.

"It's not going to happen, Olly. You are stuck with me. Face it, I'm your wifey for lifey." She grins, not moving away from my neck.

"Mmmhhmm." I hum, placing a kiss on the top of her head. "I do like the sound of that." Fuck, do I ever.

"Someday."

We just lie there together, the scent of her coconut body wash relaxing me.

"Olly?" She whispers.

"Yes, Baby Girl?"

"Are you okay?" She asks.

"What do you mean?"

She moves so that she's leaning up on her arm and looking up at me. "Your nightmares, Olly. They haven't gotten worse, but there's no sign of them getting any better. I worry about you. Sometimes I can't sleep, because all I can think about is being here with you in case you wake up screaming for me."

Fuck! I don't want to cause her any worry or pain. I know I have a lot of things I need to work out and I can't keep bottling it up. Talon saw the school counselor about his issues with his dad, and he's been doing amazing since. I mean, the shooting set him back a little, but he didn't go through what I did, so it's different for me than it is for him.

I don't think a regular old school counselor will be able to help me.

"Would you be willing to see someone?" She questions, biting her lip. "I don't want to tell you what to do. But I'm worried, and I just want you to be healthy and happy. Not just for you or me, but for Melody." She tucks her face back into my neck, giving it a kiss that sends a shiver of pleasure down my spine.

She's right. Melody may have slept through my first outburst, but the next one woke her up screaming and crying. I felt like shit after. Emmy told me it wasn't my fault and helped her to fall back asleep, but I don't want to feel like a burden to my family.

"I'll see someone." I agree. "If Talon can see someone to be the best he can be for our family, then so can I."

"I'm sorry." She sniffs and my body reacts, panic flushing through me instantly.

"What for?" I ask. "Are you crying?"

She looks at me, and I can see the tears shining in her eyes as the moonlight reflects off them.

"I'm sorry for what you felt when I was hurt, especially if it was even half as soul crushing as what I felt when you got shot. Oliver, I was so afraid." She sobs.

"Shhh, Baby Girl." I say, holding her hand to my chest as I comfort her. "I'm okay. You will never lose me. I won't let that happen."

"But you can't promise me that." She sniffles again.

"I can, and I will." I say, leaving no room for arguing. "No matter how much you don't want me to, I still blame myself for what happened to you."

"Oliver-" She starts to protest.

"But..." I say, not wanting her to try and convince me otherwise right now. "It was not your fault, not any of our faults that the shooting happened. Brittany wasn't sane and whatever issues she had were beyond needing meds. Sometimes people can't be helped. So don't be sorry, because it was not your fault."

She doesn't say anything, just nods against my neck.

"Now let's get some sleep. We have school in the morning... yay!" I say with fake enthusiasm. She giggles sleepily, and before long, her breathing evens out as little puffs of hair fan my neck.

Being at peace, with less worries, and my saving grace tucked tightly in my arms, I have a nightmare free night, for the first time in a long time. She will always be my anchor to my sanity. The one who banishes my inner demons. Even just for a moment.

CHAPTER 13
Oliver

MY ALARM GOES off at six for my morning work out. Normally, I get up, work out, shower then meet up with the rest of the group to eat breakfast before heading off to our first class.

But this morning, as I blindly look for my phone and shut off my alarm, my eyes are still not willing to open up just yet. That's when I feel the warmth of a body snuggling into my side and I smile.

"Morning." Emmy mumbles into my side, the sleepiness makes her voice sound sexy as hell and goes directly to my dick, which is already painfully hard thanks to my daily morning wood.

"Good morning, Firefly." I say back, wrapping my arm around her, pulling her closer to my body for a hug. "Always a good morning when I get to wake up to your gorgeousness."

"Lies!" She huffs in a laugh. "My hair is crazy, my breath probably smells like ass, and I didn't take my makeup off yesterday, so I probably look like a trash panda."

"I fail to see how any of that would make you less sexy."

"You're crazy." She laughs again.

"Only for you."

"You gonna choose cornflakes for breakfast to go along with all that corny coming out of your mouth?" She jokes.

I give her ass a tap, making her groan and causing my dick to react again. "Oh, shhh. You love my lovey-dovey, corny bullshit."

"I do, very much so. And I love you." She says, moving her head up to look at me. She puckers her lips for a kiss and squints her eyes, being goofy. Never wanting to leave my girl hanging, I lean in and give her a kiss. When I try to take it further, she pulls back.

"I wasn't kidding about the morning breath." She says, narrowing her eyes.

"Fine." I smirk, then lean to the side so that I can grab something from my bedside table drawer. When I find what I want, I hold out a breath mint. "Not that I give a shit about morning breath, and you know it, but here, since you insist."

She grins, then sticks out her tongue. I place the mint on it, and she quickly closes her mouth around my fingers, sucking them and twirling her tongue around them before pulling back with a pop.

"You know, Baby Girl. You better watch yourself. Nothing's holding me back anymore from taking that sweet pussy of yours. You can't get me all worked up like that, it's not fair." I growl.

"You're all worked up?" She says in mock shock. "Let me see." She reaches her hand under the blanket and finds me rock hard and wanting for her. "Oh, you know what, I think you're right." She says, gripping my shaft and giving it a good squeeze, making me groan as she starts to pump me.

"Fuck." I hiss.

"Maybe if you ask nicely." She says seductively.

"You think you're funny, don't you, Baby Girl?"

She tightens her grip on me. "Maybe." She smirks. Man, Tyson is gonna have his hands full with this one.

"That's it." I growl. I pull her hand off my cock and flip her onto her back, bringing her arm up above her head and pinning it to the bed before finding the other one and doing the same. That way she is trapped under my body, just how I like it.

"You got me." She pants, her eyes filling with lust as her breaths start to pick up. "Now what are you going to do with me?"

"I'm going to reap the rewards of my prize, Baby Girl. I've been waiting far too long to have you again. Now that you're in my hold, I'm never letting you go." I say before smashing my lips to her. She moans against my lips before opening for me. I dip my tongue into her mouth, tasting the minty flavor of the mint on her tongue as it clashes with mine.

We kiss, hot, messy, and full of passion before I pull back, leaving us both panting. She looks up at me with her wide brown eyes, and I can see that she is delirious for her release. After all these weeks of not being able to have sex, she needs this. And I plan on taking care of every inch of my girl.

I kiss her neck, sucking and nipping at her flesh, making her moan my name. I gather both her wrists in one hand and use the other to lift her top up to expose her bare breasts to me.

"Oliver..." She pants. "I haven't pumped yet. That's...that's not a good idea."

I smirk wickedly at her. She's kissed Talon after taking a load of Ben's cum, but is afraid of me tasting a little breast milk. I don't plan on drinking any, but I can see her achingly hard nipples that are just begging to be touched.

I lean down, never breaking eye contact, and flick her nipple with the tip of my tongue. She sucks in a gasp and I move to the other one, doing the same thing. This time a little bit of milk leaks out.

A deep blush settles on her cheeks. "It tastes kind of sweet." I say. "And enough of that. Don't be embarrassed, Firefly. You have no reason to be." I tell her sternly.

Not wasting any more time, I kiss a line downwards between her breasts all the way down her belly, only stopping when I get to her mound. I let go of her wrists, sliding my hands down the length of her body, needing to feel her everywhere. Pulling off her panties, I toss them to the side, before helping her out of my t-shirt.

"I'm going to taste you now." I warn. "Be a good girl and spread them wide for me."

Her eyes flash with heat as she bites her lower lip and opens her thighs for me. I almost cum right then as I take in her dripping pussy. "Is this all for me, Baby Girl?" I growl. She nods frantically, her chest rising and falling rapidly. "So fucking wet for me, Sweet Girl."

Needing her now, and unable to hold back anymore, I dive between her perfect thighs to devour that gorgeous pussy of hers. I slip my tongue between her folds, moving it upwards to swirl around her sensitive bundle of nerves, but before she gets too close to the edge, I back off to lick her bud like a lollipop. She moans my name, her hands flying to my head as she takes handfuls of my hair to hold onto for dear life as I eat her out, not wanting to waste a single drop of her inevitable release.

"Olly!" She cries. "Fuck, oh fuck! I'm not gonna last much longer." She heaves now as my tongue dips in and out of her before going right back to her swollen clit. I suck it into my mouth and she cries out again, her body starting to shake as her orgasm quickly starts to take over her entire body. I missed this, the sounds of her pleasure filled cries; the taste of her pussy.

A grunt on the other side of the room catches both our attention. I peer up over Emmy's thigh to see Ben on his side, and Talon behind him. The blanket is covering them, but it's not hard to tell what they are doing.

"Make her cum, Oliver." Talon grits his teeth as he pumps into his boyfriend. "Then make love to her. She needs you, just look at her."

Emmy's eyes plead with me for her release. A moan from Ben has her attention on them again, so I take the moment to dive back down, and take her clit into my mouth, followed by inserting two of my thick fingers into her flooded center.

I make sure to go slowly and carefully, knowing that they are the first things to be inside her in a while.

"Fuck!" She gasps as I crook my fingers at just the right angle. I suck and nip her clit as my tongue works with my hand to bring her to the brink of ecstasy.

"I'm gonna cum!" She screams. "Fuck! Oh god, Oliver!" She grips my hair so hard that it hurts, but the pain makes me moan against her pussy and the vibration along with my mouth and fingers is just what she needs to be pushed over the edge into oblivion.

She screams so damn loud I have to quickly cover her mouth with the hand that's not deep inside her pussy to muffle the sound before she wakes up the entire floor.

Her body arches, and I can feel her trying to move away from the intensity of the pleasure. I remove my fingers and use that hand to hold her still as I continue to eat her out, drawing out her climax. Talon lets out a moan of his own, telling me the sight of our girl cumming has triggered his own release. How can it not? Even I'm trying not to cum in my boxers from all the sounds I was able to coax out of her.

I let Emmy come down from her high as she relaxes back into the bed. Her eyes are sleepy and hooded, but I'm not done with my girl just yet.

Emmy turns her head, watching as Talon takes care of Ben, sucking him off, so he can find his release too.

"Are you ready, Sweet Girl?" I ask, slipping off my boxers, needing to know she's ready for what's to come.

"Yes." She breathes. "I need you inside me, Oliver. God, I've missed your cock so fucking much." She cries. I can tell the hormones are heightening her emotions, making her even more needy than ever.

"Shhh, I got you." I say, placing a kiss on her lips. Ben and Talon each slide into a spot beside her, now dressed in boxers, which tells me they don't plan on joining in.

"Hey there, My Love." Ben says, cupping her face, and placing a sweet kiss on her lips. "Oliver's gonna take real good care of you, okay? He won't let it hurt. We got you. Just relax."

Her eyes soften at his gentle way with her, and she nods.

I adjust us so that we are in a comfortable position, and take the tip of my pre-cum covered cock and rub it against her soaked core.

"I'm gonna push in. If it hurts, and you want to stop, let me know." She gives me a nod before closing her eyes. I can see her willing her body to relax for me.

I push inwards and slowly inch inside her. She gasps and I pause. "Are you okay? Does it hurt?"

"Only a little." She pants. "Fuck, it feels like I'm losing my virginity all over again." She huffs out a laugh.

"At least this time he will let you cum." Talon says, making Emmy laugh. I narrow my eyes at him. "What? It's true." He throws back at me.

"Keep going." She begs. And I do, biting the inside of my cheek as I try to hold back the groan from feeling her hot, wet pussy wrapped around my cock.

God, I missed this so fucking much. She feels so fucking perfect, like she was made for me.

"I need you to move, Oliver. Please." Not wanting her to have to beg me anymore, I do what she wants. I'm determined to make love to my girl. I'm not stopping until we are both cumming *and* are left gasping for breath as we come apart together.

I start to move, thrusting in and out of her, keeping a careful, but steady pace.

"Yes." She cries. "Oh, yes!"

I keep pumping into her, grunting and moaning. I don't think my cock has ever been as hard as it is right fucking now. I need to cum, but she has to first.

Ben and Talon stroke her hair, whispering words of praise, telling her how amazing she is doing and what a good girl she is, taking my cock like a goddess. And she is a goddess, and she's all of ours.

I start to circle her clit with my thumb, adding pressure as I do. "Oh, oh, oh. Fuck!" She chants, her eyes are wide and frenzied. I can tell she's close as her core grips my cock. Her fingernails dig into my thighs and I hiss at the pain, but it only turns me on.

Feeling my own release ready for her, I thrust into her faster. "Cum for him, Emmy. Let the ecstasy wash over you. Let him make you feel good." Ben encourages.

With that, Emmy's body starts to quake beneath me. Leaning over I kiss her, hard and demanding, with my hips still slapping against her thighs.

She whimpers and whines into my mouth, her hands clawing at my back. Then she cums, so fucking hard that I feel like she's strangling my cock, while I swallow her screams and hold her tightly as she comes apart in my arms.

Following after her, I give her one last thrust before stilling and cumming so intensely that I think I'm about to pass out.

I feel my cum coat her insides, claiming her as mine once again. When I'm sure she's milked every last drop of me, I collapse on top of her, making sure not to crush her with my weight.

"Fuck. One of the hottest things I've ever experienced, hands down." Talon groans as he cups his cock like he's ready to take Ben for another ride. "You did amazing, Shorty." Talon gives her a kiss on the lips before getting off the bed.

"So proud of you, Butterfly." Ben praises, kissing her as well. They take off into the bathroom, most likely to clean up from their activities from before.

Emmy grins up at me, looking blissed out and content as fuck.

"How are you feeling, Firefly?" I ask.

"Amazing." She breathes sleepily.

"Welcome back." I grin. "Are you ready for the all-you-can-handle orgasms and fuck-fest that are coming your way?"

"Bring it on." She laughs softly.

I pull out of her, and she whimpers at the loss. "Now, now, Sweet Girl. You need to take it easy. We will go back to our sexcapade ways soon, but for now, let's not push it."

She gives me an adorable pout, but nods anyway. I lean down, nipping her plump bottom lip, and making her moan. Not wanting to tease her, I get off the bed and slip my boxers back on. "I'll be right back." I promise her.

Heading into the bathroom, ignoring the two who are, in fact, going for round two in the shower, I fill up the tub with warm water and grab a washcloth.

When I get back, Emmy is asleep. I chuckle, my heart feeling full at the peaceful look on her face as she sleeps.

I clean her up enough so that nothing makes a mess on the way to the tub, before scooping her up into my arms.

She blinks up at me. "Sorry Firefly, I wish I could let you sleep more, but we have to get cleaned up and grab something to eat before class." She nods against my chest.

Placing her in the tub, I get to work cleaning every inch of her, washing her body and even her hair, before rinsing her off and gathering her in a towel.

She lets me take care of her right up until we have to leave.

When we get to the dining room, we grab a tray and get in line for our food. When we get to our table, Charlie is there playing on her phone as Ethan sits a few chairs over. He gets her attention before nodding to us. When she looks up, she spots Emmy, and a smile a mile wide slides across Charlie's face at the sight of our very satiated girl.

"And so it begins." Charlie says as we sit down. Emmy just smiles at her, giving her a kiss hello, before taking a seat between Charlie and Ethan.

She says hi to him, before turning to kiss Charlie. Emmy cuddles into Charlie's arm as Charlie starts to talk to us about something, but I'm not paying attention. All my attention is on my girl. My Firefly.

She grins at me. A grin that has so much fucking love and happiness in it that my heart threatens to burst out of my chest.

"I love you." She mouths to me.

"I love you, too." I mouth back.

A piece of me falls back into place as I look around at everyone, happy and laughing. Something I haven't seen for so long.

I plan on doing whatever I can to keep the expression on Emmy's face right now, firmly planted there for the rest of our lives. One that says she doesn't have a care in the world. One that is filled with contentment.

We all know it's not going to last, it never does; but I will do my damnedest for as long as I can.

CHAPTER 14
Emmy

IT'S ALMOST TOO good to be true. Yeah sure, there's still my crazy-ass sperm donor hiding in the shadows, waiting to pounce, and the fact that I don't get to be with my daughter every day, but my life at the moment is pretty damn tame compared to how it has been. And I don't mean just the past few years, but even beyond that.

No crazy bitches, no people trying to kill me... for now. I have amazing lovers, the best of friends, kick ass parents, a sister who would literally kill people to protect me, and the most perfect baby girl anyone could ask for.

Then there's this fucking prick. There always has to be that one dickhead to ruin any happy buzz.

"I have your math tests from last week. Most of you did okay, some of you not so much." Mr. Park says as he gathers a pile of papers from his desk and then stands up.

My eyes follow him as he hands back the tests in order. Or at least, it was in order until he got to me. He just skips right past me and proceeds to the next student. Once all the tests are passed back, he walks to the front of the room.

Charlie nudges me and raises a brow as if to ask what's going on. I just shrug and look back to the front of the room.

"All but one student at least had a passing grade. All but you, Miss Knox." Mr. Park says as he turns his gaze to me, eyes filled with disdain. "48%? This is one of the most pathetic grades I've seen a student your age get in math, or any subject, really. You do this to yourself, you know that, don't you? Your potential wouldn't be wasted, if you'd spend less time on your personal life, and put that amount of energy into your school work, instead of partaking in all of your *extracurricular* activities with your multiple lovers. It's only then that you might have a better chance at learning something."

My eyes go wide as my stomach sinks. I just gape at him, too stunned to do anything else. Charlie is vibrating in her seat, cursing a mile a minute under her breath.

She's ready to get up there and drop-kick his ass or something. Knowing I need to calm her down, I get a hold of myself. Schooling my features, I grab Charlie's hand and give it a squeeze.

She looks at me with tears of anger in her eyes. I give her a shake of my head, knowing that this asshole is just looking to get a reaction from us.

But I'm not near my guys in this class, and no one holds Oliver back as he jumps out of his seat which sends his chair flying back.

Like fucking lightning, Oliver is at the front of the room with Mr. Prick's shirt fisted in his hand as he slams him against the wall.

"Don't you ever fucking talk to or about her like that again." Oliver growls, his words filled with so much venom that if there weren't other students in here, Oliver would most likely have already beaten him to a bloody pulp.

"Get your hands off me, Mr. Price." Mr. Park hisses. "I don't care that your brother is a teacher here, or who your father is. You are here on probation, and unless you would like to fuck that up and go to jail after you leave here, then I suggest you let go of me, right now."

Oliver is breathing heavily. He doesn't move. I'm on the edge of my seat, and Ben is holding Talon back.

"Oliver!" Tyson barks from the doorway. Oliver's gaze snaps over to his brother's confused and pissed face. "I don't know what's going on, but I think it's best you let go of him, brother." The look Tyson is giving his brother holds so many unspoken words.

My body is shaking in fear of all the trouble this asshole could cause for Oliver. Those words shouldn't have hurt me but they did, and now I just want to get up and wrap my arms around Oliver. But I can't move. I'm still frozen in shock.

Oliver lets go at his brother's words, pushing Mr. Park back as he does.

"Come with me." Tyson demands of his brother. With one last glare that would send any smart man to his knees, Oliver storms out the room and past Tyson.

Mr. Park straightens out his shirt and looks around the room before looking at Tyson. "Be sure to tell your brother that he has just earned himself two weeks of detention."

Tyson just nods, but I can tell he's struggling to keep his own mouth shut. Tyson's gaze lands on me, and I can see a flash of concern mixed with the fury in his eyes as he takes in the state of me, but it's gone just as fast.

I know he will be demanding the whole story later.

Tyson follows Oliver, and all I can do is just stare at the spot where he was only moments ago.

"Miss Knox, See me after class." Mr. Park says, not bothering to look in my direction.

Ben and Talon look over at me like they want to drag my chair in between them and smother me in love and protection. Charlie has a death grip on my hand, and when I look over at Ethan on the other side of the room, he's shooting daggers at the back of Mr. Park's head.

For some reason, that makes me crack a smile. Knowing that my new friend cares enough to be so pissed off on my behalf.

As if he could feel me watching him, Ethan turns his head and looks at me. His mask of fury melts away, and he gives me a lopsided smile, which I return. He mouths, "Are you okay?"

I do a quick shake of my head, not bothering to put on a fake act, but I smile at him, letting him know I will be.

When class is over, Charlie, Ben, and Talon stay seated, and Ethan comes over and stops in front of my desk. "I'll see you after school, okay? Meet you in the kitchen, and we can get that dessert ready for our presentation tomorrow."

"Yup." I smile brightly at him. Ethan looks over at Mr. Park, who has a nasty scowl on his face, then over to the guys and Charlie. "I see I'm not needed. Later, Emmy."

Ethan leaves, and Mr. Park looks at the others. "You can leave, too." He tells them.

"Not a fucking chance." Talon growls.

Mr. Park narrows his eyes. "Would you like to join your buddy in detention? I'm sure it will look good for your probation officer to see you get in trouble yet again in the few short weeks you have been back. You only have a month left, and you don't want to fuck it up now, do you?"

"You guys, I'll be fine. Wait for me outside." I tell them, giving Charlie a kiss on the cheek.

"I don't want you alone with him." Ben tells me.

"Well, sorry, Mr. Parker, but you don't get a say." The asshole adds, making Ben's body tense.

"I'll be okay." I kiss Ben next, then Talon. "Take him out of here before he does something he regrets." I instruct Ben.

"I'd regret nothing when it comes to fucking up that jackass." Talon mutters, thankfully not loud enough for the prick to hear.

Slowly they leave, making sure to shoot dirty looks at the teacher. "We will be right outside." Talon adds.

Gathering my books and slipping my bag onto my shoulder, I make my way to his desk.

"Why did you want to see me after class?" I ask, looking down at my nails to avoid making eye contact.

"You're failing my class. And I wouldn't be doing my job if I didn't make sure I offered you all the help I could." He says. "So, until you can at least reach a passing grade in my class, you will be seeing me after school for extra help every Tuesday and Thursday."

"What?" I protest.

"Seeing as how even my best student in this class can't get over an 80%, you won't have much luck with any of the other students assisting you, and the school isn't offering any tutoring sessions this close to the end of the school year. Especially not after everything that's happened." He explains. "You only have yourself to blame."

"Excuse me?" I ask, taken by surprise at his words.

"I may not have been a teacher at this school before the shooting happened, but I've heard enough. You're not as innocent as you try to claim to be, Emmy. I see you." Those last words send an uneasy chill down my spine.

"So I have no choice in this? What if I don't care if I pass math?"

"None. You know as well as I do, if you do not pass my class then you will not be able to graduate and you won't be failing if I have anything to do about it."

Biting my tongue, I try not to say anything that will get me in trouble. Unlike the guys, I can't risk it. I can't risk losing my privileges to go back home and see Melody on the weekends.

"Fine." I grit out through my teeth.

"We will start Tuesday of next week. In the meantime, I suggest maybe spending less time with your... friends, and more time attempting to study."

"Sure thing." I say, forcing a smile. "Is that all?"

He looks at the door for a moment before looking back at me. "Yes. Try and behave yourself. You're a role model for your daughter now, maybe you should try and act like it." He moves away and sits back behind his desk, then starts typing on his laptop.

What the fuck does he mean by that? Whatever, it doesn't matter. *Stupid prick.*

When I leave the room, I find Ben, Talon, and Charlie having a heated discussion in hushed tones.

"Everything okay?" I ask. They all stop talking at once and look over at me. I see some of the tension leave their bodies at the sight of me.

"What did the asshole want?" Talon growls.

"Let's walk and talk. I wanna see Oliver and make sure he's okay."

We start to head away from the classroom, and I pull out my phone to text Oliver and tell him to meet us in my room.

"Emmy, what did the asshole want?" Charlie urges, slipping her hand into mine.

Letting out a frustrated sigh and pressing send on my text, I kiss her hand before glancing over at her.

"He said that I'm failing his class. And he wants to do his job as a teacher and offer me help." I roll my eyes.

"His job as a teacher?" She scoffs. "Maybe the fucker should try to be more respectful, and not call out his students like that in front of each other."

"Tell me you said no." Ben pleads from behind me.

"I couldn't. He told me I had to. And I wasn't going to risk arguing with him and have my weekend pass to see Melody taken away. I'll put up with that asshole two times a week for the next month if I have to. That's what, eight times? I'd rather that than have to go a few weeks without seeing Melly."

"Fuck's sake." Talon curses. "I don't like the idea of you spending time alone with him." Ben and Charlie both agree. "And I know for a fact that Oliver and Tyson won't either."

Boy, was he right. For the next hour, Tyson and Oliver argue back and forth being all sexy and grumpy while looking all murdery. The look in their eyes as they talk about how much they hate Mr. Prick for how he's treating me is a big turn on though.

Cuddling into Charlie, I clench my thighs together and try not to squirm as I take in their bulging, tattooed muscles. The way they flex as Oliver crosses his arms, and Tyson roughly shoving a hand through his hair.

"How are you doing, My Queen?" Charlie asks, a hint of amusement in her voice. "Are you getting all hot and bothered by the bad-boy brothers over there?

Do you want them to do naughty things to you?" Charlie teases, but damn she's not wrong. I do want that, and so much more.

Charlie was not very subtle with her teasing, and now it's caught their attention. They both stare at me with heat in their eyes, and I need to get the fuck out of here before we end up in a never-ending sex fest. I mean, I'm not opposed to it, but I was supposed to meet Ethan in the kitchen about five minutes ago.

"Nope, nope, nope." I say, detangling myself from Charlie and crawling over Talon and Ben's laps. Of course Talon sees this as a perfect opportunity to give my ass a slap, and in doing so, sends me flying face-first into Ben's crotch.

"If you wanted to suck our boy off, Baby Girl, all you had to do was ask. I don't think he would mind at all." Ben helps me up with a chuckle, and I turn to glare at Talon, but there's no heat behind it.

Well, I actually would like to suck any one of their...

Damn it, Emmy. No time to be dick-matized.

"Haha, very funny." I reply, getting off the bed. "I gotta go. I'm late."

"Late for what?" Tyson asks.

"Ethan and I have to make our dessert tonight for tomorrow's presentation."

"I'll come with you." Oliver says, stepping forward.

"Olly, I'll be fine." I warn.

"Fine." He grumbles before walking over to me, gripping my face tightly and placing a hard kiss that has me moaning. "Run along, Little Firefly. Or I'll just keep you here all to myself for the night." He says against my lips.

Fuck. Fuck. Fuck. That does sound amazing... *NO! Damn being dick drunk!*

Oliver chuckles wickedly, like he knows what he's doing to me before spinning me around and nudging me towards the door with a parting tap on my ass.

I'm in my own little lust trance all the way to the kitchen.

"How are you?" Ethan asks. "You've been kind of quiet since you got here."

I give him a half smile. "Sorry about that, I know I haven't been the best company tonight."

"I get it. Trust me, it took everything in me not to say something to that asshole." He huffs, shaking his head as we work together to stack all the cream puffs into a tower.

"What's this dessert called again?" I ask, eating one of the cream puffs.

"Croquembouche." He laughs. "And don't eat the tower." He tries to take the puff away from me, but I shove the rest of it in my mouth and smile at him as I chew.

"Not like it could be any worse." I sigh, looking at our very sad-looking tower. "The thing looks like a limp dick."

Ethan chokes on a laugh. "Girl, you have no filter, do you?"

"Nope." I chirp.

"Oh, well. What matters is that they taste good. We still need to add the caramel drizzle and spun sugar."

"What?! Now I want more when it's done." I pout.

"Tomorrow. After the presentation."

"Fine." I pout.

Ethan gently bumps me with his shoulder, as we continue to laugh and talk while finishing the tower. By the time we are done, it looks a little bit better, but nothing like the photo he showed me.

"So, did you guys pick out a name yet?" I ask, closing the big walk-in freezer. We put the tower in there to keep it fresh until tomorrow.

"We went with Mason." Ethan grins.

"Aww, that's a cute name."

"Yeah, her mother tried to get Leah to name him Alfred." He cringes at the name.

I make a funny face. "No. Just... No." I laugh.

"That's what I told Leah." He laughs back. "She said it was her grandfather's name, and as much as she loved him, she does not want that name for our son. And I totally agree."

"I'm super picky when it comes to boy names. When we were picking out names before we found out Melody's gender, none of us could agree. But with her name, we knew right away. It was like that when picking Elijah's name too. It was a perfect fit." My face falls, and my heart breaks as I think about my son. It's been so long since I've allowed myself to, and I feel like a shitty parent for letting myself forget, even for just a moment.

"Elijah?" Ethan asks.

"Yeah." I sniff, wiping the moisture forming in the corner of my eyes. Taking a deep breath to calm myself before I break out in tears. "My angel baby." I smile, my eyes now completely watery.

"Oh, Emmy." Ethan breathes.

"He would have been going into kindergarten at the start of the next school year." *Fuck.* It's too much the way Ethan is looking at me, and all the 'what if's' floating through my mind... wondering if he would have looked just like Oliver. What his little voice would have sounded like as he said 'I love you.'

"Come here." Ethan says, pulling me into his arms. I break, letting the tears flow and the sobs break loose.

Ethan holds me as I let myself break for the loss of my son.

"Sorry." I say, letting out a shaky laugh after I've cried myself dry. "I kind of soaked your shirt." I point to the wet spot on his black tee.

"That's okay. What's a few tears and some boogers between besties." He grins, and just like that, I'm smiling again, breaking into a fit of laughter.

"Alright, enough of that. Show me some photos." I grin at him.

He shows me all the photos that Leah sent him and a few videos too. By the end of it, I'm all mushy and excited for my baby cuddles tomorrow night.

"Ugh, he's just so cute!" I say.

"Who's just so cute?" Charlie asks from the kitchen door.

"Mason, Ethan's son." I smile at my beautiful girl.

"Oh, baby photos? Show me!" She squeals.

Ethan shows her everything he just showed me and she lets out a bunch of *'Awws'* or *'Oh my god, he's so adorable!'*

"So, are you all done with your little baking date?" Charlie asks, sticking her finger in the bowl that has the leftover caramel in it and scooping up a finger full before sucking it off. My eyes follow the movement, watching intently as she works her finger clean and all I can think of is that tongue of hers with all the amazing, mind-blowingly talented things it can do.

"Her eyes are up there." Ethan says, moving my head for me so that I'm looking into Charlie's eyes. Charlie grins around her finger before pulling it out with a pop.

"Not in front of the boy, dirty girl." Charlie purrs.

My cheeks flush, and I bite my lip.

"So... you're the new bestie? Are you sure that's all you want with my girl? Because, I mean, if it was more I'd be supportive like I have been with all the others; but damn, there are already enough guys. I'm drowning in dicks, and not in the fun way that Emmy is."

"Charlie!" I yelp, gaping at her.

Ethan laughs. "Nope, just besties. But, I mean, sure, if I was into girls, Emmy would be top of my list." He winks at me, and I grin.

"Wait. What?" Charlie's eyes flash with surprise. "You're gay?"

"Yup." Ethan smirks.

"Fuck, yes! I always wanted to have a gay bestie." Charlie cheers while fist pumping the air. "You do have enough room for another one, right?" She asks, but it isn't really up for discussion. Charlie is about to adopt my Ethan, and there is nothing he can do about it.

"Fine, you can join our little merry band of misfits." He sighs dramatically.

Charlie whoops and high-fives me. "Look, Babe, there's actually a guy we get to share."

"Oh my god." I laugh. "What am I gonna do with you?"

"You could always spank me?" She shrugs nonchalantly, dipping her fingers into the bowl again to take another taste. She moans this time trying to get to me, and it's working.

"Well, this was fun, and I can't wait to taste the sad tower of cream puffs we made tomorrow, but right now we gotta go."

I go to drag Charlie out of the room, but stop when I realize the mess we made that still needs to be cleaned up.

"Go." Ethan says. "I got this."

"No, I made the mess too, I'll help clean it too."

"It's okay. I'll blast some music while I clean, and it will be done in no time."

"Really?" I ask, chewing on my lip, feeling like a shitty friend.

"Yes, go. This is my way of making you feel better for what happened earlier with Mr. Jackass."

I let go of Charlie's hand to give Ethan a hug. "Thank you, you're the best. And thank you for just being there for me."

"Always." He grins.

CHAPTER 15
Emmy

"DO YOU HAVE any idea what I had to promise those guys in order for them to let me have you for the night after what happened earlier?" Charlie asks, opening the door to our room.

Following behind her, I close and lock the door. She tosses the room key on the table beside the door and turns to me.

"Umm, no?" I laugh.

"Get this... I had to bribe them with cookies. *Freshly baked* cookies. Like children! But did they *all* want the same kind? Noooo! Of course not, that would be *all* too easy." Charlie says dramatically, flopping back onto the bed.

Biting my lip, I hold back a giggle as she keeps going.

"Oliver demanded chocolate chips. Ben requested red velvet. Talon would only accept snickerdoodles!" She says, exasperated. "And do you know what kind Tyson wanted?" She asks, moving up on her elbows, face dead serious.

"No." I giggle again, biting my lip.

"Oatmeal. Oat-fucking-meal! Oh, and *here's* the kicker, not oatmeal chocolate chip, no, oatmeal raisin. RAISINS! What is he, 70?"

I burst out laughing. The look of disgust on her face is hilarious.

"I like oatmeal raisin." I shrug. She looks at me like I have three heads, and I erupt into yet another fit of giggles.

"You're crazy, and maybe a little weird." She says, getting off the bed. "But those are just some of the many things I love about you." She grins, pulling me into a heated kiss before pulling back and heading to the bathroom leaving me dazed and confused.

The tap to the tub squeaks, and a smile slips across my face. "I'm gonna run us a bath. Then we can snuggle and watch a movie before bed." She calls out to me.

Yeah, as much as I'd love that. I have a better idea. Bath, and lots of sex. She's been so amazing with letting the guys have any of our free time since I've been able to have sex again, but tonight's gonna be all about my girl and me for a change.

She starts talking about a conversation she and Felicity had on the phone about Felicity's new school, and how she and Miles are trying this long-distance thing. I try to pay attention, but I'm too busy stripping off my clothes until I'm fully naked.

"You know, we'll have to invite her down this summer. It would be easier for her just to come here-" Charlie starts but cuts off her words as she takes in my naked body, leaning against the door frame.

"Well, hello." Her eyes darken with desire. She stands up from the side of the tub and stalks towards me.

A flutter in my belly starts to break into thousands of butterflies the closer she gets to me. The look of hunger has me rubbing my thighs together as my pussy starts to pulse.

She slowly looks me up and down, committing every inch to memory.

"You wanna know something?" She asks, trailing the tips of her fingers down the curves of my breasts.

"W-what?" I ask, gasping as she takes the pad of her thumbs and brushes them over the tips of my nipples, making them pebble.

"Every time I look at you, think about you, my heart feels like it's going to explode from all the love and happiness you bring me, that I want to bring into your life." She looks from my nipples up to my eyes. My heart starts to pick up at the intensity of the emotions shining bright in her captivating green eyes.

"Charlie." I breathe, my eyes tearing up a little.

She steps closer, pressing herself against me. "I'm so proud of you. Of how hard you love. How strong you are. The fact that you will go to the ends of the earth for the ones that you love. You are what I strive to be. The hero our daughter gets to grow up alongside. You, my Queen, are perfect in my eyes. Faults and all. And these." She says, trailing her finger down the stretch marks on my breasts, to the ones on my belly, and down to the scar on my side, only stopping when she gets to the ones on my legs.

"Are just bonus beauty marks on an already stunning masterpiece." She whispers against my lips, before biting my lower one that's trembling at her words.

Fuck. Fuck! How the hell am I so damn lucky to call her mine. I don't deserve this amazing woman, but I'll be damned if I ever take her for granted for even a moment.

"I love you, Charlie." I whimper as she starts to kiss down my neck.

Alisha Williams

"There are no words to describe how I feel about you, but love will have to do. I love you too, my Queen." Her breath tickles my skin, making my body quiver with need. I feel like everything is humming with energy with every touch and caress. She kisses down my cheek sucking and licking as she goes, stopping when she reaches my peaked nipple and taking it into her mouth.

Moaning, I toss my head back against the wall with a thud, not caring about the pain because what she is doing is far too good for me to care.

Her tongue swirls around my nipple before flicking it with the tip as one of her hands trails down the side of my body to grip my ass cheek, and the other slips between my thighs.

"Mmmm..." She hums against my breast, releasing my nipple with a pop. "So wet for me." She groans as she pays attention to my other nipple, giving it the same treatment, while slipping her fingers into me.

"Charlie." I moan, my knees threatening to buckle as she starts to pump in and out while using her thumb to play with my swollen clit.

"You know, I've never cared too much for my name, but when you say it, especially like this... fuck, it's the best damn name in the world."

She kisses me, sucking my bottom lip into her mouth before plunging her tongue into my mouth.

I thread my fingers through her hair, gripping the back of her head, holding her as close to me as I can, not letting her go, not wanting to end this kiss.

When she pulls back we're both panting, her eyes are half-lidded with desire, a mirror image of mine.

She takes a step back, her gaze never leaving mine, as she starts to remove her clothes. She slowly pulls down her leggings and my eyes follow, taking in every inch of her creamy thighs.

Tossing her pants to the side, she takes off her top next and I lick my lips as I take in her sexy body, standing there in only a thong and a bra that pushes her breasts up just right.

It takes everything in me not to go over there and shove my face between them. She unhooks her bra, letting it slide to the floor, and my eyes zero in on her raised nipples. Next to go is her barely there underwear.

My eyes go wide as I take in the neatly trimmed patch of hair above her perfect pussy. "You dyed your pussy purple?" I laugh in disbelief.

"Yup." She wiggles her eyebrows. "Thought I'd have the carpet match the drapes." She winks.

"Fuck, I love you. Marry me." I say it jokingly, but her eyes tell me that she wishes I wasn't.

"You wanna marry me, Miss Knox? Make an honest woman out of me?" Charlie bats her eyelashes.

"When life calms down, and no one is out to get me." I smile. "Yeah, I really would."

Her face explodes into a giddy smile. "Come." She says, holding out her hand. "Let's take that bath while the water is still warm."

Grasping her hand in mine, she helps me into the tub. I moan as my body settles into the water. "God, I love hot baths. We need a hot tub when we get our own place. I'll never want to leave."

Charlie slips in behind me, pulling my body back so that I can settle against her as she wraps her arms around me.

"Thank you." I whisper, closing my eyes and relaxing.

"You had a shitty day. I thought a relaxing bath might help." She says. I tilt my head to the side so that it's resting back against her shoulder. Her lips trail across my skin as she peppers light kisses down my neck.

"You know what else would help me relax?" I ask her.

"What?" Her lips grazed my neck before kissing me again.

"This." I take her hand that's resting on my thigh and slide it down between my legs.

"I can help with that." She growls, her tone telling me she wants to do very dirty things right now, and I want whatever she's willing to give.

She slips her fingers inside me, thrusting a few times before pulling out and rubbing my clit.

"Charlie." I moan, already needy and desperate for some kind of release from when she got me all worked up, just before the bath.

"Shhh, My Queen. I got you." She murmurs against my neck.

She massages my breast with her free hand, pinching and pulling at my nipple as her fingers continue to work magic on my pussy.

It doesn't take me long before I feel the heat curl low in my belly, my orgasm teetering on the edge. Just as I'm about to hit my highest point before falling into my climax, she pulls her fingers free.

"Nooo." I cry at the loss. "I was so close."

Charlie laughs. "Get behind me, against the back of the tub." She instructs me. Narrowing my eyes at her, I do as she says, hoping that whatever she plans on doing gives me some sort of release.

"Put your arms over the edge and use the sides of the tub to hold you up."

"Hold me up for what?" I ask, but get my answer as she lowers herself in the water and moves until my legs are draped over her shoulders before rising up a little. My arms grip the side of the tub just in time for her head to disappear between my legs and surprise me with the intensity she brings to her task at hand.

I toss my head back with a cry of pleasure when her mouth moves upwards, and finally makes contact with my sensitive bundle of nerves. She sucks it into her mouth, and the sensations exploding through my body has me gripping the tub harder as I use all of my strength to lock my legs around her head, holding her face to my pussy.

She laughs as she pries my legs off her, placing them back in the tub.

"Babe, I'm gonna need to be able to breathe if I'm gonna make you cum." She grins.

"Sorry." I pant. "You're just really good with your mouth." I huff out a laugh.

"Turn around, on your knees, lean against the edge of the tub, ass facing me."

Really needing to fucking cum, I do what she tells me to, yet again.

Once my ass is in the air for her, I wait. When nothing happens, I open my mouth to ask her what's going on when I feel something start to push inside me.

"What the-" I stop mid-sentence, moaning as it starts to vibrate.

"Maybe I got tired of being the only one that doesn't have a dick to fuck you with." Her husky voice purrs into my ear as I feel her press against my back.

She thrusts her hips forward, causing me to groan at the mixture of her filling me and the dirty talk she whispers against my ear. All of it just raises me higher and higher and makes it hard to focus on anything.

"Do you-" She pulls out, taking my breath with her before she thrusts back in again. I struggle to think, to speak, but the one thing I know with full certinty is that the fake cock inside me feels so fucking good. I try again to put the puzzle pieces together.

"Do you have... are you wearing... a strap-on?" I barely manage to ask between heaving breaths, trying to suck in air.

"Double-sided." She pants as she starts to pump into me.

"Fuck." I cry as she angles it in the right spot. "That's so fucking hot."

We talked about using one, and we both agreed it was something we wanted to try, but we never got the chance to do it with everything that's been going on.

"God, this feels so fucking good." She moans. "I can never hit this angle with a dildo."

"Fuck me, Charlie." I beg, and she does. She fucks, finding a rhythm that works for both of us.

We're both panting and moaning by the time I feel my orgasm building again.

"I'm gonna cum." I cry. "Fuck! Please don't stop this time."

"I won't." She grabs my hips, adjusting herself a bit. "I'm close too." Her fingers dig into my skin and the pain just makes me wetter.

"Yes." I pant. "Yes, god... YES!" I grip the edge of the tub so tight that my fingers turn white. I scream out Charlie's name as I cum hard. She holds my hips to keep me from slipping as she continues fucking me. A moment later, she finds her own release.

"Fuuuuck!" She cries, her forehead hitting my back as she grips me for dear life, twitching out her orgasm.

Our breathing is ragged, and I feel like my body is boneless. Charlie pulls out of me, and falls backwards in the tub. Exhausted, I clumsily turn myself around and slip into the water.

"Wow." Charlie says, taking the strap-on off and tossing it out of the tub. It hits the ground with a thud, making me burst out laughing. "Look. I'm not into dudes; *hell*, I'm not even into other women anymore. You are the only person who turns me on. But, *fuck*, I think I'm missing out." She breathes, running a hand down her face.

"Well." I say, moving over to her, draping my body over hers and placing a kiss on her lips. "How about next time *I* fuck *you*."

"Yes, please." Her eyes light up.

We get out of the tub on shaky legs and dry off. Charlie tosses me a shirt and panties and we dress before climbing into bed together.

"Do the guys ever have dick measuring contests?" Charlie asks as she strokes my hair. My head is on her chest, and I feel so relaxed, just listening to her heart beat.

"Um. No?" At least I don't think they do. *Is that really a thing?* "But I'm sure they have compared sizes before." I think back to how Oliver knew what size Tyson is. I'm sure the others have had the same conversation.

"Good. I want in on that." She states, matter-of-factly.

"What?" I laugh.

"And I'm gonna brag about how hard you came on my dick, just like they all do."

"You're nuts." I giggle into her chest.

"I mean it is a pretty good size. I think the box said seven inches."

"Well, I'm sorry to burst your bubble babe, but the guys are eight, and Tyson is ten."

"What?!" She says in disbelief. "You mean you've had bigger than what I just fucked you with? God, even with that I felt my insides take a beating. I'll be sure to set up a nice funeral for your pussy after Tyson finally gets his hands on you. Poor girl won't ever be the same." We both dissolve into a fit of giggles before falling asleep in each other's arms.

CHAPTER 16
Talon

"ALRIGHT. UP NEXT are Talon and Seth."

My partner, some quiet kid named Seth, and I make our way to the front. I hate doing these kinds of assignments, but normally I have one of my friends or Emmy, which at least makes them bearable. Working with this kid has been so pointless. He did nothing, and every time I asked him questions, all he said was "sure". To almost every single thing I asked him.

So, I just ended up doing it myself.

"Hello, wonderful people." I greet, bowing dramatically. "Today I've come to tell you all about the fabulous country of England. Chip, chip, cheerios and fish, or what-not."

Emmy bursts into giggles, and I grin as she slaps a hand over her mouth. Giving her a wink, I keep going. "Sorry, we don't have a spot of tea for you to enjoy."

Ben snorts out a laugh shaking his head.

Maybe if I make it entertaining, they won't know I got all my information from the Wikipedia page.

"Now let's begin, shall we. England is a country that is part of the United Kingdom. It shares land borders with Wales to its west and Scotland to its north....." I keep going, reading half way down the page until the teacher stops me.

"Excuse me, I'm going to stop you for a moment. Talon, did you just copy and paste what was written on the Wikipedia page?" He asks, raising a brow. *Fuck. So much for humor being my saving grace.* Maybe someday, but not today.

"Umm, yeah, kind of?" I answer more like a question, giving him a guilty smile as I scratch the back of my head.

He lets out a sigh. "What have you and your partner been doing this whole time? You had more than enough time to come up with something more original."

"Look, man, I tried. But you gave me a useless partner." I sigh, then look at Seth. "No offense."

"Sure." He says, his voice coming out monotone, with a shrug.

"Seeeee." I say to the teacher, waving my hands at Seth.

"Seth, was Talon forced to do this on his own because you would not cooperate and work with him?"

"Sure." Seth says again.

"Oh, dear god." The teacher sighs. "Okay, fine. I'll give you a passing grade if you at least have a decent dessert."

"Well, I personally think it tastes amazing." I say, taking out the container that has the dessert I made. I went with the simplest recipe that looked good. "I present to you the Jam Roly-Poly."

He leans over to take a look. "Talon, half of it is gone."

"Well, I kind of got hungry while waiting for everyone to present their assignment. But I left you just enough for today." I shrug with a half smile.

"Fine." He says, taking the fork I have held out for him and taking a bite. "Not bad. Alright. I'll give you a 75%."

"Nice!" Seth says, finally saying something else for once.

"Not you, Seth. You will have to write a paper on England. And all the information must be found within books from the library. Oh, and don't forget to cite your sources."

"Dammit." Seth says, stalking off to his desk.

I follow after him, dumb founded. "Dude... so you *can* say more the one fucking word?"

"Yeah." He rolls his eyes.

I start to bitch him out, but Emmy and Ethan get called up next. "You know what? Never mind." I grumble, knowing that after today I won't have to work with him ever again.

"Hello." Emmy greets, giving a shy smile and an awkward wave. "I'm Emmy, and this is Ethan." Ethan gives her an amused smile, making her roll her eyes at him. "Anyways, our country is France."

"My grandmother was from France. We used to..." Ethan goes on telling a few stories about Paris and the adventures that he had there. Then Emmy takes over and talks a little about the culture and history. Honestly, it is a really well done project and even has me interested. Or maybe it's just because of the smokin' hot MILF speaking that's holding my attention.

Emmy ends their presentation, and we all clap. Of course, I do more and give her a few whoops. Gotta cheer on my Shorty. She smiles and sticks her tongue out at me. Fuck, she's adorable.

"So, what dessert do you guys have today?" The teacher asks. "And hopefully it's not already half eaten?"

"No." She laughs. She goes to the door and opens it. Tyson wheels in the tower of the cream puffs that Ethan and Emmy made last night. It's a little lopsided but otherwise looks good.

Tyson gives Emmy a lingering glance as he walks by. To anyone else it may seem friendly, but I know that blush on my girl's cheeks and how she's trying not to give herself away by avoiding eye contact. They just need to fuck already. I have a feeling by the end of this weekend Tyson will be one happy man. I mean he's about to get the best sex he will ever have. He should be grateful.

"Pour notre dessert, nous avons choisi le croquembouche." She says with an adorable, confident smile. I have no idea what she said, only picking up the dessert name; but fuck, it's so damn hot coming from those sexy lips of hers.

"For our dessert, we chose the croquembouche." Ethan repeats in English, but I liked it better the way she said it.

"Well done." The teacher nods his approval as he walks around.

"Yeah, it's not the prettiest. But it tastes good." She shrugs. "There should be enough for everyone if they want to try."

"Thank you." The teacher takes one and bites into it. "Wow. These really are good."

The teacher pushes the cart around until everyone has one of the little puffs. I shove all of mine in my mouth, and moan as the flavor hits my tongue.

Both Ben and Emmy's head snap towards me, and there's no mistaking the desire in their eyes.

I give them a knowing grin, but it probably looks weird with my mouth full. Emmy smiles wide as she covers her mouth with her hand, trying to hold back her laughter.

"Well done, you two. The presentation was very well executed. The personal stories added a nice touch, and the dessert tasted phenomenal. I see no reason not to give you guys 100%. You should be proud."

Emmy's eyes go wide as she turns to Ethan. He grins back before Emmy launches herself at him. He chuckles as she squeals her excitement.

"Alright, everyone. That's it for today. You can leave early. Enjoy a break before your next class." The teacher dismisses us.

"You did amazing, Shorty." I tell her, pulling her into my arms. She wraps her arms around my neck and places a kiss on my lips.

"Thank you, baby." She grins.

"And you speaking French? Fuck, that was sexy." I groan.

She laughs. "Don't get used to it. It took forever for me to remember just that one line."

"I know a little French too." I say, gripping her ass.

"Oh, really?"

"Voulez-vous coucher avec moi." I purr, not having any idea what it means. I heard it from a TV show, and it's something that's always stuck with me.

Lust flashes in her eyes. "I do, very much so, but you will have to wait until I get back from my weekend visit." She says, giving me a passionate kiss before moving away from me and grabbing Charlie's hand. The two of them take off to our next class in a fit of giggles.

I stand there confused, and a little turned on. "Okay. Truth time, what the fuck did I just say to her?" I ask, looking at Oliver. He just shrugs and heads off after the girls.

Ben comes up behind me, wrapping his arms around my waist. "You just asked her if she wanted to sleep with you."

"Oh..." My eyes pop open as I remember why that one French girl got really excited back before I met Emmy. I was just trying to impress the girl. I guess I kind of did? Let's not go there.

"How about I fill in for her while she's gone?" He whispers against my neck.

"Oui. S'il vous plaît." I say. Hey, more French I remember, and this time I actually know the meaning.

Emmy

"My dad wants to see Melody, if that's okay." Tyson says. Our hands are interlocked as he uses his other one to drive. His thumb rubs back and forth on the back of mine and I get butterflies in my belly just by being around him.

"Are we allowed to leave the house?" I ask.

"I talked to Mr. Tucker, he got in contact with your probation officer, and as long as you're with me at all times, and back by curfew, they will allow it since he is the baby's grandfather."

"Then yeah, of course, it would be nice to see everyone."

"And he says the Old Ladies have been hounding him to see her." He chuckles, looking over at me with a smile. "But he's also excited to show off his grandbaby."

We get to the house, and I leave Tyson in the dust as I sprint inside, excited to see my baby girl. Also, I talked to Amy before we left, and she was just giving Melody a bottle, so I didn't pump. My breasts are ready to burst.

"Hello!" I call out as I enter the house.

"Look who's here." Amy coos to Melody as they walk out of the living room.

"Melly Belly!" I grin, scooping up my little lady. "Mama missed you so much!" I hold her close to my chest, snuggling her close and kissing the top of her head. She sucks on her hand, and I know she's hungry.

"Just in time." Tyson chuckles. "Hello, My Little Princess." His voice is so soft and sweet, and the look in his eyes has me '*awwing*' like crazy inside. He kisses her, then me.

"Come. Let's feed her, then we can go to my dad's." Tyson says '*hi*' to Amy before heading up to go get Melody's bag ready. I tell Amy our plans for the night, and she tells us to have a good time and that she will be taking full advantage of her free time with Rick. I scrunch my face up, knowing exactly what she means. I don't want to know about my parents' sex life.

"She won't stop texting." Tyson says, his phone pinging like crazy. He sits next to me on the bed as I feed Melody, and shows me his phone. The name Crazy Bitch fills the screen.

His phone starts to ring, and I can see it's a video request. "Oh, boy." He looks at me with a raised brow.

"Answer it, she's done eating anyways." I say, putting Melody over my shoulder to burp her.

"Alright." He presses accept, and Harlow's face pops up.

"Oh, don't you try and put that camera on my sister. Face me like a real man, Ty Ty." Harlow castigates.

"Ohhhh, someone's in trouble." A male's voice comes from the other end as Neo pops into view over Harlow's head. "Oh, hello there, Baby Sis!" He grins. "About damn time I see that pretty little thing. Show me her face."

Tyson moves the camera to show Harlow and Neo Melody's face.

"Awwwww!" Harlow gushes. "I could just eat those little cheeks right up."

"My Queen, I'm down for almost anything. But I draw the line at cannibalism." Neo grins.

"Oh hush, you." She waves him off.

"She is pretty damn cute. Don't you want one for yourself?" Neo asks.

"Don't you start with that shit. Get." Harlow growls.

Neo leaves the camera view but I can still hear him in the background. "I will get you barefoot and pregnant one way or another. If not me, one of the others. It's gonna happen!" He calls out.

"Bite me!" She shouts back.

"Or you can bite me." He says, and I can hear the sexual desire in his voice. *Man, they are fucked up.*

"Deal." She says. And I can hear a groan.

"Low. I love you, but please, can we skip the sex shit. I'm still scarred from your last visit here." Tyson sighs.

"That was pretty damn good sex though." She grins, then looks at me. "How are you, baby sis?"

"I'm doing good. Only a month left and we are free." I grin, looking down at my sweet girl who is now asleep.

"Perfect! We are planning a week-long trip around your birthday." She announces.

"Who's we?" Tyson asks.

"It's a surprise." She wiggles her brows.

We talk for a little while and Rosie comes on to see the baby, and falls in love with her right away. Something tells me this little one is gonna be a mother hen to Melody. I can't wait.

We say our goodbyes and plan for our next weekly Facetime. We try to at least. She's pretty busy, but I love talking to her even if it's *only* for five minutes. She may not be the typical sister, but she's pretty fucking awesome. And I'm glad she's mine.

We change Melody and load her in the car. When she starts to fuss, Tyson starts singing *Hush Little Baby*, and it's adorable, even if he does not have the voice for singing it. But it does the trick. She's such a daddy's girl.

"There she is!" Steel cheers as he stands up from the table he was sitting at with some other members. "My girl."

Okay, this man has murdered people, beaten them to a bloody pulp, and he has this look that he gets when he's pissed that could make a grown man shit their pants; but the look on his face right now screams teddy bear. *How fucking cute!*

Steel takes the car seat out of Tyson's hand, and places it on the table.

"Hello, Sweet Pea." Steel grins as he unbuckles Melody, and carefully picks her up. "Look at you. Aren't you just the sweetest."

Tyson and I stand back and watch as everyone fusses over our baby girl.

"You know, Princess. By the end of this weekend, I *will* have you. Be ready. Because I won't be able to hold myself back." He whispers against my neck.

Whimpering, I push my ass against him as a needy feeling takes over me. Sure we love to mess around with each other.

141

I love to be sassy and a bit of a brat to get him going, but there's also a part of me that wants to fully surrender myself to this man. To offer my body to him on a platter and let him have his fill of whatever his heart desires.

"Will you give yourself to me? Do you trust me with your body?" He buries his face into my neck, kissing me. His tongue flicks out, tasting my skin.

"Yes." I breathe, my eyes watching our surroundings to see if anyone is watching us. But no one is, they are all too focused on the baby.

"Good. Because I want to own you. Every inch of you. Mind, body, soul." His fingers brush my thigh before he slips his hand back and over my ass. "And I still need to punish your sweet ass for that little stunt you pulled." He growls, making goosebumps erupt over my skin as my core grows slick. "But not yet Princess, now I want to make you wait." He bites my ear lobe before heading off to greet some of the guys which leaves me standing there, a completely needy mess.

"I'm so fucked." I say to myself. But I'm not complaining.

We hang out at the club house for a few hours. The Old Ladies smother Melody with kisses and cuddles while Tyson and I play a few games of pool.

"Dammit." I huff, tossing my cue stick on the table. "I *never* win against you." I pout.

"Oh, don't be like that, Princess. It's okay, no one has beaten me yet, don't feel bad." He pulls me into his arms, nipping at my bottom lip. I hiss at the bite of pain, but moan as he sucks away the sting.

"I think this little one is ready to call it a night." Steel says, a sleeping Melody in his arms.

"Yeah, I think it's about time we head home." I say, taking my little girl from her Papa's arms.

"Thanks for bringing her by. I miss the little munchkin. I can't wait until you guys are done with that school."

"Same." I laugh. "I'm excited to see how life is gonna be outside of there, now that everything is different, for the better, of course."

"I'd just like you nearby so that I know you're safe. I don't like you in that school where we can't protect you guys. Dagger might be quiet right now, but I just know that fucker is waiting to strike."

And just like that, my good mood from earlier tonight is gone. I don't want to think about that man. I want to live a normal fucking life for once, or at least one where I'm not constantly in fear for myself or my family.

Tyson and his dad talk for a few more minutes while I get Melody ready to go.

"Hey." Tyson says, drawing my attention as I mindlessly gaze out the window. "What are you thinking?"

"Just how I can't wait for the day when no one's out to get me." I give him a weak smile.

"No matter what, we have each other." He takes my hand, placing a kiss on the back of it. "I know I can say without a doubt that I won't let anything bad happen to you, but our track record doesn't seem to be so great." He lets out a humorless laugh. "But I will die trying to keep you safe."

"Don't talk about dying." I interrupt him. "We've come close one too many times. Only happy things until we have no other choice; we'll face the shitty ones together as they come, okay?"

"Okay." He agrees.

The rest of the weekend was calm and relaxing. Tyson and I just hung out at home with Melody while it rained the whole time. I loved it. Just cuddling. I can't wait until next weekend so I can do the same with the others.

"Where do you think you're going?" Tyson asks as I head towards the school.

We left a little later than normal, so by the time we got back to school, it was already 10 p.m. and dark as hell.

"Umm... to the girls' dorm? Where else would I be going this late at night on a school night?" I laugh and start walking away again.

"Yeah, I don't think so." He says, grabbing my hand and pulling me in the direction of the teachers' cabins.

"Where are we going?" I ask, trying to keep up with him. He's pulling me along like a man on a mission.

"I told you, Princess. By the time this weekend was over, I would have you. It's not Monday yet." He grins. It's sinful, sexy, and holds all kinds of dirty promises.

He grabs me and throws me over his shoulder. I squeal at the sudden movement, and he slaps my ass, hard.

"Quiet." He commands. My pussy clenches at his tone. *I guess we're starting now.* Fuck this is gonna be fun.

He carries me all the way to his cabin; and thankfully, his is further away from everyone else's.

I'm quiet as he gets his key out of his pocket. My belly is flipping with anticipation. I already know I won't be sassing back this time. I'm ready to obey his every command. The excitement for it has my body humming.

When we get inside the door, he slams it shut. In one quick motion he pulls me off his shoulder, and shoves me against the door. My legs wrap around his waist as he grinds his hard cock into my pussy.

"Fuck, Princess." He hisses. "Do you feel what you do to me? Emmy, baby, this isn't gonna be soft, sweet, or tender, that's not me. At least not with you, not yet. You drive me fucking mad. Your taste, your scent. Just looking at you makes me want to bend you over and rut into you like a wild man. I've waited too damn long for you.

And I would have waited forever if I had to. But hopefully you're not gonna make me wait now that I finally have you alone, are you?"

"No." I whimper. "I'm yours, Tyson. Yours to do with as you please."

He lets out a primal growl that has my pussy gushing. *Fuck.* I've been waiting for him too. He's perfect; tattoos, muscles, those bright blue eyes, and shaggy jet black hair. And that grin, that sexy fucking grin that always makes me *so* weak in the knees.

His mouth is on me. Savage and dirty, and oh-so-fucking delicious. I moan as his tongue takes charge of mine, demanding dominance that I was more than happy to give him.

He pulls back with wild eyes, leaving my lips swollen and bruised in all the best ways. This is not the Tyson I'm used to. This is an unhinged man who sees what he wants and is about to take it. Excitement mixed with arousal flushes through my body. My pussy pulses with need for him to be inside me already. To fuck me until I can't think straight.

He pins me to the wall with his hips, and uses his hands to remove my top and bra, so that my breasts are exposed to him.

The way he looks at me, with awe and hunger, makes me realize he hasn't seen me naked, not this way anyway. Not in a sexual way.

"Fuck." He groans. "Do you know how much I want to suck those pretty pink nipples into my mouth?"

Knowing he can't, because it would activate my tits to start leaking like a fountain, he kisses them all over instead and leaves little bites as he goes. I moan from the pain, loving every moment of it.

"Good girl for wearing this skirt like I told you." He praises me, licking a line between my breasts. "Good girls get rewarded."

He maneuvers around until he has his pants open, cock in his hand and my panties pulled to the side.

"I can't wait anymore." He growls. "I need to be inside you. Right. Fucking. Now." *Yes, please!* "Hold on, Princess."

I wrap my arms around his neck, still leaving enough space so that I can see his feral eyes as he places the tip of his cock against my soaked entrance.

"I'm gonna try to go slow. I know I'm bigger than the others and you just healed, but I feel my control slipping, wanting to get lost in you, and I don't know how much longer I'll be able to hold back." I can see the indecision in his eyes, knowing he doesn't want to hurt me.

"Don't hold back, Ty." I breathe, already so worked up even before we've really started. "You never have to be anyone else but yourself with me. I want you, all of you. Whatever side you are willing to give."

With my words, his pupils dilate growing black and something snaps. My sweet, silly biker boy is gone, replaced with this wild beast, and the change is more than welcome.

With a snarl that was far sexier than I ever imagined it could be, he thrusts inside me.

I cry out as I feel his cock stretch my pussy and it tries to accommodate him, but she's not used to this. He is so fucking big, I feel like he's tearing me in two.

The groan Tyson lets out has me panting to please him more. "Fuck. God!" He shouts as he bottoms out, filling every inch of me with his massive cock. "So. Fucking. Tight." He says, his teeth gritted tight. My fingers are digging into his shoulder, and I'm sure my nails draw blood, but if Tyson has an issue with that, he sure as hell isn't voicing it.

"Tyson." I moan as he pulls out and trusts back in.

"You want my cock don't you, Princess?" He grunts as he starts to fuck me into the door.

"Yes, Sir." I cry. He growls with his approval at my choice of words, which spurs him on to go faster.

"Take it, Princess, take every inch of my cock. It's yours, all fucking yours."

My orgasm hits me out of nowhere as I clamp down on his dick, cumming hard as I feel my release gush out and coat his cock.

"So fucking beautiful when you come." He says, walking me over to the couch. He pulls me off of him, making me cry out from the loss. "Shh. You will have me again soon, trust me; but first, I want you to get on your knees and face the couch, ass out."

Trying my hardest with my trembling legs, I get into the position he demands me to. Once my ass is out for him to see, he grips my hips, getting down on his knees so that his face is level with my ass and dripping pussy.

"No need for all this to go to waste." He laps at my cunt, cleaning my release before working me into another climax until I'm coming all over his face.

"I could eat your pussy all day, Princess." His voice is deep and husky, making my already weak knees threaten to give out. "But you still need your punishment."

Without notice, he spanks me on the ass. I let out a cry. It's not from the pain though, no that sting is just turning me on more. My scream came from the sudden contact. I was not expecting him to do that.

"Did you... did you just spank me?" I ask, looking over my shoulder to see him with a very serious expression. He is not playing, and I just fucked up.

"Just for that back sass, I'm going to give you three more." His large hand comes down on my ass in three consecutive spanks. Each time is a little harder than before, and by the last one, I'm moaning and panting for him, dying to feel his cock deep inside me again.

He rubs the sting away, bending over and kissing my sore ass cheek.

"Such a good girl." He praises, gripping a handful of my hair. "I'm going to fuck you again, are you ready?"

"Yes, Mr. Kingston." I moan as he pulls my head back, and yanks on my hip, placing me where he wants me.

"Fuck." Tyson groans in response. He places the tip of his cock at my entrance and slowly pushes in, inch by glorious inch.

"Ty..." I beg. "Fuck me. I need you."

"I have you, Baby. I'm gonna take good care of you." He soothes, pulling me up by the hair, so that my back is to his toned abs. When I'm parallel with his body, he thrusts the rest of the way in.

"Oh, god." I moan.

"No god here, Princess. Just me." He whispers against my neck, sucking and licking as he massages my breast, pulling at my nipples until he's forced to stop, not wanting to make a mess.

146

"Even better." I sigh as he starts to fuck me. First it's slow, but as he picks up speed he starts making sexy grunting sounds. Fuck, listening to how I effect him is such a turn on. My pussy is on fire as it re-molds itself to accommodate his perfect cock.

His hips slap against my ass, a hand sliding up my neck and I'm fucking delirious right now, unable to think straight.

"Tyson. Oh Baby, I'm so close." I moan as I feel another orgasm building.

"Cum for me." He demands. "Cum all over my cock, scream my name." He pinches my clit and I fucking explode like a firework, screaming his name just like he wanted.

I'm a sobbing mess as my knees finally give out as I twitch out my release in his arms.

"I got you." He whispers, holding me tight as I come down from my high.

When I start to come back to reality, he carefully removes himself from me, pulls me up so that I'm standing, and picks me up bridal style.

I say nothing as he carries me to his room. He tosses me on the bed like a man with only one goal. He digs around in his bedside table for something. When he finds what he's looking for, he tosses it on the bed. Only now, do I realize that at some point in my sex haze he stripped off all his clothes and is now kneeling before me, hard cock bobbing like a fucking god.

His rippling muscles gleam with sweat from our previous activities. My eyes travel over the tattoos covering his body, and a part of me wants to push him down and trail my tongue along every one.

But not right now. He's in charge and I'm just along for the ride.

"Arms up, Princess." He commands. "Against the headboard." I give him a questioning look at the silk rope in his hand. "Do you trust me?"

My eyes find his, and I can see them soften slightly. "Always. With my life." I breathe. Then I do as he asked, waiting, with my arms above my head.

"Now, I'm not into much BDSM. But as you can tell I do like being in charge, and I would like to try a few things with you. Nothing too out there, but I would like to tie you up. If that's okay?"

His dominant self is gone for a moment, and replaced by a man who's unsure of what's going on within this new relationship.

"I'm open to trying anything you want to do, Tyson. I love you and trust you."

"I love you, too." He says, leaning over to kiss me, then taking my hands and tying them to the bed frame.

I am expecting his dominant side to come back, but it doesn't. He places soft random kisses all over my chest.

"Out there, I fucked you. I owned your body. And thank you for trusting me to do that." He kisses me sweetly. "But now, I want to worship your body and make love to you."

"Please." I gasp as he starts to eat me out again. He devours my pussy until I'm a shaking mess. Just as I'm about to cum, he moves away, and replaces his mouth with his cock.

"So beautiful." He kisses me. "So perfect." He kisses me again. "And right this moment, you're all mine."

He puts his forehead to mine and starts to make love to my body. He whispers words of endearment and I return them right back.

It doesn't take me long until I'm a frantic mess, begging him not to stop.

"I'll never stop making you feel good." He says, before letting out one of the sexiest moans as he cums, hard, inside me, filling me up just how I like, until I can feel it leaking out of me.

His release triggers mine, and I cry out as I squeeze every last drop from him.

He rolls to the side, both of us breathing hard, and he unties me then pulls me onto his chest. We both lay there, listening to each other's breathing before he kisses my forehead and leaves to go get a washcloth. He washes me up before crawling back into bed.

"Emmy." He says, stroking my head when I'm almost asleep.

"Mmm." I murmur back.

"I know I've said this before, but I'll say it again. Thank you. For choosing me too and letting me love you."

"I'll always choose you too, Tyson. Always."

CHAPTER 17
Emmy

I WAS WALKING on cloud nine as Tyson helped sneak me back into school the next morning. I'd imagined what it would be like to finally have him so many times, but nothing could compare to the actual thing.

The way his hands caressed my body, how he took control, and his cock. God, his cock! *So fucking big and perfect.* But it's not about the size with me, even though all my guys are a little above average, it's how they use it. And they know how to use it, sometimes *too* damn well.

Tyson owns my body. Oliver gives as much as he takes. Talon is all dirty and delicious. Then there is Ben, my sweet Ben is tender and caring, but throw Talon in between us, and you get a whole new side of Ben. And I fucking love it.

Then there's Charlie, my feisty wild cat. She can read me better than anyone, and knows just what I need in the moment. Soft and sweet, dirty and sinful. She's a woman of all trades.

It felt like I was floating on clouds all day Monday. Now today is Tuesday, and I just fell right off that cloud, plummeting to earth with a deadly crash. The moment I step into Mr. Park's class, I realize today is the first day he planned to start his stupid "tutoring." More like torturing. The man clearly hates me, why the fuck would he want to spend more time with me? *To hurl insults like they're going out of style.*

The guys want to say something to him, if not to him directly, then to Mr. Tucker, but I told them no. A few insults here and there isn't worth the drama. We have less than four weeks left until we are out of here for good, and I plan on having nothing holding me back.

The class felt like it was going on forever. I really did try to pay attention, because I thought that the more I got done in class, then maybe the less time I had to spend with him afterwards.

"Alright class, that's enough for today. Do pages 89 to 96 in your textbooks tonight."

"So..." I say, walking up to his desk. He raises his gaze to look at me with annoyance, then back to my guys and Charlie behind me, who are all giving him dirty looks of their own. "Do I meet you in the library after school or...?"

"No. You can meet me here in this classroom. I have things to do that I can work on while I help you." He says, then looks back at his laptop.

"Okay, then." I say, turning around and heading out the door.

"I don't want you alone with that guy." Oliver says, crossing his arms with a pissed off look.

"Dude gives me bad vibes. I'm not kidding." Talon says, wrapping his arms around me, placing a kiss on my head.

"I'll be fine, guys. I'll go there, do my work, then we can eat and maybe go for a swim or something, okay?"

The rest of the day goes by way too fast and before I know it, I'm knocking on Mr. Park's door.

"Come in."

Pushing the door open, I find him at the table in the corner of the room, and an empty seat right next to him.

I hesitantly make my way over and take that seat.

"We won't be going back and redoing work from before. That would be a waste of time. So from now on, anything I assign, we will work on that during our hour together. That should be enough to bring up your grade so you at least have a passing grade by the end of the month."

"Okay. That sounds reasonable." I say, taking out my textbook from my bag and placing what I need on the table to do today's homework.

"Reasonable? I'd say it's more than that. You clearly needed help way before I took over this class, but your previous teacher didn't seem to care enough about his students. Now I'm left to clean up the mess he left behind." He scoffs.

Wow. Tell me what you really think, asshole.

"Well, thanks I guess... for helping me and everything." I mutter, flipping to the right page.

"You know, Emmy. From what I've seen of your other class grades, you seem like a bright young lady."

Oh... well there's something nice.

"But not everything comes easy. And if you spent half as much time studying in the classes you don't excel at, instead of I don't know, fucking around with your little boyfriends or that girl that hangs off your side like a leech, then maybe you could be an exceptional student." He says so casually.

I gape at him in shock. This man really does not have a filter on him. *How the hell is he even able to be a teacher and work with kids? So fucking rude.*

Trying not to let his words get to me, I ignore him, and we get started.

Surprisingly, I understand the work a lot better when I'm able to ask simple questions to help my brain process everything. Even with a bit of an attitude, he is actually helpful.

"I'm impressed. I told you, Emmy, you are smart. And when you actually try, you seem to know what you're doing."

"Thanks." I say, packing up my bag.

"But..." He says, reaching out and grabbing my wrist as I start to stand.

"More time with me will allow you to do so much better." I didn't like the way he was looking at me. He didn't say anything to raise any alarms, but the chill that's running down my back tells me to keep my guard up around this guy.

I pull my wrist out of his grip and quickly leave the room. Maybe I'm thinking too much into this, so I'll keep it to myself. For now.

Tyson

I haven't had the chance to be alone with Emmy since our night at my cabin last week, with the exception of the couple days our precious daughter was with us visiting. Every time I look at her, all I want to do is push her up against the nearest surface and ram my cock into her over and over again until she's a shaking mess in my arms, screaming my name.

Finally having her wrapped around me as I fucked her until I felt our souls connect was better than anything I've ever felt.

Any of the women that came before her are only distant memories now, because they will never compare to her, never even come close to how she makes me feel.

When we are together, I own her body. And I feel so fucking honored that she trusts me not to hurt her or take advantage of the power she gives me. She lets me explore my wants and needs with her. On the other hand, she owns me in every other way. My mind, body, heart, and soul. I'm addicted to her. I'm so fucking high on her, and I never want to come down.

Oliver texted me about her first meeting with her math teacher. I fucking hate that guy.

Emerald Lake Prep – Book Three: Shattered Pieces

The amount of times I wanted to go over there and smash his face in for how he talked to my girl? Well that number doesn't exist.

But I couldn't. At least not yet. One way or another, the moment my girl walks across that stage, that fucker will get a piece of my mind.

Right now, I'm in hell. Sweet, glorious hell. Because everyone is in my gym class and it's raining again, which means the hiking trip we were going to take got pushed to tomorrow, causing half the class to go to the weight room, including Emmy's guys, while the rest choose to swim.

And I choose to follow my heart to the pool because why the hell would I turn down a chance to see my girl in a two piece suit? Even if I'm trying to hide the mother of all boners as I watch her breasts bounce when she dives off the diving board, and then again when she comes up out of the water like a sexy siren.

I'm fucked right now, and not in the way I want to be.

"You got a little drool right... there." Charlie says, pretending to wipe something from the corner of my mouth.

I swat her hand away, and she sits down next to me with a laugh.

"What do you want, Miss Ross?" I ask, raising a brow at her.

"To thank you." She says with a shrug, looking out at Emmy as she swims laps. She's come a long way with swimming since she's gotten here and I'm so fucking proud of her that she didn't let that incident with Brittany last year keep her from getting back in the water. Now she's swimming like she's been doing it her whole life, and she loves it.

"For what?" I ask, not wanting to take my eyes off my girl.

"For putting the last piece in place that makes up Emmy's heart. As corny as I might sound, you two crossing that line last weekend changed things. I can tell she finally feels complete."

Looking around to make sure no one is watching, I look at Charlie.

"I'm just lucky she has enough love in her heart for me like she does with all of you. She's the best thing to happen to me, to any of us, really."

"No arguing with you there." She says, watching Emmy do the flip she's been practicing for a while.

"Did you see that?" Emmy asks, coming up out of the water with a big smile.

"I did, baby, you were amazing." Charlie beams back.

When class is over, the girls get out of the water and dry off. My eyes roam over Emmy, watching the water drip down her breasts, her nipples pebbling through her swim top.

They take off into the locker room. I just stand there, running my hand over my face, debating whether what I'm about to do is a good idea or not. But I need her. I feel like a junkie coming down from my high, and I need my next fix. Even just to touch her. Who am I kidding, the moment I lay a finger on her, I'll be consumed by her.

I watch as each student comes out of the change rooms, until the only two left in there are Emmy and Charlie. A few moments later Charlie comes out with a big smile on her face, especially when she sees me still here.

"You know, she's the only one left in there, right? She's standing in the shower, naked and soapy. I was gonna have some fun with her, but I had a feeling you would want the opportunity instead. Go get her, Tiger." She winks at me and leaves the room, shutting off the lights as she goes. I have a few moments to slip into that change room before the cameras on the wall trigger the night vision.

Saying *fuck it*, I rip open the change room door with only one thing in mind. My cock being buried deep inside my girl.

The sounds of the shower fill the room mixed with Emmy's sweet voice as she softly sings Fancy Like by Walker Hayes. I grin because it's her new favorite song, but so not her normal type of music.

When she comes into view, she's rinsing her hair with the shower curtain wide open. I guess she didn't care since she was the only one in the room. Until now. Her head is tilted under the water, pushing her breasts out. She's a vision, one I have imprinted into my mind.

Leaning against the locker on the other end of the room, I watch her hands glide over her body as she washes the soap off her.

My cock is rock hard right now, aching to be surrounded by her. Whenever she's around, my brain stops working. She's all I can think of, and after taking it to the next level with her last weekend, it's even worse. It's a new, scary feeling, but it's also very exhilarating.

She turns off the shower, wrapping her towel around her and heads for her gym bag.

"Look what I found." I whisper against her neck as I wrap my arms around her waist, pulling her against my erection as I grind it into her ass. She lets out a startled gasp, but quickly relaxes into my touch when she realizes it's me. "A lonely Princess in need of a dark knight. I've been watching you for a while, and you didn't even notice." I kiss her neck, a little moan releasing from her throat.

"Tyson." She breathes, and I can tell she wants me.

Tugging the towel off her, I let it fall to the ground. She arches into me, pressing her ass into my hardness.

I groan into her neck, kissing it as I start to massage her breasts. "Looks like someone needs to be punished for being so careless."

She shudders in my arms, a lusty whimper slipping past her luscious lips.

"You're right." She breathes. "I've been a bad girl, Mr. Kingston. I deserve your punishment, Sir."

Fuck. My cock jerks in my pants at her words, desperate to be released. My dirty girl likes to play along, even if it's just for my enjoyment. But I can tell that she enjoys it just as much.

I growl in her ear, nipping at her lobe before playing with her clit until she's dripping down her own thighs. Just as she's about to cum, I pull away. She lets out a frustrated sigh, but says nothing.

"On the bench. Hands and knees." I instruct her. She quickly obeys, like the good girl that she is. She gets down, her ass on display and her heavy breasts falling free below her.

"Fuck me, Princess, you're so fucking stunning." I say just before slapping her ass hard. The sound echoes around the room. I don't have time to do everything I want to because I don't want to risk spending too much time here and someone to come searching and possibly find us, even if I did lock the door behind me. I go over to one of the showers, turning it on full blast to drown out any sounds we are about to make.

She's at the perfect height for my cock now. And from what my brother has told me, she loves it when they are rough with her while she sucks their cock.

I'll go a little easy on her because of my size, but fuck I wanna see her choke on it, tears steaming from her beautiful brown eyes, cunt dripping just for me.

She looks up at me, eyes wide with need, waiting for me to make my next move. My eyes trail over her curves. She angles herself away, trying to hide her little baby belly.

"Don't you dare try to hide that beautiful body from me, Princess." I growl. She looks at me with a light blush tinting her cheeks. I trail my fingertips along her body, starting at the globes of her ass, covering all of her back and down under to her belly.

"You're perfect. Don't ever think for a moment we don't love you just the way you are. Any changes to your body mean nothing. You are still beautiful in every way, shape, and form. Do you understand me?" I ask, kneeling down so that I'm at eye level with her. She blinks, which tells me she is holding back tears.

"Yes." She wipes at her eyes.

"Good." I kiss her hard, making her moan as I suck her bottom lip into my mouth, giving it a bite before letting it go. I stand up and undo my pants, pulling them down along with my boxers.

She looks up at me as I stand there before her, stroking my cock. "Lick." I tell her, referring to the bead of pre-cum leaking from the tip of my cock. She licks her lips before lapping up the salty liquid.

I moan at the contact, unable to hold back anymore. I take off my shoes and pants before straddling the bench and sitting down with my cock right in front of her face.

She looks at it with hungry eyes. "Do you want this, Princess? Do you wanna suck my cock?" My voice is husky and deep with want.

"Yes." She groans.

"Then get to work." I encourage her.

With that, she lowers her head, and wastes no time trying to take me all the way in, gagging when she can only get half way down, but she simply pulls back and tries again.

"Fuck!" I hiss, leaning back on my arms. She starts to suck me off, her head bobbing with her determination to take me all the way in. "Look at you. Choking on my cock, such a good girl trying to please me." I praise her, stroking the hair out of her face and gathering it in my hand. "I'm gonna fuck that throat now. If it gets too much just slap my thigh, okay?" I don't want her to feel pain or keep going if she's uncomfortable.

I might love being in control and pushing her to her limits, but I would never force her to do something she was not completely comfortable with.

She nods with my cock in her mouth. I get a good grip on her hair and start to control her movements, shoving her head up and down on my cock. I toss my head back and moan as her hot, wet mouth does unthinkable things to my body. *Fuck.* I've gotten blow jobs before, and I've had sex with a lot of women, but nothing comes close to how it feels doing this with the woman I'm madly in love with.

She moans, enjoying every moment as she slurps and gags on my cock, saliva running down the corners of her lips and all around my cock. I'm breathing heavily, and I can feel the tingling in my balls telling me I'm close to cumming.

"I don't want to cum in your mouth, Princess." I say, pulling her off my cock. She wipes the spit from her mouth with the back of her hand. I stand up to move behind her. She looks back at me over her shoulder, her eyes drooping in a haze of lust.

I adjust my position behind her, slapping her ass, and making her moan before pressing the tip of my cock against her entrance.

"I've been dying to put my cock back where it belongs." Then I start to push inside her. She cries out as she is forced to adjust to my size.

"Yes." She breathes. "Ty, you feel so fucking good inside me. I feel so full." She moans as I bottom out.

"That's it, Baby Girl, take my cock. Fuck, you look so good, your pussy is swallowing my cock whole."

"Fuck me, Ty. Please." She begs.

Slapping her ass again, I start to thrust into her. Before long, I'm lost in the feel of her. Gripping her hip, I hold her in the position I want with one hand, while I use the other to grab a handful of her hair and pull her head back.

"I'm gonna cum." She cries as I fuck her, hitting just the right angle. "Don't stop, please."

"Don't worry, Baby Girl, I got you." Grunting, I fuck her harder, faster, until she's squirting all over my cock, screaming my name.

I catch her body as she falls forward. I'm not done with her yet. I still need to cum, but I want to look her in the eyes as I fill her up.

Pulling out, I help her turn onto her back. I lift her legs up and over my shoulder before I push back into her.

"God. Fuck." She moans as I start to fuck her as hard as before. I lick my lips then bite my lower one as I watch her get lost in the ecstasy my cock is bringing her, her breasts bouncing with every thrust.

Sweat coats her body, and I lean over, making her bend like a pretzel, and lick the bead of moisture between her breasts. I stay in this position, my cock hitting deep inside her. Fuck, it feels so fucking good I don't think I'm gonna be able to last much longer. Normally I would make this go on forever if I could, but we really do have to clean up and leave soon before anyone comes looking for us.

I kiss her, swallowing her cries of pleasure, fucking her through another orgasm. She pulses around my cock, squeezing it for dear life.

Unable to hold on any longer, I pull away from her, sitting up so that I can see her body. I thrust into her a few more times before gripping her hip, digging my fingertips in, and letting out a roar as I cum so fucking hard that I see stars.

When I empty every last drop inside her, I slowly pull out, watching as my cum leaks out of her before pushing it back in with my cock.

"Ty." She whines. "Too sensitive."

"Okay, baby." I say, pulling out. I lean over her, putting my forehead against hers and kissing her softly. "You did so fucking good, Princess."

"I love you." She breathes against my lips.

"I love you to the moon and back." I whisper, kissing her again, stroking her cheek. My thumb meets something wet, and I pull back to see tears in her eyes.

"Are you crying?" I ask, my stomach falling as I feel like a fucking monster for hurting her. "I'm so sorry, Baby. I didn't mean to hurt you. Fuck!"

"Ty." She says, grabbing my hands. "Stop." She laughs.

I look at her in confusion, eyes wide. "But, I obviously hurt you."

"No, you didn't." She smiles. "I'm not crying because I'm in pain. I feel the total opposite, actually. My body is on fire with all the best, indescribable feelings."

"Then why the tears?" I ask, kissing her hands.

"Because, Ty." She starts, giving me a watery smile. "Sometimes the emotions are so powerful my body doesn't know what to do with them. Being here with you, like this, is so overwhelming in the best possible way.

All the love, passion, and ecstasy I feel when I'm with you, well... sometimes I just don't know how to deal with it all. You didn't hurt me, Baby. You made me feel so fucking good."

I sigh, relaxing, now that I know I didn't hurt her. Fuck, the fear I just felt was something I never want to feel again.

"Come on. You're dirty. You need to shower again." I scoop her up, and take her to the shower that's still running, adjusting the water to the perfect temperature before putting her under.

"What, don't you want me to be your dirty girl?" She asks, a smile forming on her lips as the water runs down her face and body. "Don't you want me to walk around with your cum inside me, your mark all over me?"

"Fuck." I growl. "Don't tempt me." I warn her, turning her around so that I can wash her back side. She giggles, then shrieks as I slap her ass. "Watch yourself, Princess."

She smirks at me over her shoulder, sticking her tongue out at me.

I huff out a laugh, shaking my head as I finish cleaning her up.

By the time we are done, I'm rock hard again from touching her sinful body. When she goes to put on her clothes, I grab her and pin her to the locker. She wraps her arms around me, locking her legs behind me as I impale her on my cock and fuck her against the lockers until we're both cumming again. Our foreheads pressing together as we scream each other's names, breathing like we are desperate for our last breath.

I pull out of her and look down, seeing my cum running down her leg. A ringing draws my attention to my phone located in my pants that are on the ground. I pick it up and see it's my dad. Quickly, I get dressed.

"So I need to take this. And you need another shower." I say before backing away with a cocky smirk. Still in a sex haze she looks down at my cum, then back at me with pure murder.

"Tyson Kingston." She growls, and fuck it sounds super hot.

"Gotta go, baby. See you later." I blow her a kiss before taking off. I feel bad for leaving her there like that, but I need to answer this phone call. It could be important.

CHAPTER 18
Emmy

"TWO MORE DAYS!" Charlie squeals, jumping up and down on the bed.

My body bounces with the bed as I crack open my eyes to see my adorable, crazy girlfriend grinning down at me.

"What time is it?" I groan.

"Time to get up." She says with one last bounce before she lands on the bed. "Two more days, baby. Then we're done with this hellhole, and free to live our lives!" She yells, flopping back onto the bed.

"I'm gonna need some help waking up." I mumble.

She pops her head up, giving me a smirk. "I can certainly help with that." She wiggles her eyebrows before pouncing on me. I let out a squeak followed by a laugh as she covers my body with hers. She kisses me hard before ripping off the blanket and diving between my legs.

Five minutes and one amazing orgasm later, we hop in the shower to start our day. After that we get dressed and head down to meet the guys in the dining room.

"So, do you think we studied enough for our finals tomorrow?" Ben asks before taking a sip of his coffee.

"My brain is already filled to the brim. If I try to add anything else to it, it's going to explode and I'm gonna lose everything. Better not risk it." Talon says, sneaking a kiss on Ben's cheek as he sits down next to him.

"I'm so over this school. I don't even care if I pass." Oliver mutters, wrapping his arm around me. We spent last night together, and my core still aches for him. When we were done, he carried me to my room so that I could wake up with Charlie. Knowing how much it stresses me out when I spend more time with one of my lovers than the others. His actions just prove to me how much he wants our arrangement to work out for the good of our family. The little things like that make me fall in love with him all over again.

He looks down at me with a heated smirk, making me clench my thighs together.

"Enough, you two." Talon tosses a piece of his muffin at Oliver. "Bad enough you two kept us up most of the night, you don't need to start round two right here on a cafeteria table."

"Actually this would be round...." He takes a moment to think, counting on his fingers. "Four." He grins back at one of his best friends.

"Rub it in, why don't you?" Talon mutters. "She's ours next."

"Don't act like you don't enjoy watching." Oliver scoffs.

"You got me there." Talon smirks back, wrapping his arm around Ben's shoulder. Ben looks at our boyfriend with a raised brow. "Oh you love it, too. Watching her get fucked makes you just as much of a horny fucker as I am."

Talon's taunts cause Ben's cheeks to flush, but when he looks at me, his eyes fill with heat and promises of fun times later.

I knew that once I was given the green light to have sex again, we would be going back to our old ways. It's just who we were, how we liked it. We were sexual beings and, as one woman with multiple partners, it makes sense that I get sex on the daily. And I fucking love it. I had a mandatory six week vacation for my pussy, now this bitch is thirsty and needs to be quenched. *I got you, girl.*

"Enough of all this sex talk." Charlie scrunches up her nose at the guys. "I don't want to hear about all your dick-scapades."

"Why, because yours is smaller than ours?" Talon teases.

"Fuck you." Charlie hisses, tossing her empty coffee cup at his head. After that time in the tub, Charlie did brag to the guys about making me cum on her cock. The looks on their faces were priceless. But when Charlie refused to tell them the size of the dildo, they started messing with her about theirs being bigger.

"And at least I can upgrade." Charlie smirks.

"Guys, can we stop talking about dicks? People are looking." I say, looking around at the few students eavesdropping.

My eyes land on Tyson. I don't know if he can hear what we were talking about, but his eyes tell me he was thinking about something along the same lines, sexual I mean.

Since the locker room sex, which by the way, was fucking amazing, Tyson has found every opportunity to eat me, lick me, kiss me, and fuck me.

The thrill of it is intoxicating. Waiting for the next moment alone. Wondering if it was just going to be a simple brush of his lips, or the full force of his cock.

Tyson tries to spend his free time with us, but with it being the end of the year, he was pretty busy.

He never did tell me what that phone call with his father was about but I can only assume it was club business, which meant it was none of mine.

We finish eating and head to our classes like normal. Most classes were just reviewing things we learned to prepare us for tomorrow.

We head into Mr. Park's class.

"Last day before exams. From what your practice exams show, all of you can expect to pass." The class lets out a few sounds of excitement. "Don't get too excited. Most of you will just barely be passing." He scoffs. Looks like I'm getting dickhead Mr. Prick today. *Yay.*

The class goes on forever as he goes over the basics of what we learned this semester, and gives us yet another practice quiz.

After class we go about our day like normal. I enjoy art and music, finding myself sad to see them no longer be a part of my day to day life. We spend the time in art class just free style painting, and in Music we get to blast whatever songs we wanted. Charlie and I dance and sing without a care in the world. It makes for some pretty good moments on our last official day.

"Why do you have to do this with him today? School is pretty much done." Charlie complains as we stop in front of Mr. Park's classroom door.

"Today is the last time. I'm pretty confident I'll at least get a passing grade. I've been doing well and every little bit helps. Even if I would rather be anywhere else but with him."

Studying with Mr. Park was a bit of a roller coaster. Today will be the 8th time that I will sit in front of him, so he can tutor me. No meeting went the same. Sometimes he was a dick and made comments that made me want to bash his head in, while other times he was quiet and only spoke to explain something to me. Those were my favorites of the meetings.

"Fine." She pouts.

"I'll be back in an hour okay?" Charlie says, giving me a kiss before looking at the teacher with a glare before she takes off.

"I don't understand why you associate yourself with people like them." Mr. Park says out of nowhere, breaking the silence we were in as I work on the practice sheet he gave me.

"Excuse me?" I ask, looking up at him with a pinched brow.

"You are so young and bright. You have the potential to do a lot of things with your life once you graduate from here. Why do you waste your time and energy with a group of people who will be lucky to get fast food jobs once they leave here?"

I just blink at him, rage filling my veins at how he's speaking about my lovers. My family. You wanna insult me? Fine, have at it; but when you start in on my people? *Fuck that shit!*

"Well, maybe not Ben. He seems smarter than the others, but not by much. Have you thought of letting your foster parents watch your daughter full-time so you can go to college and better your life?"

Am I being pranked? I used to watch the MTV show that Ashton Kutcher was the host of years ago, and this is giving me hardcore *Punked* vibes because this joker can't be for real.

"We're done here." I say through clenched teeth, packing up my bag.

"Oh relax, Amelia. You are overreacting and taking a simple observation to heart." He grabs my arm and pulls me back into my seat. "With all those lovers, it's obvious that you have been paying more attention to them than they have to you. You deserve so much more than what they are currently giving you or what they could potentially give you down the road."

The fingers of his free hand feather over my thigh, making me tense up and causing bile to rise in my throat.

"I can be that for you." He says, leaning in to whisper in my ear. The lust in his eyes makes me want to puke.

"You know what you can do?" I whisper back.

"What?" His eyes light up.

"You can fuck off. Touch me again, and I'll chop your fucking dick off and ram it down your perverted throat." I snap before punching him in the dick. He lets out a pained grunt.

I scramble to grab my bag and run out of there, not wanting to be near that fucking creep any longer.

How fucking dare *he?! Who the fuck does he think he is?* I mumble angrily as I walk down to the beach, needing to cool down before meeting the others. I send Charlie a text that I left early and that I'll meet her in our room in a little bit. She texts me back asking if everything was okay, and I tell her I will explain everything later.

Still focused on my phone, I'm not paying attention when I walk right into something hard. "Woah, there!" Someone says, catching my arms, keeping me from falling as I bounce off of them.

"Shit, sorry." I say, looking up to see that it's Tyson I bumped into.

"What's wrong?" He growls, going into defence mode at the look on my face.

162

I look down and chew on my lip, debating on whether or not I should tell him. If I do, it means without a doubt he will track down Mr. Prick and kick his ass. It's just how it would be. *But does it matter?* We are done with school after tomorrow anyways.

"He is such a fucking creep." I hiss.

"Who?" Tyson grips my shoulders, giving them a little shake to get me to look back up at him.

"Mr. Prick. He went on about how I'm too good for the others. How I would be better off without them and that they were only holding me back. Then the fucker goes and tells me I should give up my child to go off and do things that would 'better' my life. My life is fucking amazing, thank you very much. I have a group of people whom I'm madly in love with, and them with me. I don't care what he thinks, they are all smart, amazing and - Ugh!" I shout.

"Shhh." He pulls me into his strong arms. His hand strokes my head, and I relax a little into him.

"Tyson." I sigh. "That's not all."

He stiffens. "What else?" He asks, his voice is stone cold, and it sends shivers down my spine.

"He... pretty much offered himself up as a replacement." I cringe.

"He what?" Tyson pulls back to look at my face, murder dancing in his eyes. I feel a little fucked up that it's totally turning me on, melting my anger for Mr. Prick into desire for him. *Maybe I am a little more like my sister than I thought.*

"Did he touch you?" He demands

I bite my lip, not saying anything.

"Emmy." He warns.

I sigh. "Yeah, he brushed his hand against my thigh."

"I'm going to fucking murder him. No, this time I'm gonna hand the fucker over to Queenie on a silver platter and let her play with him. Maybe I'll fucking join her." He's seething mad right now.

"Tyson! Don't do anything that will get you arrested. I need you." I say, eyes pleading with the truth of that statement.

His face softens a little. "Fine." He grits out. "No killing. At least not me."

"Tyson."

"I *am* going to smash his face in though." He promises.

"I know." I sigh, hugging him again. "I just want to go home. I want to be done with this school of nightmares and just *be* at home; free to be a mother to my child. To be able to go where I please with my lovers. Is that too much to ask?" I mumble into his chest.

"No, Princess. It's not. You have every right to all of that, and more. And I will make sure you get it... After I make him look like a bloody pug."

"What?" I laugh.

"You know, those dogs that look like they had their face rammed into a wall or something, with smushy faces?"

I burst out laughing. Maybe this is me losing it after everything that just happened, but fuck, that comparison sets me off into deep belly laughs. It took me a couple of moments before I could compose myself.

"God, I needed that." I say, wiping the tears from my eyes.

"Glad I could help." He smirks, then drops a quick kiss on my lips. "Come on. I'll walk you to your room. Then I have a fucking piece of shit to track down and take care of."

Tyson and I walk into my room to see the others are sitting around the room, waiting. I'm sure Charlie told them I left early. I'm surprised Oliver didn't come looking for me.

"I was about to come looking for you." Oliver growls. *Well, then.* Fuck, he looks just like his brother right now. All hot and scary with his tattooed muscles flexing as he clenches his hands. The dark gleam in his blue eyes, making me all hot and bothered.

Really, Emmy, what the fuck is wrong with you?

"Don't look at me like that, Firefly." Oliver grumbles, pulling me into his arms.

"You gonna tell them, or should I?" Tyson asks.

"Tell us what?" Oliver asks, looking between me and his brother.

I tell him everything I told Tyson, still fuming about all the bullshit Mr. Prick was spewing about them. I hate hearing people talk bad about my loved ones, how they weren't good enough for me. Because they were, they are. *They are fucking perfect for me and everyone else can just go fuck off.*

"I'm coming with you." Oliver says when Tyson tells the rest of them what he plans on doing after he leaves here. They both give me a kiss goodbye after making sure I'm okay with them leaving but they know I'm in good hands.

"Babe." Charlie says, getting my attention. "Why don't you go back to the boys' room. Let Ben and Talon take care of you tonight."

I look around at all of them, not knowing what to do.

"Go. I'll just spend the night listening to music and packing up our room so we can get the fuck out of here the second we are allowed." She grins. I know she's trying to make light of the situation and that she can see just how much this whole thing is bothering me.

164

"Please?" Ben asks from behind me. "Come back to our room. Let us distract you, Butterfly. Let us love you."

His green eyes shine with so much love and need to be here for me while I'm upset; there's no way I can say no.

"Alright. Let's go." I give Charlie a loving kiss before taking Ben and Talon's hands, letting them lead me back to their room.

"As much as I want to rant and rave about that scumbag, I'd much rather help you take your mind off him." Talon says, helping me take my shoes off, while Ben helps strip me until I'm in my bra and underwear. Talon goes to his dresser and grabs one of his shirts and slips it on over my head before they both strip down to their boxers. I lick my lips as I take in Ben's inked body, and Talon's toned abs as they crawl in bed and lean back against the headboard.

Ben pulls me up onto their bed so that I'm settled between both of them. I snuggle into Talon's side and drape my legs over Ben's

We put *365 Days* on Netflix. We haven't watched it yet, but I've heard people say good things about it online.

Once we get to the sexier scenes, I start to feel a familiar warmth in my belly and tingling down below. Any time I watch a movie or TV show with sex, I can't help but feel slightly turned on. But this movie... God, I have no chance with this one. It has a very BDSM vibe, and all I can think about is Tyson tying me up like the girl in the movie, and having his dirty ways with me like he did in the locker room.

"Shorty, you okay down there?" Talon asks. I look up and he's still watching the movie, but I see the sexy smirk on his lips.

"No." I admit because I don't care if it makes me look like a sex crazed person, I haven't had the two of them together in a very long time, and that is exactly what I want, more like need, right now.

"What do you need, my Little Butterfly?" Ben leans over to kiss my neck, his hands sliding up my naked thighs.

"You." I shiver with pleasure at his touch. "Both of you."

Talon shuts the movie off, and puts on some music using the remote, then moves me so that I'm laying on my back with both of them looming over me.

"We can help with that." Talon's voice is husky and deep, dripping with need and it has my thighs clenching together.

"Okay?" I squeak. The way they are looking at me, like two hungry predators trapping their prey, ready to pounce and devour, has me anxious but excited.

Talon leans down and captures my lips with his, making me moan as he caresses my tongue with his.

When he pulls back, my brain is hazy and I feel all light and airy. I turn to Ben. "Hi." I smile.

"Hello, My Love." He says softly before kissing me. I grip the back of his head, holding him to me as we battle with our lips and tongues.

Talon pulls my top up to expose my upper half. His warm hands start to massage my aching breasts and I find myself opening my thighs as they pleasure my body.

Ben continues to kiss me, heated and lazy. I moan into his mouth as Talon takes one of my nipples into his mouth.

He sucks and nips, but when he swirls the tip of his tongue around my hardening peak, it sends shockwaves to my clit. I lift my hips, needing the delicious friction from his hard cock. He grinds back, making us both groan.

"You know, it's not actually that bad." Talon says. I break the kiss from Ben to look up at Talon licking his lips, then down to my breasts that are now leaking.

"Fuck. I'm sorry. I didn't pump." I say, trying to get up to find something to clean them up, but Talon pushes me back down.

"Hey. It's okay. It's natural. You're creating nutritious food for our baby girl and that's amazing. It's not gonna turn me off during sex, and I don't think it would with the others, either." Talon says, taking some tissues from the side table and cleaning me up before holding them to my breast to stop the flow.

"But it's so embarrassing." I groan, trying to cover my face, but Ben grabs my hands and brings them up to his lips, placing a kiss on the back of each of them.

"No, it's not. If it makes you feel better I'll leave your breasts alone, but baby, do you know how hard that is? They are so fucking perfect, and those perky, pink nipples are just begging to be touched..."

"Talon." I groan, interrupting him and taking in the lust filling his eyes.

"Arms up." He instructs. I do as he asks. He takes my shirt off, then kisses me hard before trailing kisses down the length of my body, stopping right above my core.

"Are you wet for us baby?" He asks as he pulls down my panties. Ben looks down at Talon's hands near my cunt and his pupils dilate.

"She's fucking soaked for us, Tal. Look at how that pussy glistens with need."

"Fuck." I breathe. "Talon, you're rubbing off on him. You have become such a dirty boy, Ben."

"Oh, I'll be rubbing something on him in just a minute." He growls, his hand snaking around the back of Ben's head as he smashes his lips to Ben's. They kiss, hot and messy, and fuck if it doesn't have me dripping even more.

"Guys..." I whine, needing them to touch me too.

Talon looks down at me with a grin. "Does our Queen need some love, too?"

"Yes." I growl.

"Oh, feisty little thing, isn't she, Ben?"

"Talon." I close my eyes and sigh. "One of you had better have a tongue or a dick in me in less than two seconds or so help m-" I get cut off, my eyes flying open as Talon plunges his tongue into my soaked center while gripping my hips so he can bury his face between my thighs without me squirming away.

"Fuck." I hiss, tangling my fingers in his blond strands as I hold him to me.

"Soon, my love. Real soon." Ben kisses me, before maneuvering his body under mine so that my back is against his chest, and his bare cock pressed against the crack in my ass. *When did he take off his boxers?*

Talon eats me out like a starving man until my legs are shaking, and my belly coils with need. "Talon." I moan. "I'm gonna cum. Fuck."

"Cum for me, baby girl. Cum all over my tongue, then I can give our boy a taste." He purrs.

I toss my head back and forth as I try to process all these feelings. It's too much, but it's so good. Ben's arms snake around my waist as his strong hands caress their way down to grasp the soft inner part of my thighs, opening them wide for Talon. Ben's grip tightens, digging into my skin as he keeps my hips pinned to his to hold me open and still. Talon sucks on my clit, before inserting two thick digits into my dripping cunt, fucking me with them. He works his fingers and tongue together until I'm screaming out my release, cumming so hard I start to feel light-headed.

"So fucking good." Talon says, lifting his head from between my thighs with a cocky satisfied smirk on his face. Breathing heavily I slump against Ben's chest, spent but still ready for more.

"Have a taste, Ben." Talon's voice is oozing pure sex, and god, things are about to get messy. I can't fucking wait.

These two might seem like some of the sweetest loving men you will ever meet; but in the bedroom they are dirty fuckers, freaks in the sheets, and I fucking *LOVE* it.

They lean over my shoulder, meeting in the middle. Ben doesn't kiss Talon. No. He licks Talon's face clean of my release, leaving nothing behind.

I whimper, making them both look down. "I think it's time we fuck our girl. Together." Talon gives me a slow sexy smile.

"I think so, too. But I have an idea," Ben says. "Talon, lay back."

"Oh, look at you taking control. I'm all for it." Talon jokes.as he lays back on the bed.

"Drape her over your body so that her ass is facing me."

Talon pulls me up and over his chest. When I'm in place, I feel Ben kiss each ass cheek.

"Now, slide that thick cock inside our girl." Ben directs. Talon doesn't question him, doing as he says. I let out a lusty moan as he pulls me down onto his cock.

"You look so beautiful with our man's cock inside you, Butterfly, although I think you would look better with both." I feel the tip of his cock start to press in, but it's not in my ass like I was expecting. No, it's pushing inside my cunt right alongside Talon's. We've never done double penetration before.

My body tenses up as I hiss at the new feeling. "Relax." Ben soothes, rubbing a hand up and down my back. "If it gets to be too much, let me know.

"Fuck, Ben." Talon breathes as Ben pushes deeper inside me. "Your cock against mine while we're in our girl's wet, warm pussy feels so... *Fuck.*"

I try to relax as my body accommodates the two cocks. Inside the same hole. Fuck, it's a tight fit, but as they start to move, one pulling out while the other thrusts in, I quickly get lost in the new sensation.

"So fucking full. God, this feels so different." I pant, clinging to Talon as he massages the globes of my ass.

"So fucking perfect." Ben says through gritted teeth.

"Yes." I breathe, drunk on cock. "Oh, oh fuck!" Together they hit all the right places. "Please, please I wanna cum." I beg, feeling my orgasm right there, just out of reach. I'm ready for them to push me over the edge, we're so fucking close.

"Suck." Prying my eyes open I see Ben slide his fingers in Talon's mouth. Talon sucks on them sexually, making me clench around their cocks, making them groan in unison.

Ben pulls his fingers out of Talon's mouth, and a moment later I feel them penetrating my tight hole.

He slides two fingers into my ass and my eyes roll back, my nails digging into Talon's arms.

"I think she likes that, Ben. Fuck her ass with your fingers, while we fuck her pussy good with our cocks."

Ben does just that, thrusting his fingers as Talon slips his hand between our bodies to play with my clit.

"Oh." I moan. "Yes, yes!"

So much is going on, I can't handle it anymore. They work together as a team to bring me to the edge. I let out a silent scream as I cum, stars bursting behind my eyes as all the energy is wrung from my body. I feel like a feather floating in the breeze, content as I gently come down from my high. Talon lets out a moaned grunt, cumming deep inside me and all over Ben's cock.

"I can feel your cum coating my cock." Ben groans. He thrusts in a few more times before pulling out, and cumming all over my back.

"Nice." Talon lets out a huffed laugh as he watches ropes of our boyfriend's cum land on my back.

"That was fucking awesome." Ben pants, running a hand through his fiery red hair, sweat coating his face and body.

"Damn right, it was. We need to do that more often. But I do enjoy taking your ass, My Lady." Talon kisses the top of my head.

"I'll go get something to clean you up." Ben says, leaning over to kiss my cheek. I give him a lazy sleepy smile.

"I love you." I whisper.

"I love you too, Butterfly." He smiles then heads for the bathroom.

Talon slides out of me and helps me lay on my stomach on the bed next to him. We just lay there for a minute but I'd like to get this off me before it dries and becomes a bitch to get off.

"Can you hurry up? I feel like a glazed toaster strudel!" I shout to Ben as he rummages around in the bathroom.

"Let me check." Talon purrs then leans over and licks a bit of Ben's cum off my back. I groan as I watch his heated eyes bore into mine. He licks his lips. "Yum. Best damn toaster strudel I've ever tasted." He winks.

A noise from behind us draws our attention. Ben stands there naked with a wet cloth in his hand, eyes glazed with lust. He tosses the cloth on my back. "Here, love. You're gonna need to clean yourself up this time." He says before pouncing on Talon.

I let out a shriek that turns into a fit of laughter as Ben attacks Talon in a battle of heated kisses. God, I love these two. I clean up the best I can, thank god I'm flexible, and toss the cloth in the dirty laundry basket next to the bed. Crawling over to the guys on my hands and knees, I prowl towards them, nowhere near finished with them tonight.

"Got room for one more?" I ask in a husky voice. They break their kiss, and look at me, ready to devour me once again.

"There's always room for you, My Lady." Talon coos before yanking me between them. Their mouths and hands find my body as they play with every inch of me. Hard cocks against my legs tell me this night is gonna be a long one and I'll enjoy every minute.

CHAPTER 19
Oliver

"I'M GOING TO fucking kill him." I seethe. We left Emmy with the others so Tyson and I could track down this fucker and make him pay for the things he said to our girl. He had no fucking reason to spew shit that he has no right to have an opinion on.

And he fucked up big time when he put his fucking hands on her. I'm gonna enjoy breaking each of his fingers.

"No." Tyson growls. "The best we can do is beat the shit out of him for now. Fucker won't press charges if he knows what's good for him, but Emmy is right. We can't risk it. You are free and clear of this place as of tomorrow. I won't let you guys risk losing your freedom; it's what you've worked so hard for."

School has only been out for a little over an hour. Most teachers should be in their classrooms getting things ready for tomorrow as well as cleaning out their classrooms for the summer break, but not Mr. Park. When we went to his classroom, he was long gone. Probably because he knew Emmy would say something and he wanted to hide like a fucking coward.

So after searching the whole school, we assumed he had to be in his cabin. Good, we can do this behind closed doors.

"Open up, fucker!" Tyson booms as he pounds on the door with his fist. Looking around, I make sure there's no witnesses. "I know you're in there. Face me like a fucking man!" Ha, a man. No man would treat, let alone talk, to anyone the way he does.

"Fuck this shit, he's not gonna open it. Fucking pussy." I scoff.

"Fine, if he won't open the door, I will." Tyson lifts his foot then with all his strength kicks the door in. The door flies open with a bang, reverberating off the wall as pieces of the wood go flying around the room. He storms in and I follow.

"What the hell do you think you are doing?" Mr. Park demands, staring at us wide-eyed as he comes out of his bathroom drying his hair with a towel.

Thank god he's dressed because I don't feel like beating the shit out of a naked man. No one wants to have a flaccid dick flopping about.

"What do I think I'm doing?" Tyson chuckles darkly. "I'm about to smash a pervert's face in." Tyson growls. "You think you can talk to my brother's girl like that and then have the balls to touch her?"

Tyson gets in his face, chest heaving and snarling like he's about to bite Mr. Park's face off.

"Your *brother's* girl? Does he know that you're fucking her too? That she was in your cabin? Or what about how you fucked her in the locker room?" He reveals with a triumphant smirk.

"*The FUCK?* Have you been spying on us? You really are a fucking pervert." Tyson grabs the guy by the neck and slams him into the wall behind him.

"You all use her like a sex doll." He coughs out a laugh. "You just see her as a body to play with."

"You don't fucking know anything about us." I snap, getting into his face as well.

He looks at me. "Really? I know a lot more than you think."

Who the hell is this guy?

"Here's the deal. I'm gonna beat you until you're gasping for your last breath. Then I'm gonna leave you on the floor of this cabin. I'm gonna walk out that door and none of us will ever waste time thinking of you again. And if you ever so much as look at Emmy again, I will put a bullet right here." Tyson roughly taps his finger between Mr. Park's eyes.

"You don't-" he struggles to breathe. "Deserve her." He gasps.

"And you do?" I look at him with pure evil, really wanting to add him to my shit list right along with Mariah.

"Yes."

"Fuck this shit." Tyson says, tightening his grip on the guy's throat. Mr. Park claws at Tyson's hands, desperately trying to get Tyson to release him. Just as he's about to pass out, Tyson lets go. Mr. Park sucks in a strangled breath, but that's all he gets before Tyson's fist is in his face. The guy falls backwards with a pained scream. His hands fly to his face as blood starts to squirt from his nose. *Yeah, that's definitely broken.*

"I will kill you if you *ever* come near her again." Tyson roars as he straddles the guy and starts pounding into him.

I've seen what he did to Todd, and if I don't stop him now he will end up killing him and we don't need to be dealing with the cops right now.

"Ty, man, stop. That's enough." I say, trying to haul him off the guy.

Tyson lets me pull him off. His eyes are wild and his breathing is out of control. He stands up, looming over the dirt bag on the floor.

"Consider this your only warning." Tyson spits on him before turning around and storming out of the cabin, not bothering to look back, or wait for me.

I lean over Mr. Park. "You messed with the wrong people. Don't make that mistake again or you won't be so lucky next time." I straighten up, and for good measure give him a good hard kick in the balls, making him cry out. Turning to walk away, I notice his hand is in the path that my feet need to take for me to exit the cabin, so I stomp on his hand with everything I've got in me. The crunch of his bones makes my heart happy. Chuckling at the bloody mess on the ground, I follow after my brother.

No one messes with our family and gets away with it. I will show no weakness when it comes to keeping my loved ones safe.

Ben

"You look so handsome." My mom gushes as she fixes my cap. My mom, dad, and sister drove in for the graduation ceremony as well as Rick and Amy, who brought Melody.

"Mom, it's fine." I laugh at her fussing.

"All of you look amazing." She smiles at Oliver and Talon before turning her attention to the girls. "And look at you." She says, her eyes starting to tear up. "So beautiful. I'm so proud of you ladies." She gives Emmy a big hug, then one to Charlie.

An announcement is made that the ceremony will start in ten minutes.

"Alright, you guys go with your class. We'll be there cheering you on. Now give me my grandbaby." She says, taking Melody from Oliver. She smothers her with kisses and baby talks to her as they leave to take their seats.

We're having the ceremony outside. It's a nice sunny day, and it's perfect. We finished packing our rooms last night. Tyson had a moving truck come early this morning to bring everything back to the compound. We didn't want to step foot back inside that place for any reason.

As soon as we get our diplomas and walk across that stage, we are leaving Emerald Lake Prep in the rearview mirror and starting our new lives.

We took our exams yesterday and they were brutal. We won't actually get our results until next week, so this is all for show. Even if we don't pass, we will still have each other and we can figure out what to do then.

"Emmy!" Ethan shouts, waving his hand. Emmy grabs mine and Oliver's, dragging us over to see him.

"Hey." Emmy smiles, giving him a hug.

"I want you to meet someone." Ethan says, then looks at the young lady next to him with the baby in her arms. "This is Leah, my best friend." He looks from Emmy to Leah. "Leah, meet Emmy, my other bestie."

"Hi, it's so wonderful to meet you. Ethan has told me so much about you." Emmy beams.

"I heard a lot about you, too." Leah smiles. "Thanks for being there for him when I couldn't."

"Of course. He's an amazing friend. I'm happy to have him around." Emmy smiles back.

"And we can't forget this little one." Ethan says, taking the baby out of Leah's arms. "Emmy, meet my son, Mason."

"Oh my god, he's so adorable!" Emmy and Charlie start fussing over him.

"How cute would it be if he and Melody got married?" Charlie says, her eyes wide with excitement.

"Fuck, no." Oliver growls. We all look at him, startled. "She's never getting married. She's gonna live with us until we die, then I'll haunt her ass and scare all the guys away."

"Oh, don't be so dramatic." Charlie scoffs.

"Olly, what if she's gay?" Emmy smirks, raising a brow.

"Then I'll chase all the women away. It doesn't matter to me either way." He shrugs.

"You're crazy." Emmy rolls her eyes, but the smile on her face tells me she's amused. She loves it when we go all 'Papa Bears' over Melly.

"So, are you ready for another one?" I ask with a grin.

"What if I am?" She challenges back.

My eyes go wide. *Oh, fuck.* Maybe it's not a good idea to joke about that right now because the way she's looking at me at this moment, tells me she's ready to try for baby number two.

We're all in pretty amazing moods right now. Knowing that we are free and that we won't have to spend one more moment under that school's roof, puts us all in good spirits.

"Come on, the ceremony is starting." Talon says, grabbing my hand and leading me to the stage.

One by one everyone's names are called. And every time it's one of ours, the parents scream and shout their praise and excitement for us. I preen at the look of pride on my mother's and father's faces.

I'm so damn lucky to have them in my life. They have always been so supportive of me. They were there for me when I told them about my sexual orientation. Then, again when I explained our unique relationship dynamic. And without thought, they opened their arms when we told them about Melody's impending arrival. They continue to be there for me every step of the way, helping and advising me through fatherhood so far. To top it all off, they took Talon in as one of their own. They truly are amazing parents. And I'm glad to call them mine.

Afterwards, we took some family photos with Melody looking so adorable in her little pink dress and all of us holding our diplomas.

"You guys ready?" Tyson calls.

"Yup, we'll meet you at the car." Emmy calls back.

"So, this is it." Charlie says.

We all turn around, standing side by side in a row as we look upon Emerald Lake Prep's big mansion style building. Its old, grey stones covered in vines were what we called home for years, at least for some of us that is.

Talon cups his hands around his mouth and shouts "FUCK YOU, EMERALD LAKE PREP! PEACE OUT, MOTHERFUCKER!" He flips off the school with both middle fingers.

Talon lets out a hoot as he wraps our girl in his arms, spinning her around before giving her a heated kiss. Emmy laughs at Talon's antics, and I find myself smiling at how happy they are.

I never had the heart to hate this school. I met my best friends here. One who later turned into my lover. And I met the mother of my child, the other half of my soul. So, as much pain as being here has caused, there were also a lot of good memories that came out of being here, too. And I will forever be grateful for the opportunities it presented me with.

"Mr. Knight. You may no longer be a student here, but this is still a place of learning, please respect that." Mr. Tucker says walking towards us from the direction of the school's front entrance.

Emmy huffs out a laugh. "With all due respect, Mr. Tucker, this may be a place of learning, but this is *not* a place you should be proud of. I appreciate the concept that you envisioned for this place. I know you wanted to make your grandmother proud by turning her dream into reality, but I think she would be pretty disappointed at what it has become. You care more about the money you get from taking in troubled or wealthy students, than you do about the students themselves. This school should have been my second chance. And yes, in a way, it was. I found the loves of my life and I've never been happier, but I also experienced a lot of pain and suffering due to the negligence of the staff, who were supposed to protect and help me. That is what I got out of your school: neglect and pain. You hired despicable monsters as teachers, and allowed unstable students to get away with far too much. I think it would be smart to take this summer to get your priorities straight before the new school year starts. And if they are not to clean up this school and turn it into what it was originally intended to be, then maybe you should just shut the whole place down."

Okay, so watching my Butterfly be all badass right now has got my cock rock hard, and from the looks on Talon and Oliver's faces, so are theirs.

"So, if you don't mind, we've said our goodbyes to the place, to this chapter in our lives, and now I'm gonna go home. I'm gonna be the best damn mother to my daughter. I'm gonna live hard and love harder. I'm gonna enjoy every second life has to offer me because the one and only lesson that I learned from coming to this school is that you never know how long you have left on this earth, so live it with all that you got and have no regrets."

With that she turns around and heads right for Tyson's car. Talon gives Mr. Tucker a massive grin before spinning around and running to catch up with our girl.

Oliver just gives Mr. Tucker a once-over, shakes his head, and takes off.

"Later Mr. T." Charlie waves. "See ya never. Peace!" She holds up a peace sign as she walks away.

"You really should take her advice. It's not fair for children to have to go through what some of us have. Also, you really need to be better at hiring people." I say, looking behind him seeing Mr. Park watching from under a tree in the distance. I can see the bruising from here, and that his broken nose is in a splint.

With a sick satisfaction, I smile at the fucker, hoping he sees it before I turn to follow after the rest of my group.

176

Farewell, Emerald Lake Prep. You will forever be a part of our past.

CHAPTER 20
Emmy

"WE'RE *FREEEEEEE!*" TALON screams out of the open window as we travel down the highway on our way home. My face splits in a giant grin as I laugh. I have never felt so relieved like I do right now. Leaving that hellish place behind we're officially free to live our lives the way we want to.

It feels like the weight of the world has been lifted off my shoulders. No more being told what to do. No longer being kept behind those fences around the school grounds like a caged animal. No longer being restricted by the adults who claim to know what's best for me. I am free. Free to go on dates, sleep in late, or go out and be with my loved ones without limitations. The feeling is amazing.

Before Emerald Lake Prep, I was alone. I spent every day working my ass off to make money, to try and keep myself alive, and a roof over my head. I did the best I could with a drug addicted mother who stole from me all the time.

This school saved me from my past only to trade it for a new type of hell. At least this school gave me something my old life didn't have. Six something's to be exact.

So, even though I had to go through things people should never have to endure, I came out with the ultimate prize. I would go through every ounce of that pain again if it meant being with my guys, Charlie, and Melody.

"We need some music. No car ride is complete without it." Charlie says, leaning over me to switch on the radio, turning it as loud as it can go. *Paradise* by Bazzi blasts through the speakers. Charlie smiles wide as she takes my hand, giving it a squeeze. I return the smile, giving her a quick kiss before we start to sing along with the song at the top of our lungs, no care in the world at this very moment.

All the windows are down, filling the car with a cool breeze. My and Charlie's hair is flying about, but we couldn't care less. The bass is vibrating around us, making my body rattle. My chest shakes in time with the beat, and I don't think I've ever felt more alive.

The guys start singing along with us and I laugh, moving my head back and forth to the beat.

Tyson grabs hold of my other hand, bringing it to his lips for a kiss. He smiles one of his bad boy sexy grins that makes me shiver with all the dirty promises those lips hold.

Hands squeeze my shoulders, and I look back to Ben who's between Talon and Oliver in the back. He gives me a content smile, and kisses me before settling back into Talon's arms.

This. This moment in time, right here, will forever be one I remember. Every little detail. Me between Tyson and Charlie, the guys in the back, the music, the trees along the side of the road as we head to the start of our new lives with our past long gone behind us. I will never take these people for granted.

I know something bad is coming. I'd only be fooling myself if I thought otherwise. I know Tyson will still be around me all the time, even if it's in the background. Dagger is planning something. We're not fooled by his silence. Now if only we could figure out what it is exactly he is planning then maybe we could prepare ourselves a little better. One thing I do know for sure is that it has something to do with me and Melody. And I'll be *damned* if that fucker gets his hands on her.

But I'm not gonna live in fear. I plan on living my life until the universe decides to throw another curveball my way. And when it comes barrelling at me, I'll have an army at my side.

"Emmy." I feel someone lightly caress my hair. "Princess, we're home." I sleepily blink my eyes open to see Tyson looming over me. "You fell asleep." He grins. Lifting my head off the seat of the car, I look out the front window. This is not Rick and Amy's house.

"Where are we?" I ask, my voice coming out groggy.

"Home." He chuckles.

"Tyson, I know it's been a week since we've been back here, but you've been to Rick and Amy's enough times to know this isn't their place." I say, taking his hand as he helps me out, closing the door behind him.

We stand in front of a two story house. It's a nice little home.

"Babe, let me be a little more clear. We are home, this is *our* home.

My dad had this place built for me or Oliver, whoever started a family first. He wanted his sons and their families close by and safe behind the compound walls."

179

"Really?" I ask, stunned. "We have our own place? This is really ours?"

"Sure is." Oliver says, standing in the doorway of the house with a big smile on his handsome face.

Looking around, I see that houses are lined on both sides of the dirt road leading up to the clubhouse off in the distance. But this one is separated, on its own.

"Why are we away from everyone else?" I ask.

"Dad wanted us to have our own space. Perks of being the Boss Man's sons. But I guess in this case it was a good idea. Don't want the neighbors hearing us." Oliver wiggles his brows, and my cheeks flush. "You can be pretty loud, Firefly."

"We all are." Talon laughs, coming out from behind Oliver. "This place is awesome!"

"Come." Tyson says, holding out his hand. "Let me show you our new home."

Tyson escorts me up the steps and into the house. The front door leads into an open floor plan. No walls or doors to separate the space. To the left is the living room with a big sectional couch separating the living room from the entryway. There is also a massive TV that's mounted to the wall with a fireplace below it.

To the right is a dining room with a cute picnic style table big enough to fit at least 10 people.

We make our way further into the house, to a massive kitchen that has state of the art stainless steel appliances. I walk around checking out everything. The fridge is huge and even makes ice!

The stove is a flat top. *Thank god, so much easier to clean.* There is a nice contrast between the wooden cabinets that are a dark brown, almost black color and the white marble countertops. This place is beautiful. Something I could see myself designing.

As I take another look around, I see some things I missed before. Over in the corner sits a brand new high chair. The living room has a little play mat off to the side, butting up next to a little toy box with baby toys in it. I smile when I realize this really is our home.

"So I know Melody is only three months old, but we wanted to be prepared.

The place has a fully furnished basement with three rooms, upstairs has four rooms and there's at least one bathroom on each floor. So there's enough room for everyone to have their own space if they want." Tyson says, leaning back against the kitchen island.

"But Ben and I are gonna share a room. I mean who wants to sleep alone? Plus if we get sick of each other, we could always just get away by going to the man cave." Talon grins. "Man cave?" I say, raising a brow.

"It's pretty awesome. We have a gaming system down there, couches and chairs, a bar, a pool table; there's even a fridge." Oliver says.

"Well, what about us girls?" I pout.

"I'm sure there's ways you could persuade us to let you hang out there." Talon says, pulling me to him and placing a heated kiss on my lips.

"Yeah, not happening. You can have your man cave." Charlie scrunches up her nose.

"Well, no one was offering for you to come in anyways." Talon sticks his tongue out at Charlie. Charlie smirks before grabbing one of Talon's nipples through his shirt and twisting.

"Ouch!" Talon shouts. I giggle at the shocked look on his face. "Did you just give me a titty twister?"

Charlie gives him a smug look. "Yeah, and a wet willy." She sticks her finger in her mouth and shoves it in Talon's ear before taking off.

"You're gonna pay for that, Charlotte Ross!" Talon growls, chasing after Charlie. "Not the man cave!" He shouts, following her down to the basement.

I can't help but smile and shake my head at their antics.

"Butterfly," Ben says, getting my attention. "I wanna show you something." He leads me up the stairs to the top level. He shows me everyone's designated room, telling me his and Talon's are in the basement. Probably because they plan on fucking any chance they get. Smart.

Melody's room is a lot like the one she has at Rick and Amy's. Charlie has her own room so whenever the guys and I do group activities she has a place to escape to. And my room is perfect. It has a big king size bed with a teal bed set much like the one I had back at school, and a TV mounted on the wall.

The whole room was exactly how I always wanted my room to be if I could afford it. I even have my own bathroom!

"This is what I wanted to show you." Ben says, leading me to another door off to the side.

"Oh my god." I breathe, looking around to see the wall lined with books and a little spot with blankets and pillows in the corner.

"I thought we could have our own little spot. You know, so we can keep reading together. It has all the books we've read already plus all the ones you told me you wanted to read."

I run my fingers along the book spines as I take in the accumulation of all my favorite stories. "It's amazing." I say, looking up at Ben with tears in my eyes. "Thank you."

"Hey," he says softly, bringing me into his arms. "Are you okay? Why are you crying?"

"I'm fine." I say into his chest. "Just happy and overwhelmed, but in a good way. So many amazing things in such a short amount of time. It's a lot to take in but I promise I'm happy with it all."

"Good." He says, squeezing me tight and placing a kiss on the top of my head.

"Knock, knock." Tyson says. "Sorry to intrude, but Rick and Amy are here."

We head downstairs to find Amy lightly crying in Rick's arms as Oliver holds Melody looking unsure what to do about Amy.

"Amy? What's wrong?" I ask, placing my hand on her shoulder.

"I'm just sad. I'm gonna miss you two." She sniffs.

My heart squeezes, and my eyes start to water. "We're not too far. Still in the same town. You're welcome over anytime. And trust me, we will be over so much you're gonna want to kick us out." I laugh.

"Never. Our home will always be yours too." Amy says. "And I expect you to abuse your free babysitting privileges any time. I mean it. You just have to hand her over and I'll watch her. Any time of the day, for any amount of time."

For a few moments we just hug and cry together. This woman is one of the best people I've ever had the privilege of having in my life. She is my hero, my role model, my mother. Blood means nothing in this case. She is everything I wish I had growing up, and I'm honored to have her in my daughter's life.

"Thank you." I say, holding back more tears. "For everything you've done for me; for Melody. You opened your home and your heart to a poor teenager with a shitty life.

You took me in and saved me from a horrible situation. You gave me a roof over my head, food in my belly, and a shoulder to cry on. You will always be my mother. My one and only mother."

She bursts into another fit of tears, and we cry some more.

"I'm so glad to call you my daughter. You're everything and more, Emmy. Always remember you were never a burden on us. You made our lives better and brighter and that little angel over there just made it all the more perfect. I'm proud to call you my daughter."

"Hey, Kiddo." Rick grins although. I see his eyes are a little glassy with his own tears.

"Hi, Dad." I smile back.

"I will never get tired of hearing that." He hugs me tight. "And everything Amy just said? Yeah, that goes for me too."

"Really, Rick?" Amy laughs and blows her nose with a tissue. "Stealing my words as your own?"

"You know I'm not good with all that stuff."

"It's okay. I feel the same way." I lean up and kiss him on the cheek.

I show them the house and we hang out for a little while with Melody in my arms, where she's meant to be.

"Emmy." Tyson says. I look up from my sleeping daughter. I just nursed her and she fell asleep quickly after that. I should have put her in the crib, but I didn't want to let go of her just yet. "I want to take you somewhere." He gives me a panty-melting smile. I can tell whatever he wants to show me has him excited.

"I got her." Charlie says, coming into the room and taking Melody from me. "She's in good hands."

"I know." I kiss Charlie and follow Tyson.

"So where are we going?" I ask as we walk down the road, hand in hand.

"To the clubhouse."

When we get to the clubhouse we are greeted with a round of cheers like always. Steel gives me a hug before Tyson drags me into the back.

"There she is." Tyson's voice is filled with excitement. "Fuck, have I ever missed wearing this." He takes a leather cut off a hook and slips it on, showing me the Phantom Reapers logo on the back. A skeleton reaper with a scythe in its hand with the name of the MC.

"Damn." I whistle. "My man is bringing sexy back in his leather jacket."

He gives me a hungry look. "You like what you see?" He prowls towards me, backing me up against the wall. I swallow hard, all forms of joking gone. My knees go weak and my pussy clenches for this sexy biker.

"Yes." I breathe.

"You know, I think I'm gonna fuck you with this on." He says while tracing his finger down my jaw. I close my eyes, trying to steady my breathing.

"I'd like that."

"And you can wear this." He says, backing away from me. I instantly feel cold from the loss of his body contact and open my eyes with a pout. It quickly changes to surprise when he pulls out a box and places it on the desk.

"What's that?" I ask.

"Open it, Princess." He says with a wolfish grin.

With an excited smile, I open my present. Inside I pull out a leather jacket of my own. "Tyson," I breathe as I open it up to see the whole thing. "It's gorgeous."

"It's a little different from ours. And you're the only woman to have one. But I want everyone to know whose girl you are, and who has your back."

I turn it over to see the back. It has the MC name only.

"Dad said no at first, because only official members can have one like mine. And I don't think you want to be a prospect. So we came to a compromise." He shrugs.

"I love it." I squeal, making him chuckle as I quickly slip it on.

"Damn, Princess." He growls, and my eyes snap up to his.

"No fucking in my office!" Steel shouts from the bar, followed by some wolf whistles and laughs.

My cheeks heat, and I bite my lip holding back a smile as I have a sexy stare down with my man.

"Cock blocker." He mutters under his breath, making me giggle. "Here, these are to go with it." Tyson says, and takes something else out of the box. Riding gloves. Then hands me a brand new helmet.

"What do I need these for?" I ask, brows pinched in confusion.

"We're going for a ride."

My eyes go wide. "On your bike?" I ask, surprised because riding a biker's baby is a big deal.

"You don't honestly think I would miss out on taking my girl out for a ride, do you?" He asks.

I bite the inside of my cheek and look down at the helmet. Last time I went for a ride was with Oliver and I was worried the whole time, clinging to him like we were about to crash at any moment. But I think the main reason for that was because Oliver had not been riding for that long when he took me out. Tyson has been riding for years, at least six or more.

"Princess." Tyson gets my attention. "Do you think I'd ever put you in harm's way?"

"No." I say without hesitation.

"Then, trust me. Let's go for a ride. I want to take you to one of my favorite places."

Alisha Williams

I take his hand and he leads me out to his bike. A sexy black Harley Davidson sits at the end of the row.

"I don't think you've ever shown me your bike." I say, hanging my helmet on the handlebars so I could run my fingers along the sleek body.

"She's been in storage. I haven't had the time to ride her." He says, slipping on his own riding gloves.

"I'm sorry."

"You have nothing to be sorry about, Princess."

"Yea I do; you haven't been here with your club brothers, doing things you love. Instead, you have been babysitting us for the past two years, almost two anyways."

"I may not have had much of a choice in the beginning, but I'm glad my dad put me on that assignment. If I never took that job at the school, never got the chance to be around you, then we may never have ended up where we are." He puts his helmet on the bike, and pulls me into his arms.

"You know, you got on my nerves a lot when you first started at the school. Always on my ass about everything." I grin.

"Yeah. I remember. I loved getting under your skin." He smirks, giving me a kiss then nipping at my bottom lip, making me putty in his arms.

"I used to bitch to the girls about you. But really, I just thought you were hot as fuck."

"Yeah." He smiles, only inches from my face. "You were a stubborn Princess. You know how many times I wanted to spank your ass for being a sassy little brat?" His voice is deep and rumbling out from inside his chest, and fuck, if my pussy doesn't quiver.

I'm wet for him, and now I'm about to go on a ride, my arms around his hard body. Fucking kill me now before I explode with need.

"Some things never change." I say, then pinch his ass.

"You little-" he growls. I dart away with a giggle, snatching my helmet from the handlebar and putting it on, snapping the visor shut so he can't see my face.

He narrows his eyes at me, silently promising punishment for that little stunt. I can't fucking wait.

"Get on, Baby Girl." He says, straddling his bike and starting it up with a growl.

I get on, wrapping my arms around him, resting my head against his back. Relaxing my mind and reminding myself I'm safe with him.

We drive for a while. The rumble of the bike is *not* doing any favors for my aching core. But there's something freeing about riding down the highway, the wind surrounding you. Nothing to box you in. Total freedom.

"See, that wasn't so bad." Tyson says, shutting off the bike, and taking off his helmet.

"No, it was actually a little relaxing." I say, taking off my own.

We went off the main road and down a narrow dirt path, stopping by a little lake.

"How did you come across this place?" I ask, taking in the beauty of the secluded lake. There are ducks swimming along the edges, but otherwise it's quiet and peaceful.

"When Oliver got sent away I was pissed. I wanted to go after Dagger and kill him. But it was all a big fucking mess. Oliver didn't know who we were, even though we knew who he was. So, I was helpless at that moment. Not wanting to be around anyone I took off with no destination in mind, just drove until I found this place. It was quiet, no one was around. I stayed here for hours. After that, it became my go-to place when I needed to just get away from everything. Sometimes I'd bring food and stuff and just stay here for the entire day."

"It's beautiful. Thank you for sharing this with me." I wrap my arms around his waist and tilt my head up to see his face.

"You're the only person to ever ride with me, you know that?" He asks, pulling me closer. "I never had another woman even touch my bike, and I never brought another soul here. Only you, Princess, always you."

"I love you." I kiss him and he quickly deepens the kiss, threading his fingers through my hair, licking the seam of my lips for me to open. And I do. His tongue dominates my mouth until I'm nothing but a boneless, needy mess in his arms.

"I love you so *fucking* much, Princess." He growls before kissing me again.

"Tyson," I whimper against his lips. "I need you." I whine. Okay, so I sound like a spoiled brat, but fuck, he's just so damn sexy and I'm always a goner when I'm with him. Hell, when I'm with any of my lovers. There's no chance for me. Leave me here to die from orgasms. It's okay, I'll happily accept my fate.

186

"What do you need from me?" He asks, his lips brushing against mine.

"You. Your lips, your tongue, your monster cock. Fuck, I don't care what at this point. I just need some part of you."

He kisses me again, before leading me over to his bike. He starts it up, but doesn't get on. I stand there confused.

"I wanna try something." He says, and the look on his face is pure sin and sex, and *fuck,* I want whatever he has in mind.

"Okay?" I answer sounding unsure, confused as to why he would need his bike running right now.

He says nothing more, crouching down to pull down my shorts and panties together. "Step out."

"Tyson!" I shout, quickly looking around, shocked that he's just exposing me out in the open.

"We're alone, Princess, now step out of these." His voice pitched low and commanding. I do as he says, still wary about this whole thing. What if some weird man lives in the woods or something? I've heard some really fucked up stories about killers in the woods. You never know.

"Emmy." He growls. "No one is gonna come out of the woods and murder us. Now stop overthinking this, and get on my bike."

Oops, I must have said that out loud.

I look at him, at his bike, and then back at him. *Why the fuck not?* He helps me up on the bike backwards, taking my arms and wrapping them around the handlebars and placing my hands on the grips. My body is up high enough that he doesn't have to move too far down to reach my pussy.

I'm laying there, pussy exposed to him, and the look of hunger on his face has my core dripping for him. "Look at that pretty pink pussy. *Fuck,* I will never get tired of eating you, devouring you until you scream my name and cream all over my face." He growls, taking my legs and hiking them up over his shoulders. "Do you know how fucking sexy you look on my bike, presenting yourself to me like the finest delicacy a man could wish for? Best thing I could ask for."

The vibrations of this bike only adds to the amazing sensations that are running through my body. My breathing is coming out quick and choppy already.

He looks so fucking sinful right now with his shaggy, raven hair. His cut fitted snugly over his muscled, toned arms. And I can see some of his tattoos sticking out at the top of his black tee. I want to sit up and trail my tongue along his collarbone, but I'm not going anywhere right now, even if I tried.

"Talk about meals on wheels." I joke. He raises a brow with a smirk of amusement. Before I can fully sink into the embarrassment of my corny-as-fuck joke, he scoots back a little before diving between my legs.

"Tyson!" I cry, tossing my head back with a moan as his tongue starts to lap at my glistening center. "Oh, god." I grip the handlebars and accidently rev the engine, making me jolt in surprise.

Tyson chuckles against my core, adding to the vibrations and it feels fucking fantastic.

"Yes. Right there." I start to whimper as his tongue and lips work me over, but he holds me in place with his big hands. My legs wrap around his head, holding him closely while my body begs me not to let him go.

"That's it, Princess." He speaks against my lower lips. "Let the world know who owns this pussy, even if there's no one around to hear you scream. Let it all out. Cum for me." He coaxes as my body begins to tremble from the wicked things that his tongue is doing to me.

"Ty." I whine, feeling my impending orgasm start to erupt.

"Let go, Princess. Give it all to me." He licks and sucks some more, taking my clit into his mouth, giving it a little nibble. My legs are shaking, my head tosses back and forth because it's all too much, but not enough at the same time; his mouth, this bike, and when he adds two thick fingers inside of me, I'm a fucking goner.

I scream out and yes, I scream his name so fucking loud it scares the damn birds in the trees, sending them flying away.

"I love it when my name comes out of your mouth that way. It's the only time I'll allow you to raise your voice at me." He snarks, licking his lips. I swallow thickly as I try to clear my vision, my head still floating on cloud nine.

He gives my ass a smack, making me squeal, and he chuckles at the threatening glare I give him. He knows I love it and I'm not fooling anyone anymore.

"We should get going." Tyson says, helping me off the bike and back to my removed clothing. "As much as I'd love to keep you here all to myself for a little while longer, Oliver has been blowing up my phone." He shows me the five missed calls and twenty unopened texts. I giggle as I look through them. Most of them consist of Oliver calling Tyson a selfish dickhead for hogging me.

I hand him back his phone with a grin. "He needs to learn how to share. He's had me since we were five." I roll my eyes.

"Trust me, I love to remind him of that whenever I get the chance."

Tyson helps me on his bike, and I look up at the sky to see that the sun is already starting to set. Wrapping my arms around him, I sigh as I feel so much emotion in this moment. Being with Tyson like this, outside the school where we can finally be a real couple, makes me so fucking happy.

We head back to the compound and by the time we get there it's dark, but as we drive through the gates and closer to the clubhouse I can see the place is packed.

Tyson parks his bike and helps me off. "Thanks for coming on a ride with me, Princess. I love seeing you on my baby." He kisses me sweetly and I melt into him, sighing against his lips.

"Let's get in there before they come out here looking for us and I have to hear them bitch and complain." He grumbles against my lip. I giggle and take his hand, allowing him to bring me into the clubhouse.

"Hey you two, it's about time." Steel greets us. "Hope you don't mind, but we felt like tonight called for an all-around celebration. It's not everyday that my son and his girl graduate."

"Oh, of course. I love being here, and everyone is amazing. I'm glad they could come by and celebrate."

"Any excuse for some beers and a BBQ!" One of the members shouts, raising his beer before downing it. I laugh and shake my head as Tyson starts to lead me out of the room after saying goodbye to his dad.

"Where are we going?" I ask as he takes me out the back door. "And where are the others?"

Tyson doesn't answer me, he just keeps leading me to wherever. When we walk around the back and into the outside lounging area, my eyes go wide with surprise as I see the whole place lit up with fairy lights.

My eyes land on the people I love most in this world. Oliver, Ben, and Talon stand there wearing dress pants and button-down shirts, looking all sexy. Charlie stands next to them in a flowy summer dress with Melody in her arms in a cute little flower romper. Her hair is in little piggy tails on the top with a headband that has a flower matching the one on her outfit.

My eyes start to tear up as I take in their happy faces.

"Surprise, Shorty!" Talon shouts. Using the perfect opportunity to combine the viral TikTok video, and my nickname.

I burst out laughing as Oliver looks at Talon like he's a fool. But he's my fool. *Fuck, I love these guys.*

CHAPTER 21
Tyson

"WHAT'S ALL THIS?" Emmy asks as she takes in everything around her with wide, excited eyes.

"Well, I told the guys about the conversation we had last week, the one about how it sucks that we didn't get a normal graduation and no prom? And they agree that it sucks, because proms always look so fun on TV; getting dressed up, with fancy hair, taking lots of photos, with all the dancing and drinking until you pass out." Charlie stops when she sees Emmy's face. Emmy is trying to hold back a fit of giggles, and I roll my eyes at a babbling Charlie.

"Anyway," Charlie laughs. "We thought we would give you your own mini prom." Charlie opens her free arm encompassing the decked out backyard. "Now there's no fancy hair or dresses, but there are pretty dresses and awesome music."

"You guys are the best!" Emmy says, rushing over to give each of them a hug and kiss. "And you," Emmy gushes at Melody. "Look at you, you are so stinkin' cute!" Emmy kisses Melody's face all over. Melly just looks at her mama like she's a crazy lady, but takes all the love with no fuss.

"Give me this cutie pie." Oliver says with a smile, taking the baby from Charlie and looking at Emmy. "Go with Charlie to get dressed."

Emmy takes Charlie's hand and they both race off down the street towards our new place with cheers and laughter.

"Thanks for taking her out so we could set this up." Ben says, taking two beers from the tub of ice.

"Trust me, man, it was all my pleasure." My grin is cocky as I take a beer for myself and crack it open, taking a sip as I take a seat in one of the fancy lawn chairs. He heads over to stand with Talon, handing him a drink as they start in on a conversation.

"Why do you look like the cat who got the cream?" Oliver asks with an accusing look on his face as he bounces the baby around to keep her from fussing.

"Oh because, brother, I got the cream alright. *All* the fucking cream." I feel like a king right now. Eating out the sweet pussy of the woman I love has while being on my bike, with her naked from the waist down and a sexy as fuck leather jacket on? My ultimate wet dream came true.

"Where the hell did you do that? Where did you guys even go?" Oliver asks.

"I took her for a ride." I smirk.

His eyes go wide. "She actually got on your bike?"

"Yup. We went to one of my favorite places, then I had me a snack." I grin behind my beer.

"You took her out to eat?" Ben asks, taking his attention away from his conversation with Talon. Poor dude has no idea what we're talking about.

"You could say that. But I was the one who got to eat."

"Why didn't you share it with her?" Ben asks, looking annoyed with me. *Fuck, this is too good.*

Talon raises a brow, looking at me, before he clues into what this whole conversation between me and Oliver is *really* about.

"Babe. I'm pretty sure the snack he's referring to is our girl, not *with* our girl." Talon wraps his arms around Ben from behind and kisses his neck. "Much like I plan on doing the next chance we get."

"Ohhh." Ben says, a flush of red growing on his cheeks.

"The mix of her purrs with my bike's roars was sweet, sweet music to my ears." These guys had her for a whole year before me, damn right I'll be rubbing my alone time with her in their faces, at least for a while.

"You ate her out on your bike?" Oliver grins. I just shrug with a smirk. "I'm doing that next time. She didn't seem like a fan of riding when I took her out that one time. But I guess that's changed now."

"Probably had something to do with the fact that you were driving for less than a year, and I've been doing it for a while now. I'm more experienced." I say with a wink.

"Doing what for a while now?" Emmy asks as she and Charlie make their way over to us.

"Riding. Tyson was just telling us all about how he kept you distracted while we set this up." Oliver taunts.

Emmy's cheeks match the color Ben's were just a moment ago, as she looks at me with her big brown eyes. But they quickly turn heated when she sees the look I'm giving her in return.

My eyes eat up her body, taking in every inch of her. She looks stunning. She has on a pair of flat, strappy sandals and a purple summer dress, while her hair is braided to the side. She's not wearing her glasses, so I guess she put in a pair of contacts. She doesn't wear them much, but I think she's beautiful no matter which she chooses.

I get up, place my beer on the table, and pull my girl into my arms. "You look gorgeous, Princess." I say, sneaking a kiss before Charlie slaps my arm.

"No messing up the makeup until after photos." She scolds me. Emmy giggles and gives me a hug before going over to the others.

One of the Old Ladies is a photographer and offered to take our pictures. She said she would love to do a baby photoshoot with Melody and was sad that she wasn't able to do new-born photos also. Emmy was over the moon excited at her offer because Emmy wants photos for everything when it comes to Melody. Her phone is full of baby pictures. Most of them look the same to me but she swears they are all different.

I stand back and enjoy the pure happiness radiating off Emmy. Her smile is so bright and beautiful I can't look away.

They get photos with everyone, doing a bunch of different poses, everyone taking turns with the baby.

"Ty, come here." Emmy shouts for me to join.

"This is your day, Princess, and theirs." I reply.

She folds her arms, giving me an adorable mad face. She knows I don't like photos, but I don't think she's gonna back down until I take some.

"Tyson Kingston! Get that sexy ass over here right now and take photos with your girlfriend and daughter, damn it!"

Okay she's gonna pay for being a little brat later but I'm not gonna lie, she's hot when she's mad.

Ignoring my growing dick, I march right over to her, get right in her face, cupping her cheeks in my hands, and kissing her so hard I can feel her knees start to buckle. Clicks of a camera tells me this is all getting documented, but she wanted photos. *Right?*

"Wow." She breathes when I pull back.

I give her a cocky smirk. "Isn't this what you wanted? Lovely couple photos?"

She nods, her eyes glazed over with lust. She looks over to Anna, the one taking the photos. "I'm gonna need those."

Anna laughs. "You can have them all."

I take Melody and quickly get over my dislike for photos as we do a few different poses.

Why make a big deal when something so little makes my girl so happy? I know I would hate myself for not having something like this to look back at later.

A million and one photos later, Emmy is beyond happy.

"Dance with me?" Charlie asks, grabbing Emmy by the hand and pressing a button on a little remote in her other hand to turn on the portable speaker.

Fancy Like by Walker Hayes starts playing and I laugh because Emmy really is obsessed with the song. They start dancing, big smiles on their faces. I grab another beer, sit down in the chair I was in earlier, and watch my girl.

They sing along, doing a horrible version of the dance moves and only end up belly laughing every time they trip over each other's feet. This is something I didn't know I needed; the chance to just relax and enjoy being with the ones I love. Even just for the night.

Talon and Ben join them, pulling Emmy away and trapping her between them, but I don't think she has an issue with it. They grind into her, and after a minute, it starts to look like they are ready to fuck her right here.

Before things get too hot and heavy, Oliver takes his turn, and the other two resume their dry humping with each other.

"It's nice to see her smile like that." Charlie says, sitting down next to me with a sleeping Melody in her arms.

"It really is." I say, taking a sip and watching my girl and my brother slow dance as they kiss, holding each other close. She breaks the kiss, smiling at him with a little giggle before tucking her face into his neck.

"I want everyday to be like today." Charlie says, grabbing my beer and taking a sip. I give her a dirty look but she just smirks and rolls her eyes. "Happy, carefree, and constantly smiling."

"I know everyday can't be like this, but I'll try my damnedest to give her as many moments as I can to make up for it."

"Same."

We sit in silence for a few minutes watching the others before I turn to her. "You know, if someone told me a few years ago that I would end up with the girl of my dreams, the one I watched from afar, whom I protected while being in the background, only to share her with not just my brother, but his best friends and hers as well, I would have laughed in their face. But now, I can't picture my life any other way. This feels... right."

"So have you changed your mind about joining in on their group activities yet?" Charlie asks, wiggling her eyebrows.

"Have you?" I ask, raising a brow.

She scrunches up her face. "Eww, no. I know what they do, and sorry but I do not want to be around when they have their confetti poppers flying about before they explode everywhere."

"Did you just refer to a dick as a confetti popper?" I laugh.

"Well, I mean." She takes one hand, makes a jerking motion before pretending it explodes with a pop. "Like confetti. But like nasty, wet, and gooey confetti."

"I don't know. I love when Ben's confetti explodes all over me." Talon says with a shrug as he grabs a beer from the tub next to me.

"Oh. My. God. Eww. Just... no." She scoffs in disgust, making Talon laugh as she gets up and takes Melody inside.

Letting Emmy have her fun, I head inside too and talk to a few people. Amy and Rick take Melody so we can all let loose and drink. We didn't want her to go too far, so Steel offered up his apartment for the night.

Amy tells me to convince Emmy to enjoy herself and have a few drinks. To explain that it's okay while breastfeeding as long as she dumps everything she pumps tomorrow, just to be safe, and feed Melody by bottle for the day.

I agree with her. Emmy deserves to let loose for the night and enjoy herself. She hasn't gotten to drink like the others in over a year. So when they walk in, I order Emmy her favorite drink, and help her let loose.

Oliver

Ok, so when Tyson told me what Amy said about convincing Emmy to have some drinks and let loose, I agreed. Emmy was all for it even though she was bummed about having to pump and dump, but because it was a special occasion, she eventually agreed.

What I didn't expect was for her to be such a lightweight. An hour and three drinks later, she was dancing on top of the bar.

My dad and the others are laughing, not caring about how she's acting, but I don't like how some of the new prospects are looking at her.

"Emmy, baby. Come down here and play pool with me." I hold my hand up to help her down.

She stops dancing and looks down at me with a big grin. "Yes!" She shouts. "I'm gonna whoop your ass!"

I laugh, helping her down. She stumbles a little on our way over to the table. She grabs a cue stick to get ready to play, but brings it back a little too freely, and smacks one of the members in the back of the head. He looks over at her with a murderous look but it disappears when he sees who hit him.

"Sorry man." I say, my voice a warning not to say anything about it.

"No problem." He says, rubbing the back of his head.

"Sorry!" She shouts at him then giggles turning to me. "He looks pissed." She imitates his pissed off look.

"Come on, Firefly, the winner gets bragging rights." I laugh.

We play a few rounds and I let her win because, let's be honest, she's too drunk to play properly and a pissed off Emmy is not what I want right now.

Just as we finish the last game, Emmy starts to rub her 'wins' in my face when an overly flirtatious laughter catches Emmy's attention.

She follows the sounds and sees a Sweet Butt standing by the bar with Tyson sitting in the seat next to her. Her beautiful smiling happy face is gone, and something really fucking scary replaces it, but before I can grab her or even say anything, she takes off towards them.

I look around and lock eyes with my dad. He shakes his head, not at my girl but at the girl who has balls to try and flirt with Tyson. He does nothing, just sits back and watches.

There's a rule here that if one woman messes with a taken man, we let the women work it out. My father let Emmy do that when Mariah tried shit with me, and he's gonna let it happen now with Emmy and this girl.

"You know, you don't have to share a girlfriend with your brother, you can have me all to yourself." Just as the girl is about to touch Tyson's arm, Emmy intercepts her by putting herself in between them.

She grabs the beer from the Sweet Butt's other hand, smashing the glass against the side of the bar then puts the broken bottle against her neck.

"You know, you're not really all that smart, are you? Everyone knows Tyson is taken. You fuck half of these bikers and that's not enough for you? You have to go after a man in a committed relationship? How fucking low can you go?" Emmy sneers at her with revulsion. The girl's eyes are wide. Every member is standing now. No one says a word, waiting to see what happens next.

"Why do you get both of them?" The very stupid Sweet Butt spits. "Don't you have enough cock as it is?"

Tyson just sits there, and from the glazed look in his eyes I can tell he's tipsy. But the look he's giving Emmy right now says he's two seconds away from bending her over the bar and fucking her right here. I know how he feels. Right now, scary Emmy is fucking hot, being all possessive and shit.

"I'm gonna fucking kill you." Emmy says in a dangerously low voice.

Okay, time to stop this before she spills blood. "Come on, Queenie 2.0." I say, snatching the bottle from her hand and tossing it behind the bar. "I think it's time we get you home and into bed." I grab her and throw her over my shoulder.

"You, go to bed before you get yourself or someone else killed." I tell Tyson.

"I was about to tell her to fuck off, but my feisty Princess got here first." Tyson slurs while a smile spreads across his face.

"I got him, take her home." My dad says, coming up next to Tyson. I nod at him and start walking out of the clubhouse with a kicking and screaming Emmy on my shoulder.

"Let me down!" She shouts, hitting my ass with her little fist. "I'm not done with her. She needs to *bleed.*"

We continue past Talon, Ben, and Charlie, who are all passed out in a booth. *They are gonna feel like shit in the morning.*

"Enough of that." I slap Emmy on the ass as we start towards our new place. "If you kill someone, then cops get involved and no one wants that. You just got free."

"Fine, then give me a phone, I'll call my sister." She argues back.

"Babe, Queenie doesn't kill for flirting." I laugh.

"She might if I ask nicely."

She keeps going on about kicking a bitch's ass and how dare she come on to her man the whole way home.

"Oliver." She says, her voice a bit panicked, stopping mid-rant. "Olly, let me down. I'm gonna be sick."

I quickly put her on her feet, and she leans over, puking up everything she's drunk and eaten tonight. I hold back her hair and rub her back.

"Eww." She whines when she's done. "Why did you guys make me drink?"

"We suggested a few drinks, the rest was on you, Firefly." I chuckle as she straightens up. "You're the one who kept downing them like they were water."

"Ugh." She groans, wiping her mouth with the back of her hand. "But they taste like pop, and are so good."

"Come on, let's get you showered and into bed." She leans against me as we stroll along, tripping over her feet every now and then. By the time we get to the house, she's pretty much sleepwalking.

Scooping her up bridal style, I carry her up the steps, get my keys out of my pocket, unlock the door, close and lock it behind me before taking her right to the shower.

Sitting her on the toilet seat, I start to strip her out of her clothes. "Are we gonna have shower sex?" She mumbles, blinking up at me.

"No." I smile. "I never have, and never will have sex with you while you're this out of it."

"Why not?" She pouts adorably. "Don't you want me?"

"Always." I say, cupping her face. "But baby, I have too much respect for you to take advantage of you in this state. I can wait until your mind is a little clearer than this to have sex. A little tipsy is one thing, but this." I shake my head.

"Fine." She sighs.

I get a toothbrush ready for her, and she brushes her teeth; while she does that, I undress and turn on the shower.

"You fucking suck." She mumbles around the toothbrush. "We can't have sex, but you can just stand there all hot as fuck and naked. Tease."

"Rinse your mouth out and get your sassy ass in here."

She rolls her eyes and puts her toothbrush away. When she gets in the shower with me, she sticks her tongue out at me, earning her a tap on the ass.

She yelps. "What is it with you and your brother and ass slapping?" She narrows her eyes.

"You like it." I grin.

She considers it for a moment. "You got me there."

I help her shower, washing her tempting body. When I scrub her hair, she lets out a sexy moan and leans into my hands. Fuck, my dick can't help but react to that.

"Are you sure we can't have sex?" She asks, grinding her plump ass against my cock. "Because he seems to have other ideas. And, I think I puked up most of the alcohol anyways. I'm only tipsy now."

"Emmy." I growl and feel her shudder in my arms. "You can go one night without sex. And as much as I'd love to sink my cock into your perfect, wet pussy, it's one in the morning, everyone else is passed out, and we should be too."

"You can't say things like that." She whines.

"I'll make it up to you tomorrow, okay?" I kiss her cheek and bring her head back under the water to rinse out the shampoo.

"Pinky promise?" She pouts, holding up her pinky.

I bite the inside of my cheek, holding back a grin as I take her pinky in mine. "Pinky promise."

"With mind-blowing orgasms on top?" Her eyes look big and hopeful, and fuck, if my heart doesn't flutter. I fucking love this girl. My best friend in the whole fucking world. My heart and soul.

"Promise."

"You have to say it!"

"Fine." I huff out a laugh. "With mind-blowing orgasms on top."

"Good." She chirps. "Now dry me off and take me to bed."

"Yes, Dear." I chuckle.

We get out and dry off. I carry her to bed in her towel and by the time I lay her down, she's already fast asleep.

Tucking her in, I go to my room and grab a clean pair of boxers then head back to crawl into bed with her.

I pull her into my arms and close my eyes, willing myself to sleep.

When the nightmares started, nothing kept them away. I would wake up in the hospital screaming every night. When I got to school, I felt bad for waking Talon and Ben up. It got to the point where I would stay up as long as my body would allow, and only then when my body was too exhausted to function, did I have a dreamless night.

After Melody's first weekend visit at the school when I woke up screaming, I would pretend to fall asleep with everyone else, and when I knew they were fast asleep, I would go down to the weight room and work out until I was ready to pass out before showering and slipping back into bed.

I've noticed that the only time I don't need to overwork myself to have nightmare-free night is when Emmy is in my arms.

I'm pretty tired right now. It has been a long-ass fucking day, but my brain is still running wild with thoughts. Even though I was at the school most of the time, I was still a prospect and soon I'll become an official member. Some might think it's too soon, but they all know this is where my life is heading and are more than happy to have me be a Phantom Reaper officially.

This is what I've wanted for a while, I just never accepted my dad's offer until I knew Emmy would be okay with it. Even when I had no idea if she would ever talk to me again, I didn't want to make life altering decisions without her opinion.

But this is where I'm meant to be. With my best friends, my brother, and the love of my life.

The others don't know what they want to do, at least that I know of. We haven't really had time to sit down and talk about things. Tyson and I know what we want. And whatever Emmy and the others decide to do, we will support them, just like they do us.

I haven't told Emmy yet, but I found a therapist that comes highly recommended. I even had Harlow look into her. So this week, I will have my first appointment to see if we can get these nightmares under control.

I want to be the best man I can be for my girl and our daughter. I'm not too prideful to admit when I need help. Not when it could put my girls at risk.

Emmy stirs in her sleep and snuggles into me. Knowing I should get some sleep, I kiss the top of her head and listen to her steady breathing until I pass out. The others and I have a jam-packed week planned for Emmy, she just doesn't know it yet.

Now that we have the freedom to do whatever we want, we each plan on getting our own alone time with her. We all have special dates planned out for her and have been putting everything together for a while now. Being in that school left shitty options for dates. Now that we are out, we want to give her some of the best memories we can, while we can.

CHAPTER 22
Charlie

GOD, MY HEAD. It feels like a million tiny people with tiny hammers are bashing in my skull. And my back, fuck, *where the hell am I?*

Opening my eyes, I almost shit my pants when I come face to face with a drooling Talon, his eyes only slightly open. *Why the fuck am I sleeping next to him? Did he sneak into bed with me and Emmy?*

I don't even remember getting home last night. *Fuck, how much did I drink?* Groaning, I push myself up into a sitting position and realize I'm not in my bed, and Emmy is nowhere near me.

I'm still in the clubhouse, in one of the booths. Ben is sitting across from me sleeping, his head tipped back and mouth wide open as he snores. Looking under the table, I see Talon's eyes are fully open now, just staring at me.

I let out a yelp, and jump back, hitting my head against the booth. "Ouch!" I complain, rubbing the back of my head. "Why the fuck do you have to be so damn creepy?" I mutter.

Talon sits up and looks at me, confused. "Where are we?" He asks, his voice hoarse.

"The moon." I deadpan.

"Har, Har." He narrows his eyes and looks around. "Why the hell are we still in the clubhouse?" He looks over to a still sleeping Ben and lightly shakes him. Ben jolts awake with a loud, choked snore.

"What, what's going on?" He looks like he's ready to attack.

"Chill out Karate Kid, no need to go all Cobra Kai on us." I roll my eyes.

"Why are we in the clubhouse?" He asks, looking from Talon to me.

"That's the million dollar question." I sigh, rubbing my eyes, willing the pounding headache to go away. "I feel like death, and my mouth tastes like ass."

"So that's what you two do while you're alone?" Talon jokes. *Nope, too early for this shit.* I give him a mocking smirk while flipping him off.

"Look who's finally up. Good morning, sleeping beauties." Steel laughs as he walks into the room from his apartment in the back.

"Too loud." I whine, covering my ears as I place my head on the table.

"Do you know why we are here?" Ben asks.

"Well, you all got loaded, sat here and laughed about some really dumb shit for an hour, then passed out." Steel smiles.

"Where's Emmy?" Talon asks.

"Oliver took her home last night. You missed your girl being a real badass last night too." He chuckles. "My boy had to take her out of here kicking and screaming before she caused a blood bath."

My head snaps up a little too fast to look at him, but I ignore the throbbing pain. "Is she okay?" I demand.

"She's fine. Tyson, on the other hand, he's gonna feel like shit, even if it wasn't his fault."

"What did he do?" Talon growls.

"Nothing." Steel promises. "Emmy was on the bartop dancing and Oliver didn't like it, so he got her to come down and play pool. Tyson went to the bar to have some drinks and watch them play."

"Oh man! I missed my girl dancing all sexy on the bar. Was it all Coyote Ugly style?" Talon asks hopefully.

"No." Steel laughs. "She was just... enjoying herself. Anyways, while they were playing, a Sweet Butt went over to Tyson and started flirting."

"Oh, no." Ben sighs.

"Yeah, not the smartest thing to do, seeing as how everyone in this compound knows my sons are in a committed relationship. Emmy saw, and well...."

"Did she kick her ass?" Talon asks, an excited gleam in his eye.

"She took the girl's beer bottle, broke it against the bar, then threatened to kill her." Steel's eyes are shining bright with amusement.

"I'm never drinking again. I miss all the good stuff." Talon says with a pout.

"I'm sure someone around here has a recording of it." Steel says.

Talon perks up again. "Thanks, I'll be sure to ask around."

"I'm dead. I am so dead." A panicked Tyson comes running out into the bar in only his boxers. He looks around frantically before noticing us. He rushes over to his dad and grabs him by his shoulders. "Please, I beg you, tell me I didn't do something stupid."

"Calm down, son. You didn't do anything wrong." Steel reassures him.

"I didn't?" Tyson relaxes a bit. "I can't remember much, *fuck*! It's all bits and pieces.

All I remember was some Sweet Butt trying to flirt with me, then Emmy's murderous glare as she came charging over. Then nothing."

Steel retells him what happened. Tyson looks less worried, but a nervous look still shows on his face.

"Come on, let's go home." I say. "Today is the start of our week-long date event, and my date is first up."

"Does Emmy even know we all pretty much planned the next week out for her?" Tyson asks after running back into the apartment, getting dressed and saying goodbye to his dad.

"Nope." I say as we head out the door and start for our awesome new house. I still can't believe we are finally out of that school. I'm so excited to leave that part of our lives behind us and start living our new lives together. Free to do what we want, and watch Melody and other future kids grow up.

"So, what do you have planned for her?" Ben asks.

"Well, first I plan on showering so I don't smell like some homeless bum, and I'm gonna take a few painkillers to take this pounding in my head away. Then I'm gonna take Emmy to the arcade downtown."

"Oh, like recreating your first date?" Ben asks.

My eyes light up, a mischievous grin creeps onto my lips as I look at Tyson. "Sure, if they have a photo booth."

Tyson smiles, shaking his head. "Fuck, that was before I even thought I had a chance with Emmy. I can't believe I'm admitting this, but that was pretty hot." He laughs.

"The blush on her face when you saw the photos." I burst out laughing. "I still have them." I wiggle my eyebrows with a smirk.

"Of course you do."

The rest of the way, Talon bitches about why Tyson got to see these mystery photos and he can't.

When we walk through the front door of the house, the smell of bacon and eggs hits me. I moan at the delicious smell. Following it, I find Oliver standing at the stove cooking. He turns around when he hears us come in.

"Well, look what the cat dragged in." He laughs. "You all look like shit."

"Thanks, ever the charmer." I mumble, taking a piece of bacon and shoving it in my mouth like a starved animal. "Coffee!" I shout, seeing a fresh pot is already made. I rush over and make myself some of my own elixir of life.

"Where's Emmy?" Tyson asks.

"Should be in the shower by now, she was pumping when I came down here." Oliver says, flipping an egg.

"Shower time!" Talon cheers and looks at Ben. "Last one there has to watch the other person make our girl scream." He starts running to the stairs, losing articles of clothing as he goes. Ben takes off after him, both racing up the stairs.

"How's she doing?" Tyson asks, taking a seat on one of the stools at the kitchen island.

"Well, after I saved that Sweet Butt with a death wish by getting Emmy out of there, she got sick on the way home. I helped her shower, then we went to bed. She seemed fine this morning. I think she got most of the alcohol out of her system when she got sick, and the rest with some sleep."

"You didn't drink?" Tyson asks.

"One of us needed to have a clear head. I didn't mind, it was still a fun night. Even with trying to avoid a murder from occurring." Oliver grins, setting two plates full of food in front of us.

"I love being a Phantom Reaper, but I do not enjoy being around Sweet Butts. It's like some of them could care less who has an Old Lady and who doesn't. They want that title and are willing to fuck whomever to get it."

"Aww, look at you. You're all grown up." Oliver teases. "It seems like just yesterday when you had a different one for every day of the week."

A slipper comes flying through the air, hitting Oliver in the head. "Oliver Price Kingston. If you want to get your dick wet any time soon, you might want to watch what past memories you care to remind people of." Emmy warns.

"Fuck, that hurt." Oliver mutters, rubbing his head.

"Good." She cocks a brow.

"I'm sorry, Firefly. That's a past that no one needs to be reminded of."

"Thank you." She kisses him and looks at Tyson.

"Hi." Tyson smiles a little unsure.

"Hi." Emmy says, climbing into Tyson's lap. "So, I guess watching other women talking to you makes my inner Queenie come out." She grins. Tyson relaxes and I huff out a laugh as a smile takes over his face.

"Is it bad that it kind of turns me on?" Tyson asks, his voice low. He nips at her ear and I can see her whole body shiver as she squirms in his lap.

"She got mad at me because I wouldn't let her kill the girl. Then she said she would get her sister to do it." Oliver smirks, taking a bite of his food.

Tyson groans. "No! Do *not* get her involved. I don't think Harlow would have killed her, but she would most likely have some fun with her and we don't need that shit right now. I love the girl, she's my best friend; but I'm never ready for her level of crazy when she gets in moods like that."

"Wait... I thought Talon and Ben went to ravish you in the shower?" I ask, just now realizing that she's here, and they are not.

She laughs. "I was already out and dressed by the time they came up. So they just showered together instead."

With perfect timing a moan makes its way down the stairs, along with a loud "Fuck!"

Emmy just grins and shrugs.

"Well, then." I laugh. "I'm gonna use the shower downstairs, then we can get ready to go."

Her brows pinch in curiosity as she tilts her head to the side. "We're going somewhere?"

"Oh, right." I laugh. "Since we are now free to come and go as we please, we have each planned out a date we want to take you on. So, every day this week you will be wined and dined by your lovers." I grin. "Well, not really wined and dined, because I don't think any of them actually have that planned, but you get the gist."

Emmy's face slips into an excited grin. My heart races over how beautiful she is when she's happy. "Really?"

"Of course." Tyson says. "But tomorrow we have to go to the court and sign some paperwork with the judge and parole officers."

"Oh, right... Them." Emmy groans. "You know, I keep forgetting we have those."

"Well, with the school taking you under their care, they weren't really involved unless you were to get in trouble with the law again." Tyson shrugs.

"Anyways, that shouldn't take too long. Then you and Talon can go on your date." I say, walking up to her and tucking a piece of hair behind her ear.

"Actually, I wanted to do something tomorrow, if it's not too much trouble?" She asks, looking at all of us, nervously biting her lip.

"What's up?" Talon asks with a smug grin as Ben trails behind him with a flushed face. Both still have wet hair from their shower.

"I was just about to see if you guys were up to going somewhere before our date tomorrow." Emmy replies.

"Oh, good you told her about our plan." He smiles at us, then looks at Emmy. "We can go wherever you want to go, babe." Talon kisses her cheek in passing.

"So... I've been wanting to go back for a while, and I think with Melody being born, it's a good time to go." Emmy's eyes start to water.

"Go where, Princess?" Tyson asks softly, seeing the change take over her mood.

"I'd like to take Melody to meet Elijah." She pauses and we all look at each other with a sad understanding. "And I want you guys to meet him too." She chews on her lip, waiting for our reaction.

"We would love to meet him, Butterfly." Ben says, taking her from my side and pulling her into his arms in a tight hug. Talon comes up behind her, wrapping his arms around her from behind.

"I'd love that." He kisses her cheeks.

"I hope he doesn't mind me talking his ear off as I tell him all about his baby sister." I smile.

She huffs out a laugh and wipes her eyes from the tears that threaten to fall. "Awesome, thank you guys. Now, let's get our day started."

Breaking away from the others, I quickly shower and get ready for the day. Thankfully after the painkillers, food, coffee, and shower I feel so much better.

"I'm ready." I tell Emmy as I walk into the living room. She and Tyson are in the middle of a heated make out session as she dry humps him. They don't hear me over their moans.

Taking the newspaper off the table by the couch, I roll it up and walk over to the couch behind Tyson, and hit him upside the head with it. "Bad boy!" I scold. "It's my day today. So keep your wiener in your pants, and give me back my girlfriend."

They break apart. Tyson lets out a grunt of pain mixed with annoyance, as he turns his head to give me a murderous look. But my girl? She hides her smile behind her hand while trying to hold in her giggles.

"Sorry, baby." She says, a smile clear in her voice. "You're right. It's our day today." She gives Tyson one last quick kiss before climbing off his lap. "Let me go say goodbye to the others, and I'll meet you in the car." She takes off into another room.

"Did you really just hit me with a rolled up newspaper like a fucking dog?" Tyson asks, looking at the evidence in my hand.

"Well, if you want to act like a horn-dog, I'll treat you like a dog." I say, crossing my arms with a raised brow. My sass game is strong at the moment.

"You're like the little sister I never wanted." He mutters.

"Aww, and you're like the big brother I'm glad my parents never gave me." I snark back.

He smiles. "But you love me anyways." *Cocky fucker.*

"I wouldn't go that far." I roll my eyes. Then the dickhead puts me in a headlock and gives me a damn noogie. "Stop! Not the hair!" I shriek.

He lets go with a chuckle and heads outside to the car. I fix my hair with a pissed off huff. He's lucky I love my girl so much.

I get into the back seat, ignoring the smirk Tyson gives me.

"So where are we going?" Emmy asks, getting in the back with me. My annoyed mood brightens up right away because she chose to sit back here with me.

"We could use a day to just have fun and play games. So, I thought we could recreate our first date."

"I love that idea." She smiles. "And we even have Tyson with us like before." She laughs.

"Yeah." I glare at him in the rear-view mirror.

"Don't give me that look. I would love to be able to give you guys your privacy. But you're not going out without protection. And as much as I love the guys at the club, if I'm able to do it myself, I'd feel better."

"Fine, you're right." I sigh. I really hate Dagger. Crazy fucker wanted nothing to do with his daughter her whole life, then out of nowhere he wants her and Melody because she's dating his enemy's sons. I hate that he's been so quiet.

Tyson said the Phantom Reapers haven't seen any of their men outside the Savage Hellhound compound. So that means they are holed up in the middle of the fucking woods on the other side of the city.

"He will be in the background keeping us safe, you won't even know he's there, just like before." Emmy says, taking my hand and giving it a kiss.

We drive for about thirty minutes and stop in front of a strip mall with the arcade at the end.

"Soooo, I kind of did something." I said, turning to her in my seat.

"What did you do?" She asks with a smile.

"I kinda booked the whole place for the next three hours."

Her eyes go wide as she laughs. "Charlie!"

"I know it's crazy, but I wanted this to be about just you and I didn't want to have to wait to play games and listen to all the kids screaming as they ran around all hyped up on sugar."

"That must have cost a lot."

"Not as much as you would think." I shrug. "Plus I have the money babe, let me spoil you."

She says nothing for a moment, then sighs. "Alright, let's go."

We get out of the car and walk inside hand in hand. The place is empty, except for the music from all the games playing, giving the room an upbeat, chaotic feel.

"What should we do first?" I ask.

She looks around eagerly. "Everything."

I laugh as she grabs my hand, dragging me to our first game. We laugh as we compete, getting overly worked up when we lose, but rush over to the Skeeball game next.

We put a token in and the white skee balls slide down. "Wish me luck." I say, taking a ball in my hand.

"You got this!" She cheers.

I throw my first ball too hard and I get nothing. The second ball hits the top of the game and as I keep going, I only get small numbers. But every time I get one, Emmy gets super excited for me. Bless her soul for being so supportive. This girl really does own my heart. When I get to the last one, I try a different angle, but just end up hitting the side of the game, making it ricochet and sending it flying into the game station next to us.

"Oh, well." Emmy says, kissing my cheek. "I'm sure we will have better luck next game."

We did not do better, not once; and after a while I started to realize that it was a really good idea to not have anyone else around, because man, we are having the worst luck with these games.

While playing air hockey, I hit the puck so hard, it flew across the room. When we played the basketball game, Emmy tossed the ball so hard, it bounced off the backboard, sending it crashing into the game behind us. When we played dance-dance revolution, Emmy did a move that sent her dress flying up, exposing her sexy ass to me.

But even with all the hiccups, we were still laughing so hard that our sides were hurting.

"I'm kind of afraid to play this." Emmy laughs as we walk up to the dart game. "With our luck, this dart is gonna end up in someone's body."

"Nah, we'll be fine." I take the darts and toss three in a row. One misses, the other one hits just under a balloon and the third one manages to bounce off a balloon and onto the floor. The worker looks at us with pity, takes the big owl plushie off the wall and hands it to me.

"Just take it." He says, shaking his head. "You look like you could use a break from all the bad luck."

I take the owl, and look at Emmy. We both burst into laughter.

"I think we should grab something to eat, then head out." Emmy says. "We've pretty much done everything, and won nothing."

"Except this." I grin, holding up the owl, then hand it to her.

"By pity." She giggles.

"Still counts!" I sing, as we head over to the concession stand. We order a hot dog and nachos, and I get an extra order for Tyson and bring it to him. He thanks me, and eats in the corner.

"That was nice of you." Emmy says, taking a bite of her food.

"Poor dude looks bored as fuck." I shrug.

We eat and talk. Today may not have gone how some might expect a date to go, but it was perfect for us. I can tell Emmy had a good time, and that's all that matters.

"Ready to go?" She asks.

"Almost. There's one thing that's missing that we haven't done yet." I grin and point to the photo booth in the back of the room.

"Ohhhh." Emmy says, her cheeks staining red.

Taking her hand, I guide her over to the photo booth. Tyson watches us step in and I give him a dirty smirk. He just shakes his head.

"Sit." I tell her, pushing on her shoulders a little until she's on the little bench. She's watching me with curiosity and lust. Locking eyes with her, I get to my knees. Running my hands up her thighs, I push her dress up to her hips, exposing her panties. Her breathing starts to pick up as she clenches her fingers around the edge of the bench.

"What are you doing?" She asks in a breathy voice as I turn to change the settings on the photo booth screen.

"Giving us as much time as we can get before the timer runs out on our photos. But even with doing that, I only have one minute to make you cum. I don't have time for foreplay, so let me get right to work." I say, before adjusting her hips so I can pull off her panties. She says nothing, waiting for me to pleasure her. "Lean back a bit." I tell her. When she does, I take her legs and put them over my shoulders.

Her pussy is already wet and waiting for me. I love how easily we affect her. Just knowing some simple touches are enough for her. With her in place, I press the button.

Not wanting to waste time, I take my first lick. She sucks in a quick breath, and I groan against her core as her flavor coats my tongue. So fucking delicious. I continue to lick her like an ice cream cone, making sure none of the sticky, sweet goodness goes to waste. She moans my name softly, trying to keep quiet. Looking up, I see she's watching me with hooded eyes.

Click. One photo down, three more to go.

I watch her as I flick my tongue back and forth against her clit. Her hips jerk forward, but her hands stay at her sides as I work her into a frenzy. Biting her lip, she closes her eyes, enjoying every lick of my tongue.

Click.

Once I have her panting, and I know she's getting close, I dip my tongue in and out of her a few times before adding two fingers, thrusting in and hooking them right on her sweet spot. She cries out, unable to keep her voice down.

Tossing her head back, her hands grip my head to hold me to her as she rides my face, chasing her impending orgasm.

"Fuck! Oh god, Charlie. I'm gonna cum. Oh, oh." She moans. Knowing I need to send her over that edge, I suck her clit into my mouth as I rub her G-spot. She locks her legs tighter around me, coming so hard I feel her squirt all over my mouth and chin. It's been a while since she's done that. I feel pretty proud that I made her do that.

Click.

Lifting my head from her spent pussy, I keep her legs in place, as I wipe my mouth with the back of my hand. Her eyes are still closed. She sags back, breathing heavy as she comes down from her high.

Looking back, I see that there's five more seconds until the last photo goes off. I look at the camera with a big, cocky as fuck smile, and give a thumps up just as the last photo is taken.

"You good, baby?" I ask, carefully lowering her legs.

"Yeah, yeah I'm good. So fucking good." She slowly blinks her eyes open.

"I love you." I laugh.

"I love you too, Love Bug." She gives me a lazy smile. I help her get up and fix her dress. She doesn't even notice that I have her panties next to me. I grab those, then the owl, and we head out.

"Have a good time in there?" Tyson asks with a smirk as he makes his way over.

Emmy blushes but nods her head. "Oh, yeah." Tyson shakes his head.

The photos are done printing and I love every single one of them. I show them to Emmy, and her eyes go wide.

"Charlie!" She laughs, her blush deepening. "That last photo." She scolds.

"Hey, it was a proud moment for me. Had to keep the memory alive." I grab the back of her head and kiss her hard until she's moaning. Still kissing her, I open my eyes and look at Tyson. Grabbing Emmy's panties from my pocket, I toss them over to Tyson. He catches her soaked fabric with a surprised look. Breaking the kiss, I grab Emmy's hand and we take off for the car.

Looking over my shoulder, I give Tyson a wink as he stares at me in slight shock before rushing after us to keep up. I can't help but laugh, and Emmy is too lost in her after sex bubble to notice.

I love our dates. No matter what, they never disappoint.

CHAPTER 23
Emmy

YESTERDAY WAS AMAZING. My date with Charlie was some of the most fun I've had in a long time and I'm excited to see what the others have planned for me. They are so damn sweet to do this for me. It makes me feel bad that they are doing all this for me when I haven't done anything for them in return.

When I voiced this to them last night, Oliver was quick to reassure me that all they wanted was to see me happy, and me being happy made them happy. He continued to tell me that after everything I went through the last two years, I deserved to be pampered.

And if this was something that made them feel good, I'm not gonna question it just to make them feel bad about it. So, I thanked them again and cuddled on the couch between Charlie and Oliver as we watched the new Conjuring movie. I almost had a heart attack when the doorbell rang, but I recovered quickly when I realized it was only Amy bringing Melody back to us. I missed my little Jelly Bean so much.

As much as I appreciate my parents watching her, now that we are out and free to care for her ourselves, we would all rather have one of us watch her, unless we are engaging in a group activity that doesn't allow children. It's less of an occurrence now that we are out because we always try to include Melody as much as we can.

I ended up falling asleep between Ben and Talon, with Melody in her crib at the foot of the bed. It was our first official night with her in our new home, and I had the guys move it in here because I wasn't ready to be away from her after just getting her back.

I don't think the others were either because when I woke up in the middle of the night to feed Melody, Charlie was sleeping at the foot of my king size bed. Tyson was asleep in the rocking recliner in the corner of the room, and Oliver was getting Melody out of her crib to bring her to me.

Crawling out from between Talon and Ben, I move to the other side of Talon, so that Oliver could lay down next to me. He hands her over to me, telling me that he loves me, and gives me a kiss before doing the same with Melody.

After feeding Melly, Oliver lays her back in her crib and comes back to cuddle into me, both of us falling back to sleep quickly.

A hushed argument wakes me the next morning.

"I want to." Talon whispers.

"It's my turn." Charlie argues.

"No, it's mine, you got to change her last night."

"That was Ben!"

Sitting up, I find them over by the changing table. Melody just lays there looking up at her Daddy T and Mama C as they actually argue over who gets to change her diaper and clean her butt. It makes my heart melt that they want to be involved as much as they can.

"Umm guys, what's going on over there?" I ask with a giggle. Their heads snap over to mine.

"She's trying to steal my turn." Talon says, narrowing his eyes and pointing at Charlie.

She gapes at him. "Am not, because it's mine."

Melody starts to baby babble, smiling at her crazy parents. We all look at her, big grins plastered on our faces. We haven't seen or heard her do these things yet.

"Did she just?" Talon asks.

"Yup." Charlie beams.

They start baby-talking to her, praising her for being such a good girl. Melody soaks up all the attention, just looking back and forth between them.

"How about you do rock paper scissors to see who goes next. Maybe we should make up a chart to keep track of who's done it last, especially if you guys are gonna fight over her."

"That's a good idea. I'll make one while you're out on your date with Talon." Ben says, walking into the room.

"Good morning, Benny Bear." I greet him with a loving smile. He smiles back, bringing me into his arms.

"Hello, my Butterfly." He places a sweet kiss on my lips, making me sigh happily against his. "How's my Little Caterpillar?" He walks over and picks Melody up. "Oh, god. She smells horrible. Has no one changed her yet?" He asks, holding Melody up in the air.

Talon and Charlie look sheepish.

"We were just deciding who gets to go next." Talon says with a guilty look.

"Figure that stuff out in your free time. She should not have to be sitting in her own shit while you guys fight like children." Ben growls, placing Melody back on the changing table. He gets out everything he needs to change her and starts to do the job himself. "Don't worry, Melly Belly. Daddy Ben will make you smell all nice and pretty again." He coos down at her.

I'm just sitting here watching in amusement. But he does have a point. She should be attended to, no matter who does it. Everything else can wait.

Charlie sits on the bed, crossing her arms with a pout, and Talon just stands back to watch. He chews on his lower lip with downcast eyes; I can tell that he feels bad.

When Ben is done, he scoops her up into his arms. "There, all better." He kisses her forehead.

"I'm sorry." Talon says.

"I know. And I know you guys are excited to be able to finally parent her. Let's try to do better next time." Then he takes the poopy diaper and hands it over to Talon. "You can dispose of this." Talon looks at it with disgust and heads out the room. Charlie follows, and they pick their bickering back up.

"I think this little one is hungry." Ben says, handing me the baby as he sits next to me. Melody is munching away on her fist.

"Thank you." Once I get her latched and she starts to nurse, I look up at Ben with heated eyes.

"You know, watching you go all Papa Bear is a bit of a turn on. I'm not used to a growly Ben. I don't hate it." I smirk.

"Fuck." Ben breathes out. "I gotta go." He gets up and starts leaving the room.

"What!? Why?" I ask in shock.

He looks back. "Because, with the way you're looking at me, and how hard I am right now, I'm seconds away from handing her over to one of the others and fucking you into the mattress. But seeing as how we have a busy day ahead of us, we don't have time for that." He turns back around, and leaves the room. Now *I'm* in the mood. I'm sure I could convince one of the others to take this feeling away, but he's right, we do have a busy day.

"You know, I would not be surprised if you ended up as a big sister within the next year." I blow out a breath. "Your daddies are too addicting for their own good." *And they're all mine.*

We were in and out of the courthouse in no time. All we had to do was sign off on a few things and parted with a few words from the judge telling us he hopes he never sees us in his courtroom again. *Me and you both, buddy.*

Now we are parked outside the cemetery.

"Are you okay, Firefly?" Oliver asks, turning around in his seat to look at me.

"I will be." I say, my voice distant as I look out at all the graves.

"We can do this another time if you're not ready." Charlie says.

"No. No more waiting. He deserves to have us visit him. It's not right that it's been so long."

Oliver nods, his face trying to mask the pain he's feeling too. We need to be strong for each other right now.

I get Melody and her car seat out of the car as Oliver gets her stroller from the trunk. He opens up the stroller and takes Melody, clicking her car seat in place.

"How the hell did you do that so easily?" Tyson asks, coming from his car. He drove Talon and Ben here separately.

"It's not that hard. You just push this little button down and pull." Oliver says, pointing to the button on the side, and shrugs.

"Fucking show off." Tyson mutters under his breath.

Talon and Ben walk over with flowers and a teddy bear in their hands. I give them a brave smile and turn to the entrance of the cemetery.

Oliver holds out his hand and I take it, Charlie taking my other one. Tyson pushes Melody and the other two walk behind us.

They all surround me like a protective human bubble. They give me strength when I'm unable to be strong. They hold me up when my knees are too weak. They love me hard when my heart feels like it's gonna break. Without them, I would be an empty shell of myself. With them, I know I'll be able to do this.

When we get to his grave and I read his little headstone with his name and date of death, I break down. Everything comes back to me full force, causing me to drop to my knees with body wrenching sobs.

Oliver holds me until I have nothing left in me. A tear splashes onto my cheek and I know it's not mine, which tells me he's crying too.

When I'm finally able to speak, I wipe my eyes and get a hold of myself. "Hi there, baby boy." I smile, running my hand on the stone, tracing his name with my fingertips. "I'm sorry I haven't been by to see you in a while. Life has been pretty crazy. But that's all behind us now, and I promise we'll come by to visit whenever we can." Tyson squats down next to me, his eyes rimmed with red. He hands me Melody, giving me a kiss on the cheek.

"You're amazing, Princess. So *fucking* strong." He whispers in my ear before stepping back.

"There's someone I want you to meet. Elijah, this is your baby sister, Melody. She's so beautiful. I know you would have been an amazing big brother, and the two of you would have been the best of friends. You would never believe how she came into this world." I laugh. For the next 10 minutes I tell him all about the good things that have happened since his passing.

"Thank you." I say. "I know you had a hand in sending me our sweet baby girl. Thank you for bringing her to us, and giving us a new light to fill our lives. But don't worry, she will never replace you in my heart. There's enough room in there for everyone."

Looking around, I see that the others have sat down next to me, listening silently as I talk.

"Oh god, I'm so sorry." I say. "Here I've been, chatting away. Does anyone else want to say anything?"

"It's okay, Firefly. You take all the time in the world. We can wait." Oliver says.

"I think he would like to hear from his daddy."

Oliver looks at the grave, placing his hand on the stone. "Hey, Buddy." He says, his voice breaking a little. "First off, I wanna say, I'm sorry for not being there for your Mama when she needed me the most. I wish I knew about you so I could have helped her through it. I wish I could have gotten to meet you. Something tells me you would have been just like your mama, stubborn and smart."

"And loving and protective like his dad." I smile at him.

Oliver goes on about all the things he wishes he could have done with him, or what he thinks Elijah would have loved or hated.

When Oliver is done, I ask the others if they want to say anything.

"Umm.. Hi. You don't know me. I'm..." Ben looks at me, not sure what to say.

"This is your Daddy Ben." I smile at him. He gives me a wide grin back, tears forming in his eyes.

"I brought you this, in case you get lonely." Ben places a plastic clear box next to the grave. It has a little teddy bear holding a heart that says 'we love you' on it. I almost break down all over again. These men never cease to amaze me. I know I say this a lot, but I'm so fucking lucky to have them.

"I know it might get a little confusing but, hi, I'm Daddy Talon. You have four daddies and two mommies. But the good thing about that is you get all the love in this world."

"Oh, and one of your dads is also your uncle." Charlie points out with a smile.

I groan with a laugh. "I didn't even think about that! God, I wonder what people are gonna say about that."

"Fuck them. If they have anything to say about it, I'll kick their ass." Tyson growls.

We sit and talk some more, the sadness slowly easing away. I know coming here will never be easy, but I'm glad we came here, and I plan to continue coming in the future.

"We better get going, you still have your date with Talon." Tyson says, kissing me on the temple. They all say their goodbyes, placing flowers on the grave before heading back to the car.

"I'll meet you there." I tell Oliver who hangs back.

He nods and takes Melody to catch up with the others.

"Now that it's just me and you, I have a favor to ask you. We don't have an easy life, and there's a very bad man who is waiting in the shadows. We don't know what's going to happen next, but I'm asking you to please watch over your sister. She needs her big brother." I kiss my fingers then place them on the headstone. "I'll be back soon. Mommy loves you."

Talon

Fuck. Nothing could have prepared me for that visit to the cemetery. I might not have known Emmy when she lost Elijah, but in my heart it feels like he is just as much my son as Melody is my daughter. Seeing her break down like that broke something in me. I might not be able to do much to ease her pain, but I will try my hardest to help her in any way I can.

"So, where do you plan on taking me for our date?" Emmy asks, taking my hand in the back seat of Tyson's car.

After we left our visit this morning, we came back home to drop everyone else off and so that I could grab the bag I packed for my surprise date with Emmy.

"I'm not telling." I smirk. "You're just gonna have to wait until we get there."

She gives me an adorable pout. Leaning forward, I pull her lower lip into my mouth, giving it a little nibble before capturing the rest of her mouth with mine, and sliding my tongue in to caress hers. She gives me a throaty moan, and my dick perks up like that is the magic word that will unleash the beast.

"Enough of that. No sex in the back seat of the car." Tyson chides, getting in and starting up the car. "Unless it's me and Emmy." He gives her a sexy grin and wink that has her breathing heavier than she already was.

"It was just a kiss." She sasses back.

Tyson narrows his eyes at her and she bites her lip in response. "I don't care, knowing you guys, it was about to become a full-on sex fest."

"I mean, he's not wrong." I laugh when she smacks my arm.

On our way there, I keep my hand locked with hers, our fingers playing together as she leans her head against my shoulder. The windows are rolled down to aid us with this summer heat. Her hair blows around, but she doesn't care, she just enjoys being next to me with her eyes closed as we ride.

"We're here!" I say, a smile splitting across my face when I see the top of one of the waterslides come into view.

Emmy lifts her head and looks out the window and gasps. "Oh, my god! We're going to the water park!?" She asks me excitedly.

"Yup." I beam back, knowing my date idea has made her happy.

Her face falls a bit. "But I didn't bring a swimsuit."

"I got it here." I say, lifting the backpack next to my feet. "Got everything we need. Suits, towels, sunscreen and a change of clothes."

Her face brightens again. "This is gonna be awesome!"

"I thought this might be a little more fun than the typical date you're used to. Plus now that you're a pro at swimming, it's time to move on to the next level."

She's practically bouncing in her seat as she looks out the front window.

The car is barely in the parking space before she hops out of the car. She runs around to my side, throws the door open and stands there vibrating like a kid hyped up on sugar.

"Come on! I don't wanna waste any more time."

Laughing, I get out and let her drag me to the entrance.

"Before we go in there, we need to set a few ground rules." Tyson says as we get in line to pay for our entrance tickets.

"Okay, *Dad.*" I roll my eyes.

He narrows his eyes at me. "Look, this is a big wide open space. Anything can happen. I'm not gonna be up your ass, but you need to let me know where you're going at all times so I can watch from the background. I can't keep you safe if I don't know where you are."

"We will." Emmy says, raising a brow at me, daring me to argue.

"Fine." I say, then pay for our tickets.

"I got mine." Tyson says, paying for his own.

When we get into the main area, Emmy looks around with a look of awe on her face.

"We can change in the family changing rooms. That way Tyson won't have a baby cow because you're alone."

"I heard that." Tyson mutters, leaning against the wall outside the changing room door.

I just roll my eyes and guide a giggling Emmy into the room. We get changed, putting everything in a locker, and then with our towels in hand, we head back out to meet Tyson.

"Doesn't our girl look sexy as fuck?" I grin, adjusting my swim shorts as I look around to make sure I don't scare any kids or old ladies.

"Fuck me, Princess." Tyson growls as he looks Emmy over in her strappy black bikini.

"You don't think it's too much?" She mindlessly touches her scars on her belly and legs.

"You look like a goddess, don't let anyone make you think otherwise." Tyson pulls her in for a heated kiss.

"Hey, this is *my* date, dude. Back off my girl." I say, pulling Emmy from his arms. "Charlie was right, you're really here on these dates so you can sneak in as much action as you can."

Emmy laughs pulling me away by our connected hands. "Let's go!"

We walk over to a sign that lists all the slides and attractions in the water park. People are running around, kids are laughing and screaming, and the smell of chlorine burns my nose.

"What should we do first?" Emmy asks. "There's the slides, the wave pool. Oh, look! They have a lazy river with tubes."

"We can do everything, but how about the wave pool to get used to the water, the slides for a while, then we can leave the lazy river for last before we have to go home."

"Good idea." She says. We hand our towels over to Tyson, who doesn't complain, surprisingly, and race over to the wave pool.

Emmy squeals with laughter as the water comes up and splashes her legs. "Fuck, that's cold!"

"There's only one way to get used to it!" I grin, then scoop her up and carry her into the water. Once our bodies are submerged up to our shoulders, she moves her body around so that she's clinging to me like a spider monkey.

Once we get used to the temperature, I ask, "Do you want to go in the waves now?"

"Yeah, let's go." We start to swim deeper into the pool.

"If you can't touch, let me know. I don't want you to get too tired." I yell to her over the screams of everyone around us.

"Okay." She calls back.

I look ahead and see an enormous wave coming towards us. I grab her hand, making sure she doesn't drift away from me. "Ready?" I ask with excitement.

She looks at me with wide excited eyes and nods eagerly.

We take a deep breath as the wave hits us and takes us under. Emmy comes up moving her hair from her face while laughing. "That was awesome!" She shouts. "Let's go again."

Grinning we swim back to where we were before just in time for the next wave, this time we stay mostly above, allowing us to just go along for the ride.

We do this for a while, sitting on the side-lines until the horn goes off again, letting us know another round of waves are coming. After a half hour of this, we decide to go ride some of the slides.

"There are five different ones. The Twister. " I point to the blue side with lots of twists and turns. "The Bullet." I point to the red one next that is straight down with a single twist at the end. "The Corkscrew." I say pointing to the one that looks like a twisty straw. "The Speed Bump. And the last one, The Rocket." I point to the tallest one. It towers over the others, and has a pretty steep drop.

"No way in hell am I going on that." She shakes her head.

"I am." I grin. "But I'll leave it for last."

We choose to go on The Twister first. We have to wait in line for ten minutes before it's our turn. It is technically two slides. Emmy goes to the entrance of one, and I go to the other.

"Winner gets to have Ben scream their name tonight." She gives me a sexy, mischievous grin.

"Oh, you are so on!" I crow just as the light turns green to go. With a whoop, I jump on the slide hoping to gain some speed on the way down.

It felt like only seconds before I was being shot into the pool at the end. When I come up out of the water, I find a smug Emmy standing on the side waiting for me.

"How the hell did you get down here before me?"

She just shrugs. "No clue, but I win!" She yells with a grin on her face and her arms thrown up in the air.

"Well, you might get to have Ben scream your name, but you're going to be screaming mine." I promise her. Her eyes light up, and just as my lips are about to meet with hers, she dodges the kiss and starts heading for the next slide.

We ride the other slides. Some more than once. As we wait in line to go down The Speed Bump, a group of guys catch my eyes. They are talking in hushed tones as they look at me and Emmy. At first I think they are checking her out, but then they start to laugh, and it takes everything in me, not to go over there and say something.

But Emmy is having fun and I don't want to ruin our date. She is oblivious to the guys as she looks over the edge at the other people going down the slide.

"You go first." I tell her, not wanting to leave her up here alone with these dicks, and it helps knowing that Tyson is waiting for her down below.

"Okay."

She goes next, screaming with excitement all the way down. Once it's my turn, I look back at the snickering assholes, and give them a death glare before taking my turn.

"So you're really going to go down that?" Emmy asks me once I catch up to her. She looks worried, her eyes bouncing between me and up at The Rocket.

"Yup. Wish me luck." I give her a kiss, and Tyson steps closer just to be safe.

After feeling like I've climbed Mount Everest, I make it all the way to the top. *Fuck, why did I think this was a good idea?* My stomach flips as I look down below. I have to squint to see Emmy waving to me, because she looks like a tiny ant.

I wave back with a shaky hand. No turning back now. With a deep breath, I go down; it's now or never, right? I scream like a little bitch all the way down because this slide is living up to its name. I'm going so fast, I feel like my cheeks should be flapping in the wind.

When I get to the bottom, I take Emmy's outstretched hand to pull myself up out of the water.

"You okay?" She asks with a laugh.

"Yeah, but fuck! My ass hurts." I go to rub it, and realize my swim trunks are up my ass, giving me a wedgie. "Yeah, I'll be feeling that for a while."

"If it helps, I'll take your mind off it later." She winks.

We go to the lazy river next, grabbing a two person tube. It's pretty relaxing. We float down the river, holding hands and splashing our feet in the water as we go, enjoying the music playing around us.

"I love you, Tal." Emmy says, her head lulling back against the tube with her face looking towards mine.

"I love you too, My Lady." I grin, bringing her hand up to my lips for a kiss.

220

"I think we should grab something to eat."

Emmy convinced me to go into the wave pool again for another hour, but now we are lying on one of the beach chairs, soaking up the sun.

"I could go for a hamburger right about now." She says sleepily, opening her eyes.

I wave Tyson over. "I'm gonna go get us something to eat. Do you want anything?" I ask.

"Just some water."

I nod and head over to the line for the concession stand. While waiting, I do my best to ignore the flirty looks from the girls in the line behind me.

"Hey." One of them says.

Sighing, because I really don't want to talk to them, I look at them, not wanting to be rude. "Hi." While giving them a forced smile.

"My friend thinks you're hot. She has a thing for snake bites. She wants to know if she can have your number." One of the girls next to her giggles.

I raise a brow at the one trying to hide behind her friends. "Well, thanks for the compliment. My girlfriend loves my snake bites too."

The girl's face drops. But the friend keeps going. "But can she suck cock like a pro?" She purrs.

Huffing out a surprised laugh, I shake my head in disbelief. "Yeah, she does, and so does my boyfriend."

They just gape at me as I turn around to order, dismissing them all together.

"Two cheeseburger meals and a bottle of water." I ask the lady behind the counter.

I pay and stand off to the side waiting for my order.

"Hey." A guy says, and I look around to see the group of guys from earlier walking over to me.

Not saying anything, I tip my head back in acknowledgement as I watch them with caution.

"So, we want to know something." One guy snickers. "That chick you're here with... Is it some kind of pity date or something?"

My eyes narrow as my blood starts to boil.

"Excuse me?" I ask in a dangerously low tone.

"You know, like are you just here with her because you felt bad or something."

"Why the fuck would you ask me that?"

"Because you're out of her league, looking way too good for her. All the scars on her body. Did you see the fucked up tattoos? And those stretch marks, she must have looked like a cow before losing the weight." The guy makes a gagging noise.

The lady calls out my order number, but her voice is drowned out by the roaring of the blood pounding in my ears. My breathing starts to pick up, and it's taking everything in my not to kill them all right here.

"Oh, is that your order?" One of the guys asks. "I don't think she should be eating one of those cheeseburgers." He makes a big belly gesture, and that's all I can take. Taking the tray of food, I toss the drinks in their faces, then smash the first guy upside the head. One guy trips trying to get out of the way, and I take my opening.

My fist pounds into his face. When his friends try to help him, I elbow one in the face, breaking his nose, sending him stumbling back onto the ground with a cry of pain. When another tries to drag me off, I leave the waste of space on the ground and start in on the last fucker left in front of me.

One against four was not the best idea, but all logic went out the window the moment he talked about my girl like that.

In a fit of rage, I black out, and the next thing I know Tyson is dragging me off one of them, yelling in my ear to calm down.

Breathing like a wild animal, I look around frantically. All four are on the ground bleeding.

Emmy's looking at me, panicked and confused.

"What happened?" She asks, approaching me as someone would a cornered animal. She lightly cups my face, wiping something away from under my nose. Blood. When did I get hit?

"Talon, baby, what happened?" She asks again.

I'm not telling her what they said. It would crush her, set her back on all the progress she made with her self-esteem. But I need to tell her something.

"They said shit they shouldn't have, and I made them bleed for it." Understanding shows in her eyes, she doesn't ask what they said.

"Crazy, fucking bastard!" One of them shouts. "I'm gonna sue your ass and throw you behind bars."

"Like fuck, you will." Tyson growls. He crouches down low, and talks so only they along with Talon and I hear him. "Have you heard of the Phantom Reapers?"

Their eyes go wide with fear.

"Ah, it seems you have. Well, if you say anything about what just happened here, they will be paying you a visit. We make house calls too, did you know that?" Tyson's normally handsome face turns into something out of nightmares. Now I know why he and Harlow get along so well. He can be just as bloodthirsty if his loved ones are involved.

One of them looks at Emmy and I kick him in the side. "Don't you fucking look at her." I growl.

"Come on, let's go." Emmy says, looking at the guys on the ground as she starts to pull me away.

Tyson follows, leaving the punks bloody and whining on the ground.

"What if they call after we leave?" Emmy asks after coming out of the changing room with our stuff.

"I'll have a few guys follow them home to scare some sense into them."

Emmy looks around the sea of cars, trying to find Tyson's. Her body tenses as her eyes lock on the fence on the edge of the parking lot. All color drains from her face.

"What is it?" I ask, trying to see what she's looking at, but nothing is there.

"A man." She points to where she was looking. "There was a man watching us."

"Emmy, what did he look like?" Tyson asks carefully.

"Short, black hair with a bushy beard. I didn't get a good look at him but, Ty, he gave me really bad vibes." She says in a shaky voice.

"Fuck!" Tyson curses.

"Tyson," Emmy asks. "What is it?" When he doesn't answer her, she asks again, adding, "Tyson, don't lie to me."

He sighs heavily. "From how you described that man, it could be Dagger. Or maybe it was just one of his men."

Emmy clings to me, and starts looking around in a panic.

"It's okay, Baby Girl. We won't let anything happen to you."

We get in the car and head back home. The whole car ride Emmy clings to me like I'm her safe place. I hold her tightly against me, still worked up over what those fuckers said.

They were wrong, so fucking wrong. Emmy is perfect. A survivor. A fucking goddess. Every scar on her body makes her even more beautiful and I'll be damned if anyone says otherwise.

"Fuck!" I hiss, burning my hand as I try to grab the hot frying pan. I'm trying to make Emmy something to eat considering our date was cut short by those disgusting bastards.

"Talon!" Emmy gasps as she rushes into the kitchen. She had gone upstairs to shower off the chlorine from the water park, while I made us some food. Although, based on how these burgers are coming out, I'm sure they wouldn't classify as food. They look more like burnt bricks of charcoal.

Emmy turns the sink faucet on, slips on a pair of oven mitts before taking the pan that is now on fire, and tossing it into the basin under the stream of water.

"Let me see." She offers, her voice soft and wavering with concern. She gently takes the hand that I have clutched to my chest, trying to pry my fingers open to get a good look at the damage I've done to myself. She sucks in a breath at how angry and bubbling the skin looks. "Well... it's not too bad, but we probably should take care of this before it gets infected. Here." Emmy pulls me to the sink, moving the tap over to the other basin, guiding my hand under the cool water. I bite back a noise at the pain which feels like I'm getting burnt all over again. "I'll be right back." Placing a kiss on my shoulder, she takes off.

Hanging my head as the cold water starts to numb my burn, I sigh heavily, exhausted from today's events. I just wanted to spend the day with my girl, to see her smile and laugh. How dare they fuck it all up with their cruel lies because that's exactly what they were: lies. Emmy is the most stunningly beautiful woman I have ever laid eyes on. It's a shame that they are too rotten-to-the-core to see it.

"Talon, baby." Emmy whispers, her hands resting on my shoulders, giving them a little squeeze. "It's okay. We can order in."

"It's not okay!" I shout, slamming my good hand down on the counter. She startles a little, but doesn't move away because she knows I would never hurt her. "Fuck. I'm sorry. I'm not mad at you, I'm just... You wanted burgers, and that's what you're gonna get." I say, moving to find my phone.

"Stop." She grabs my hand with one of hers, using the other to force me to look at her. "I don't care about that right now. I don't know what happened back at the water park, and what those stupid boys said but it doesn't matter.

What does matter is getting this hand taken care of. Then I want to go upstairs and relax with my man. Can you do that for me?" She leans in, rubbing her nose against mine. My body relaxes at her calming presence. She is perfect for me, Oliver, and Tyson. She knows just how to tame our anger, our inner beasts.

"Yeah. I'd like that." I give her a soft kiss before pulling back and licking my lips, tasting her vanilla mint lip balm.

Giving me a sweet smile, she gets to work on my hand, cleaning it, putting some cream on it then wrapping it up in a bandage. "I don't think you're gonna scar."

"It doesn't hurt." I lie. Because it does hurt; like a bitch. I just don't want her to worry about me. I should be the one taking care of her, not the other way around. She was a little shaken up after seeing that man watching her in the parking lot. Dagger or not, I believe she saw someone. I don't like seeing all that fear swimming in her eyes.

"Okay." She smiles, amusement showing me she doesn't quite believe me. "Come." She holds out her hand, waiting for me. I wrap my hand around hers, letting her lead me upstairs. Oliver and Tyson are at the clubhouse letting Steel know what Emmy saw. Charlie is around the compound somewhere with the baby.

Just as I'm about to disappear up the stairs, I see Ben standing in the doorway to the basement. He smiles at me, then looks at our girl before turning around and heading back down. I know Ben and I know he wants to be here with us, taking care of us, but he also knows that I need this alone time with our girl. With how busy life has gotten in such a short amount of time, I haven't had much of that. Melody is a really good baby and almost never cries, she sleeps through the night most nights, but that doesn't change the fact that she is still a baby and needs a lot of work. Even with all the extra hands, it's still a full time job. One I'd never want to quit.

We enter Emmy's room and she lets go of my hand, heading over to her dresser to take out one of my t-shirts. I smile as I watch her strip, then slip the t-shirt over her sexy naked body.

"What's that smile for?" She asks, walking over to me and wrapping her arms around my waste.

"I think it's cute that you're changing into something comfy, and that the something comfy that you choose also happens to be one of *my* shirts." I nip at her bottom lip.

"Why not? We're cuddling and watching a movie. Jeans are not cuddling clothes." She gives me a look laced with fake innocence.

I chuckle deeply at her comeback. She shivers at the sound, biting her lower lip and trying hard to keep her little game going but I see right past it. "You're right, jeans are not meant for cuddling. But we're not cuddling."

"Were not?" She cocks her head to the side, her pupils dilating as I pull her flush to my body. She lets out a little whimper as I tuck my face into the crook of her neck, lightly kissing and sucking behind her ear. My thumbs rub little curls on her curvy waist before sliding down over her bare ass. She's wearing a g-string, leaving me access to her plump juicy cheeks.

She groans as I grind my hard cock into her belly. Pulling back I look down at her flushed face. "So, did you still want to cuddle?" I grin like a wolf toying with its prey. She shakes her head no. "Then what do you want?" I breathe against her lips, lightly brushing mine against hers.

"You." She sighs, shifting in my hold. "Make love to me Talon." Her eyes are vulnerable and pleading. She needs this, needs me. She doesn't want my alpha bullshit. No, she needs soft and sweet tonight. That might not be what I'm used to because both my lovers are dirty little freaks and I love it, but I can be whatever she needs me to be when it's needed.

Pulling her shirt back over her head, I toss it to the floor, followed by her g string. She wraps her arms around my neck as I pick her up by the globes of her ass, carrying her to the bed.

My mouth finds hers as I swallow her moans. Her hands find my pants, quickly undoing them and pulling them over my ass, boxers and all. I try to maneuver out of them without breaking away from her by kicking my legs out to the side. She giggles against my lips as I get nowhere trying to rid myself of these jeans completely.

With a grunt, I reluctantly break the kiss and roll off her. Huffing out a breath of annoyance, I pull my pants off the rest of the way, tossing them to the side before prowling back over to my girl.

"You think that was funny?" I growl, hovering over her. She bites her lip, trying to hide her smile as she shakes her head. *Well, let's see if she thinks* this *is funny.* Giving her a feral grin, I slide down her body to her pretty little pussy and lap at her soaked core. She moans my name, her hands flying into my hair, as she tightly grips handfuls. *Not laughing now, are we?*

I lick and suck, flicking the tip of my tongue against her swollen clit until she's a withering, panting mess beneath me. She cums, her release coating my face and tongue, and makes my name sound like a sweet symphony on her lips.

"More." She begs, her breathing ragged. "I need you inside me."

"Gladly."

Not bothering to wipe her from my face I kiss her hard, making her taste herself on my lips. She groans as I trace her with the tip of my cock, smearing the pre-cum against her swollen pussy.

Her hands find my ass pulling me towards her, telling me where she wants me. Not wanting to keep her waiting, I push into her, loving every whimper and cry of pleasure that spills from her lips.

She claws at my back, begging me to go harder, faster. With all the self control I have, I give her just enough of what she's asking for while also being careful not to change it from making love to something more primal and savage.

It doesn't take long before I feel her pussy gripping my cock. Burying my face into her neck, I thrust into her again and again, completely focused on the feel of her sweet cunt around my length and the sounds of her loving every moment of it.

"Oh, Talon." She cries, biting my shoulder in an attempt to smother her scream as she breaks apart beneath me, taking me over the edge with her.

"Fuck! Emmy." I groan, giving her a few more thrusts before shuddering and emptying myself deep inside her.

We lay there until our breathing evens out, just enjoying being in each other's arms.

"I love you, Talon." Emmy says, her voice husky and slow. "Thank you. I don't know what they said to make you act that way, but I have a feeling it was because of something they said. It doesn't matter what they think, but thank you for being one of my knights in shining armor."

"You mean your dark knight." I kiss her shoulder, moving to pull out of her.

"Doesn't matter, you are perfect any way you choose to be."

"I love you, too. So fucking much. I'll always be there to defend you."

"I know." She gives me a sleepy smile.

Giving her one last kiss, I grab a washcloth to clean her up. When I get back, I find her fast asleep. Smiling, I carefully clean her up not wanting to wake her. Today was a long day and she deserves to sleep.

After I'm done, I toss the dirty cloth in the hamper and tuck her into bed, before making my way downstairs.

"How was your day?" Ben asks as I take a seat next to him on the couch in the basement.

I give him a look that conveys exactly how my day went. "Oh no. What happened?" He pulls me into his arms and I tell him everything.

"I know you're trying to control your anger, but thank you." He kisses the side of my head.

"For what?" I ask, looking up at him.

He gives me a smile. "For kicking their asses. I would have done the same."

I smile back, letting out a laugh. "I know you have gotten into a fight in the past, but it's still hard to picture you like that." He lets out a grunt, making me laugh again. "I know I'd totally be turned on."

"Of course, you would." He shakes his head with a smirk.

"I'll always fight for her. In every way. And I'd do the same thing for you."

"I know you would." He leans down and kisses me. "As would I. For the both of you."

CHAPTER 24
Oliver

THE DAY THAT I get to take Emmy on my date has arrived, and she has no clue what I have planned. The others do, and will be staying at home with Melody while I take Emmy out of town for the night. Our bags are packed and in the car waiting.

This is something that Emmy has been dreaming about for a while. Something she has wished she could do since she was little and we were too piss poor to ever expect this dream to come true. Where we are going is about four hours away, so we will need to get a head start now, so we can be there by check-in time for our hotel and I know Emmy is going to want to have some time to get ready.

I don't mind that my brother is coming, but I don't plan on having him in the background like the others did. I do enjoy being around him, and I know we haven't had time to hang out much, so I kept that in mind when I planned my night with my girl.

Also, I have a goal. Emmy wants that brother sandwich, and it's my mission to give that to her by the end of this little trip. I have no issues having sex with her in front of him or any of the others. Plus, the two of us sharing her is one of her favorite things to fantasize about. She says it makes her feel loved, being surrounded by us. She pretty much says the more the merrier.

Everyone is already up and downstairs eating. Melody is fed and changed thanks to Charlie, so we decided to let Emmy sleep in. She was up late last night with the baby, and made all of us go back to sleep, no matter how much we wanted to stay up with her.

"Firefly." My voice soft as I caress her cheek. It's just past 10 a.m., and by the time she gets up and gets dressed we will be able to leave and make it to the hotel just in time for check-in. "Time to get up."

She blinks her long lashes and looks up at me. "Hi." She murmurs sleepily. "What time is it?"

"Ten." I say, sitting next to her on the bed.

"Ten?!" She shouts, popping up, looking fully awake now. "Why did you let me sleep in? Where's the baby?"

"You needed sleep. And she's with the others downstairs. You do remember Melody has six parents to care for her, right?"

"I know." She mumbles, rubbing her eyes.

"Plus, it's our day today." I grin wide at her.

She mimics my expression. "That's right! So what are we doing?"

"We are going on a little trip."

"And..." She encourages.

"And we are staying there for the night. I got us a hotel."

"Really?" She questions excitedly. "Come on. Tell me, tell me!"

Grabbing the envelope on the bedside table, I hand it to her. She looks at it curiously for a moment before opening it and taking three concert tickets out and reading the band's name on the ticket. She lets out a high pitched squeal as she stands up on the bed and starts jumping around.

"SYSTEM RISING! I'm going to see System Rising. Fuck yeah!" She punches the air with both fists. I only have a second to react before she launches herself in my arms. "I love you. I fucking love you so much. You're the best!" She starts kissing me all over my face, making me chuckle, before ramming her tongue down my throat. I grip her ass, grinding her against my cock, moaning as she continues to make me harder by the second.

"Fuck, Baby Girl. As much as I want to let you show your appreciation in a very fun way, you need to get ready. It's a four-hour drive, and we need to be at the hotel by a certain time."

"Right." She says, quickly detaching herself from me. She hands over the tickets. "Guard these with your life." She says seriously before rushing into the bathroom.

Shaking my head with a smile, I head downstairs.

"I take it she likes the date you're taking her on." Ben says, smiling into his coffee.

"Yeah, we would be fucking right now if we didn't have to leave soon." I laugh.

"I knew she would love it." Charlie grins.

"Well, thank you for letting me know they were coming this way. I knew she loved the band, but I didn't think about keeping tabs on them."

"You're very welcome." Charlie smirks triumphantly. "And you're lucky that I didn't use this idea for myself. But I'm not a fan of big crowds, so I don't think it'd be as much fun for me as it would for you."

Ben passes me a plate of food, and I thank him before digging in. Ten minutes later, Emmy comes bouncing down the stairs.

"I'm going to see-" Emmy's words get cut off as she trips on something and hits the floor. Tyson tries to help her up, but she jumps up quickly, a smile still glued to her face. "System Rising!" She finishes.

We all burst out laughing. "Come eat, you nut job." I say, pushing a plate of food towards her. She sits next to me and practically inhales her food.

"Slow down, Butterfly, you're gonna choke eating like that." Ben says.

"No. Time." Emmy mumbles around a mouth full of food. "We need to go."

"We have time." I say, putting my hand on her shoulder.

She turns and glares at me. "I'm not risking it! What if we get a flat, or run out of gas? Every minute is valuable."

She finishes off her plate and gets up, going over to see Melody who's in Charlie's arms. She takes her, cuddling her close. "Mama's gonna miss you, Melly Belly." She kisses her all over, but Melody just babbles, getting a hold of Emmy's hair and starts chewing on it. Emmy laughs and hands her back to Charlie. "Someone is hungry."

"My turn!" Talon says, going to heat up a bottle.

Emmy says goodbye to everyone and just as she's about to leave me and Tyson behind to head out to the car, she runs back and gives Melody one last kiss. "I expect you to send hourly updates. Even if it's just to tell me she's sleeping."

"We will." Ben laughs.

Emmy says goodbye again, grabbing Tyson's and my hand and starts dragging us towards the door. "Let's go!"

"Princess, relax. It's a long ride." Tyson says, getting into the car. Emmy and I slide into the back.

"Just drive!" She demands.

"Excuse me?" He turns around and gives her a look. Her eyes go wide, but I see heat behind it. "You wanna rephrase that, Princess?"

"Please?" She shrugs.

"Brat." Tyson mutters, giving her another look that promises punishment, but at least she's more relaxed now.

"Ooooooh, someone's in trouble." I joke, leaning in to whisper in her ear, so only she can hear.

She looks at me with a cocky smirk. "I know, I can't wait."

"You're bad." I chuckle deeply. "Maybe I should punish you too?"

She says nothing, her eyes growing more heated by the second as she squirms in her seat. Oh this is gonna be a fun night for all of us.

Emmy ended up falling asleep for most of the ride. I'm glad she got some extra sleep, now she will be able to enjoy her night without being tired. Tyson and I just talked or listened to music to help the time pass by more quickly.

"Emmy, baby, we're here." I say, giving her shoulder a little shake.

We get out, grab our bags, and head inside to the check-in counter. Once we get our key, we head to our room.

"See, we got here on time. Nothing went wrong, and you were freaking out over nothing." Tyson says, tossing his bag on the bed.

Emmy gasps, and covers her ears. "La la la, I can't hear you!" She says, then goes over to the bedside table, and knocks on it.

"Umm, baby, what are you doing?" I laugh.

"Knocking on wood so that big guy over there doesn't jinx this whole trip." Emmy says, sitting on the edge of the bed with a bounce.

"A little dramatic, aren't we?" Tyson smirks, raising a brow at Emmy's quirky habits.

"Better safe than sorry." She shrugs. "This is a nice room." She flops back onto the bed. "God, this bed is comfy." She sits up against the headboard and looks around. "There's only one bed. Are we all sharing?"

"Is that a problem?" Tyson asks.

"Nope." She smiles wide. "Sleeping between my biker boys? Sign me the fuck up." Tyson chuckles and heads into the bathroom.

She's right, this room is nice. It has a couch, a little kitchen and a big screen TV on the wall. The king-size bed has more than enough room for the three of us.

"There's a jet tub in there." Tyson comments as he comes out of the bathroom.

"Really?!" Emmy jumps up and goes to check it out. "Sweet!" She calls out before coming back into the room. "I wanna try that out before we leave."

"I think that can be arranged." I say, my voice low and husky.

"Great." She breathes, biting her lip. "But right now, I'm starving, and not for cock this time." She pauses. "Okay, for cock too, but that can be dessert."

We go out to eat, enjoying a good meal at a nice restaurant. It's relaxing. You would think sharing a girl with your brother would be awkward, but in our case, it's not. It feels right, natural. Maybe it's because it's similar to sharing with the others. It's something we are used to by now. Tyson has adjusted to the unique dynamic of our group really well. And in all the years I've known him, I don't think I've ever seen him this happy.

After we eat, we come back to our hotel room to get ready for the concert that starts at 7 p.m. I got her VIP tickets, but I left that as a surprise.

"Alright, I'm good to go." Emmy comes out of the bathroom, and I almost choke on my beer. Fuck me, how the hell am I gonna keep my eyes off her all night. *Easy, I won't. How can I?*

She has on a pair of black lace shorts that hug her in all the right places and a white crop top that shows off a little cleavage along with her under boob tattoo. A silver belly button ring with a butterfly shimmers in the light and draws my attention to her sexy belly. She still has some baby weight, but fuck if it doesn't make her yummier than before. Her thighs and ass have gotten thicker, her hips a little wider, and, fuck, her breasts were always plump but now they overflow in my hand. I just want to shove my face between them and stay there all day. *Great, now I sound like Talon.*

Her long brown hair is down, flowing in beach waves, and she's wearing her contacts. Her makeup completes the whole look.

"Close that mouth, big boy." She says, gripping my chin, and wiping the corner of my mouth. "Got a little drool there." She smirks.

"That's it, you're staying here with me. I'm burying my cock deep inside of you for the rest of the night." I growl, going to grab her. Her eyes widen and she slips just out of reach, running to hide behind Tyson while laughing.

"Save me from the big, bad, *hungry* wolf."

"I don't think I'm gonna be much help here, Princess, he has a point. You look fucking edible."

Emmy groans. "Not now! Don't get me wrong, I want to have sex right now too, actually I have wanted to all fucking day, but we really have to get going. The line is gonna be a bitch."

She moves away from Tyson, watching me with caution as she grabs her purse, and heads for the door, expecting us to follow behind. And that's *exactly* what we do.

"Holy fuck, it's packed." Emmy says. "I told you we should have gotten here earlier. Now we have to wait in this mile-long line." She looks so sad and disappointed. It makes me grin, knowing that we will *not* be waiting in that line.

"What the fuck are you smiling about?" She sasses, annoyed with me.

"Come with me." I tell her, dragging her out of the line.

"Oliver! What the fuck, now we've lost our spot in line."

"Trust me, Firefly."

She mutters angrily at me as I bring her over to the VIP entrance, Tyson close behind us.

"Here we are." I say, stopping in front of a door that has a big sign indicating the VIP entrance.

"This is the VIP line." She deadpans. "We can't go in there."

"Or can we?" I grin, pulling three VIP passes out of my back pocket and looping one around her neck. She looks down in disbelief.

"I get to... I get to meet them?!" She looks up at me with tears in her eyes. "Have I mentioned I love you?" She cries out, tossing her arms around me in a bone crushing hug.

"Only the best for my girl." I kiss her neck. "Now, let's meet those guys you love so much."

"Not nearly as much as I love you and the others." She smiles.

We show the security people our passes, and they let us in. We follow the signs until we get to a room.

"Oh my god, it's Patrick Ramsay." Emmy breathes.

"Well, go say hi." I say, gently pushing her forward.

She looks down at herself, and back to me with a panicked look. "Oh god, why did I wear this? He's gonna think I'm some sleazy girl."

"Hey." Tyson says, cupping her face. "Don't say things like that about yourself. You look amazingly perfect. So stop it." He growls. Emmy relaxes at his touch, and nods.

"You're right. I got this. They're just normal people, right?" She takes a deep breath, straightens her shoulders and heads over to meet the band. *There's my Firefly.*

Tyson and I watch Emmy fan girl over the band. She talks a mile a minute about how much she loves their music, and how some of their songs got her through rough times. She takes photos with each of them, then one with the whole band.

After that they tell her she can go to any of the tables lining the room, and pick out any merch that she wanted. She came back to us with a big bag and a new winter hat on her head.

"Look at what I got." She smiles brightly, her excitement reminds me of a kid on Christmas.

"You took one of everything, didn't you?" I grin, loving how happy she is.

"Fuck, yeah! They said I could and you damn well better believe I did."

"Princess, it's the middle of June, and you have a winter hat on." Tyson points out, grinning.

"I wanted to put on the hoodie too, but it's too hot for that. I am gonna put this band tee on, though." She pulls out a shirt from the bag and slips it on over her outfit. I pout a little inside as her stunning breasts are hidden behind the fabric.

We head out to our VIP seats to enjoy the pre-show bands. We get the luxury of having reclining chairs in the front row, with enough space so that we are not straining our necks to see the performers. I don't plan on telling Emmy about the grand I spent on getting these tickets. She deserves all this and more.

Emmy sits in my lap instead of her seat, snuggling into me as she listens to the music. We haven't heard any of these bands before, but they are pretty good.

When System Rising comes on, Emmy jumps up and starts cheering with the crowd.

They start to play their opening song, and Emmy joins in, belting out every word. As the night goes on, we dance and scream, having one of the best nights ever.

As the show comes to an end, they start playing a slow song, and Emmy sits back down on my lap, swaying back and forth to the music.

My body is on fire, energy is humming through my veins for my girl. Her being in my arms all night, watching her smile and enjoying herself without a care in the world is one of the hottest things I've ever seen.

She shifts in my lap, making my cock start to grow. I'm love drunk for this girl, and I just want to go back to the hotel room and fuck her brains out.

I sit up, wrapping my arms around her, tucking my face into her neck. I start to kiss her, making her moan in return. The music is loud, but I'm so close that I can easily hear all the little noises she's making as she grinds her ass back into my cock, while I continue to kiss her neck. My hands rub up and down her thighs, going higher and higher each time. She grabs my hands, and turns in my lap to look at me.

There's raw lust in her eyes. I can tell she's just as affected by tonight as I am. The song ends and they say their goodbyes, thanking everyone for coming to see them. The crowd loses it as the band departs, but Emmy doesn't move. She doesn't cheer with everyone else. She just stares at me with hungry eyes, like she's waging a war within herself whether she wants to fuck me here in front of everyone or not. After a few more moments, she leans forward to whisper in my ear.

"Let's go back to the hotel room." Her voice is so raspy and sexy that it has my cock twitching to be free. Not saying anything else, we get up and start heading out of the building; of course, with Tyson only steps behind us.

When we get outside to our car, Emmy catches me by surprise by pushing me against the car before attacking my mouth with hers. We kiss hard, messing around until she's grinding against my thigh.

"Guys, get in the fucking car. People are stopping to watch." Tyson grumbles, slamming the car door behind him. Emmy pulls back from me, both of us breathing heavily. She looks around and bites her lip when she sees the people who are turning to leave now that the show we were putting on is over.

"Let's pick this back up at the hotel." I open the back door, and Emmy gets in. We both sit as far away from each other as we can, knowing if we didn't, we would be fucking in the back seat right about now. The need to touch her, to fuck her, to love her is so damn strong right now. This woman is my everything, and there is never a time that I don't want to be worshiping her body. Tonight isn't any different.

When we get to the hotel, we leave Tyson behind to grab Emmy's merch, and race up to our room. The moment the door shuts behind us, our mouths are back on each other, kissing, sucking, and nipping like our lives depend on it. We rip away each other's clothes like wild animals until we are both in our underwear. Gripping her by the ass, I lift her up. She locks her legs around my hips, grinding her hot pussy into my hard cock. She moans into my mouth as I carry her over to the bed.

I drop her down on the bed and slide my hand under her back, undoing her bra and tossing it across the room. She watches me, her pupils blown so wide that her eyes almost look black. Her breathing is ragged already and fuck, I can't wait to make her pant and scream my name.

I rip off her panties before I get to my knees, kneeling before my goddess. Sliding her legs over my shoulder, I open her wide enough for me to see that she's soaked for me.

"Please, Olly." She begs. Not wanting to leave my girl unsatisfied, I lower my head, and start to lick her clean. She moans my name as she grabs handfuls of my hair. I eat her out, desperately wanting her to cum on my face, and for her to break apart before my eyes so I can put her back together.

Her breathing starts to pick up, and she grips my hair even tighter. Looking up to watch her, I see her eyes are not on me, nor are they closed. They are hyper aware of something behind me.

Looking over my shoulder, I see Tyson watching us. His eyes show just as much lust as ours. He likes what he sees, but the question of the lifetime is: will he want a part of this? A part of rocking our girl's world?

"Care to join us, brother?"

CHAPTER 25
Emmy

"CARE TO JOIN us, brother?" Oliver asks Tyson. Ty stands against the hotel room door, his pupils blown wide, and his hands fisted at his side. His eyes flick from his brother, who has his head between my legs as my thighs rest on his shoulders, over to me, laying here, desperate and wanting. Wanting both of them.

"I'll go wait in the lobby until you're done." Tyson mutters, his voice strained as he tries to get himself under control. He turns around, reaching for the door handle, prepared to leave, but I don't want him to go. I want to feel them both, in me, on me, everywhere.

"Tyson..." I plead as I reach my hand out to him. "Please stay... Sir?"

He pauses, his hand hovering over the handle. I don't say anything more, giving him the chance to leave if this really is something he doesn't want to do. I don't want to pressure him into this, or make him feel guilty for not giving into my whims.

He slowly turns around. "Is this what you want, Princess? Me and Oliver, at the same time?"

"Yes." I breathe. "But only if you feel comfortable."

He looks at Oliver. "I'll do this, for her, under one condition. I'm in control. You do as I say, both of you, or this won't work."

"I'll do anything for her. You're in control." Oliver promises.

Tyson hesitates only for a minute before slipping his jacket off. Then he takes off his shoes before grabbing the hem of his black tee and bringing it up and over his head, allowing me a full view of his delicious ink covered abs. I whimper and Tyson's eyes flick to mine, flashing with hunger. "Oliver, I don't believe you're finished with your meal, I haven't heard her scream your name yet."

Fuck. Fuck me, please, with a cherry on top.

Oliver looks at me with a sexy as fuck grin before diving back down to finish what he started. I suck in a gasp of air as his hot, wet tongue laps at my pussy, and his fingers grip my hips to hold me in place when I start to squirm.

"Do you like what he's doing to you? Are you gonna cum for my brother?" Tyson asks, his voice low and husky, and I gush at the sound of it, which has Oliver chuckling against my core while he licks up my juices, making sure nothing goes to waste.

I nod frantically, unable to say a single word. Oliver takes my clit into his mouth at the same time he thrusts two thick fingers inside me. I cry out, tossing my head back and squeezing my eyes shut as my body quivers in intense pleasure.

"Cum for him, Princess. Scream his name, and then, and only then, will I spank that bratty ass for how you spoke to me earlier today."

My eyes snap open, meeting the eyes of my sinful, biker boy. No, not boy. Everything about him is all man. And he's all mine.

Tyson reaches over and tweaks my nipple between his calloused fingers. The shock of pain turns to pleasure, when Oliver crooks his fingers in just the right way, and I do as I'm told, cumming hard. "Oliver!" I scream in a desperate plea. His hold tightens into a bruising grip when I try to move from the intense feeling, making me ride out my orgasm while I try my hardest to ride his face.

My climax reaches its highest peak, and then I'm tumbling down, breathing like I ran for miles. Sweat coats my hair line, my chest heaves with every breath, and with the way Tyson is looking at me, I feel like the sexiest person alive. It's a confidence boost for sure.

"So fucking beautiful, Princess." He says, his voice low as he cups my face in his big hand. "Now, on your knees." He commands, and my pussy clenches in response to his assertive tone.

He takes his pants off, leaving him in only his skin tight boxers. They do nothing to hide his monster cock, and my mouth salivates at the sight before me. I want to taste it. To lick it like it's my favorite flavored lollipop while he comes apart by my hand.

But that will have to wait. Right now, I'm about to get my ass spanked, and to that I say, *Yes, please!*

Oliver helps remove my legs from his shoulders, and I roll over, getting up on all fours, wobbling like a baby deer as I make my way over to Tyson. My limbs feel like jelly.

Tyson sits in the middle of the bed and pats his lap. I lay across it, waiting for his next move. "You know that sassy mouth of yours is just gonna get you in trouble. The others might let it slide, but not me, Princess, and you know it. So I'm going to give you something better to do with that mouth. But first..."

He gives me no notice before bringing his hand down on my ass. I jolt, with a little yelp, at the sudden contact.

He rubs away the sting before bringing his hand down again, but on the other cheek this time. I moan when I feel Oliver's lips kiss the sore spot as Tyson rubs the opposite cheek.

"Look at you, taking it like a good girl." Tyson runs his fingers through my hair, gripping it slightly before bringing his hand down again. It hurts, but feels so fucking good at the same time.

"Three more, then you're gonna suck our dicks, how does that sound, Princess, do you want our cocks?" Tyson turns my head to face him. His eyes are hooded, dripping with lust.

"Yes, Sir." I breathe. He groans, and I can feel his cock twitch from underneath me. His palm makes contact in three quick strikes, causing me to whimper. My pussy is flooded, and Oliver kindly points that out to his big brother.

"Look at this, Ty. Look how fucking soaked she is. I think she enjoys being punished." He chuckles deeply. Fuck, these two are gonna wreck me, but in all the right ways.

"Is that right, Princess, are you wet for us?" He asks, but I know he doesn't expect an answer this time when he instantly slides his fingers against my lower lips, dipping them into me before holding them up for all to see. "You're right, brother, she is." Tyson brings his fingers to his mouth, sucking my juices clean. I moan at the sight. I need a dick in me, and soon. This is fucking torture. Do they know how fucking drop dead gorgeous they are? The bad boy biker thing does wonders for them. And seeing Oliver's dominant side? Show me more! Fuck, it's everything I knew I fucking wanted.

"Get between us." Tyson tells me, and Oliver moves to sit next to his brother, leaving enough room for me to be on my knees. Tyson pulls his boxers down, revealing his glorious cock that I've come to love so much. He grips it tightly, giving it a few strokes. "You're gonna take turns sucking our cocks. Then I'm gonna fuck your perfect pussy, while Oliver fucks your tight ass." He leaves no room for discussion, but you won't hear me objecting.

I look at Oliver. He's watching me with an intense look, revealing all the emotions he feels for me. I have to look away before I get choked up. Locking eyes with Tyson, I wrap my fingers tightly around his length just below his hand.

He moves away, his hands falling to his side as I lean forward and flick my tongue out, licking the bead of pre-cum away. He groans, nostrils flaring and I can tell he's trying really hard to hold back.

I swirl my tongue around the head of his cock, before lowering myself, taking as much of him as I can. I only manage to get halfway down before it hits the back of my throat.

Alisha Williams

Locking my lips around his velvety shaft, I start to bob my head, making sure to lick and suck him, the way I know he loves. He makes another sound of pleasure, while he slides his hand into my hair, holding my head down until I'm gagging with drool running down my chin.

"Fuck, Princess, look at you taking my cock. So fucking sexy." He lets me up, and I gasp for air, my chest heaving, but I'm fucking loving this. "You didn't forget about Oliver, did you?" Tyson smirks. I look down at Oliver's cock in his hand, then back up at him.

"I will never forget about him." I purr before taking Oliver's cock in my mouth, giving it the same attention I did Tyson's.

I take turns going back and forth, switching when they start to make some of the sexiest noises I have ever heard.

"That's enough." Tyson demands, pulling my mouth off his cock. "Come here."

I crawl up his body until my pussy is over his cock. Placing my hands on his shoulders for support, I thrust my hips so that my wet core slides against his hot smooth length. He groans, gripping my hips and lifting me up. He removes one of his hands to line himself up with my entrance. He lowers me so that just the tip is in, keeping his cock where he wants it. He snakes his hand behind my head, and brings it towards his face. He captures my lips with his, plunging his tongue inside just as he uses his other hand that's on my waist to force me down, impaling me on his thick cock.

He swallows my cry as he rocks me on to him. He's so fucking big, and every time I'm with him, it feels like the first time. My body slowly adjusts to his size as he uses my body to fuck himself.

"So tight." He grunts against my lips. I lean back, changing the position so I can start to ride him, my chest bouncing as I move. His eyes drop to my breasts, as his hands come up to grasp them. He starts to massage them, using his fingers to pinch and tug at my nipples.

"Oh, god." I moan, closing my eyes and tilting my head back as I focus on all the sensations running through my body. It's not enough, I need more, I need Oliver too.

"More." I pant, searching for Oliver.

"Fuck her, Oliver, don't leave our girl waiting." Tyson orders.

"I'm right here, Baby Girl." He comes up behind me, slipping his hand between my thighs to rub my clit while leaving little open mouth kisses on my neck, and making me moan at this touch.

"Lean forward, Princess, make room for Oliver." Tyson directs, adjusting himself, getting ready for a wild fucking ride.

Leaning over Tyson's muscular abs, I balance myself on my arms before lowering my head to lick a line up his toned abs. I can't help it, they are just too damn tempting.

Oliver's fingers scoop up my cream that's running down my thighs, and brings some to lube up my ring of muscles.

"Fuck, Firefly, you're so worked up we don't even need any lube, you have enough here to coat my entire cock." He says, before pressing the tip of said cock against my puckered hole.

"Relax, Princess." Tyson soothes, bringing my body flush to his, running his hand up and down my spine.

I suck in a deep breath as Oliver starts to push in. Full, that's how I feel; so *fucking* full. God, it's amazing, the stretch of their cocks has my body buzzing like I'm hooked up to live wires that are emitting a small electric current.

"Oh, god." I moan as Oliver bottoms out deep in my ass.

After a moment Oliver pulls out and starts to thrust into me, knowing just what I like. "Fuck me." I beg "Use my body, make me scream, and cum so fucking hard in me that I'll be dripping with your mark for days."

Tyson groans, gripping my hips, and starts to fuck me, not holding back anymore. They work together until I'm a shaking mess.

"Oliver." I scream. "Fuck. Tyson!" My orgasm is building rapidly. "Fuck, fuck, fuck." I chant, feeling each of their cocks with every thrust. My inner muscles clamp down around them, as I dig my nails into Tyson's side.

"Cum, Princess, all over my cock. Squeeze Oliver's with that tight, perfect ass."

Oliver thrusts harder, rubbing my clit faster and faster. I can't hold back anymore. With a hoarse cry, my body tightens around both their cocks, and I cum hard. I can feel myself explode all over Tyson's cock and thighs. I collapse forward, exhausted from the events of today mixed with these two dangerous men and their earth-shattering orgasms.

"I'll never get tired of hearing you scream, Baby Girl." Oliver whispers, leaning over to kiss my spine. As if he knows that I want more but am unable to do much else, he says, "Just lay there, Baby Girl, let us do the rest of the work." And I do just that. They fuck me hard, making me babble out nonsense, and working me over until I feel my third orgasm build to a crescendo. The sounds of their ragged breathing, grunts and groans only add to my impending release.

"Amazing, Princess, taking both our cocks like a pro, stretching to fit us, like you were made for us."

"I need to cum." I sob, feeling my orgasm just out of reach. Oliver adjusts himself behind me, and Tyson moves me so that he can capture my lips with his. He kisses me with a desperate passion, his fingers scraping red lines on my hips. Every thrust from Oliver sends Tyson's cock deeper inside me, rubbing all the right spots.

Tyson breaks the kiss, and just as I'm about to lay my hand back down on his chest, he grips my chin, making me look at him. "Eyes on me, Princess."

I stare at him, panting hard, trying to catch my breath between each jolt of pleasure. My eyes bounce from his eyes to his lips, to his gritted jaw.

"Cum for us, Firefly." Oliver coaxes, running his hand up my back until his fingers are in my hair. He pulls my head back, giving me an even better view of Tyson with his chest heaving like he's ready to follow me over the edge.

Oliver pounds into me from behind, while Tyson starts to thrust up into me.

"He said cum, Princess. Now, cum." Tyson growls his demand, then slaps my ass, hard.

My eyes roll back in my head as I let out one last lust filled cry of pleasure. My body tensing up as I squeeze both their cocks so hard they groan, cumming too.

Jets of Tyson's hot cum coat my core, as Oliver's release fills my ass. I can feel it start to leak out as they slowly thrust a few more times as we all come down, completely spent.

I collapse onto Tyson's chest, brain fuzzy and feeling like I'm floating on air.

"Well, I guess it wasn't *so* bad." Tyson huffs out a laugh, his chest vibrating with a sexy chuckle.

"Maybe it's something you'd be willing to do again?" Oliver asks, slowly pulling out of me, using the tissues he snatched from the nightstand to catch his cum so it doesn't get on his brother. I can tell Oliver is trying to make this as minimally awkward for Tyson as possible, and I love him for that.

Tyson chews on his lower lip, sweat gleaming on his sexy face as he looks from his brother to me, then back to Oliver. "Only with you. I don't think I could do this with the others around, that would be pushing it."

"Only with us." I smile up at him, happiness filling me that he would think about doing this again. Having them together was mind blowing, and I would hate for this to be our one and only time.

"I think that's doable." Oliver laughs, getting off the bed and heading to the bathroom. I just lay on Tyson, his softening cock still inside of me. His fingertips caressing my spine, and I sigh, happy and content.

"I love you, Princess." Tyson says, kissing the top of my head.

"I love you too, big guy." I kiss his chest.

The water to the tub starts up and Oliver peaks his head out of the bathroom. "Ty, clean her up then come give her a bath, I'm gonna hop in the shower to clean up."

Oliver tosses a washcloth, and Tyson catches it, glaring at his brother. "I thought I was in charge."

Oliver grins. "Yeah, during sex. Now that it's after care it's fair game." He says before disappearing back into the bathroom.

Tyson wraps his arms around me, rolling us so that I'm on my back, before putting the washcloth under his dick and slowly pulling out. A surge of his cum follows and my body shivers. I love when they're bare inside me, no condom getting in the way.

Tyson carefully cleans me up, then when he's done, he scoops me up and brings me into the jacuzzi tub. I enjoy a relaxing bath in Tyson's arms. When he's done washing me, he dries me, dresses me, and places me on the bed between them. I'm grateful for his help because my body feels boneless, and I don't think I'd be much help.

I fall asleep between two of the four men I love with all my heart. The way I'm feeling right now is the best, and I'll never get tired of being surrounded by the ones I love.

When morning comes, we clean up the hotel room the best we can, making sure we have everything we brought with us. Oliver goes downstairs to get us some free breakfast.

Once he comes back we eat and have a cup of coffee before heading out for our four-hour ride home.

"Are you sure you have everything? You got your phone, charger, your toothbrush?" Tyson asks, closing the hotel room door as we start down the hall.

"Yes, Sir. I've got everything." I roll my eyes. He already asked me this three times before.

I jump with a squeak when his hand comes down on my ass, slapping it hard as he passes me. "Watch your tone with me, Princess." He warns, and a delicious shiver runs down my spine.

I stick my tongue out at him. His eyes narrow, promising me that I will pay for that later. But it's not a threat anymore, he's just giving me what I love. "Brat." He mutters, shaking his head.

Just as I'm about to go into the stairwell, the feeling that someone is watching me takes over my body. Looking back, my eyes find a man on the other end of the hall standing in the exit on that side. My eyes widen, and I suck in a gasp. I can't really make out much because of the distance, but I do know that this is the same man from the water park.

"What is it?" Tyson asks from the top of the stairs.

"The guy from the water park..." That's all I can say before looking back. He's gone.

Tyson rushes past me, and looks around. "Where?" His voice is hard.

"The exit at the end of the hall, but he's gone now."

Tyson looks to Oliver. "Take her down this way. Here are my keys, go right to the car. Do you have your gun?" Gun? When the hell did he get a fucking gun? *Oh, we will be having a talk about that!*

Oliver nods, and grabs my elbow, leading me out of the hall and down the stairs. "Come on, Firefly. If the guy is here, Tyson will find him."

We head down to the lobby and check out. My nerves are shot as I hold on to Oliver's arm, my eyes watching everything.

We wait in the car for ten minutes before Tyson comes back. "I didn't find anything." He curses, punching the steering wheel.

"Do you really think it's him? Would he follow us and come all this way?" Oliver asks.

"Knowing that crazy fucker, I would not be surprised."

"I think we need to call church. I have a feeling that the calm before the storm just might be coming to an end." Oliver says, seizing my hand.

We ride home in silence, our perfect date ruined by that despicable man. I won't let him dictate my life. I will not hide. He will never control me; not now, not ever.

CHAPTER 26
Ben

"WE'RE AT A library." Emmy says, looking out the car window at the big public library in the next city over from our little town.

"Yes." I laugh. "Very observant." I tease.

She gives me a glare. "Is our date here?"

"Yes." I grin.

"Oh. Okay, cool." She nods her head, trying to act excited, but I can tell she looks a little let down. That will change in just a moment. She looks around the parking lot. "It seems a little busy for the middle of the week."

"That's because today is not just any regular day. There's an event going on."

"There is?" She looks back out the window, finally noticing the sign on the side of the building that says 'Smutty Books Got Me Hooked' Author Meet and Greet. Her head snaps around to me, her eyes wide with excitement. "No fucking way!"

"I was looking up things to do online and this event came up. I looked at the attending authors list and saw a bunch of authors you love, and decided this would be the perfect date."

"I love you!" She squeals before leaning over the console and giving me a bear hug.

She scrambles to get out of the car. "Come on, Dude. What are you waiting for?!" She says, popping her head back into the car. Shaking my head with a chuckle, I follow after her.

"Oh, wait!" I stop and head to the trunk of the car and grab a big bag.

"What's in there?" She asks.

"Look for yourself." I grin.

She opens the bag and takes out a book, then another, then another. "Ben, these are all my books." She raises a brow.

"I know, and with them here, you can get them signed."

"Wait... The authors of *these* books are *here*?"

"Yup. So, let's go so you can fan-girl it up."

She does a little happy dance, puts the books back in the bag, then grabs my hand and drags me into the building.

Once we get into the building, I see that the event isn't in the actual library, but in its massive lobby. There have to be about thirty authors here. Not as big as some other events, but big enough for a little city like this one.

Emmy's eyes are all over the place as she sees which authors are here. "Babe, who do I meet first?"

"How about we start on one side and work our way to the other." I shrug.

"Good idea."

We head over to the first author. Reading the banner, I see her name is Quell T. Fox. "I love her *The Road to Truth* series!" She takes the bag and picks out six books.

"You're getting all of these signed?" I chuckle.

She looks at me with eyes widening slightly. "Do you think that's too much? I can't just get one and not the others, it would feel wrong."

"I'm sure it would be fine, Butterfly." I say, kissing the side of her head. When it's our turn, I stand to the side. Emmy plops down all her books on the table with a thunk. Quell gives Emmy a smile as she apologizes for having so many, but Quell tells her that she's more than happy to sign all of them for her.

When she's done she gets a quick selfie, and then I see her eyeing up some of the merch on the table. "Get whatever you want, this date is on me." She only hesitates for a moment before buying a few things. Emmy says her goodbyes and we move on to the next author.

We make our way around the room until we've stopped at almost every table. Emmy says she doesn't know of all the authors, but she did say the ones she knows and loves were Amber Nicole, KH Helens, Cassandra Featherstone, Taya Rune, Tammi Lynn, and Drea Denae just to name a few.

"Almost done? You already have almost all of your books signed and a tote full of other merch." I laugh.

"I know. Isn't it awesome?" She beams up at me, her brown eyes sparkling with excitement.

"Who do we have left?" I ask, looking at the pamphlet with all the author's names on it.

"Umm." Emmy looks at it with me. "Oh. My. God. It's Jaye Pratt and Crystal North. They wrote the *Knox Academy* series we started."

"You mean the one with that Baxter guy you love so much, that's also linked to another series."

"Yeah, that one! Oh, this is so exciting!"

We get in line and wait. When Emmy gets up there, she does her little fan-girl thing and I can't help but smile.

She tells them how much we love their series and how she's reading it with her boyfriend. When they look at me and smile, I can't help but blush a little.

Emmy buys more swag, telling me she's sorry for all that she's spending on my behalf, but she just can't help it. I tell her not to worry about it, that this is her day.

"Alright, last person." I read the banner. "Melinda Terranova. Who's that?" I ask Emmy, looking down at her.

She just gaps at me. "Are you kidding me?"

"No? I don't remember reading any books by her."

"Oh." Her face falls. "I must have read it when we were off from school after I gave birth." She sighs. "You have to read it. I'll even re-read it with you. It's called Corrupt Temptation. Soooo good. It has a stepbrother who is also a teacher in the harem."

"You and your love for a good stepbrother romance." I laugh.

"I have a thing for teacher romances, too." She smirks. "Mine just came true."

After the last author, we grab a bite to eat at the little concession stand before going into the main part of the library. There were a few books Emmy bought that were just released, and she wanted to cuddle up with me and read, if only for a little while.

We find a couch and snuggle in. We read for an hour just enjoying being in each other's company. I get to a part where the main girl is giving one of her boyfriends a blowjob in the back of their school library, and my mind instantly pictures Emmy doing these things to me. The more I read, the more I find myself getting hard. With this book describing everything, I can't help but want Emmy to do all of it to me.

"Ben," Emmy whispers my name with a little amusement in her tone. "Is this scene affecting you?"

We're reading the same book, so she's reading the same scene as I am. "Maybe." I clear my throat, knowing it's useless to lie, seeing as how she's sitting sideways on my lap and my cock is digging into her thigh.

She looks up at me with heat in her eyes. I can tell this scene is getting to her too. They always do; she loves reading smutty books, and it's fun to have sex after scenes like this. If we were home right now, I would have already been balls deep inside her.

Emmy closes the book, setting it to the side before standing up and looking around. "Come with me." She says as she drags me deeper into the library until we are at the very back.

"What about all your stuff?" I ask, looking back to where we left everything, not wanting anyone to steal it.

"Tyson can watch it. I know he's creeping around here somewhere." She grins.

Tyson let me take her myself, and followed on his bike along with a few other club members. After what happened at the hotel, Tyson and Oliver have been extra cautious. But because everyone excluding me and Tyson had their date already, Emmy argued that it wasn't fair if I didn't get to have mine. In the end, Tyson agreed but brought backup to have more eyes on the place. If this fucker was here, he would not be getting away this time.

"You know, we just so happen to be in a library right now. So, I see no reason why we can't live out this little fantasy." Emmy purrs, locking her arms around my neck so that her breasts are thrusted upwards towards my face.

My eyes go wide. I mean we've had sex in some interesting places, but this place is packed. "Emmy, baby, we can't. There's too many people around."

"It's just a blowjob. No clothes have to come off. And we can tuck ourselves in the dark corner over there. We're in the very back with all the encyclopedias, no one will be coming back here any time soon."

Biting my lip, I contemplate if it's worth it. I mean, that scene was pretty hot. And having my girl recreate it would be fucking heaven.

"Fine."

Emmy's face splits into a wide, mischievous grin. She leans up a little until she's on her tippy toes so she can kiss me. Her warm soft lips feel so good against mine. I moan as she slips her tongue in, slowly caressing mine. Once we are practically panting, she breaks the kiss and slowly lowers to her knees.

She looks like a sexy vixen kneeling before me, and I can tell she wants this too. She's very excited and eager to suck me off, to please me, and that makes me even harder.

"Remember, it's a library, so..." She places her finger up to her lips with a smirk, then reaches for my zipper.

My heart pounds as she slowly undoes my pants. I look around, making sure no one is close by. She takes my cock out, and I hiss as she gives it a tight squeeze before pumping it a few times. "Sometimes I forget you have this." She rubs her thumb over my cock piercing. "But I love to play with it when I get to play with you." Her voice is seductive, sending a shiver down my spine.

Biting my lip, I hold back a moan when she leans forward, licking the bead of pre-cum off the tip. She locks eyes with me, lifting my cock up so that she can take her tongue and slowly lick me from base all the way to tip.

After swirling her tongue around the tip, she finally takes me into her mouth. I slip my fingers into her hair and close my eyes as I try to hold back the moan that's threatening to escape past my lips.

My chest starts to heave as she bobs her head. My cock hits the back of her throat. My eyes open and I look down at my girl with hooded eyes as she starts to do what the girl in the book did. She pulls back, grasping my cock in her hand with a firm grip. Drool drips from the corner of her mouth, and I use my thumb to wipe it away. She lifts up my cock again, making me think she's going to do what she did before, only this time she goes for my balls instead. I bite my knuckle as she sucks one of my balls into her mouth and pumps my cock. She does the same thing to the other one before taking my shaft back into her mouth. Her hands slowly run up my thighs and around them to grip my ass. She gives it a hard squeeze and starts to massage it as she forces herself to deep throat me. I'm so damn glad this girl doesn't have much of a gag reflex anymore.

"I'm close, My Love." I pant, already feeling my body trembling, my balls starting to draw up. She starts to bob faster, kneading my ass. My fingers tugs on her hair as I help control her movements. She does this dance with her tongue that drives me crazy. Closing my eyes as I toss my head back, and I hold her in place as I cum hard down the back of her throat. My cock twitches out my release, and I bite my lip to keep from calling out her name. I can feel her throat closing around me to swallow my load.

When I'm sure she's sucked every last drop out of me, I slowly open my eyes and... lock eyes with a little old lady across the aisle.

My body tenses up at the horrified expression on her face. She looks from me to Emmy. "Umm. Emmy, Baby." I say, frantically tapping her cheek.

Emmy pulls back, letting my cock go with a pop. Her hooded eyes lift to mine. "So fucking delicious." She licks her lips.

"I'm glad you think so, Love, but umm..." I point to the old lady, who is still standing there, shell shocked. Emmy looks behind herself and freezes. Only now my cock is on full display for this lady to see. She finally snaps out of her trance, letting out a loud gasp.

"Dear, god!" She cries. "I just wanted a book!" She turns around and races away, mumbling something about God having mercy on our souls.

Neither of us move for a moment, then Emmy lets out a loud snort before falling to the ground in a fit of laughter. I just stand here, my mouth gaping, and my cock still hanging out, stunned that this just happened.

"Dude, put that thing away." Someone says. My gaze snaps up to Tyson, who's standing there with a scrunched up face. I scramble to tuck myself away and do my pants up as Tyson bends over to help Emmy up.

Her face is streaked with tears. "Fuck, that was gold. Did you see her face?" Emmy makes a shocked face, mimicking the old lady before laughing again.

"I had a feeling it was you two." Tyson shakes his head with a grin. "Some old lady came running by blabbering something about tattooed hooligans performing sinful acts for the world to see." That sends Emmy into another fit of laughter. "Alright, Miss Giggles, let's get you guys home. The event was over thirty minutes ago."

Once the initial shock is over, I'm not even sorry. That was one of the best blowjobs she's ever given me.

Tyson walks us out to our car, opens the door to let Emmy in. He leans over, giving her a kiss on the head, then shuts the door after she gets in.

"So, see anyone?" I ask, looking at the other bikers behind Tyson, waiting to leave but still on alert.

"A black car did slow down, but took off when they saw we were here. It had tinted windows, so no one got a good look at the person inside. Some guys tried to follow but they lost him pretty quickly. Could have been a random person, but we're not taking any risks." I nod. "Anyways, get going. We will follow behind."

He hands me Emmy's bags of merch before walking to his bike. Getting in the car, I put the stuff in the backseat, and start up the car.

"Thank you for today." Emmy says with a smile. Leaning over I give her a heated kiss before pulling back, and putting my forehead against hers.

"Anything for you, Butterfly. Forever and always."

"Oh, I could put it here!" Emmy says, rushing over to one of the book shelves, taking some of her books out and placing them in their spots. She takes out a few more, looking them over. "These can go here." She rushes over to another bookshelf. "No, no room. Here." Over to another one.

I lean against the doorway to the reading room that I made for Emmy with a smile on my face, my arms crossed as I watch her race around like an overly caffeinated squirrel as she tries to find space for all her new stuff from the book signing, rearranging where all her books used to sit.

"Shit." She sighs. "I don't have any room for the merch."

She needs to calm down from her high of the day before she crashes hard.

"Hey." I say stepping forward, putting my hands on her shoulders. I can feel her body vibrating with energy. "Everything will get a place. I can get another bookshelf if we need it."

"I know, but I want everything put away now. I don't want to just keep them in the bag, I want them proudly displayed."

Grabbing the bag with the remaining items from her hand, I place them in the corner of the room.

"Hey!" She huffs.

Turning around, I walk back over to her, pulling her into my arms, hugging her close, rubbing my hand up and down her back in an attempt to help her chill out.

"Shh. Don't get stressed out over nothing. You're still hyped up from all the excitement over today. Let's worry about that later." I kiss the side of her head. She relaxes in my arms, her heart still racing like a drum. She wraps her arms around me, placing them on my lower back.

"Thank you." She says into my chest, moving her head back and tilting her head to the side, allowing me to place light kisses against her neck.

"I'm glad you had fun." I murmur, sucking the spot behind her ear.

"Don't tell the others, but that is one of my favorite dates so far." She whispers

"Just between you and I. Promise." I smile against her neck. "I love you."

She pulls back to look into my eyes, her wild look gone, replaced by affection with a heavy dose of lust.

"I love you, too." She pulls me in for a kiss. I groan against her lips as she licks mine, asking for access that I happily grant. We kiss like lost lovers for a bit before she pulls back. Her lips are swollen and she looks so beautiful. "Let me show you just how much I appreciate everything you did for me today."

"I think you did that back in the library." I chuckle, shuddering when an image of the poor traumatized elderly lady pops up in my mind.

"Are you saying you don't want me to show you more?" She asks, taking a step back and lowering her dress, making it drop to the ground.

Swallowing hard, my eyes drop to her luscious breast. She stands there looking like a goddess, one with a look in her eyes saying that she would really like me to be her play toy, and I'm all for it.

I love this side of Emmy. Confident and sexy. When it comes to sex, she's more submissive and I know she loves when we dominate her. But it's times like this, when she takes control, takes what we are offering her, I love it. Times like this make me feel like that virgin boy I was back when we had our first time together. She took the lead and rocked my fucking world, and has every day since.

She prowls towards me, taking off her panties as she goes, tossing them to join her dress on the floor. There is something about her looking so fierce that makes my dick rock hard. It has me wanting to fall to my knees and bow to my queen.

"Are you gonna let me show you Ben?" She asks, her voice seductive, sending a shiver down my spine. *She's* the one to drop to *her* knees. Looking up at me with her big brown eyes, she undoes my pants, slowly pulling them down taking my boxers with them. My cock springs free. She looks at it, licking her lips before slowly rising, and running her hands up underneath my shirt, her fingers gliding over my abs as she goes. I can feel every caress and stroke of her fingers like my body is hyper aware of her touch.

She pulls my shirt off, leaning over to trace her tongue along the tattoos on my peck. Her tongue flicks my nipple, making them pebble and stand at attention. She sucks it into her mouth, and I groan.

"You like that don't you?" She smiles. "I've seen Talon do it to you and I loved the look of pure bliss that takes over your face when he does. I have to say, it's pretty fucking sexy being the one to make you look like this."

She kisses me, dipping her tongue into my mouth, dancing with mine. It's quick and hot, leaving me panting for her, for more. Emmy grabs my hand, leading me over to the corner of the room where she has blankets and pillows arranged on the floor for when we cuddle and read together in here.

"Sit." She commands me, giving me a little nudge. I quickly comply, keen to see where this is going. When I'm sitting, she moves to straddle me. Putting her hands on the windowsill behind me, she starts to grind her dripping pussy against my cock.

Gripping it, she gives it a few firm strokes before placing the tip to her entrance.

"Remember?" She asks, her breath tickling my ear before giving my lobe a nibble. "Remember when I rode your cock for the first time. The feeling of your piercing dragging along my walls and hitting me in all the right places. The thickness of your massive cock stretching my cunt so good.

I loved seeing how I affected you, like how our whole experience together sounded like the best thing that's ever happened to you."

"Because it was. It is." I grind out, my fingers twitching to grab her hips so I can impale her on my cock.

"I'm gonna ride you Ben. I'm gonna fuck you good until you're screaming my name, cumming deep inside me, filling me up with your cum." She purrs.

Fuckkkkk. Talon is the dirty talker in our relationship. From conversations with Charlie, I know Emmy can be this way with her, but it's not something we normally do when it's just us. And fuck I'd be lying if I said I didn't love it.

"Yes." I breath. "Fuck me Emmy, ride my cock. Grip me with that tight pussy."

And she does. She stops teasing me, lowering herself down on my aching length until I'm fully sheathed inside her. "Holy fuck." I moan, gripping her hips, my eyes rolling into the back of my head. She always feels so tight and ready for us. I love the feeling of her hot, wet center around my cock.

Emmy starts off slow, building me up, making me feel every ounce of pleasure before the feeling of being unable to hold back takes over. Moving faster, her breasts start to bounce with every thrust of her hips. I'm delirious with each stroke of her inner walls sliding against my cock. So wet, so perfect. She works us both over until we are both panting messes, blubbering curses.

"I- I'm gonna cum." She whimpers. As her climax gets closer, I can feel her tightening in little pulses around my cock. "Help." She breathes, her eyes wide, her mouth panting out little harsh breaths. "Fuck."

I know what she needs. Her mind is taken over by pleasure; she's unable to concentrate on her movements anymore. Gripping her hips, I help her move, lifting my hips to thrust up into her. "Oh god. Ben, fuck yes, Ben." She chants as I get us into a rhythm. After a few more thrusts, Emmy tosses her head back, letting out a cry that could shatter glass. My name never sounded so fucking good as it does right now coming from her swollen, pink lips.

I help her ride out her wave of pleasure before she collapses against me, her chest heaving from her climax. I hold her to my body as I thrust up into her a few more times before grunting out a curse and cumming hard deep inside her. Jets of hot cum filling her, marking her as mine. My fingers gripping her hard enough to leave bruises, only she moans at the contact.

My fingers lazily run up and down her spine as we snuggle together with my cock still buried inside her, my cum dripping from her; we don't have to move yet, though. It's perfect; having her in my arms, her steady breathing, her heart beating in sync with mine. I would stay here like this forever if I could.

"I love you." She mummers, snuggling deeper into me like she can't get close enough.

"I love you too, Butterfly. My bright, beautiful, vibrant Butterfly."

This moment, right here, right now, this will be something I won't soon forget.

Tyson

"Why do we have to go in there?" Emmy whines, looking out the window at the Reaper Tattoo Shop. "Are the same people still working there?" She asks, turning to look at me.

"Yes, but it's been over two years, Princess. They know you're with me, and they know you felt bad about the whole thing."

"But I worked with these people, got to know them, they trusted me, and then I fucked them over by stealing from them." She nibbles on her bottom lip, looking back out of the window.

"And like I said, they know everything, and they don't hate you. They understood why you did what you did. It's over and done with; it's in the past. We have to go in there, so let's just *go*."

"But why?"

"Because." I grin. "This is our date." She narrows her eyes at me in confusion, making me laugh. "Stop being a baby, and let's go." I get out and check my surroundings. I see a few of my men around, which lets me know we're all good for the moment.

Opening her car door, I hear her mumbling to herself that I'm the baby. "Excuse me?" I say, and her head snaps up to me, eyes wide. "You're being a brat, get out." My voice is stern now, leaving no room for an argument. She's thinking too much into this.

"Fine." She sasses. She gets out and starts walking towards the shop. Going to walk by her side, I slap her ass hard, making her jump.

"What was that for?" She gasps.

"For calling me a baby." I say before grabbing the back of her head and kissing the ever-loving fuck out of her right in the middle of the parking lot. She moans against my lips, leaning into me for support. Pulling back, I nip at her bottom lip with a growl.

She blinks at me in a lust hazed spell. "Better?" I ask. I know she's nervous, and I don't want to dismiss her feelings, but she's overthinking this and I don't want her to miss out on coming here because of it. I know she wants more tattoos, and she can get them for free, right here.

"Not really." She sighs. "Now my panties are soaked. This date isn't gonna be very comfortable."

"Is getting a tattoo ever really that comfortable?" I smirk.

"Wait. Am I getting a tattoo?" Her eyes light up with excitement.

"Yes, and I'm gonna be the one to do it."

Turning away from her confused face, I pull her into the shop.

"Tyson, my man. Long time no see!" Ren, the shop manager, greets.

"Hey, Ren. Life's been pretty crazy."

"I've heard. How's being a Papa?" He laughs. "Still crazy that you're a dad now. But what's even harder to believe is that you managed to get this pretty lady. Hey, Emmy." Ren grins.

"Hi." Emmy says with a small smile.

"You know, this guy has been pining over you since you first stepped foot in this shop. He never talked about you, but we could all see it in the way he watched you." I give Ren an evil glare. "Dude, don't even try to deny it." He laughs. He wasn't necessarily wrong.

"You're making me sound like a creeper." I say.

"Why? Because I was 17, and you were 23?" Emmy giggles.

"Yeah, that just sounds bad."

"My birthday is in two weeks, so we both will be in our 20s and you won't have to feel like you're robbing the cradle anymore." She tries to hold back a laugh.

"You're on thin ice, Princess." I growl.

"What are you gonna do? Spank me? We both know that threat is just an encouragement at this point." She raises a brow. Fuck, she is one sassy little brat. She's lucky I love her.

"Table. Sit. Now!" I command, pointing to where she will be getting her tattoo.

"Yes, Sir." She purrs, finally doing something I ask.

"You two are adorable. And damn near perfect for each other." Ren chuckles.

"Don't call me adorable. I'm the fucking Enforcer for the Phantom Reapers, I don't do adorable."

"Yes, you do!" Emmy calls out, but quickly shuts her mouth when I give her a look.

I go over to where Emmy is, and get everything set up. I put my gloves on, wrap all the equipment, and get the colors out that I will be using for this particular piece.

"So you're a tattoo artist. I don't know if I should be excited that my man can give me free tattoos." She smirks, and I smile. "Or mad because that's a pretty big thing to not tell me."

I shrug. "I was just an apprentice when we met. I was going to make a career out of it, but then I took on a bigger role in the MC. For a while I tried to do both, but I got too busy."

"So that means you can draw?"

"Yes." I say, taking a seat next to her.

"Do you have a portfolio of your drawings?" She inquires, and I nod. "Can I see it sometime?"

"Yeah, if you want to."

"If I see something I want, can I get it as a tattoo?" She asks hopefully.

"I don't see why not. Now lift up your dress."

"Why?" She asks.

"Because I need to clean your leg for the tattoo."

She lifts up her dress, and I start to wipe down the leg that has all her Disney tattoos on it, the ones that got ruined from her stabbing.

"Tyson." She says, grabbing my hand to stop me.

"Do you trust me?" She pauses for a second, then nods. "Then let me."

She lets go of my hand, and I get to work. She hisses in pain when I first make contact, but after a moment she just lays her head back and closes her eyes.

"I love getting tattoos. Some hurt, but the pain is what I crave. I don't know how to explain it."

"I get it. I feel the same." The tattoo gun hums, and I get lost in my work. I've missed this. "I'm glad I'm able to do this for you."

It took me a few hours, but overall it turned out just as I was hoping it would.

"All done." I say, wiping the blood and ink away. She hasn't looked at it once since I started.

She looks down and inspects the new artwork on her leg. When she doesn't say anything, I start to get worried. Dipping my head down and to the side so that I'm able to see her face, I take note of the tears gathering in her eyes.

"What's wrong? Don't you like it?" My stomach drops at the thought of me making this worse.

"No." She sniffs and my heart drops. "I love it." She looks up at me, and I get a good look at her expression. Seeing the love and appreciation for what I was able to give back to her by fixing her tattoos, has my heart filling up with pure happiness. "Thank you." She whispers, finally letting the liquid free to roll down her cheeks. She pulls me to her, giving me a bone crushing hug. I hug her back, enjoying the love she's given me.

"You can't even tell." She says, pulling back. "You can't see the scars anymore."

"I had to go over a few characters in order to be able to do what I had planned. I'm sorry if I fucked it up." I explain.

"No, it's perfect. You replaced it with Disney characters I like, but didn't get the chance to add. We can just add the ones you covered to another place."

"I'm glad you like it." I smile, feeling a hell of a lot better about everything.

She cups my face, taking me by surprise. "Ty, you have no idea how much this means to me. I've learned to love my scars, but you, being able to do this, takes that little bit of the doubt in the back of my mind away. I don't have to worry if people are staring and talking about me behind my back anymore."

She kisses me with every emotion she has inside of her. She's my Princess and I'll do anything to make her smile.

CHAPTER 27
Ben

"YOU KNOW, WE'RE pretty much crashing their date." I tell Talon as we walk from the car to the front entrance of Reaper's Tattoo Shop. Talon thought it would be a perfect place to get his first tattoo, and because Tyson and Emmy were there already, he chose now as the perfect time to get it done.

"It's more convenient this way. May as well get it out of the way." He shrugs.

"Do you even know what you want?"

"Kind of."

Cracking a grin, I shake my head. "Do you want to get this tattoo for you, or because you're the only guy without one?" I ask.

"Both, maybe? I mean, I don't want to be covered like you guys. Although I do find yours and Emmy's tattoos very fucking sexy." He stops me to pull me in for a kiss, giving my ass a squeeze. Chuckling against his lips, I bite his lower one, making him groan before pulling back. "Alright. Let's go get you some ink."

Entering the shop, I look around at the place that meant so much to Emmy in her past. It's a nice shop. Very clean and edgy. I don't know why I thought it would be a little more grungy than it is. I guess you can't judge a book by its cover.

"Hey, sorry, but we're closed today. Owner has the place booked out for personal use." A man says when we walk into the shop. As I get a good look at him I notice tattoos cover him from head to toe and he has black shaggy hair with light brown eyes. Underneath it all, he's a nice looking man. I can tell he's checking Talon out while he's looking for Emmy.

"It's okay, we know the owner. We're his girlfriend's boyfriends." Talon says, strutting in like he owns the place. The guy's brows shoot up, before a look of understanding replaces his surprise.

"Ah, you guys must be the other two men in Emmy's harem. I gotta say, she's one lucky bitch." The guy says, looking me up and down.

"Hey now, I'd watch what you say and do, Ren. Did you hear what Emmy did to that Sweet Butt who tried to hit on me last weekend?" Tyson says, coming out from a little blocked off cubby with Emmy trailing behind him.

"You're a cool guy, Ren, but don't think I won't cut you for flirting with my guys." Emmy grins. She has a black bandage on her leg. The one with all the scars. *What did she get done?*

"Well then, I'll keep my eyes to myself, can't risk this pretty face now, can we?" Ren laughs before heading into the back room.

"What are you guys doing here?" Emmy grins.

"Thought I'd get my first tattoo today, since you guys were already here."

"Really?" Emmy asks. "Gonna break that virgin skin? I think you will look sexy with ink." Her eyes heat as she looks him over. "I mean you're fucking sexy already, but I got a thing for ink, what can I say?" She shrugs with a laugh.

"So what did you get?" I ask her, wrapping her in my arms for a hug. She looks up at me with a beaming smile. I can't help but kiss those soft, perfect lips of hers.

She steps back to bend over and pull back her bandage. My eyes go wide when I see that the images that were distorted from her scars are covered up with new characters.

"Holy fuck!" Talon breathes. "They look amazing."

"And you can't even tell where the scars are unless you get really close. Tyson did an amazing job." She looks so happy and it makes my heart feel full.

"Wait. Tyson?" Talon asks, looking up at the man in question. "You can do tattoos? How the fuck didn't we know this?"

"I didn't even know until today." Emmy laughs.

"It's not a big deal. It was something I wanted to do in the past, but the MC came first, and it got pushed to the side until one day I just... stopped." He shrugs like it's no big deal.

"Can you do mine?" Talon asks.

"Yeah, I guess. I don't see why that would be a problem. Do you have an idea of what you want? I might be able to sketch something up quickly, depending on how intricate what you're wanting to get is."

Talon and Tyson head over to the cubby Emmy just came out of.

"It looks amazing, Butterfly." I tell her as she covers it back up.

"Does it make me shallow that I'm glad it covers my scars?" She asks, worry etching her features.

"What, no. Why would you think that?"

She nibbles on her lip before answering. "Because it's not that I think I look bad with them, I've accepted and grown to love them. It has nothing to do with my appearance. But every time I'd look down, or see them in the mirror, I'm reminded of that night, and everything that happened."

"Then, definitely not. Being happy for not having that reminder anymore doesn't make you shallow, My Love, it makes you human." I pull her into my arms and hold her. She sighs and relaxes into my body. We take a seat on the leather couch in the waiting room for a bit until Tyson comes out.

"Alright, we're good to go. You can come back and watch if you want."

We follow Tyson to his work area where Talon's waiting. He is sitting on the table that's propped up in a chair position, and his arm is lying out on an arm rest that's attached. Tyson puts on a pair of gloves and cleans Talon's arm as I take a seat, pulling Emmy down into my lap.

"I'm excited." Talon says.

"Alright, ready?" Tyson asks. We can't see the design he's chosen, so when I try to stretch and get a look, Talon snaps his fingers at me.

"Sit! It's a surprise." He growls, turning me on a little, but then he looks at Tyson. "I'm good."

The tattoo gun comes to life, and it gives me a little thrill. It's been a while since I got some fresh ink, I think I'm due for more soon. Tyson brings it down onto Talon's arm causing his smile to slide off his face. As Tyson keeps going, Talon's face gradually starts to change into a grimace filled with pain. I can tell he's trying to put on a brave face. It's like he didn't expect this to hurt at all.

He only lasts a few more seconds before yelling, "Stop! Just stop." Tyson lifts the gun up in the air like he's surrendering. "Holy, sweet mother of Moses. How the fuck are you guys covered in tattoos?" He beseeches us, his face honestly astonished.

Emmy bursts into giggles at the look on Talon's face, while I hide my smile behind her shoulder.

"Baby, what did you think it would feel like, being tickled by a feather or getting puppy kisses?" Emmy questions him.

"No!" He says, annoyed that we're finding humor in his pain. "But I didn't think it would feel like-"

"You're getting stabbed with a needle three thousand times in a minute?" I ask, cocking a brow.

"Well, yeah. *That.*" He huffs.

"Dude, I already started, and it's gonna look like shit if I don't finish. We need to at least do the outlining today, then I can do the shading another time. But I can tell you, once you get used to it, it's not so bad. It starts to feel kind of numb after a bit." Tyson says.

"It's true. That's part of the reason why I don't mind getting them. Depending on the place, eventually it just becomes a dull tingle. Like when your foot falls asleep." Emmy says. "But, if you need a distraction from the pain, I'm more than happy to help." She purrs. Talon's eyes light up at the idea.

"That might work." He smirks.

"Hey guys, I'm heading out. Nice to see you, Emmy. You're locking up, right?" Ren says, directing his question to Tyson.

"Yup, you're good to go. I'll clean up here afterwards and shut the place down." Tyson replies.

"Nice. Alright, well, hope to see ya around. Later."

"Bye!" We all reply.

"So where were we on that distracting thing? I mean, it's just us now. I won't say no if you want to help ease my pain." Talon wiggles his eyebrows suggestively.

"I don't know, that depends on if Tyson is okay with it." Emmy says, turning her attention to Tyson.

He raises a brow, giving her a look before sighing. "Fine. But go get the privacy sheet in the back room, and no sex. Too much movement." *He really can't deny her anything, can he?*

"Fuck, yes!" Talon fist pumps the air. Emmy giggles and runs off to get the sheet.

"So, what are you gonna do to keep my mind off the pain?" Talon asks me with heated eyes.

"Well. You know, that little game you thought would be so much fun to play while we had our last 'fun time' with Emmy." I grin.

"Yesssss...?" Talon says, his tone coming off with a bit of caution.

"Well, I think I wanna play that. But change a few things around."

"Like what?" His eyes narrow.

"Every time you make a sound from the pain, Emmy will stop sucking your cock. Which means I'll stop fucking her from behind, and you won't get to watch the show anymore."

"Oh, I like that game." Emmy says with a laugh as she wheels in a cart with a sheet attached.

"Of course, you do. You guys just want to see me suffer." Talon pouts.

"Oh, totally, that's why I'm going to suck your cock to take the pain away." Emmy rolls her eyes.

Tyson chuckles and puts the gun down. He takes the screen from Emmy and places it so that it completely blocks him from view. There's a slit in the middle that allows Talon's arm to poke through.

"Alright, I'm good on my end." Tyson says, and it sounds like he's snapping on a clean pair of gloves. "Just let me know when you're good to go on your end."

"You ready for me, baby?" Emmy's voice is seductive and sexy. I love when she gets in playful moods like this. One thing Emmy is not afraid of is embracing her sexuality. She likes what she likes, and she doesn't care what anyone thinks. Her sister Harlow is a lot like that; but, from what I heard, a little more adventurous than Emmy.

"I'm always ready for you." Talon groans as Emmy palms his cock.

"You're already hard for me?"

"Ben painted a picture that I really, *really* liked." He grins.

"Look, enough with the foreplay, I don't have all day." Tyson says in a bored tone.

"Alright, grumpy ass, jumping right in it is." Emmy sasses back.

"Princess." Tyson warns.

She turns back to me, rolling her eyes. I stifle a laugh as she turns back to Talon. "Good thing you wore a dress today. Makes this a lot easier."

"It's like she was hoping this would happen." Talon grins.

"It's because I told her to, you idiot. Made tattooing her leg easier. Which, by the way, be careful with it. Now enough chit-chat, Princess, suck your man's cock, so I can finish the big baby's tattoo." Tyson says, sounding impatient.

Talon goes to say something, but cuts himself off with a moan as Emmy wastes no more time, taking him into her mouth. "Fuck." Talon hisses.

Tyson takes that as his green light to get back to work and the buzz of the tattoo gun starts back up. Talon starts to make a noise as if in pain, but Emmy starts bobbing her head. "Yes." Talon moans, but I can see the flinches of pain on his face.

"You keep sucking him, My Love. I'm gonna take this sweet pussy we all love so much." I tell her, running my hand down her back before lifting her dress above her hips. Kneeling down, I can see her red panties are a little damp already.

"Does sucking our man off turn you on, Butterfly?" I ask, running my nose over her covered pussy. She whimpers as her answer. I'll take that as a *yes*.

"Taste her, Ben. Tell me how it is." Talon commands, lust clear in his voice.

"With pleasure." I pull down her panties until they are around her ankles. Her pink pussy lips glisten with need. I give her a lick, lapping up what's waiting for me. "So fucking delicious." Emmy groans around Talon's cock, making him moan.

Standing up, I take out my cock. I'm hard as steel. Seeing my girl with my guy always gets me going. It's one of my favorite sights to see.

"Fuck her." Talon groans, gripping Emmy's hair, making her take him deeper. "Fuck!" He screeches out of pain, not pleasure. Fear flashing in his eyes.

"Do that again, and I stop." I narrow my eyes.

"You know, I'm spanking your ass after this. I know you love it just as much as Emmy." He says through gritted teeth. My cock twitches at his threat. He's right, I fucking love it, and so does our girl. To prove his point, I give her ass a swat, and she jolts forward gagging on Talon's cock. I'm normally not the one to do the ass slapping, but I love how responsive she is.

I run the tip of my cock against her wet pussy, before slipping past her entrance and bottoming out in one quick thrust. She cries out and clenches around me at the sudden intrusion. "Fuck." She moans, pulling away from Talon. "I fucking love your cock. Fuck me, Ben; make me cum and I'll make our man cum."

"Yes, ma'am." I grin before pulling back and thrusting back in. I fuck her just the way she loves it, but I have to be careful not to move Talon too much. Gripping her hips for control, I focus so that my thrusts are slow and hard.

Emmy is making sounds that are driving me crazy. And watching the look on Talon's face just makes it all that much better.

I get a steady pace going, enjoying how every time I hit her G-spot, she clenches a little tighter. It's a tease for my dick, but it feels so fucking good. Then Talon ruins it. I almost forgot about our little game, and wish I kept my mouth shut about it.

"Ouch, *fuck*." Talon hisses, looking towards Tyson, but the screen is blocking him from our view.

I stop mid-stroke, making Emmy whine, and release Talon's cock.

"What? No no no, don't stop. Please! I was so close." Talon begs, his eyes wide.

"How about we make a deal, no more games like these in the bedroom, and we can end it now, and everyone cums."

"Deal!" He responds quickly. "Now, Baby, please stick me back in your sexy-as-fuck mouth and keep working that magic, I was *so* close." He pouts.

"Only because I need to cum too." She looks over her shoulder giving me a glare. I just lean over to give her a kiss, which makes the pissy look melt from her face. "Not fair, you know your kisses are my weakness."

"I know." I smile, thrusting back into her, making her eyes roll back.

"Can you all hurry the fuck up? It's becoming distracting." Tyson mutters.

Emmy chokes out a laugh. "I kind of forgot you were there, sorry." She says before taking Talon back into his mouth.

"That's it, Baby Girl. Take my cock." Talon groans, gripping her hair, and controlling her movements. He leans his head back and closes his eyes, enjoying everything she's doing to him.

I start pounding into her again. It doesn't take long until I feel that familiar tingle. "Fuck, I'm gonna cum." I grit out, trying not to be the first one to find our release.

"Same." Talon pants, his breathing getting heavier, before he grips Emmy's hair harder, forcing her down as he lets out a long, lusty moan, and cumming down her throat. "Fuck! Swallow that cum."

Emmy is next to reach her climax, causing her to grip my cock so hard she's practically strangling it. I can't take it anymore. When she pulls away from Talon to cry out our names, making his still rock-hard cock slap against his abs, I lose it.

I pull her up with her back flush to my front, and angle her face so that I can kiss her while ramming my tongue into her mouth to taste Talon. I fuck her like a wild beast until I'm cumming so hard, I need to break the kiss so I can breathe. Tucking my face into her neck, I twitch out the last of my release, holding her to me. We're all breathing hard as we come down from our highs.

"God, that was amazing. And I don't even really feel much of the tattoo anymore. I mean I do, but you were right, it's more of a numb, dull pain now."

"Told you." Emmy smirks, licking her lips. I grab the box of tissues on the table next to us as I carefully slide out of Emmy and clean her up the best I can before tossing them in the trash.

"Go pee and clean up more thoroughly." I tell Emmy, kissing her hard, tasting Talon's release on her tongue, which makes me groan. She takes off towards the bathroom, and I turn back to find Talon smirking at me. "What?" I ask with a smirk of my own.

"It's hot to see you take a little more control during sex. I mean, I love having you two at my mercy, but seeing you like that with her..." He bites his lip.

"I don't know what came over me. Just watching you two brought it out in me, I guess."

"Maybe we can bring it out again, sometime soon."

"Alright, enough! I just had to listen to my girl choke on your cock, while your boyfriend fucked her. I don't want to hear any more than I have to. I get enough of it at home."

Emmy laughs coming back from the bathroom as Tyson removes the screen and Talon tucks himself away. She sits on my lap as we talk to Talon for the rest of his tattoo. An hour later, it's done.

"Alright, I wanna see." Emmy says, bouncing in my lap.

Tyson cleans up the tattoo before Talon sits up, and angles his arm towards us. At the top of his shoulder it looks like a crack in a wall, and growing out of it is a vine. It's not a very long vine, but it has two leaves growing out of it. Leaning forward, I see that the leaves have names. One says Elijah and the other says Melody.

Fuck. My heart skips a beat as I lock eyes with my guy. He gives me a lopsided smile filled with emotion.

"You...you got our babies' names?" Emmy sniffs. "I love it. It's beautiful." Emmy hugs Talon, careful of his arm, and softly cries happy tears.

"You're amazing, you know that?" I grin, my eyes watering a little.

This man who was so afraid of becoming a father, a man who has been through so much with his own, has ended up being one of the best dads anyone could ask for. He overcame his fears for our girl, and I can tell that he never regretted his change of heart since the moment he laid eyes on Melody. That moment changed us all in some way, for the better.

I'm so proud to call him mine, and I can't wait to spend the rest of my life with him, our girl, and our kids.

CHAPTER 28
Emmy

MY BIRTHDAY IS Friday, and I am actually pretty excited about it for once. After all the dates with each of my lovers, the weeks that followed have been pretty relaxing. Tyson and Oliver have been spending a lot of time at the clubhouse with their dad and the others. They're preparing for a war, but with no idea when it will come. Since seeing that man who apparently looks like Dagger, the guys have been on high alert. As much as I enjoyed getting out and doing things with the others, it's been nice to just hang out at home with the knowledge that we have nothing to worry about here.

Harlow is set to come down and will arrive later today. I can't wait to spend time with her. I missed my batshit crazy, big sister. Harlow has been demanding baby pictures daily and we have been sticking to our weekly phone calls.

Tyson has told Harlow about my Dagger sightings, and said she prays the fucker has the balls to show his face while I'm out with her. She's been itching to put a bullet between his eyes for a while now but has waited, albeit not so patiently. She rules LA and its surroundings, but this is Canada, so it makes things a little more tricky; but for her, it's not impossible.

Harlow did end up buying the strip club we went to for Charlie's birthday last year, but instead of keeping it a strip club, or even turning it into one of her burlesque clubs, she decided to make it a regular nightclub. She doesn't like the idea of girls working in that industry under her name and not being able to be as involved like she is with the others.

She also told me the grand opening would be this weekend just in time for my birthday; making it a win-win for her to come now. She wants us all to come and enjoy a night out with her. This will be my first time going clubbing, same with the others, so this should be interesting.

Today is just another lazy Thursday. Talon and Ben are gaming while Charlie and I are just hanging out with Melody while doing some housework.

As I'm sweeping, the doorbell rings.

"I'll get it!" I call out to the guys who are yelling at the TV from the basement.

I can hear them aggressively pressing buttons on their controllers. I don't think they even heard the door. Rolling my eyes at them with a smile, I answer the door.

"Surprise!" The voice of one of my best friends in the whole world cheers.

"Felicity!" I squeal and launch myself at her. "What are you doing here?" I ask, taking a step back to get a good look at my beautiful bestie.

"Well, as you know, I'm leaving for Harvard next week; I have no idea when I'll be back in the country, so I had to see my girls before I left. Also, I had to officially meet my niece. You know, now that she's not all covered in goo, while some crazy bitch is hunting us down."

I snort a laugh at her comment. "Well I'm glad you came. I would have been pretty bummed if I didn't get to see you. It's been months and I miss you."

"I miss you too, boo." She gives me a sad smile.

"Come in, I know Charlie will be excited to see you." Felicity follows me into the house, and just as I close the door, Charlie comes to check on things.

"Babe, who's at the-" Charlie stops mid sentence when she sees Felicity. Her eyes go wide and she lets out an excited girly scream. It scares Melody, who bursts into tears and starts to cry.

"Shit, Mama C is so sorry, Baby Girl." Charlie says, rocking Melody to try to calm her down.

"What's wrong, what's going on?" Talon and Ben come running up the stairs and into the entryway.

"Everything is fine." I tell him, going over to Charlie. She looks at me with a guilty look. "It's okay, I did the same thing when I saw her too." I take the baby from Charlie, and pull down my shirt. The moment she latches on and starts to nurse, her cries go silent. She gives us a few hitched breaths before slowly blinking her eyes closed and falling asleep. Once Charlie was satisfied that Melody was in fact okay, she rushes over to our bestie and gives her the same greeting.

They talk for a moment while Felicity tells her everything she just told me.

"Well, hey there, little lady. We missed you." Talon greets her with a smile, pulling her in for a hug.

"Hey there, manwhore, how's life treating you?" Felicity grins.

"You know, living the dad life, minus the dad bod. Getting my D wet daily per usual though." Felicity cocks a brow, shaking her head at my wild man.

"Don't mind him." Ben says with a laugh, giving Felicity a quick hug. "It's good to see you. I know the girls have missed you like crazy."

"Just the girls?" Felicity teases.

"Us too, of course." Ben grins.

"Where are your biker boys?" Felicity asks me, wiggling her eyebrows making me laugh.

"MC shit. Girl, we have so much to tell you."

We sit in our backyard on the porch swing and talk for what feels like hours. I tell her all about the shit with Dagger, and she tells us about what's going on in her life. She is going off to school to study astronomy, no surprise there. She said that she and Miles are going to try the long distance thing, but he wants to stay here and eventually become a partner in his father's company. Something about proving he's better than his past mistakes. I hope they can make it work, they're pretty amazing together, but if life has other plans, what can you do?

"Look who's up from her little nap." I coo to Melody. "Someone wants to meet you, Melly Belly." I say, handing her over to a very eager Felicity.

"Oh my god." She gushes. "She's so adorable."

"Isn't she just the cutest baby you have ever seen?" I smile, brushing the hair out of Melody's face. It's crazy long for a three-month-old.

"It's still so red." Felicity looks around. "So, do you guys think she's Ben's?"

Talon looks at Ben and smiles. "Well, she's all of ours. Although it would be no surprise to us if, when we do a paternity test, it comes back verifying that she has his DNA. I mean, we *do* plan on doing it eventually."

"You do?" Felicity looks at me with a pinched brow.

"We talked about it, and when we are ready for more kids, we want them each to have an equal chance at having a baby." I shrug. "So we would need to find out whose DNA makes up a part of Melody. But, like Talon said, she is 100 percent all of theirs. I don't think I've ever doubted that for a moment." I grin up at Talon. He gives me a look filled with so much love that my heart almost stops.

"So you want three more kids?" Felicity asks in disbelief. "Oh, girl, I'm so sorry for your lady bits." She says, sounding genuinely concerned. I burst out laughing at the look on her face.

"It's gonna happen to you one day." I point out.

"Nope. No kids for me. I have a lot of plans for my life, and so far none of them include kids. Not that I don't like them, I just don't see them as part of my future right now. Maybe that will change someday.

But for now, I'll just enjoy being an auntie to this cutie, and any others you have. I'll give her back at the end of the day." We all laugh and talk some more. Tyson calls and tells me they won't be home in time for supper, but to go by the clubhouse in an hour for the barbecue they are having in celebration for a member's birthday.

We invite Felicity too, and she accepts. We all head over to the clubhouse and mingle with some people, and it isn't long before the Old Ladies take Melody like they always do. The girls and I take advantage of the moment, and grab a bite to eat. Ben and Talon are off doing their own thing, so we head inside and play a game of darts.

"Charlie!" Felicity shrieks, jumping out of the way of the dart that is headed towards her. "Are you trying to kill me?" Her eyes are wide as she watches the dart hit the wall right where her head was only a second ago.

"Sorry." Charlie cringes. "I told you, I'm not the best at this game. You were standing too close."

"I was five feet away from the board." Felicity says with a blank face.

"Okay, so I'm *really* bad at this game."

"Ya think?" I can't help but giggle at their banter.

"Emmy." Someone calls my name. Turning around, I see Steel heading towards me.

"Hey, what's up?" I smile at him.

"I have a surprise for you." He says, then steps to the side to reveal Ethan. My eyes go wide, and my face splits into a huge smile.

"Oh my god." I breathe before pulling him into a hug.

"Hey, girl. I missed you." He says, hugging me tightly.

"I missed you, too." I pull back to look at him. "What are you doing here? Where are Leah and Mason?"

"They are at our new apartment down the street." Ethan grins.

"You moved here?" I ask excitedly.

"Yup, Steel gave me a call the other day. He said he heard that Leah and I were looking to break away from our parents and needed a place of our own. He offered us a place in one of the buildings he owns. Even offered us jobs. Leah is going to work at the daycare they have here in the compound, that way she can still watch Mason. And I'm going to be working at the corner store that's under our apartment. It's nothing fancy, but it's something that will help us start our new lives."

"Oh, I'm so happy for you." I give his hand a squeeze. Then my brain processes what he just said. "Wait, you said Steel did all this, how did he know anything about you?"

"Looks like your tall, dark and handsome MC man said something. I'm grateful he did. I take pride in providing for my son and Leah, but I'm not stupid enough not to take help when we really need it."

"Sooooo, did you forget about us?" Charlie says from behind me. I turn around and see Charlie standing there with her hip popped, hands resting on top of them, and brow cocked.

"Hey, Charlie." Ethan says with amusement, then opens his arms for a hug.

"That's better." Charlie nods her head in approval and gives him a hug.

"Anyone gonna introduce me?" Felicity asks.

"Of course." I chuckle. "Ethan, meet Felicity, my ride or die bitch. Felicity, meet Ethan, the guy who kept me from going crazy when the stupid place sent you away."

"Nice to meet you." Felicity says as they shake hands. "Thanks for keeping this one from killing one of her guys. Or Charlie."

"Thanks." Charlie says, rolling her eyes.

"We're not that bad." Tyson says, coming out of nowhere, making me jump. "Did I scare you, Princess?" Tyson pulls me to his body, wrapping his arms around me. I can smell him, mint and tobacco. He's cut down a lot since we got together, but he still smokes on occasion, mostly when he's with the other members. I don't mind the smell, it's the lasting effects that bother me.

"A little." I lean up and kiss him. "I missed you today." I breathe, lightly brushing my lips against his. An excited shiver runs down my spine when he growls low and deep, nipping at my lower lip.

"I missed you too, Princess. All I could think about during church was going home, bending you over my knee, and spanking that plump ass until you were dripping down your thighs. Then fucking you into a coma."

Well, fuck me silly. There go my panties. I wonder if that offer is still on the table. Wait, never mind, it will have to wait, we have company.

"But I didn't do anything to deserve a spanking." I say trying to sound innocent, my voice light and airy while I'm lust drunk on the idea of him doing naughty things to me.

"Do you really need a reason?" He gives me a dangerously sexy grin. And to prove his point, I was about to present my ass to him right here and now.

Ethan's laugh snaps me out of my haze, reminding me of what Ethan said. "Did you talk to your dad about everything going on with Ethan?"

"Maybe." My broody bastard grunts.

"Why?" I smile.

He says nothing, giving me a resting bitch face before sighing and giving in. "Because he is one of your best friends. He means a lot to you, therefore, by default, he means at least something to me. Plus, he is a good kid in a very shitty situation and we have the power to make his life a little less shitty, so why not? If it makes you happy, then I'm happy."

"Fuck, I love you so damn much." I really was seconds away from climbing this man like a tree and begging him to ruin me with his monster cock.

"I love you too, Princess. You know I'd do anything for you." He kisses me hard and fast, lifting me up by my thighs, as I wrap my legs around his waist. Pushing me against the wall, he grinds his thick cock against my throbbing pussy. I don't care if anyone is around, I want him. Now.

My horny bubble dies, as well as any plans of getting off tonight, at what happens next.

The doors to the clubhouse burst open, and in walks one of the scariest people you will ever meet. Or so I'm told. "Bow down, Peasants! Your Queen is here." My sister, Harlow, a.k.a. Queenie, or as the underworld knows her, one of the craziest serial killers to ever exist, greets the room full of bikers with a really fucking creepy smile. She's fucking beautiful, so she pulls it off.

Everyone is quiet. No one dares to say a word. They know who she is. And when her just-as-crazy man, Neo, walks in behind her, I think I see a few hardened club members ready to pass out or run away.

Well, this night just got a whole *hell* of a lot more interesting.

CHAPTER 29
Tyson

LEAVE IT TO Queenie to make a dramatic entrance that also has people wanting to shit their pants.

She looks around the room until her eyes lock on me and Emmy. Emmy's legs are still wrapped around my waist, my cock still straining against my jeans. Never thought Low would be the one to be a cock blocker.

"Ty-Ty!" Queenie cheers. "Is that you over there in the darkly lit corner, defiling my baby sister?" She asks with a wicked smirk. Everyone looks at us and Emmy lets out a groan of embarrassment. She drops her legs from around my waist and tucks her head into my chest to hide her reddening cheeks.

"No defiling here, Queenie, thanks to you." I give her a blank stare. A few people gasp at how I am talking to her, but being best friends allows me some leeway in public, but I know never to try and test how much I can get away with.

"Well what kind of big sister would I be if I didn't get in the way of my baby sis getting some D at least once?" She winks.

"My Queen, where should I put this?" a gruff voice asks as a giant six-foot stuffed llama makes its way through the front door. It takes me a second to see that it's actually Neo behind the damn thing.

"Umm." Harlow hums, putting her finger on her chin as she looks around the room. "There." She points to a booth full of people. She walks over, and all it takes is for her to make eye contact with everyone to make them scatter like mice. She sweeps her arm over the table, taking all the cups and food with it. "You can put it here for now until we bring it over to Emmy's."

Neo sets it down, making sure it's sitting up perfectly before taking a step back, admiring the stuffie. "Will she like it?" Neo asks with a hopeful look on his face.

"I think she will love it, you did good." She nods her head. Neo gives her this intense stare, before grabbing the back of her head, kissing her hard and dirty.

She moans loudly into his mouth before jumping up to wrap her legs around his waist. He sits her on top of the table, the same one with the stuffie, and she starts to fucking dry hump him. Seriously, what is the matter with these two? They really don't care who's watching.

Needing to put a stop to this before Emmy is scarred for life seeing her sister get fucked like a crazed animal, I clear my throat.

"Queenie." I say, trying to get her attention. But I'm just met with a moan. So I try again, a little louder this time. "Queenie."

"Mhmm, what?" She asks, pulling back from Neo, looking at me with this drunk and horny expression. She looks at me, then around the room. "Oops. Sorry, sometimes we get a little carried away."

A little? It was about to become a graphic porno in here.

"Why is there a giant llama in here?" I ask, pointing to the thing.

"Alpaca!" They both shout at me, making me jump a little.

"My bad." I say, holding my hands up. They seem really offended by my misnaming.

"And it's a gift from Neo to Melody." Harlow beams.

"Speaking of Melody, where is she?" Neo huffs, looking around. He spots Melody across the room in an Old Lady's arms. The poor woman looks like she wants to run and hide, but that would not be a smart idea. Neo seems like the kind of guy who enjoys the chase.

Neo starts storming over in their direction. I look at Emmy when she grabs my hand. Her face has a slightly concerned look as she watches this big, buff, scary killer stomp towards our daughter.

When he gets to Melody, he glares at the woman. "Give her to me." He demands. She has a panicked look on her face, but doesn't hand her over, not until she looks over at Emmy and sees the nod that it's okay. She holds out a cooing Melody for Neo to take with shaking arms.

He takes her, and the moment Melody is in his hands, his face goes from crazy demon to utter mush.

"Look at you." He coos. "Who's a gorgeous little princess? You are. Yes, you are." He starts to kiss her face. Melody lets out an excited squeal, then starts to laugh. My face splits into a wide smile. That was her first laugh. Emmy is grinning from ear to ear. Neo looks up, and sees the whole room watching him. "The fuck you looking at?!" He barks. "Mind your own damn business before I cut you!" He warns. Just like that, everyone looks away, conversations start up, and the whole room tries their hardest not to look at him. All but the fucker at the bar, who has had one too many drinks.

"Aren't you supposed to be some kind of crazy killer?" The dead-man-walking asks. John is an MC member, and my dad is watching with fear in his eyes that he might just lose a brother. "You look more like one of those little fairy boys." He chuckles.

Oh, John... Stupid, stupid John. I never liked the guy, he is very openly homophobic. Dad has banned him from making crude comments about Emmy, Charlie, Ben, and Talon and how they choose to live their lives, but that doesn't change his view on the subject.

"Mistress." Neo calls for Harlow, his voice void of any expression.

"Yes, My Pet?" Harlow asks, going to stand next to him.

"Can you please take this little ball of sunshine?"

"Of course." Harlow says, taking Melody into her arms, then immediately goes all mushy.

Neo turns to the guy. One moment he is standing a few feet away, the next he's at the guy's side, grabbing the back of his head and smashing it into the bar top. John lets out a roar of pain. No one does anything to help him. He dug his own grave, but I can see the pain on my dad's face. Neo grabs John's hair, ripping his head up so that his face is visible. Neo slips his hand into his back pocket, retrieving a pocket knife.

"Oh." Harlow says, raising her hand up to cover Melody's eyes. "Auntie Q does not want you to see what Uncle Neo is about to do. Although, that red *is* a very pretty color." She says, watching the blood gush from John's mouth, over his broken teeth, mixing with the blood dripping from his broken nose, like she was in some kind of trance. *Damn, she really has a thing for blood.*

Neo takes the knife and does something to John with it, but I'm unable to see because of where I'm standing. John lets out a horrible cry, and I see Emmy move away from me and over to her sister. She takes her hands and covers Melody's ears.

"Good idea! I guess four arms would have come in handy right about now." Harlow giggles. Emmy just smiles at her sister, and looks down at Melody, talking to her while trying to avoid the blood fest.

When Neo is done doing whatever the fuck he's doing, he moves away a little, allowing me to get a good look at John. Across his forehead the word 'homophobe' is carved into his skin. "I don't take kindly to people who make fun of the LGBTQ plus community. So I suggest if you want to keep your tongue in that trashy mouth of yours, you should avoid making comments like that in the future.

The *ONLY* reason you are getting to live today is because I like to play with my victims, and I don't have time right now because I'm spending time with my niece, which you so rudely interrupted. But I want you to have something to remember me by." Neo gives him a crazy-as-fuck smile that sends an uneasy shiver down my spin. Neo takes the knife in his hand and rams it into John's side, giving it a twist before yanking it out and tossing him to the ground.

Neo turns to my dad. "You're a good guy, Steel. I respect you. But I think you need to watch the company you keep. Or, I'll be more than happy to take them off your hands for a play date."

"Oh, me too, me too!" Harlow says, her eyes lighting up. Neo walks over to the sink behind the bar and washes his hands, ridding himself of the blood. When he's done, Neo is back at Harlow's side.

"Little Bug, please." Neo holds his hands out with a blank face. Harlow giggles, shaking her head as she hands Melody to the man who just stabbed a guy after he bashed said guy's face in, like it was no big deal. Even Emmy doesn't blink. She knows Harlow would never put her child in harm's way. I love how they already have such a strong sisterly bond.

"I'm not getting my baby back any time soon, am I?" Emmy asks Harlow.

"Nope." Harlow says, popping the p. "I think at this point even I might have to stab the fucker for some time with her." Harlow leans over closer to Emmy and covers the side of her mouth. "But between me and you, he would enjoy that way too much." Emmy's eyes widen slightly as she processes what Harlow means by that. Harlow just gives her a wink.

"Why did he come with us? You know you can't bring him anywhere." A red haired woman says, walking toward Harlow.

"Because you know he would never leave my side for that long." Harlow rolls her eyes. She pulls the woman to her, then places her hand on her cheek lightly before giving her a soft, but heated, kiss. The woman blushes and bites her lip, looking at Harlow like she's her whole world.

"Emmy, I'd like you to officially meet Evie, my girlfriend." Harlow beams.

"It's nice to finally meet you." Emmy says, giving Evie a bright smile.

"Same here. This one can't shut up about you." Evie laughs.

"You know you love finding ways to put my mouth to better use when I get chatty." Harlow gives her a sexy grin, making Evie blush again.

"Is it safe?" Ethan asks, coming up next to me.

"Yeah, because I wanna meet this girlfriend too!" Charlie says, pushing her way into the little circle that has formed around us. "Hi, I'm Charlie, the little sister's girlfriend." Charlie greets Evie. They shake hands. Emmy introduces Felicity to Harlow and Evie next. The five of them get lost in conversation and take off to sit in a booth next to Neo, who is taking selfies with Melody. *Am I in the twilight zone or some shit?*

Ethan tells me he's gotta go home, and to tell Emmy he will call her tomorrow. I'm glad he's living closer. Emmy needs some friends who live close by.

"Wow, what happened here?" Talon asks, coming into the clubhouse and stopping next to John who is still on the ground bleeding. Neo shouts for someone to get rid of John, because his crying is annoying him. My dad takes that as the okay to get John help. Talon notices Neo and Harlow and starts to laugh. "Ah, that makes *so much* more sense now. At least this time it's not me."

"So, what were you two doing that would make you late to the party?" I ask with a smirk, taking in their messy hair, and Ben's flushed cheeks.

"He... uhhh... was helping me with something." Ben says awkwardly. I don't get why he still has shy moments around me when it comes to sex. I mean the guy fucked our girl while she sucked Talon off with nothing but a paper thin sheet separating us. I think we're past that shit.

"If you mean helping you get rid of your massive boner by sucking it dry, then yes, I helped you." Talon grins at Ben. Ben groans, swiping a hand down his face.

"Where's Oliver? Is he not back from his appointment yet?" Ben asks. Oliver has been seeing someone about his nightmares, and they have been improving a lot. With how relaxed our lives have been for the past few weeks, I think he's been allowing himself to worry a little less about Emmy so he can get the help he needs. But he still wakes up every few nights. Thankfully, he's not screaming bloody murder anymore, but I have found him working out in the basement a few times, unable to go back to sleep.

He's opened up a lot to me, and I feel bad for him. I worry for Emmy too, we all do. We want to keep her safe and protected. Oliver has been through the most if you include his own trauma mixed with hers. Most of the time I think he's just waiting for the other shoe to drop. And, to be honest, sometimes I am too. With so many looming threats, it's hard to really relax and live.

277

"He should be back any time now." I say, heading over to the bar for a drink. "Tammy, can you get someone to clean this up please? I don't want it to stain the wood, and it's a safety hazard. Someone could slip and fall." Tammy, the bartender, heads off to find someone. I hop behind the bar and make the guys some drinks.

We talk for a bit until Oliver gets here. When he arrives, we fill him in on what happened between Neo and John.

"So where's Neo now?" Oliver asks, looking around. I look over at the booth he was in, but he's not there anymore. The girls are still in the same spot, and Harlow has Melody now. Knowing Neo must be nearby, I search harder. Then I find him. The crazy fucker is in the back corner, sitting in the dark of a shadow, glaring at Harlow, pouting like someone stole his favorite toy.

"You know, we win the 'Most Fucked-Up In-laws' award." Oliver sighs, shaking his head before downing a shot. "And what is up with the life-sized llama?"

"Alpaca!" Harlow and Neo yell out in unison. *How the fuck did they hear that?* You know what, I don't even wanna know.

CHAPTER 30
Charlie

"THIS PLACE LOOKS amazing and I've only seen the outside so far." I say, looking around in awe. People are lined up around the building and across the street. I can feel the bass music seeping from within the building and vibrating through my feet. The building is black brick with no windows, at least not on this side, along with a bright blood red door.

"At least we don't have to wait in that." Emmy laughs, pointing at the poor fools who probably won't even see the inside of the club tonight. Harlow made a really smart choice by having the opening night be on a Friday. I'm just lucky that it also happens to be Emmy's birthday.

"Where is Harlow anyways?" I ask.

"She's in there somewhere. Neo and Evie came with her to make sure everything was set for tonight. She told me we could just go in." She shrugs.

"Come on, then. Let's get in there and find them. Can't keep the birthday girl waiting." Tyson says, pulling Emmy to his side and giving her a kiss on the top of her head as he leads us towards the VIP line.

"VIP pass?" The guy asks, looking us up and down with a judgy stare. *What the fuck is his problem?*

"That's okay, we don't need one. We know the owner." Emmy says with a friendly smile.

The guy huffs out a laugh. "Yeah? So did the last 20 people I just turned away without a pass. You're not getting in here without a VIP pass."

"We don't need one. We know the fucking owner." Tyson growls.

"Look buddy, I know that line of people looks intimidating, but that's life. You really should have gotten here a few hours ago if you wanted a chance to get inside." This dude has a lot of nerve to talk to Tyson like that.

Normally he's in his Phantom Reaper's cut, and people take one look at him and do what he asks, but seeing how it's his girlfriend's birthday, he wanted to dress up a little. I mean, he's wearing black jeans and a black shirt, but at least they are clean.

The bouncer guy doesn't have much of a size difference from Tyson. He's a little shorter than Tyson, but has more stock to him.

"And I said, we know the damn owner. Now let us the fuck in before we are forced to bring her out here. And I don't think Queenie would like that." Tyson snaps.

"Look, Queenie is my sister. I've texted her that I'm here, and she said to come in. See?" Emmy holds up the phone to show the guy the texts. The asshole doesn't even look at them.

"You're pissing me off now. You don't have a pass, so get lost." The guy says in a frustrated tone while grinding his teeth together.

Then out of the shadows, like a fucking ninja, Harlow appears behind bouncer dude. None of us say anything. I know the reason I'm keeping my mouth shut is because I very much want to see what she does to him for being a douche canoe, and I'm pretty sure that goes for our whole group.

"Now, is that anyway to talk to my baby sister?" Harlow asks, stepping up to the guy's side, trailing her dagger down the side of the guy's neck. The bouncer freezes, as his body starts to shake in fear. "Didn't your mommy teach you how to use your manners?"

"S-sorry. I didn't know she was your sister." The guy stammers, terror coating every word.

"Well that's funny." Harlow giggles. And it's not a cute girly giggle. No, I feel like we are in a horror movie. Thank God she's on our side, because *fuck*. "I'm pretty sure I just heard her tell you. She even showed you the text messages. Are you calling me a liar?"

"N-o ma'am. I mean Queenie. Never." I'm trying not to laugh because the guy is sweating like a pig and sounds like he's about to cry. Looks really can be deceiving in his case. A shadow catches my attention. Without a sound, Neo creeps up behind the guy, towering over him. He looks over at us and puts his finger to his lips for us to be quiet, giving us a sinister grin as well.

"Good, because I would hate to have to kill you on my sister's birthday. Today is about happy thoughts and fun times. But him, on the other hand, he might be willing to play." Harlow looks behind the guy pointing her dagger up at Neo. The bouncer slowly turns around, and when he looks up, he lets out a high pitched scream.

You know, like one of those dumb chicks from those cheesy horror movies, who always ends up dying first. Except I can't blame this guy, both Harlow and Neo are scary motherfuckers. The guy drops to the ground and instantly folds into the fetal possession. Then the smell of fresh urine hits my nose, making me scrunch it up in disgust.

"Fucking gold." Talon howls with laughter. "He screamed like a little bitch!"

"So did you the first time you met Queenie." Tyson taunts with a smile on his face.

"Yeah, okay, but I didn't piss myself." He puffs out his chest, proud of that fact.

"My Queen, I think we broke the guy, and we didn't even have to touch him." Neo gives her an excited grin.

"Nice!" She says, and they high five each other. Okay, they might be terrifying but these two are some of my favorite people. Never a dull moment. "Okay. You deal with that, and get someone to take his place. My sister and I have a night of dancing and drinking to attend to."

"Yes, My Queen." Neo growls, but not out of anger. No, the guy looks like he's about to rip her clothes off.

"I bet you spit-up cleaning duty for a week that they fuck on the dance floor tonight." Oliver says, coming up next to me.

"No fair! You damn well *know* that's gonna happen." I glare at him.

"I know, why do you think I made the bet?" Oliver chuckles, following after Emmy, who is being dragged by her sister towards the entrance, and away from the horny serial killer.

When we get in, the bass crashes into me like a wave, causing my heart to feel like it's rattling in my chest as my whole body hums. I love it.

The place is so packed I can barely see anything but bodies, but as we follow Harlow, it's as if she's fucking Moses or some shit; the whole crowd parting for her like the Red Sea.

"Order whatever you want." Harlow yells over the music, then turns to the bartender. "This group here drinks free all night. Understood?"

"Of course, Queenie." The woman says. "What will it be?" She asks, turning to us.

Once we all order our drinks, Harlow leads us to the VIP section. Black leather couches make a semi circle with a table in the middle.

"You guys can chill over here if you want, we're gonna go dance." Harlow says, then grabs Emmy's and Evie's hands as she starts to drag them to the dance floor. Emmy looks back to see if Felicity and I are following, but Felicity is sitting on the couch, nursing her drink. I wave her off, and mouth 'Have fun'. I'll join her afterwards, so she can spend some time with her sister before she has to leave in a few days.

"You don't want to dance?" I ask Felicity, sitting down next to her on the couch.

"I do, but I think I need a few drinks in me before I can be around Emmy's sister without thinking that if I say or do one small thing wrong, she's gonna stab me or something." Felicity laughs, then panic takes over her face as she looks around, making sure none of Queenie's people overheard her.

I laugh. "You're good. You're pretty much automatically on her good side by being Emmy's best friend. I think it would take a lot before she would go all crazy killer on your ass."

"Still. She's terrifying. But she's also fascinating at the same time. I'm so confused." She takes a sip of her drink, trying to calm her nerves.

Looking over at the guys, I find the two horny lovers, Ben and Talon, already tonguing each other as they have a hardcore make out session on the couch. Tyson and Oliver, on the other hand, are on high alert. I have a feeling they won't be having much fun tonight, but I don't think they care. They are here to keep an eye on Emmy and to keep her safe. They aren't much of the club type anyways.

"You good?" I ask Felicity after we both have another drink in our hands.

"Yeah. I think I am." I help her up, and we let the guys know where we are going, and join Emmy.

She's dancing on stage with Harlow with the biggest smile on her face. But Evie isn't with them. I find her sitting on a couch off to the side, watching Harlow with such a loving expression that I can't help but smile myself.

Evie is a bubbly, flirty person but all it takes is one heated look from Harlow and she turns into this submissive blushing virgin. It's adorable. I can tell that the love they have for each other is a lot like mine and Emmy's. It's soul consuming, heart stopping, mind-blowing love. The kind of love that you would kill for, you would die for. The kind that you would suffer through any amount of pain if it means seeing the person you love smile, even just once.

Felicity and I join them up on the stage, and Harlow grins wide, grabbing Felicity's arm and spinning her around. Felicity lets out a laugh, and she and Harlow start to dance.

But not like how I plan to with Emmy. I can tell she's had a few drinks, but she's not drunk. Tipsy maybe. "Hi, Love Bug." She purrs, pulling me close so that our chests are pressed together. "Dance with me."

"Anything for you, my Queen. You're the birthday girl after all."

"Then kiss me. The birthday girl demands it."

And I do. With everything I have, I kiss my girl so hard and so good that she moans, melting into me. We dance for a while, just enjoying each other's closeness. When I look around to see how Felicity is doing, I see she's not here anymore, but over on the couch talking to Evie. Now Harlow and Neo are dancing together. *Or are they... oh god. Yup, they are definitely fucking.*

Looking away quickly, I laugh and Emmy gives me a funny look, then sees what I was looking at. The horror on her face only makes me laugh harder.

The song changes, and Bang by AJR filters through the speakers.

"Fuck yeah!" Harlow crows, detaching herself from Neo like he didn't just have his dick inside her. Neo has a massive grin on his face as he watches Harlow with fascination and awe. She starts dancing around the stage, and holy shit, she's amazing!

Neo comes and stands next to us. "You should see her dance to this song when she has guns and people to play with." Neo grins, turning his attention back to his queen.

Something tells me I really *don't* want to see that and if I did, it would be something that would haunt my dreams.

Emmy

After a while, my sister ends up somewhere with Evie. Knowing her, she's probably in the back office doing things little sisters shouldn't know the details of.

Neo is around here as well, but he's most likely keeping things running smoothly. He's already had to kick a group of people out. At first they looked like they were wanting to argue but they changed their tune rather quickly.

Charlie, Felicity, and I continued dancing for a while, but the girls were drinking more than me, so Steel, bless his heart, sent a car to pick them up and take them home. I was ready and willing to go back with them, but the guys said the girls would be fine, and it was their turn with me.

They are right, I did spend most of the night with the girls. Tyson and Oliver are still watching the place like hawks.

Now, I'm in the middle of the dance floor with two of my sexy-as-sin men grinding up on me. My panties are soaked and I'm panting like a bitch in heat, sweating like crazy while two massive cocks grind into me, making me lose my fucking mind.

I haven't been this horny in a very long time. It's my birthday, and this birthday girl wants three of my men, all at once.

We all move our bodies against each other to the beat of the music. Ben and Talon are kissing my neck, getting me all worked up, and every once in a while, they will move away from my neck to make out with each other before going back to tasting the fuck out of me.

"That's it. I can't take it anymore." I pant.

"What's wrong, My Lady?" Talon murmurs against my neck.

"I need you. Like now. As in your cocks inside me. I wanna go home."

Talon looks at Ben over my head. They have a silent conversation before nodding and grabbing my hand to lead me off the dance floor and over to Tyson and Oliver.

"Are you guys good to go?" Talon asks.

"Yeah, we're ready to go whenever you guys wanna leave. Everything okay?" Tyson asks, looking at my flushed body and red face.

Oliver gives me a once over before a knowing smirk takes over his face. "Yeah, brother, she's fine. These two got her worked up. Now it's time to take her home so we can take care of her properly."

"Right." Tyson nods. "You guys can have her room tonight, but try not to keep me up all night with your screaming orgasms."

"No promises." Talon chuckles before leading me towards the exit.

The car windows are rolled down the whole ride home. Between my overheated body from the club and the warm summer air, the cool breeze coming in from the windows feels amazing against my skin. Talon, Ben, and I had a few drinks, but nothing like the others. I wasn't drunk, although I was tipsy enough to make me easily turned on. But let's be honest, with my lovers, it doesn't take all that much.

When we get home, the guys pull me out of the car and lead me right to the bedroom. However, when we get up there, Felicity and Charlie are passed out on my bed.

"Fuck. Let's go to the basement." Talon suggests.

When we get to the basement, we are about to walk into Talon and Ben's room, but Oliver stops us. "Wait. I have an idea." Oliver says with a sly grin.

"I'm listening." Talon says, with a grin of his own.

Oliver makes his way over to me, his stride filled with this cocky swagger. He's so full of himself right now. Fuck, he's so sexy. He unbuttons his dress shirt before pulling his undershirt off in one swift motion and tossing it to the floor. My breathing starts to pick up as my eyes eat him up. His tattoos are on full display covering every inch of his tan skin, which has gotten darker because he's been working out in the sun since we've gotten back. It just adds to all the yum that is him. His black messy hair falls into his face, and I just want to run my hands through his silky strands, preferably while I hold his face to my pussy.

"Hey, Baby Girl." He says, prowling towards me like a predator. He doesn't stop until I hit something hard behind me, and our bodies are flush up against each other, letting me feel all of his delectable muscles. Tilting my head up, I see a very hungry Talon, his blond locks falling forward, tickling my forehead. Another body steps up to me. Ben. I love when his sex-crazed side comes out to play.

I'm trapped between three sinfully delicious men. A shiver racks my body at their nearness.

"It might be past midnight, but your birthday isn't over until you've cum at least once." Oliver's voice is low and husky. I swallow hard, and nod, making me look like a bobble head. He dips his head down, capturing my lips with his in a hungry kiss. As Oliver ravages me with his tongue, the others work together to strip me naked, then themselves.

I see we are not wasting any time.

Oliver steps back and rids himself of his dark wash jeans and boxers. His cock bobs free, slapping his belly. My eyes snap down to his thick length and I lick my lips, making him groan.

"Come with me, Baby Girl." He holds his hand out, and I follow him to the couch. He sits down, and pulls me into his lap. My bare wet pussy straddles his hot length. I roll my hips, grinding against him, making him grab my hips tightly and moaning out loud.

"Fuck, Baby Girl, I need to be inside you." He breathes. I sit up and grab his length, lining it up with my entrance and sink down on him, taking his fat cock in me in one smooth motion. We both groan as I give my hips another rock. "Ben, come behind me. Talon, on your knees behind our girl."

The guys listen to Oliver immediately and move into position. Ben grips his cock in his hand, giving it a few strokes as he looks down at me with lust filled eyes. The couch is just the right height, so that if I lean over Oliver a little I can take Ben into my mouth.

Talon gets something out of the little side table next to us, and when I feel the coolness against my ass, I realize it's lube. "Bend over, Emmy. Let me prepare you for my cock."

Leaning over, I press my tits into Oliver's face so that I can reach Ben's dick. I wrap my hand around it, squeezing lightly, and giving it a few strokes before licking the pre-cum off the tip, making him groan as I swirl my tongue around the base of his cock. Just as I take Ben completely in my mouth, Talon presses a finger into my ass, making me moan against Ben's cock as my pussy grips Oliver's. Talon chuckles as they both let out a hiss.

I slowly bob, sucking Ben's cock as Oliver helps me rock against him. Talon works his way in and out of my puckered hole before adding another finger.

It's not enough. I want all of their cocks inside me. Pulling back from Ben, I look over my shoulder to Talon. "Please." I pant. "Get inside me. Now."

"Okay, My Lady. Your wish is my command." He pulls his fingers out, replacing it with the tip of his shaft. Oliver widens his legs a little more so Talon has room to get up nice and close. Talon slowly starts to press inside me, making sounds of pleasure as he does. When he's all the way in, I feel so fucking full. It's indescribable.

"Fuck..." I whine. My pussy is throbbing with need. I have to move. "Please, I need to move."

"We got you, Firefly." Oliver says, rubbing soothing circles on my back. They are in control and make all the movements, the rest is out of my hands right now.

"Open up, Butterfly." Ben says, his voice husky, making my core clench as he paints his tip against my lips. "Time to finish what you started."

Leaning forward, I take Ben back into my mouth. His fingers slip over my hair, wrapping his hand around a chunk of it, and holding me where he wants me as he starts to thrust in and out of my mouth. He makes a sexy sound as he closes his eyes.

Talon moves next. He pulls out of my ass, before pumping back in, making me rock into Oliver. We all let out collective groans.

Oliver and Talon start working together, getting a good rhythm going. My body is alive, every nerve ending on fire. The feeling is intense and overwhelming, but in a good way. After a few minutes, I'm practically useless. My brain can't think straight. I'm trying to give Ben's cock the attention it deserves but the other two have me doing no better than babbling nonsense around Ben's length.

He seems to know that I'm unable to do much at this point, because he starts to take complete control, fucking my mouth hard. Not as hard as the others do, but I still love it.

"So fucking beautiful, Butterfly." He groans, stroking my face.

"You feel amazing, Baby Girl." Talon grunts, pushing into me, hard.

"You drive me crazy, Firefly." Oliver says, his face in my chest because of the position we are in. He takes one of my nipples into his mouth, swirling his tongue around the peaked point before giving it a little bite. That's all it takes. Everything has been building slowly up to this point, and I fucking erupt like a volcano.

I cum hard. My eyes roll into the back of my head as I scream around Ben's shaft. My pussy clamps down on Oliver's cock and my ass tightens around Talon.

"Fuck, fuck, fuck." Ben says, thrusting into me with each word before holding me to him on the last one. He lets out a long groan, his cock twitching in my mouth, sending jets of cum down my throat. I try to swallow the best I can, but there's only so much I can do as I'm still shaking from my own release.

"I love you." Ben pulls out of me. I gasp for air before he steals it away again with a passionate kiss.

"One more, Baby Girl." Talon pants, giving me a slap on the ass. "Cum for us one more time so that we can fill you up."

I groan, resting my head against Oliver's chest. "I can't." I say, exhausted from the night, and then them fucking me senseless.

"Just let us do the work, all you gotta do is squeeze our dicks, and scream our names." Talon says with a sexy chuckle. *Cocky fucker.*

Ben comes around the couch to my side, bending over, and slips his hand between me and Oliver to find my clit. "Oh, oh fuck. Oh god." I pant as his big finger rubs my swollen bud in firm circles. The others resume fucking me hard. One thrusts in as the other pulls out, and all I can do is repeat 'Oh fuck' over and over again.

"Cum, Firefly. I don't know how much more I can take, you feel too fucking good. So hot and wet. You're fucking dripping down my cock." Oliver says through gritted teeth. Ben pinches my clit, sending me into another climax. And just like they asked, I scream their names as I feel my soul leave my body before slamming back into me.

"Fuck!" Oliver shouts, holding me to him as he starts to cum deep inside me. I can feel his warm release inside me start to drip out as he gives a few little thrusts to extend the feeling of ecstasy. Talon pulls out of me, causing me to cry out at the sudden loss, and then I feel his warm liquid hit my back as he paints my body with his release.

"Damn, Baby Girl. You look so fucking sexy covered in my cum." He takes his fingers and smears it into my skin.

"Really?" I ask, my voice hoarse from screaming. "That's gonna be a bitch to get off."

"What can I say, I wanted to mark my girl." He gives me a wicked hot grin.

"Come on, Firefly, let's get you cleaned up." Oliver pulls out of me, his cum gushing out as well. "Well *shit*, now we're gonna need to invest in a carpet cleaner."

I laugh. Way too fucking hard because it wasn't that funny, but I'm overtired and my body is like jelly from the orgasms.

"I think this one has officially lost it." Talon laughs. "We're gonna go shower upstairs then game for a bit before bed. I love you, My Queen." Talon gives me a kiss, then licks the side of my mouth. I give him a funny look. "You had a little bit of Ben on you." He winks before walking away.

"Good night, My Love." Ben whispers, kissing me hard. "I love you so fucking much. Never forget that."

"Never." I breathe, giving him a sleepy smile.

Oliver carries me into the upstairs bathroom and we get in the hot shower together. He sits on the built-in bench and cleans me without ever letting me go. I love being held by him. He makes me feel safe and loved when I'm in his arms. They all do.

When we're done, Oliver wraps me in a towel and carries me to his room. He places me on his bed while he gets dressed. Then he dresses me in one of his shirts before placing me in the middle of his bed. He crawls underneath the blankets and cuddles beside me, pulling me to his chest.

"I love you, Firefly. I hope you had a good birthday." He whispers, kissing the back of my neck. I'm almost asleep so I don't think I respond, even though I want to tell him I had an amazing birthday. I got to spend the night with my sister, one of my best friends, and all my lovers, what more can I ask for?

A few moments later I feel the bed dip in front of me. Forcing my eyes open, I see Tyson laying there. "I just wanted to be near you." He says, kissing me on the nose.

I give him a smile. Taking his hand in mine, we fall asleep.

Perfect ending to a perfect day.

CHAPTER 31
Emmy

"TYSON, ARE YOU ready?" I call into the house. We have an appointment at noon for Melody's four month shots. The original appointment was supposed to be earlier this week, before my birthday celebration and Harlow's arrival, but due to a booking issue they had to reschedule us for the Saturday after my b-day. It sucks because I would have loved to have slept in, but my baby comes first. I still can't believe she's already four months old. She is growing so fast, right before our very eyes. She loves tummy time and can hold herself up really well.

Whenever she's playing on the floor, the guys will get down on the ground with her, on their bellies, and play too. I love watching how they are with her. They love her so much. There are no better dads out there for her; she's one lucky Princess.

She's a sassy one, for sure. Loves to babble almost every minute that she's awake. Tyson loves to have full on conversations with her as if she's actually answering back.

After all the hell we went through these past two years, it feels amazing to just relax and live as a family as we raise our daughter together. My favorite moments with Melody are her late night feedings. Just having snuggles with her while she breastfeeds, just her and me while everyone else is asleep. I'm gonna miss that when I switch her to formula and solid foods.

"Yup, I just had to find her favorite bunny." Tyson says, coming to the front door holding up a plush brown bunny. "Thought it might make her feel better after that dick stabs our daughter." He growls before putting the bunny in Melody's car seat beside her with a big loving smile on his face.

"Babe, it's just a needle. A quick prick. She'll be fine." I laugh.

"Is it just you two coming?" Amy asks.

Amy wanted to come with us, since she was there to take Melody to get her first few shots, and she loves being a hands-on Nana, so of course I said yes.

"Ben and Talon are still sleeping. They were up all night gaming." I roll my eyes, and Amy laughs. "Charlie hates needles, and would most likely end up crying harder than Melly, so she said she will be happy to spoil her and give her whatever she needs when we get back.

And Oliver is with his dad up at the clubhouse. Steel wants him to spend some time doing MC stuff since he missed a lot being at school." I shrug

"I'm shocked your sister isn't coming" Amy comments.

"Oh, trust me, she wanted to but the office has a limit as to how many people can come. Plus, Evie convinced her that there was stuff to do at the club, so we just agreed to meet up to have dinner later tonight." I inform her.

"Then it's just us?" Amy smiles. "We should go out for ice cream after. I know she can't have any, but I think mom and dad might need something for being brave too." She winks, making me laugh.

The car ride was all giggles from Melody. Poor girl doesn't even know what's about to happen.

When we get there, Tyson takes Melody out of the car seat and carries her in himself. I give him a funny smile. "What?" He grunts. "I want to make my baby girl feel safe, sue me."

"Alright, Papa Bear." I laugh.

When we get into the waiting room, we check in at the window and then have a seat to wait for Melody's name to be called.

Kids are running around, playing with the toys. I smile as a little girl walks up to Tyson and says hi.

"I like your jacket." She says. "I have one with pink gemstones on it."

"I bet it's pretty, just like you." He smiles, and ugh, seeing my big, bad, biker boy being all sweet with kids always hits my heart in the best of ways.

"Come away from that man, Robin." A lady, I'm guessing this little girl's mother, says, pulling her away by the arm with a haughty look directed at Tyson. She's judging him by his looks. This lady has no clue that Tyson is one of the most loving people when it comes to kids. When she makes eye contact with me, I give her a smile, and slowly flip her off. Thankfully, no kids were paying attention to us. She gasps in shock. She's about to say something when the nurse calls out, "Melody Knox."

We all follow her to an exam room. Tyson's leg is bouncing as he stares off into nothing while we wait for the nurse to come back.

"Hey." I say, slipping my hand in his. "She's going to be fine. Everything is going to be fine."

"I know." He lets out a sigh. "I just don't want to see our baby girl cry."

He really doesn't. Melody has him wrapped around her little finger. Same with the others. Any time she cries, they scoop her up and do whatever they can to make her stop.

"Hello." The nurse greets as she walks into the room. "So, today we will be doing the second dose of the same shots she received last visit. Are you breastfeeding?"

"Yes."

"Wonderful. If you're comfortable with it, sometimes we find it helps to breastfeed them. It gives them comfort and distracts them a little. I'll go as quickly as I can."

Taking Melody from Tyson, I get her latched on. The nurse cleans the spot on her leg, and is about to administer the shot, when Tyson lets out a growl. The nurse stops and looks up at Tyson with wide eyes.

"Enough." I hiss. "Let the poor woman do her job. If you can't behave, I'm going to kick you out and make you wait in the waiting room." I glare at him.

"Fine." He huffs, sitting back in his seat, but does not take his eyes off the nurse.

"You're okay to continue." I say, trying to make her less freaked out with a friendly smile.

She hesitates for a moment, but then proceeds. Melody doesn't flinch at the first two but by the time we get to the last one, she has detached herself from my breast, letting out a high pitched wail and has tears streaming down her face.

"Alright, that's enough. Give me my baby." Tyson says, taking Melody from me. I quickly put my boob away and roll my eyes at my drama king. "It's okay, Little Princess. Daddy Ty's got you. You're safe from those mean, mean people."

"Really?" I look at Amy who's trying to hold back a giggle.

"Men." She laughs.

"There's a little ice cream shop down the street so we can just walk there." Amy says as we exit the building.

"Yeah, alright that's fine. Here." Tyson hands the baby over to Amy. "Hold her, I'll go get her stroller."

"Need any help?" I snicker, knowing he sucks at getting that thing unfolded.

"No, I think I can get the stroller myself." He growls.

"Sure, if you say so." He gives me a look that promises all the spankings later. Joke's on him, he knows I love that.

It's hot out, and the sun is beaming down on Melody, so we walk over to the shady spot under the tree.

"Emmy!" Tyson roars. My head whips over in his direction. He's fighting off three men that look to be in cuts, but it's clearly not the Phantom Reapers.

No. No. Not now. This can't be happening. *He's here.*

I'm frozen in fear as I watch the guys gang up on Tyson. He's holding his own pretty well, but where the fuck is his gun? Why hasn't he shot them already?

A grunt next to me, followed by Melody's cry snaps me out of my mind. Looking next to me, Amy isn't there anymore. My eyes flick down to the ground, where Amy is lying unconscious.

Where is Melody? "Melody!" I start to scream. I have never felt this kind of fear before. Pure terror is racing through my mind. Tyson needs help, but my baby is gone. *Where the fuck is my daughter?* This can't be happening. This isn't real!

He took her. He fucking took her! I'm going to kill that man and enjoy every fucking second. He fucked with the wrong person.

I don't know where to look. I don't know what direction she was taken in. I run down the street and back, screaming her name. Why hasn't anyone come out to see what's going on?

Once I get a moment to think, I pull out my phone and dial Oliver as I race back to the parking lot where Tyson is still fighting.

"Hey, Firefly. How's our baby girl doing? I wish I could have been there with you guys." Oliver says when he answers the phone.

"Oliver, we're at the doctor's office. They have-" Only I don't get to finish my sentence. My phone is snatched from my hands.

"I don't think so." A familiar voice says, from behind me. Whirling around, I come face to face with my math teacher, the fucking creep who made a pass at me.

"Mr. Park. What the...?" I can't think straight.

"You know, it took a lot longer to get to this point than we wanted. But finally, after months of waiting for just the right moment, the Phantom Reapers got lazy, just once. But that's all we needed. We were ready." He gives me a slimy smile.

"We? What the fuck is going on. Where is my daughter? What are *you* doing here?" I scream in his face.

"He will answer all your questions."

That's the last thing I hear before feeling a sharp pain in my neck. My eyelids start to get heavy, and my knees give out. Then everything goes black.

My head is pounding, I feel like I'm going to puke, and with a pained groan, I open my eyes.

A man stands over me, tall with long black hair fanning his face. He oozes power and death. He looks at me with a sinister smirk. Something sick and evil gleaming in his eyes. "Hello, daughter. Welcome to Hades, home of the Savage Hellhounds. And your new home."

The End...

Just kidding. You didn't think I would just leave you all hanging like that? Make sure to come back and read Redemption Found to find out what wild ride is waiting for Emmy behind the enemy's walls.

BOOKS BY ALISHA WILLIAMS

Emerald Lake Prep – Series:

> Book One: Second Chances (February 2021)

> Book Two: Into The Unknown (May 2021)

> Book Three: Shattered Pieces (September 2021)

> Book Four: Redemption Found (Coming Soon)

Blood Empire – Series:

> Book One: Rising Queen (July 2021)

> Book Two: Crowned Queen (Coming Soon)

Silver Valley University – Series:

> Book One: Hidden Secrets (Coming Soon)

Angelic Academy – Series:

> Book One: Tainted Wings (Coming Soon)

ACKNOWLEDGEMENTS

I would love to give a huge thank you to anyone who has supported me on this journey. A big thank you to every single person who helped Emerald Lake Prep be what it is now. Without each and everyone of you, this second book would not be possible.

I'm also beyond grateful for Jessica Pollio-Napoles You are more than just my Alpha, you're family! Thank you for all the time and energy you put into this book, and helping it become what it is! I don't think I would have had as much fun writing it without you! Can't wait to make more books with you!

Special shout out to Tamara! Thank you for taking on my crazy ass, and being the best damn PA a girl could ask for. You're not only that, but a best friend and wifey. Love you, babe!

Many thanks to my Beta and ARC teams. You all helped me make my book even better, and I look forward to sending you more work in the future.

And finally, thank you to all my readers. It was an honor to write this book for you. Thank you for loving book one - and I hope you will follow Emmy, Charlie, and the guys on their final chapter in _Emerald Lake Prep (Redemption Found Book Four)_

ABOUT ALISHA

Romance author, Alisha Williams, lives in Alberta, Canada, with her husband and her two headstrong kids, and two kitties. When she isn't writing or creating her own gorgeous graphic content, she loves to read books by her favorite authors.

Writing has been a lifelong dream of hers, and this book was made despite the people who prayed for it to fail, but because Alisha is not afraid to go for what she wants, she has proven that dreams do come true.

Wanna see what all her characters look like, hear all the latest gossip about her new books or even get a chance to become a part of one of her teams? Join her readers group on Facebook called **Alisha's Ally Cats**, or find her author's page - **Alisha Williams Author**.

Of course, she also has an Instagram account to show all her cool graphics, videos, and more book related goodies, just look for **Alisha Williams Author**.

Made in the USA
Middletown, DE
30 October 2021